# DEACON
## A DARK COWBOY ROMANCE
## RAYA MORRIS EDWARDS

Deacon

By Raya Morris Edwards

Copyright © 2025 Morris Edwards Publishing

All rights reserved. No part of this publication may be reproduced, stored, or transmitted without prior permission of the publisher of this book.

This is a work of fiction. Names, characters, places, and incidents either are the product of the author's imagination or are used fictitiously. Any resemblance to actual persons, living or dead, events, or locales is entirely coincidental.

FIRST EDITION

Developmental editing by Lexie at Morally Gray Author Services

Proof and copy editing by Alexa at The Fiction Fix

Cover design by Maldo Designs

This book is for everyone who wants a tatted up, unhinged cowboy daddy with a special piercing. Deacon is for you.

# Contents

1. CHAPTER ONE — 1
2. CHAPTER TWO — 14
3. CHAPTER THREE — 21
4. CHAPTER FOUR — 36
5. CHAPTER FIVE — 45
6. CHAPTER SIX — 57
7. CHAPTER SEVEN — 66
8. CHAPTER EIGHT — 77
9. CHAPTER NINE — 84
10. CHAPTER TEN — 98
11. CHAPTER ELEVEN — 107
12. CHAPTER TWELVE — 119
13. CHAPTER THIRTEEN — 122
14. CHAPTER FOURTEEN — 127
15. CHAPTER FIFTEEN — 137
16. CHAPTER SIXTEEN — 146

| | | |
|---|---|---|
| 17. | CHAPTER SEVENTEEN | 150 |
| 18. | CHAPTER EIGHTEEN | 157 |
| 19. | CHAPTER NINETEEN | 165 |
| 20. | CHAPTER TWENTY | 174 |
| 21. | CHAPTER TWENTY-ONE | 187 |
| 22. | CHAPTER TWENTY-TWO | 193 |
| 23. | CHAPTER TWENTY-THREE | 199 |
| 24. | CHAPTER TWENTY-FOUR | 205 |
| 25. | CHAPTER TWENTY-FIVE | 216 |
| 26. | CHAPTER TWENTY-SIX | 223 |
| 27. | CHAPTER TWENTY-SEVEN | 228 |
| 28. | CHAPTER TWENTY-EIGHT | 242 |
| 29. | CHAPTER TWENTY-NINE | 246 |
| 30. | CHAPTER THIRTY | 253 |
| 31. | CHAPTER THIRTY-ONE | 261 |
| 32. | CHAPTER THIRTY-TWO | 268 |
| 33. | CHAPTER THIRTY-THREE | 270 |
| 34. | CHAPTER THIRTY-FOUR | 275 |
| 35. | CHAPTER THIRTY-FIVE | 280 |
| 36. | CHAPTER THIRTY-SIX | 288 |
| 37. | CHAPTER THIRTY-SEVEN | 292 |
| 38. | CHAPTER THIRTY-EIGHT | 301 |

| | | |
|---|---|---|
| 39. | CHAPTER THIRTY-NINE | 313 |
| 40. | CHAPTER FORTY | 320 |
| 41. | CHAPTER FORTY-ONE | 325 |
| 42. | CHAPTER FORTY-TWO | 330 |
| 43. | CHAPTER FORTY-THREE | 338 |
| 44. | CHAPTER FORTY-FOUR | 345 |
| 45. | CHAPTER FORTY-FIVE | 356 |
| 46. | CHAPTER FORTY-SIX | 361 |
| 47. | CHAPTER FORTY-SEVEN | 366 |
| 48. | CHAPTER FORTY-EIGHT | 372 |
| 49. | CHAPTER FORTY-NINE | 383 |
| | Acknowledgements | 389 |

# Author's Note

This book is a BDSM romance, however for the purposes of plot and character development, BDSM is not always depicted exactly as it should be practiced in real life. Please do not look to fiction for education on BDSM.

This book contains Appalachian characters and themes, which means throughout you will find instances of dialect that may be unfamiliar to you. It's not a mistake and is intentional and correct.

## Important Content Information

This book is intended for adults only. There are frequent themes, discussions, and depictions of heavy content regarding violence, toxic relationships, abuse, and more. There are also explicit sexual descriptions throughout.

Please visit rayamorrisedwards.com/deacon to read a detailed list of the content tags before reading.

# CHAPTER ONE
# FREYA

## BEFORE

"What's the worst profanity there is?"

I'm newly eighteen, plus one month—too old not to know about this kind of thing, but nobody talks to me in a house of men who don't notice me any more than they take note of the flies on the wall. That's why I'm asking the one person I can trust with sensitive questions—my only good stepbrother, Bittern.

He's sitting on the stoop, like always. There's an unlit cigarette hanging from his lip. His colorless hair falls in his russet eyes. I need to take the buzzer and give him a haircut soon.

"Why do you want to know that, Frey?" he drawls.

He talks real slow since the accident. I don't know why that is. The doctor said there wasn't anything wrong with him except a few broken ribs, and those healed a while back.

"I just do," I say.

Bittern flicks his lighter absently, on then off again.

"Cunt, probably," he says.

I've heard that around but only on the periphery of my understanding.

"What does it mean?" I squint up at him.

The sun filters around his head. Overhead, the far-reaching arms of the oak trees are dappled with late afternoon sun. Everyone is gone at work except for Bittern—he can't work at the factory anymore. They won't take him on account of his slowness around the machines.

"It's like pussy," he says. "You should know this by now."

I frown. "Are you sure there's not another? What about...cock? That's bad. Or fuck?"

He shakes his head. "No, I reckon cunt is the worst one."

"Why?"

It's his turn to frown. "Hell if I know, Frey. It just is."

He gets up, and the screen door flaps shut. It doesn't latch. Instead, it just flaps on the hinges. Aiden, my stepfather, has slammed it too many times. I keep quiet on the porch for a while. The reason I wanted to know is because I'm becoming aware of an uncomfortable fact.

There appears to be a disadvantage to being a girl. Not the kind I understand, where Aiden rages on about how he didn't want to be left with his dead wife's daughter who's not even his blood. Or where I get stuck at the back of the line. Or get the plate with the least food.

No, this is an awareness of the structure of everything.

The worst word Bittern knows is a name for a part of my body. Maybe that means something, maybe it doesn't.

I stare into the woods, to where the trees open and show the goldenrod clearing below, for a long time. Then, I get up, because I have to start dinner. Hungry stomachs wait for nothing, not even groundbreaking revelations.

It's seven when the table is set. There's breakfast for dinner—sausage, sweet boiled apples, gravy, biscuits. I lay everything out and go to the porch to see if I can hear Aiden's truck.

They must have snuck in while I had the radio on. Ryland, my oldest living stepbrother, stands in the yard, talking on his phone. Walking around the side of the house, head down, is my stepfather, Aiden.

He's a brutal man in his mid-forties. His wavy dark hair is crisp with the same sweat that eats away at his collar every day in the factory. All up and down his arms and neck are tattoos he got for a bag of pills and a bottle of moonshine.

He pauses when he sees me and fixes those cold eyes on my face.

"Dinner?" he says.

I nod. "Breakfast. It's set out on the table."

He doesn't respond; he just goes up the steps and disappears inside. Ryland hangs up his phone, and I duck back into the hallway. If he's in a good mood, he'll taunt me a little, but not in a way that hurts too bad. If it's a bad mood, he'll eviscerate me over the meal until my nails are so deep in my palms, I break skin.

We sit at the table. Aiden starts talking to Ryland about something that went on at work. Bittern eats and tells me it's good but nothing else. I clean my plate and get to picking up afterward, while the men talk at the table.

The moonshine and cigarettes come out. I go down the dark hall and into my room, shutting the door. Inside, in short stacks, sits my collection of insects, moths, and butterflies. I've been working on it since I was a little girl. They're my one solace in a world that doesn't make room for me.

I used to keep them under the porch. After Wayland, Aiden's eldest, died and I got his room, I had space for more cases. Now, I put them behind the door and cover them with a drop cloth.

I lift it, just to look. Orange wings, iridescent shells, and yellow antennas glimmer in their cases.

A spot of beauty. A place to call my own.

In bed, I lay on my side, staring up through the window facing the road. Trucks whiz by sometimes. There's a deadly curve a few yards past the house, and I sometimes hear their brakes wheeze as they take it.

A car pulls up outside, and I get up and look out. It's one of Ryland's friends, Braxton Whitaker. He's from over the border, but he works at the factory during the summers. It's been a while since I've seen him, maybe a few years. I watch as he gets out of his truck and walks around the back door. Then, I hear his boots on the porch, and laughter sounds from the kitchen.

I lay back down. From here, I can see a sliver of the hall.

Aiden passes by, going upstairs. He's headed to bed. Bittern follows, and I hear the door to his room click shut. Then, it's just Ryland and Braxton in the kitchen, shooting the shit. They're talking about women—in detail.

My stomach turns.

There it is—a greater awareness.

I listen for a while and hear all the words Bittern and I discussed. Then, I get up and shut the door, curling up against my pillows. There's a blanket tacked over my window, but through the crack, I can see the outline of the mountains.

There are two places I feel at home: the one-room church three miles down the road, and the mountains. Without those two places where Aiden never goes, I swear, I'd lose my mind.

Nothing is consistent inside these walls. Outside of them, I have an anchor in these soft, green hills. In the dust that settles on church pews. In the beam of sunlight falling across my lap while the preacher drones far away.

I close my eyes. In my mind, I fall asleep curled up on the doorstep of the church, mountains folding me in like soft flannel sheets, dotted with the wings of butterflies.

My safe space.

The next morning, I run into Aiden as he busts out of the back door on his way to work. He's having a cigarette, coffee cup hanging from his fingers. He clears his throat, and I pause, knowing he's about to speak. I don't know what's going on with him, but he seems annoyed.

"Here," he says, holding out his empty mug.

I take it. He has worn-out tattoos down his fingers. Burn marks. Callouses from the factory. Every man I know is beat up like him.

He waves a hand toward the hills. "All this fucking shit."

"What?" I whisper.

"The farm," he says. "I'd sell this land if I could get anybody to take it off my hands."

I know he doesn't want his family farm. That's not the part that's surprising. No, it's that he's talking to me like I'm human. Normally, I'm more of a maid, somebody he can point at when things go wrong.

"Property taxes," he says, walking away and disappearing around the corner of the house.

That makes sense. He inherited the land, but the property taxes still flow out. I turn just as Ryland and Braxton walk out. That's my sign to get lost. My stepbrother is terrible, and his friends are just as bad. I try to skirt around them, but Braxton blocks me.

I drag my eyes up to his smirk. He's got the same colorless hair, the same washed-out eyes. I'd call him handsome, though. He sports a strong build, from his baseball hat to his steel-tipped boots.

"Hey," he says, giving me a look that takes its time.

I'm in my sleep shorts and one of Bittern's t-shirts—not exactly my Sunday best. Out of nowhere, I'm aware of every curve of my body.

He's looking at me like he's hungry and I'm something to eat. Alarmed, I duck around him and force my way into the hall. He steps aside, grinning.

"Freya," Ryland calls.

I put my head back out. "What?"

"Bittern's coming to work to help us today," he says. "Braxton's coming back around noon to get his shit before he leaves for his aunt's house. You make something for lunch."

"Fine," I say, slamming the door.

My heart is thumping. I don't want to be alone with Braxton, but there's not much I can do. So, I watch Bittern go, and then I make sandwiches to leave on the table. Then, I strip all the beds and haul the sheets out to the tobacco barn. I usually wash the bedding once a month, but I need an excuse to be out of the house.

I'm halfway through the second load when I hear boots on the floor. I glance up. Braxton is standing in the doorway, arms crossed over his chest.

"Hey, pretty girl," he drawls.

I turn back around, mouth dry. He gets closer, leaning on the dryer to my left.

"Hey," I say, voice low.

"I gotta be going soon," he says. "Headed up to my aunt's, then back to West Virginia."

"West Virginia is where my mom's family is from," I blurt out.

I don't know where that came from. Rarely do I talk about my mother, because there's nothing to say. She left when I was barely more than a toddler. The memories I have of her are like photocopies, blurred with age. I'm not even sure they're real memories anymore.

"Oh yeah?"

I nod, trying to make small talk. "And the preacher at the church I go to."

"You go to church?" he says, taking a step closer.

"Yeah," I whisper. "The one-room down the road."

The corner of his mouth curls in a lopsided grin. I wonder if the church thing turns him on. I wonder if he thinks I'm something pure to ruin. The world has made it clear that sex will change me, but men, they reincarnate themselves before the bed is cold. Sin doesn't stick to them, somehow.

I want to believe that's bullshit. Who taught me that anyway? Not the dusty, dry preacher who refuses to even discuss sex.

Maybe Aiden?

All my self-hatred leads back to Aiden. I know that well.

"You a good girl, huh?" Braxton drawls, pulling me from my mind.

I'm not really an anything girl—I've barely started living. I look over; he's close. The washing machine thumps, making it hard to think. Warm summer air comes in through the slats of the tobacco barn and blood pumps in my ears. I see his hand come up and touch my cheek.

"Think you could give me something to think about later before I go?" His voice is low, oddly persuasive.

I wet my lips. "What kind of thing?"

His eyes flick down. "Maybe something quick."

My stomach swoops. "Like...sex?"

He flashes a grin. "Yeah, you don't have to do anything. Just spread those legs. It's real easy."

"I haven't done that before," I blurt out.

He cocks his head, hand working down my face to my neck. I got dressed in my favorite jeans and shirt after everybody left. His finger traces down the line of my cleavage.

"It's alright. I won't tell anybody," he says.

My mind goes back to all the things I heard him say to Ryland last night. He clearly knows what he's doing. All the men I know do is talk about sex—about how good it is, how they always want more of it, who's willing to give it freely and who's not.

I'm eighteen, grown up. I think I'm ready.

I swallow hard. "Okay."

What follows is the most bewildering, startling experience of my life. When he's gone, I go inside, ball my clothes up, and push them into a grocery bag. I never want to see my perfectly broken-in pair of jeans again.

I'm spun around. Ashamed, disappointed.

Aiden gets home first, before Bittern and Ryland. I've just finished putting the clean sheets on the beds and getting dinner on the table. His truck rumbles, exhaust rattling as he parks it.

I pour a shot of moonshine. It's the third since Braxton left.

Aiden walks in and goes to the sink to wash up. I hate when he does that in the kitchen, but nobody criticizes Aiden, least of all me.

I sink down at the table. He pulls his shirt off and dries himself with it.

"What's the matter with you?" he asks roughly.

I shake my head, wordless. Clearly, something is off—this isn't my normal silence. He comes closer, still drying his hands.

"Speak up," he orders.

"Nothing," I whisper. "Braxton left this afternoon."

He stares at me and I stare back at him. Aiden doesn't like me, never has. I'm the stepdaughter left behind after his second wife became the second wife to leave him. He barely noticed me until I was an adult, old enough to start working.

But now, he's looking, forehead creased.

"What?" he presses.

I wish he'd just go. Aiden has made my life hell. He calls me a whore and taught Ryland to do the same. Now that I'm thinking about it, I'm pretty sure the idea of my body being ruined from sex originated with Aiden.

"Nothing," I say again. "He just… It's nothing."

My voice cracks. The room is so still, I'm aware of the sudden dilation of the dark center of Aiden's blue eyes.

"He rape you?" he says.

I startle. He says that word like it's nothing, but I know that's not so. Aiden might hate my guts, but if Braxton raped me, Aiden is honor-bound by these hills to put the cold end of a gun in his mouth and pull the trigger.

Aiden will do it too. He cuts his teeth on violence. His rap sheet is probably longer than his inked-up arm at this point.

But Braxton isn't a criminal. No, he's just negligent.

"No," I whisper. "He fucked me. I didn't like it, but he didn't…you know."

In his face, something ugly sparks. We stare at each other for at least a full minute. Aiden calls me a whore almost daily, so it's shocking to me that he doesn't say a word. He just picks up his shirt, clearly thinking hard.

"Okay," he says finally. "Alright."

He turns around and walks out, leaving me open-mouthed. I regret telling him, because he's weird around me for the next few days. Then, he disappears, saying he's got business in Pikeville. When he returns, it's like we hit the reset and he's back to hating me as hard as he can.

I never mention Braxton Whitaker to anybody after that. His name comes up once while Ryland is talking a few months later, and Aiden gives him a death stare until he shuts up.

Nobody ever speaks of Braxton Whitaker again.

# NOW

It's winter, I'm twenty-two years old, and Aiden sold every acre of his land to a developer from California. He's loaded from it. It happened all up and down our valley. The developers came in and wrote a check—more money than any of us ever dreamed of. Now, our land is being logged and leveled.

Aiden sold my home, my soft green hills.

Which is why I'm standing outside Bittern's truck in the middle of rural Montana, staring up at the nicest house I've ever seen, a hundred times nicer than the farmhouse we grew up in. In one hand, I have my purse. The other sits on my insect collection cases on the floor of the passenger seat.

There's a row of brand-new trucks in the drive, the kind that costs fifty thousand a pop.

Bittern circles the truck, my suitcase in hand. We stayed back while Ryland and Aiden went ahead to develop the acreage. It was the most peaceful time of our lives. Aiden never worked well with Bittern, so I doubt he noticed his absence. I know my absence in the last six months has probably been a relief.

I'm glad he stayed. I'd hate to have to face Aiden alone.

Bittern wasn't exactly present growing up, but he was the buffer who kept Aiden from dumping me when I was nothing but a birdlike child. Even after the accident in the mine, when Aiden got too violent, he'd rouse himself. Not to hit back, but to shove me outside to keep me from getting decked by a flying plate.

"All good?" Bittern asks.

The front door slams before I can answer. We both look up.

Aiden stands at the edge of the steps. He's in different clothes, the blue-collar working kind, but nicer than I've ever seen. His steel-toe boots are new, his shirt collar not eaten up by sweat yet.

My stomach has a pit in it. If anything, getting money has made Aiden more of a threat to me. Now, he's got a superiority complex and a plan to keep his bank account growing via a fresh start in Montana.

Who knew Aiden had it in him to make good business choices?

Aiden looks at me. He's got that stare, the washed-out one that comes from years of desperation. A chill goes down my spine.

"You make it here alright?" he says to Bittern.

"Yeah. Long haul, but we're good," Bittern says, eyes down.

Aiden jerks his head. "Bring her shit in."

Bittern reaches past me for my collection. My stomach flips as he pulls it out. Aiden goes to the door and takes a dolly from inside, dragging it down the steps. My fists clench as he picks up my cases. They're all wrapped up in sheets. He doesn't know they're my insects, but luckily, he sets them down without slamming them.

Aiden hates it when I have things that make me happy. I do my best so he never sees my insects. Because if he does, the next time he wants to hurt me, he'll go right for them.

My heart flutters as he hauls them into the front doorway and sets them down. Breath caught, I walk into a house that looks like it's right out of a magazine. Only, it's mostly empty. I wonder if Aiden is going to order furniture; it's over an hour to the city as far as I know.

Bittern skirts around me. "Come on upstairs."

Silently, I go with him, pulling the dolly behind me. I'm surprised to see the upper floor is furnished. All the rooms are set up, all eight of them, with beds and a dresser and a rug. I stand there in awe.

"You can pick whatever room you like," says Bittern. "At least the ones that aren't occupied."

Right away, I know which room I want. At the end of the hall is a door on the left side. I pick up my bag and float down to it, pushing the door open. Inside is a twin bed and a desk by the window. There's no dresser, but there is a closet and a bathroom. Distantly, I hear Bittern's boots ring out as he joins me.

"I want this one," I whisper.

"Good choice," he says, putting my bags on the ground.

Bittern disappears, and I go to the window and pull the curtain aside. My stomach is a cold knot. Outside is a barren, desolate landscape, with low hills for miles, flat gray-green land, inky mountains in the distance.

Another set of boots sound on the stairs, not Bittern's. I know everyone by the timbre of their steps. I turn, tucking my hands to my sides. Aiden comes back with the dolly I left at the bottom of the stairs. He locks it with his boot and shifts the boxes off.

I glance up, and he stares back at me, eyes narrowed like he's trying to find something to pick at. Aiden is like a name-brand version of himself, but I know he's just as mean as ever inside.

"I'm going out," Aiden says. "I'll be back late. Bittern and Ryland are going with me. Leave dinner in the microwave."

I nod. "Yes, sir."

He goes downstairs. I stand, fists clenched, and wait for him to go. After a bit, there's quiet. I get changed into jeans and a t-shirt and creep down to explore the kitchen.

My stomach sinks—he hasn't left. He's leaning in the doorway, cigarette in his fingers. His pale eyes are locked on the horizon, one foot inside, one foot out. I halt, contemplating going back upstairs, but he turns, narrowing his gaze.

"Come here," he says.

Dragging my feet, I move closer and stop. There's no way in hell I'm getting within arm's reach. He takes a pull on the cigarette, tilting his head.

"This is a fresh start for all of us," he says. "Back home, we were nothing. Here, I've got a business, land to develop. I don't want the shit you do to blow back on me."

I don't know what he means. Mouth dry, I tuck my hands behind my back.

"I...won't do anything," I whisper.

He kicks the door shut and comes closer, until he's towering over me by over a foot. "You keep your legs and your mouth shut. Put your head down, get a job, pay your rent. Don't be a whore under my roof."

In my chest, it aches. It shouldn't ache anymore. This is nothing new, but it still opens the doors to a flood of shame.

"I haven't done anything," I whisper.

That's a mistake. It's better to just accept Aiden's point of view. His jaw twitches, a glint appearing in his eye. He points at me.

"I know your type," he says. "I married your type."

If I had a dime for every time he's said that, I'd be loaded. It still doesn't make sense. He acts like I'm prowling the streets, trying to get myself knocked up. I've had sex once in my life. It wasn't good, and I haven't tried it since.

But Aiden doesn't have to make sense. He's the patriarch, the bill-payer, the end-all-be-all. Whatever he says is gospel.

"Yes, sir," I say. "I can behave."

"Can? Or will?"

His jaw works again, like he's gritting his teeth.

"Both," I burst out. "And I'll start looking for a job right away."

"Good." The word falls from his lips, short and cold. He taps out the cigarette in the sink and tosses it. I draw back against the counter, watching as he gathers up his keys and wallet.

Then, he's gone—Hurricane Aiden off to ruin somebody else's day.

I'm left in the quiet house, alone. My shoulders sink. I got off easy, and now I can finally relax.

Alone is my favorite place. Quiet is my favorite sound.

I make dinner and eat. Then, I put together three plates and set them in the microwave. When the kitchen is spotless, I tread through the silence up to my room and lock the door.

Carefully, I unwrap the specimen cases. A familiar sense of safety slips over me. There are over two hundred different kinds of insects here, and hundreds of butterflies. My little jewelry box, a piece of my beloved Appalachia.

My mouth tugs up into a smile.

The wind whistles against the house. It's winter and dry-cold outside, not like the breeze that trails through the soft green valleys of the Appalachian Mountains. No, this is a brutal cold I know will chap my skin raw.

A heavy feeling fills my chest. It takes me a moment to identify it.

I'm homesick—not for the aging farmhouse, but for the hills that raised me. My home, despite everything.

That makes me stop and stare out the window at the distant mountains that aren't like the ones I grew up with. I miss the pines, the grass that ripples when a storm comes through. I miss being tucked away in the hills, high up enough so I can see the rivers snaking below.

I miss what I know.

And I dread what I don't.

# CHAPTER TWO
# FREYA

The days that follow my arrival in Montana are a disappointment. Maybe I thought Aiden would calm down now that he has something more than factory work, but he's as big and brutal a presence as ever. The only difference is, he's got a nice truck, lots of money, and land.

The first day after I get home from job hunting, I make dinner—beef, egg noodles, fresh bread—and serve it. When I come back into the kitchen after getting dressed, he's setting his plate in the sink. I reach for it, but my eyes fall on the countertop.

A thin line of dust. Leftovers.

Our eyes meet over the plate. My stomach sinks. Aiden isn't really an addict. He drinks nightly, but he snorts sparingly.

That doesn't mean, behind closed doors, high Aiden isn't terrifying. He's already like a landmine. One wrong move, and *boom*, somebody's getting the shit beat out of them.

Luckily, he doesn't hit me. If he did, I'd be dead.

"You got something to say?" His jaw twitches.

I shake my head. His pupils dilate, and I'm so close, I can see it. Then, he snorts and walks, leaving me standing there, shaking inside. I need to get a job so I'm out of this house. I'm always on eggshells here, and Aiden could turn on me at any moment.

The next morning, I get Bittern to drop me off in Knifley so I can submit more applications. I'm in jeans, boots, and a jacket. My hair is loose to keep my neck warm, pinned with a wool cap. The ground crunches with snow, the gutters a mess of salty ice.

It's a bad time of year to look for work. I've already made my way down the street, applying to every business that will take an application. And I've come up with nothing but dead ends since I started.

The scent of warm vanilla hits my nose. I stop short, looking around. A few yards ahead, to my right, is a café. Right away, it draws me in like a magnet.

The door is fern-green, my favorite color. Entranced, I push it open. Inside is a tiny room with shelves lining the walls and a cash register. On either side of it are glass cases full of pastries, and behind it sits a woman with a motherly face and big, leopard print glasses.

She looks up. "Hey there."

Her voice is soft. She reminds me a little of one of the women from church back home. I gather my courage, extending my hand over the counter.

"I'm Freya Hatfield," I say. "I'm looking for a job. I have experience."

The words rush out. I want to work at this café that smells like a home. The woman shakes my hand, a crease between her brows. There's a short silence, and then she offers me a smile.

"Well, I wasn't hiring, but my husband was just saying how I'm never home, so maybe this is a sign," she says. "We don't get a lot of newcomers in the dead of winter. Why're you here?"

"My family bought a parcel of the old ranch that got divided up and sold off," I say. "We're doing some land development, like building, construction."

Her brows rise.

"I wanted to stay, but I don't...can't," I whisper.

Her eyes soften. "Where are you from?"

"Eastern Kentucky." The word catches in my throat.

"Rough place," she says.

I shake my head, defensive. "It's the most beautiful place in the world."

"No offense meant. You homesick?" She gives me a kind smile.

I nod, unable to speak past the lump in my throat. There's no way I'll let myself tear up. Aiden taught me good and hard not to cry.

"I'm Tracy. I own the place," she says. "I live here in town with my husband. You got anybody?"

"Just my stepfather and his sons," I say.

That doesn't sit right with her; I see it in her eyes. "Your parents not together?"

I shake my head. "She...left, then passed away."

Tracy clears her throat and dusts her hands off. "You said you have experience?"

I nod. "I worked at an ice cream shop back home for five years. I can work a cash register. And I can cook and bake."

She leans on the counter and studies me. It's like being put under a microscope. Then, she sighs and lifts her hands.

"I'll give you a trial," she says. "Lord knows I can use some help. I've got three other businesses downtown."

I dip my head, a shock moving through me. "I promise I'll do it right."

She nods, reaching under the counter and taking out an apron. "You look responsible. Don't disappoint me."

Hardly able to believe my luck, I set my purse down and take the apron. She watches while I take my coat off and put it over my fern-green sweater.

"Thank you," I whisper.

She nods, giving me a smile I hold onto for the whole day. People have been kind to me before, but I'm still in shock when it happens. I'm going to make sure she doesn't regret taking me on.

She gets out a bowl and starts teaching me how to make blueberry scones. I've spent my life cooking and baking, so I know my way around a kitchen. Tracy talks, and I do my best to respond. She's curious about me, but I don't know that I'm very interesting at all.

By the end of the day, Tracy is impressed. We have an entire case of goods ready for tomorrow. The shop is so warm and smells so nice, there's a pit in my stomach as I drag my apron off, hoping she'll say I can stay. I hold out the apron.

Tracy smiles and shakes her head. "It's yours now. You be here tomorrow, bright and early at seven."

I nod, unable to speak. This job gives me money, but it also offers me a place to go that isn't the house.

Bittern picks me up by the courthouse. He's tired, I can see it in his face, so I keep quiet for the drive. Bittern is always so sad. I hoped moving would help, but since the accident…he's just broken.

It happened when I was little. When the recession hit, the factory closed briefly. Aiden and Ryland started a handyman business. Maybe it was just a cover for other things, but Bittern and Wayland went to the mines in Harlan County.

They were gone for months. I wrote to Bittern. He sent me back the wings of moths he found underground and notes stained with coal dust.

Then, one day, the call came. The ground had collapsed, Wayland and Bittern trapped for days. When they pulled up Wayland's body, it was clear he'd died instantly. But Bittern, he'd laid in the dark with nothing but a pack of saltine crackers and a bottle of water for too long.

He broke ribs, but it was his heart that really needed fixing, and not even the compensation check of two hundred and fifty government dollars could put it back together again.

Bittern pulls up to the house and gets out. I follow. It's snowy, ice cold. I don't stand on the porch longer than it takes to tap off my boots. Inside, I can hear Aiden in the kitchen. I put my head down and try to hurry past the doorway. Bittern goes in to sit at the table.

"Come here," Aiden barks.

My stomach sinks. I back up until I'm standing just inside the kitchen. It's dark out, making the kitchen look small. Aiden has his arms crossed, and he's leaning against the counter. Bittern is sprawled out in his seat. He's got a cigarette hanging from his lip, but he's just staring at the wall without lighting it.

Bittern has a kind face, unlike Ryland, who looks more like his father. Aiden is a handsome man, but not even that perk could make his wives stay. He's over six feet, with wavy dark hair dusted with gray and bright blue eyes. Years of manual labor have made him strong. Rough living has put scars and tattoos all over his body.

"Yes?" I say, keeping my tone low, respectful.

"Where were you?" Aiden asks.

"I got a job," I say.

Bittern smiles. "Hey, that's great."

"Thank you," I whisper.

Aiden doesn't reply—he was gearing up to chew me out about being jobless.

"I'm just gonna go wash up," I say, backing up. "Then I'll make dinner."

Aiden jerks his chin. Bittern has gone back to staring at the wall. I put my head down and go upstairs to put my purse and coat away. In the bathroom, I splash my face with cold water and tie my curls on top of my head to keep them away from the stove.

I drag myself into the empty kitchen. Through the window, I see Aiden standing on the side porch—my favorite place when he's not occupying it. Bittern sits on the bench just outside the door. He's smoking again.

I put pork chops on the stove, fry potatoes, and make biscuits. Aiden and Bittern are still outside when I start plating food and drizzling it with gravy made of pork grease and flour. In the distance, I hear Ryland's truck come up the drive and rumble to a halt.

They all have these big trucks with huge wheels now. I had to get into Aiden's a few days ago, and Ryland laughed at me because I was too short to climb in. Bittern silently helped me up. He has to pretend he's not too nice to me in front of Aiden, but I saw him give Ryland a shove.

The front door swings open. I get Ryland's plate, fill it, and put it down. He walks in and sits down at the head of the table. There isn't much to say about Ryland, except he's a less intelligent version of his father.

I stare at him sitting in Aiden's seat.

"What're you looking at?" He cocks his head. He's tired, like he's been working hard all day. I know they've been clearing land on the northern side in preparation for paving a road.

The side door kicks open, and my stepfather appears, smelling of winter and cigarettes.

"She's looking because she's well trained enough to know you shouldn't be sitting in that fucking seat unless you're paying the bills," says Aiden.

Ryland gives me a dirty look and moves. Aiden takes his patriarchal throne, leaning back and spreading his knees. Bittern sinks down at his brother's other side. I set the plates down, along with a beer each. Finally, I sit down with my food.

"Go get me a bottle opener," says Aiden.

I get up, taking the opener from the counter and handing it to him. Ryland leans back, freezing me with his stare.

"I'd like a cold glass," he says.

Obediently, I go to the fridge. I put three glasses in there earlier, but they're nowhere to be found.

"Did anybody take the glasses from the fridge?" I ask.

"I did," says Aiden. "I needed the space."

"Put another in," says Ryland.

I'm unsure what he wants me to do. It'll take a good ten minutes for the glass to get cold in the freezer. Ryland cocks his head, like he's daring me to disobey in front of Aiden.

Bittern coughs, hitting his chest with his fist. He's got bad lungs from the mines, and on top of it, he smokes worse than a chimney.

"Stop fucking with her," he rasps.

Ryland's lip curls. "It's all in good fun."

Bittern jerks his head at my chair, and I go to sit down, but Aiden lifts a hand.

"Get the salt and butter while you're up," he says.

Silently, I go to the fridge again, but the butter dish is empty. In the laundry room is a secondary freezer, so I go there and dig through until I find another pack of butter. The men are talking when I get back, and

I'm glad they're not focused on me. I warm the butter and set it by Aiden with the salt.

I sink down, and Bittern gives me a look, like he's trying to apologize for the others. I offer the tiniest smile back. My food is cold, but it's still good. Eyes on my plate, I cut some pork and put it in my mouth.

Chairs scrape back. Aiden and Ryland get up, Bittern at their heels, their plates and beer bottles empty.

"Let's get the barn locked up," Ryland said. "Fucking cold out."

They leave, and the house is silent. I eat steadily, surrounded by the mess of dinner. I'm at peace inside because I met my little goal and found a job, which means when I wake up, I get to leave this house for eight wonderful hours.

I clean up the table, scrub the kitchen spotless. Outside, the men are fed and happy for the night, standing around on the porch. The smell of cigarettes and the sound of rough male laughter is so familiar, I barely notice it anymore.

That night, I lie on my side and stare into the star-laden sky.

Is this it? Did we go all the way across America just to be the same broken people on the other side? Because nothing changed for me except my belly is full, and now I'm miserably homesick at night.

I close my eyes.

Everything could still change. I want to believe it can.

# CHAPTER THREE
# DEACON

**BEFORE**

Every person who's ever hurt me was a man.

Women, on the other hand, haven't been anything but good to me.

It started with Amie, my foster mother, way back when I was John Williamson, not yet Deacon Ryder. Amie wanted two boys, but she only gave birth to one. I was the rejected twelve year old she landed on to fill that empty spot. God knows why. I'd been given back after an adoption and kicked around the foster system for years.

I was trouble. Even I knew that.

Her husband, Phil, was awful. Good women like Amie usually end up with awful men like Phil. It's the way of things. He fucked around on her, fucked up her life, and fathered a piece of shit son to keep her from leaving.

He hated me. Amie told me it wasn't my fault—we were just too alike.

Fifteen years old, I sit on the back of the ranch's prize stallion, Deacon. Phil bought him a few years back and never did anything with him. Then, I started working with him every day in the morning before chores, on my own time. A year later, I won a state championship and a lot of money with him.

Turned out, I was the best trainer in that part of Montana—I just hadn't discovered it yet.

Now, I train all the horses, and Phil cashes the checks.

The front door opens, and Henderson walks out, hat pulled low. He's the biological son of Phil, the heir of Three Point Ranch. He's like Phil but meaner than a snake, just tied up in knots about everything and everyone.

Behind him comes Phil. He used to kick me around and holler at me until I put his ranch on the map with Deacon and the other horses. Now, I'm the favored son, and Henderson is chopped fucking liver because he doesn't bring in any income. I don't like that much.

"John," Phil barks.

"Yes, sir?" I take my baseball cap off, shoving it in my coat pocket.

"Paperwork's done," he says. "We're going to the courthouse."

Henderson gives me a disgusted glance and slinks away. My stomach turns over. I slide down and bring Deacon into the barn to strip his tack off. Phil joins me, holding out a handful of papers. There's a coffee stain on the corner from where they sat at the breakfast table.

I stare down at them. I've never had a real name. John is the one the nurse who found me on the hospital steps gave me. I've never considered it mine. It doesn't fit my face.

On the top line of the second document is a new name.

*Deacon Ryder.*

I stare at it, mouth dry. I know who John Williamson is. I've been him all my life. He's a hard headed troublemaker with a talent for horses. I don't know this Deacon Ryder.

I also don't know why I couldn't just have Phil and Amie's surname. That would make the most sense.

"Why not your last name?" I ask.

"We'll see how much you make at the fair next weekend," Phil says, taking Deacon into his stall and shutting the gate.

It clicks into place—Deacon's rider. That's what I am to Phil, just the person who put his ranch on the map. He's made so much money in stud fees from Deacon, it makes me half sick to think about.

"You should be thanking me," Phil says. "I gave you a home."

I clear my throat. "Thank you, sir."

Phil walks past me. "Come on, Deacon Ryder. Get in the truck so we can get this finalized."

I'm not too torn up over it. I've never been loved, so I don't know what I'm missing, even if, deep down, I want it. Amie tries to love me, and I'm always kind to her because she's a good woman, but the damage is done.

I've got thick armor, and Deacon Ryder is a hell of a name.

I'm freshly eighteen when something happens that changes everything. Phil is sick, Amie gone. Henderson is thinking he might go to college, but Phil says he's lazy and it's no use. I tell him college won't do shit for him out here, and he tries to hit me in the face.

We end up fighting in the barn, and Phil pulls us apart, but only after we both have split lips and black eyes.

I go inside after Phil chews us out. Henderson and I fight all the time now. The hint of camaraderie that grew between us before Phil found out I was a cash cow is dead, killed by jealousy. Amie's death was the nail in the coffin. We were pretending to get along for her, but there's no point in it now.

I go upstairs and pull my shirt off to splash water on my bloody nose.

A car door slams. I hear a woman's voice. Intrigued, I go to the window. Henderson stands in the yard, still bloody from my fists. There's a pretty blonde girl in the open door of a pickup.

She's mad, waving her arms. Henderson yells back, the veins in his neck popping. Cowed, she backs up, but he closes the gap.

I pull my shirt over my wet torso and go downstairs to the porch.

"You alright?" I call.

Henderson lifts a hand at me. "You fucking stay out of this."

Warning bells go off in my head. I've seen Phil look that way at Amie a few too many times. Not doing anything about it is the biggest regret I have now that she's gone.

"Get in the truck," I say, coming down the steps.

"What the hell?" Henderson turns on me.

"Not talking to you," I say, turning to the blonde gazing open-mouthed at me. "You get in that truck and go. Don't come around him anymore."

Henderson is speechless. I stare the girl down until she obeys and the truck's engine roars down the drive. I go inside before Henderson can fly off the handle again. Dinner that night is a cold half hour, and then I go to bed.

The next day, I go to the gas station to refill a propane tank. I'm standing in the parking lot, talking and smoking with one of the men from the auction in Knifley, when I see a flash of blonde disappear into the store.

I flick that cigarette away and head inside.

Everything changes after I lose my virginity to Henderson's ex-girlfriend in the bed of my truck parked in a field behind the gas station.

After that, it's like a whole new world.

Men either like me or they don't. I got buddies who barrel race, people I can drink with on the weekends, and I like them fine. Then, there's Phil and Henderson and all the other men who've fucked me over and fucked me up.

Until now, I've been so busy trying to survive that I haven't had any time to do more than look at women.

Turns out, women are so much better in real life. I've never experienced intimacy before, and I can't get enough of skin on skin. They're soft, they're sweet, and God, do they feel good when they come on my dick. Even that pales in comparison, though, when I figure out they'll let me put my head between their legs. That's better than liquor, maybe better than barrel racing.

I have a new purpose in life.

I'm good at two things: making women come and raising the best barrel racers in the state of Montana. It tracks that Henderson can do neither. When he finds out I'm fucking his ex, he's livid.

So, I fuck all the rest of them. He's worked his way through all the girls he graduated with at this point. The town is small.

In retrospect, it was an asshole move, but he made it so easy by being the biggest piece of shit in the county.

I'm twenty one when Phil dies and leaves the farm to both of us. Henderson is back together with Calli, the girl I lost my virginity to, and it's put a rift between us to the point we barely speak. She tells him to mend it, he screams at her, and she breaks up with him.

An hour later, she's in my bed with her thighs wrapped around my head.

Henderson and I go back and forth, fighting over her, because Phil was an asshole who used his love like currency to manipulate us. He breaks my nose three times, and I don't have to retaliate, because I am everything he wants to be. I'm bigger, smarter, and I run the ranch and train the horses that sell for hundreds of thousands.

He can't seem to get anything off the ground.

And I fuck his women when he's done with them. That's the thing that keeps us at each other's throats.

Until it goes too far, and I do something that ends this cold war once and for all.

I carry that ugly, terrible thing inside me forever.

# NOW

I'm standing in the dirty alley between the café and the general store. It's ice cold, the air dead. There's a point in winter out here when the cold doesn't ache. It stands still, drier than dust, too cold for more snow to fall.

That's January in north-west Montana, specifically Knifley, unbuffered by the mountains.

My fingers aren't cold. They're too fucked for that. I flick my lighter and hold it to the tip of my cigarette. It flares, I inhale.

From here, I can see the back door of the café. It has two parts: a side for hot coffee and a side for ice cream in the summer. I smoke here once a week when I come into town to pick up cattle and horse feed. Andy, my manager, goes into the general store to get whatever his wife, Ginny, wants. I stay outside to have a quick cigarette.

Today is the first time anybody has ever walked out the back door of the ice cream parlor. I see it from the corner of my eye—the swing of the metal door, a flash of fern-green, the brightest ice blue eyes I've ever seen.

All at once, I'm wide awake.

The person who just stepped into the alley, her cold hand wrapped around a steaming paper cup, is the prettiest girl I've ever seen. My breath hitches. I take the cigarette out of my mouth. I don't want her to see me smoking.

I don't think I want her to see me at all. I need a chance to gawk, so I step back until I'm behind the corner of the building. She's visible, but she can't see me around the edge.

She's got a petite but curvy body—a narrow waist, thick hips and thighs. My eyes drag higher, over her tight, fern-green sweater, over the swell of her hips, and linger on her breasts. I can't help it. They're perfect. I've always had a type, and she's it—short, sweet, and sturdy.

And pretty.

Goddamn, she's a knockout. Big, pale blue eyes with stark lashes. A small nose with a straight bridge, a heart shaped face, a full mouth. Her hair is rich bark brown. It's braided, but it's clear she's got a head of curls by the bits around her ears.

She leans against the dirty wall. Her fingers tighten around the cup.

There's something sad about her, like the last breath of autumn before a freeze. Her skin looks cold, her mouth pale pink. Her lashes flutter, her eyes turning up to fix overhead. I glance up, taking in a flock of geese cutting through the winter sky.

She looks up at them like she wishes she could hitch a ride.

I don't think she was made for this cold.

Entranced, I flick away my cigarette and lean against the corner. She takes a sip from her paper cup. The back door opens, and the store owner, Tracy, leans her head out and says something to her. She nods before the door shuts.

I consider walking up and introducing myself. After all, there's no cure like just doing it. I've always been straightforward.

But something holds me back.

Something tells me this is different.

She flicks away something on her cheek. Then, she throws out the dregs of her cup and pulls open the heavy door, disappearing. My stomach sinks, and the heaviest disappointment I've felt in years sets in. I've always relied on my instincts. They've gotten me to forty without letting me down, And my instincts are telling me not to walk away.

"You alright?"

I look up. Andy stands at the corner, four bags hanging from his hands. He's a tall, wiry man with white hair. Today, he's wrapped up in a thick coat, the collar poking up to his jawline.

"Hell, you look like you've seen a ghost," he says.

I shake my head. "No, just cold. You go on to the truck, and I'll grab a coffee."

"Get me one," he says, skirting around me.

He heads to the back parking lot. I give myself a short pep talk and cross the side street, alighting at the curb on the opposite side. When I circle around to the front window of the café, the crowd has died down. I pull open the door and step into the cramped space.

It's just Tracy standing behind the counter. We've spoken at city meetings plenty of times before. She's a kind woman of about sixty who owns a handful of businesses downtown. The café is her baby, so she spends most of her time here. It surprises me she hired someone to help.

There's a man waiting ahead. He wants to shoot the shit with Tracy. He keeps talking about the weather, and it's really fucking grating on me, but I stand as patiently as I can until he heads out the door.

Tracy looks up, tucking a strand of reddish hair behind her ear. "Look who the devil dragged in," she says.

I lean on the counter. "I know a coffee is two dollars, but how much is information?"

Her brows push together. She goes to fill a paper cup with black coffee. "What do you want to know?"

"You hired somebody," I point out. "Make that two coffees. I got Andy in the truck."

She nods. "I did, from the new family who moved here from Kentucky. What about it?"

"I want to know about her," I say firmly.

Tracy sets my cup down, brow raised. "No."

"What?"

"No," she says. "You're a bit of a whore. And a menace."

"Tracy," I say, giving her my best pleading eyes. "That hurts."

She presses her lips together and crosses her arms. I'm losing her, I can tell.

"I just want to ask. I won't touch," I promise.

I'm lying. I'd like to touch that girl, maybe convince her to let me take her out and spend some time touching her in my truck.

Or take her home.

That trips me up. I never take women home. Ever. I prefer to fornicate in neutral locations, like the bathrooms of bars or sex clubs. The realization that I'd like to take this girl to my home, bring her up to my bed, after a single look at her is unsettling.

This isn't normal for me. My eyes drop, and everything comes to a screeching halt. There's a ribbon on the countertop. Fern-green, one side velvet. The shade is so familiar, but I can't place where I know it from.

"Deacon?"

I bring my focus back to Tracy. She's watching me with a pitying expression.

"What's her name?" I press.

Her lips thin. "Freya Hatfield."

Her face swims into my mind. It's the perfect name for a girl like her—soft but strong. A little wild.

"I know she's pretty, Deacon," she says, "but she's been through a lot. I don't want you making it worse. I like her. She's real sweet, the customers love her. I'm hoping she can be trained to run the shop on her own a few days a week."

She must be special. Tracy's territorial about her café.

"I won't fuck around with her," I say. "I just want to talk."

"Deacon..." Tracy says, voice lowering. "She's twenty-two. Maybe stay away from this one."

I have all the excuses in the world about that. I could bring up how Andy and his wife have twelve years between them, but I don't.

"Just one thing," I say.

Her jaw works. "Fine, I'll tell you something that scares you right off," she says. "She goes to the Methodist church on the state route."

My interest is piqued. "So she's religious?"

Tracy gives a heavy sigh, like she's giving up. "Not so much. She's more of a social religious person. She told me she went growing up because she could walk there and it was a way to get out of the house."

I open my mouth to ask another question, but she frowns.

"You stop wheedling away at me," she says. "I've told you too much already. That coffee is free if you take yourself out of my shop and stop trying to sleep with my employees."

I set four dollars on the counter. "I won't hurt her, I promise. Whose ribbon is that?"

She frowns, following where I point. "Freya's. She left it here."

"Mine now." I shove it in my pocket and grab the coffee. "Thanks."

Tracy watches, jaw slack, as I leave the shop. I'm quiet all the way back to Ryder Ranch. The ribbon burns a hole in my pocket. Andy sits in the passenger side, leafing through the Farmer's Almanac and rambling about the weather. It feels like all everybody is talking about today is the weather. It bothers me because I want to discuss what happened to me when I laid eyes on that girl.

I'm all shaken up, down in my bones.

That night, I don't sleep. After a while, I get up and pull my sweats on and go downstairs. The gas fireplace in the living room glows orange, and I pour a little whiskey in the bottom of a glass and sink down before it.

My house is big and empty, a lonely fortress on a lonely hill.

The firelight glimmers.

Maybe I could do it right this time. I know I'm rough, too old for her. But maybe if I do it right this time and don't come on too strong, I could have a possibility of a relationship. I've always been headstrong and brash. It's how I survived years of being on my own as a child. Those walls keep me safe.

But they've also kept people out.

I don't want that anymore. I have a dark empty house. I want a wife, I want kids.

I think I want her specifically.

The next morning, I peel myself off the couch where I fell asleep and go out to get my chores done. Andy is already up, breaking the ice in the paddock. I go into the barn, where Bones And All, my stallion, waits.

I run my hand over his nose, and he bops my palm. Andy's boots crunch on the gravel as he enters the barn.

"Do you know about the family from Kentucky?" I ask.

"What's that?"

I turn, leaning on the stall door. "Do you know about the family who moved here from Kentucky?"

Andy takes off his hat and sinks onto a straw bale. "The Hatfields. They're the ones who bought the land to the west of you. Not the southern strip you're having problems with, the one up above the main road, closest to our western side."

It's been a year of fighting back encroachments on my land. A few years ago, the man who owned the enormous ranch to the south-west of Ryder Ranch parceled it up and sold it off. It's caused me thousands in lawyer fees and surveyors to keep developers from moving up from the south and putting houses between me and the highway. The last thing I want is to drive through a subdivision to get into town.

Makes me sick to my stomach.

I run a hand over my face. "So they bought the land that goes up to the McClaine's ranch?"

Andy nods. "I never paid much attention to it because it's not all that much acreage. It doesn't seem to be much of a threat to you. It's just a strip between the highway and the McClaine's."

I know the land. It shouldn't bother me much to have a small farm sitting there. The only thing I need to keep an eye on is if the Hatfields start getting friendly with the McClaines.

The McClaines have been trying to turn their land into a housing development for over a year. They lacked the funds. I need to make sure they don't get an idea to make an unholy alliance with the Hatfields.

That would provide a clear path to the main road.

"So Deacon's Hill is the only thing between those two farms," I say. "Means my land touches theirs a bit."

Andy nods again, rising. Deacon's Hill, named for my first horse, is the furthermost northern corner of Ryder Ranch. It's a strip of land that tapers to a point where the land gets rocky. Underneath is a cave system. In the winter, the animals congregate there because it's dry and sheltered from the wind with all the high rocks. Just below is a little valley with a stream running through it for a water source.

It's also sandwiched right between the Hatfields and the McClaines.

"Why do you want to know?" Andy asks.

I shrug. "Just keeping stock of who's in the neighborhood."

The breakfast bell rings in the main housing area. To the left of my house, about a half mile down, is my employee housing. I only need a staff of about forty people full time, and they all live on site. During the branding and breeding seasons, we borrow wranglers from the surrounding ranches.

"You go on to breakfast," I say. "I'll feed the horses."

He disappears, and I finish up with the barn chores. Instead of going to eat with everyone else, I head to town. Knifely is only about thirty minutes down the highway. The roads are clear, the sun is out, and it gives me time to think.

I've had a copious amount of sex in my life, but I've never dated anybody. I know it involves asking a girl out for coffee or something, but I don't know the etiquette.

Maybe I'm scared I'll come on too strong. I don't want to fuck this up.

In Knifley, I park my truck across from the café. She's inside. I see her through the window. This time, she wears a tight plaid skirt that falls to her knee. Her boots come up, and there's a strip of fern-green tights showing. They match her green sweater—and the ribbon in my pocket.

I lean back and watch her through the window as she works.

And the next day, I do it again.

This time, I park my truck in a different spot so she doesn't notice it two days in a row. I get a coffee in a paper cup from the diner and drink it so I have something to do with my hands.

The ribbon burns against my thigh.

My chest is tight, like my heart beats sideways.

She's quiet but animated, a far cry from the cold, pale face in the alley where nobody could see her sadness. When she's at work, she smiles sweetly and listens as customers talk. She's patient, she's kind. She's everything I'm not.

And that makes me want her more.

My cup is empty when I finally start my truck's engine and head back to Ryder Ranch. Once there, I go inside and start pulling my keys out of my pocket to toss them on the table. The ribbon comes out along with them.

I hold it to my face.

Warm vanilla, the way a home should smell.

Something in me breaks. Still in my boots and coat, I head up the stairs and down the hall. At the end is the attic room. I climb the steps and walk down the center of the large room with vaulted ceilings.

When I built the blueprints of this room, I intended for it to be for the woman I married. While I laid down the floorboards, I saw her watching me, curled up on the couch in the corner, gazing at me sleepily while I worked. I swear, I felt her presence, like I knew her already.

I know it was all rooted in my loneliness, my desire to finally have a home.

But it felt like a real possibility at the time.

I planned this room out, but I only got as far as painting the walls. In a haze, my boots carry me across the floor to the far wall. I lift the ribbon and place it against the paint.

It's the same shade. The color of ferns, deep in the woods.

A dark, peaceful shade for a beautiful woman.

I shake my head hard. Either I'm getting some kind of sign from the universe, or I'm so horny, I'm making connections that aren't there.

I stand in the attic by the window and watch the snow fall for a while. The house is quiet. I'm alone again, and I'm sick of it. I think, whether it's a sign or not, I'm going to make it one.

She could be mine. All I have to do is play my cards right, and I can make it happen. I have a place for her already built. She's the missing piece, I'm sure of it.

I go downstairs to my bathroom to get undressed and wash up for bed. When I was younger, I picked up a lot of tattoos, some when I was sober, most when I was drunk or high. I went through a phase where I did a lot of coke and spent too much money on ink. They're stuck on me now. I don't hate them, but I do wish I'd been more careful.

Over the last ten years, I've fixed my arms with cover ups, but I still need to figure out what to do with my chest and stomach.

My mind dips into my baser thoughts.

If I meet her and she's willing to see me, like a date, the way regular people do, it could lead to more. To sex, where she sees all of me. The scars, the smashed knuckles, the scars on my thigh and shoulder—a reminder of the worst moment of my life.

A moment I came back from.

I should have died, but I didn't.

Maybe that means I can do this and do it right.

I splash my face with cold water to bring myself back. The ribbon sits on the sink, staring at me while I dry my neck and chest. I pick it up and bring it to my face again, inhaling.

This time, a surge of arousal follows the warm scent. In my boxer briefs, my cock lengthens and goes rock hard. I push my free hand in them and grip it, groaning softly at the pressure.

It's been a while since I got laid, and I have a feeling it'll be a while until I do again.

I'm going to wait for her.

My eyes shut, and the image of her burned onto my eyelids swims into focus. Beautiful curves on display as she leans across the counter. Tapered waist. Full hips and thighs. Full breasts. An elegant neck with curls falling around it.

*Goddamn it.*

I come all over the sink, three and a half strokes in.

That's when I realize I'm fucked. It hammers it home when I get up the next day and do that again before getting dressed. I put the ribbon beneath my pillow because I don't want her scent to wear off in my pocket.

When chores are done, I find myself in my truck on the way to town. This time, I tell myself, I've got a good excuse, but I can't remember what it was when I park and sit down at the diner across from the café. From my seat by the window, I can see her standing on the doorstep with Tracy.

She's in the same fern-green sweater and skirt with a mug in her hand. Her hair is loose, out in the sun there's a little red in it. She wears these brown boots with laces and tights that show off her legs.

Tracy says something. Freya laughs, flashing a row of white teeth. Then she shifts, like she's nervous showing emotion.

I like those little plaid skirts on her. Maybe I like the thought of pushing her up against something, sliding my hand underneath, and tugging those tights down. Bending her over and getting on my knees behind her—

I need to stop.

They're talking about the shop window. I can see Tracy gesturing at the lettering. I want to go over and introduce myself, but I can't, and not just because Tracy will run me off with a broom. No, there's a real possibility that if I play my cards right, I can get everything I've ever wanted.

I didn't realize up until now that that was Freya.

The next day, I have coffee in town again. She wears jeans this time and a cream sweatshirt. The next day, it's a skirt and tights again.

I have a lot of coffee that week. By the end of it, I'm wired and horny.

A week later, I decide not to go into town after morning chores. It's Sunday, and the ranch is quiet. I wake up feeling frustrated. I've got plenty going on with the land to the north-west of Ryder Ranch. I've seen a few friends about it this week, one of them being my lawyer.

Truthfully, I got a glimpse of something good. Now, I'm bored with everything else. I'm dying for a glimpse of Freya.

I think, for the first time in my life, I'll go to church. I won't go inside—that's a step too far—but I'll watch her walk in. When I realize that, it starts to sink in that this is real, and I'm ready to do some desperate things.

# CHAPTER FOUR
## DEACON

I go to church here and there. Sometimes, I just sit in my truck and watch her from the parking lot. At first, she gets dropped off by her brother. I've seen him around town—Andy pointed both brothers out to me one day. One is taller, dark-haired, and the other is blond with vacant eyes. He's the one who drives her to work and church.

After a while, Tracy starts going with her. Not every time, but once or twice a month. There's something special about this girl. Tracy sure as shit isn't religious, but here she is, taking time out of her Sunday for Freya.

I'm distracted, the closer we get to spring. It's a hard season at Ryder Ranch, and I'm up working from dawn to dusk. Pretty soon, I don't have time to go into town as often as I'd like, but I still make sure that when I do, I drive by the café and see her through the window.

It's a month and a half after I first saw her when something puts the brakes on my slow plan to approach her in a normal manner. I'm up half the night with one of my mares, trying to birth a foal.

Andy takes over around three, and I get a few hours of sleep in, waking to find the mare and foal are alright and the worst is over. Andy goes back to his house, and I get in my truck to pick up supplies in South Platte, the town a few hours east.

It's cold, but I feel a hint of spring. It takes me a while to get through the store, and I'm feeling restless.

I've been restless since the day I saw Freya. It's making me feel my oats a lot more than usual, like I've got a whole lot of something with nowhere for it to go. So, I decide it can't hurt to drive down to West Lancaster. I need to get out of my head, and I've got friends in the area.

The Brass Terrier sits on a street corner, a neon sign signaling it's open. I park around the back and enter through the side door. It comes out beneath the stairs, the L-shaped bar to my left and an open area of round tables to my right. I sink down at the bar, adjusting the seat so I can fit my legs in.

The door above my head opens. Boots clatter down the stairs. A tall, slender figure appears on the other side of the bar. He wears a dark button-up, black hair brushed back over his head. His moss green eyes are always distracted, like he's a million miles away.

"Bit early for you, Ryder," he says.

He's got a low unnerving voice, but everything about Jack Russell is unnerving, just a little too smooth. He leans his elbows on the counter, exposing the necklace hanging under his shirt collar—a silver terrier.

"Just roaming," I say. "Got any bourbon?"

"It's a bar, Ryder," he says. "I've got everything."

"Hit me with it."

He obliges, shoving the glass toward me. "You've got a girl."

I frown, leaning back. "Why would you think that?"

He crosses his arms. "It's my job to know things," he says. "You're tripping after that Hatfield girl."

My stomach sinks. "Who told you that?"

"You're not hiding it," he says. "Word of advice—keep your enemies close, preferably in your bed, because the Hatfields are going to fuck you over before the winter is out."

I take a beat, making sure my next words are careful. Jack knows everything about everyone. He's tight-lipped most of the time, reluctant to spill secrets he can use as currency, so it means something that he's volunteering information.

"Why are you telling me this?" I ask.

His eyes narrow. "I want your white horse," he says. "And when the time comes, I'll repay the favor."

That gives me pause. A favor from Jack Russell is worth thousands, maybe millions.

"Are you talking about the stallion I bought from Texas last year?" I ask.

"Apocalypse In Exile," he says. "Yes, I want him."

"Exile is an expensive horse," I say. "I only got one season from him."

"You can still breed him. I won't charge a stud fee," Jack says.

"Exile is a barrel racer," I say. "And I won't sell him until the fall. I don't sell until the end of the season. I need to get stock of what I have going into winter first."

"He's a distance runner, not just a sprinter," Jack says, undeterred. "I know sooner rather than later, you will need me. Give me Exile, and you have my help, free of charge."

I know better than to say no. Out of everyone I know, I've known Jack Russell the longest. He's the best gun for hire in the country, and he's gotten me out of some of the tightest binds in my life. He shows up at the eleventh hour, fires a bullet, eliminates a problem, and he's gone before the smoke clears.

In that way, he has everyone in his pocket.

He's also my friend. I might be one of the few people who can genuinely call him that.

"Come up to Ryder Ranch," I say. "We'll see if Exile likes you. I don't sell horses that don't want to be sold."

The corner of his mouth turns up. "Exile loves me."

"We'll see." I shake my head. "You're a hard man to refuse."

"It's my best trait."

"Can you get me a coffee to go?"

He nods, going to fire up the coffee pot. "You need to go see Jensen Childress about the Hatfields while you're in the area."

It's been a few months since I've spoken with Jensen, but he's a good friend. He's from Kentucky but now lives and runs a construction company here in South Platte.

"Why?" I ask.

Jack sets a paper cup of coffee down. "Because he built the Hatfield's house that sits right by your property."

I flick my wrist to check my watch. "I wonder if he's home."

"Make sure to knock before you walk in," says Jack, yawning. "Last time, I didn't knock, and there were naked women in his kitchen."

"Plural?"

"Plural."

"Interesting." I pick up my coffee and stand. "You take a look at Exile when the weather breaks."

"I'll come up this summer," he says. "Or fall. I'm busy."

I nod and step out onto the street to head back to my truck. Snow drifts, wet enough to signal spring isn't far off.

I'm heading down the main road when I see a familiar sight—the tailgate of Jensen's construction truck disappearing around the bend. He's heading up toward the main state route. Making a U-turn, I follow him out of West Lancaster and out onto the flat stretch of road heading east.

It takes him ten minutes to pull up beside a construction site near the road. I bring my truck behind him and get out, but he takes his sweet time.

"Why're you stalking me, Ryder?" he calls over his shoulder.

The snow is falling harder but not hard enough to worry about. I follow him as he heads up to the foundation of a house with walls, doors, but no siding.

"Jack said you knew about the Hatfields."

He pushes in the door, turning around. "Yeah, I built their house. What about it?"

He dips inside and I follow. The half-finished house is dusty and smells of pine. It's fucking cold in here. I push my hands into my pockets and go after him as he takes out a measuring tape and gets to work in the kitchen.

"What can you tell me about the Hatfields?" I say.

Jensen straightens, flicking the toothpick from one side of his mouth to the other. "They've got two sons, but the patriarch, Aiden, said there were three. They're all from one of the south-east counties in Kentucky."

"He's got a daughter, right?"

The words fall from my mouth before I can bite them back. Jensen's brow rises, and he leans back, crossing his arms.

"Looking for a girlfriend?" he drawls.

"I need to know about the Hatfields," I say. "Jack said so."

Jensen doesn't stop smiling. "Sure it don't have anything to do with that pretty little brunette who lives right next door to you now?"

"I'll beat your ass," I threaten. "Have you met her?"

"No, but I know she exists. I helped build their house," he says, shrugging.

I sigh, crossing my arms too. "Jack's being all fucking mysterious about them. I need to know what's going on."

"Nothing," Jensen says. "But I'd be careful trying to fuck around with Freya. She's got an insulated wall of asshole men around her, and I'd put my money on Aiden trying to hook her up with one of the McClaines."

The McClaine farm sits above mine. They're part of the reason I've had too much trouble keeping the roads and developments off Ryder Ranch. Elijah McClaine wants to put a development on his land. It would make him a multimillionaire, but to do that, he'd have to... No, this is what I was hoping wouldn't happen.

My mind goes back to the conversation I had with Andy about the Hatfields. Aiden would have to own or have legal access to the Hatfield land, which he could get through the McClaines.

I take my hat off. "Is Aiden Hatfield friendly with the McClaines?"

"Very," says Jensen.

"Fuck," I say.

Jensen's jaw works, and he runs his hand over it. "You think they're planning on going in on a development?" he says. "But you would still have Deacon's Hill as a buffer between whatever road Hatfield tries to run across his land up to the McClaine property."

He's right—there's still a solid strip of land separating the Hatfield's and McClaine's land. It belongs to me, and there's no way in hell I'll sell it. But this may mean I get to spend this coming summer worrying about that on top of the city council member and real estate developer pushing at my property from the other end.

Somebody is about to get a bullet to the temple.

I'm tired of courtrooms.

I stare, thinking hard, and Jensen goes back to measuring the spots for the kitchen appliances. We fall into a hollow silence until he's done. Then, he straightens, dusts off his hands, and puts his hat back on.

"Want to get some food? I need to head into Knifely, so I can meet you there," he says.

"Does your business have something to do with the naked women Jack said you had in your house?" I say, following him back outside.

"Aw, shut up. You're jealous," he says, locking up and shoving the keys in his pocket.

We pause beside the trucks. "Not jealous," I say. "I think those days might be over for me."

Jensen's brows rise. "Why's that?"

I clear my throat, unsure how to answer. "I just...think I'm ready to settle down."

His eyes narrow in thought as he pulls open the truck door. "You've been ready for a while now," he says, getting in.

It gives me a lot to think about as we both head to Knifely. Not just that I'm ready to settle down and I have an idea the girl I want is one I've never even spoken to, but her family buying that farm might have opened up hell on Earth for my ranch.

I have to be careful. I can't go in there like a bull busting through the gate for many reasons.

I blink hard, running a hand over my face. The truck is hot, and I'm sweating. I crack the window as we get into Knifely and pull up beside the curb. Jensen gets out, and we meet on the sidewalk outside the general store.

"What are you looking at?" Jensen asks.

I tear my eyes from the café window. Through it, I can see the back of Freya's head—long dark hair, braided, leaning on the counter as she talks to a customer. There's the prettiest little arch to her lower back, right before her perfect ass I've spent too much time thinking about.

I swallow. I can do this. I can handle this without fucking up.

"I said, what're you gawking at?" Jensen says, louder than he needs to because I'm standing three feet from him.

I jerk my head toward the café. "That's where Freya works."

"Well, let's go in then."

Jensen starts walking, and I grab him by the elbow and haul him into the general store. He stumbles in, hat askew.

"Jesus, what's wrong with you?" he spits.

"Don't talk to her."

"Why the fuck not?"

"Because I haven't talked to her yet," I say. "I don't want to scare her off."

He looks at me like I've lost my mind—and maybe I have, but I want this so bad that nothing can fuck it up for me. I need time to figure out what's going on with her family and then do this right, with the flowers and gifts and shit.

I'm pretty sure that's the way it's supposed to go.

Jensen's jaw works. "Alright," he says. "But I'm a great wingman."

"And I'll let you know when I need assistance," I say.

He's satisfied by that, and we head to the diner a few blocks away. We talk for a while, not about Freya, thankfully. The waitress serves us watery coffee, but it's hot, so we both have two cups. It's helping me get my head on straight to get off my ranch and out of my truck.

Jensen and I have been up to Sovereign Mountain more than usual in our spare time. I don't know if I would call myself friends with Gerard Sovereign. He's a hard man to befriend, but I like his land manager and close friend, Westin Quinn, a lot. I would pay good money to get him out to Ryder Ranch to work for me, but he's loyal to a fault.

Maybe I just need to spend more time in South Platte and at Sovereign Mountain. I think being holed up at Ryder Ranch is making me lonely.

We part ways. Jensen has some work to do, and I should be getting back. I'm almost to my truck when I see something through the general store window—a bolt of soft green fabric, the same color she always wears. It wouldn't be strange for me to buy it because, if I'm being upfront, I have a whole trunk in the attic of little things that remind me of her. I can't help it. Everything I see that reminds me of her makes me feel like this could be more than delusion.

Like it's all part of a path I can follow straight to her.

So, I buy it, because I'm pussy whipped for a girl I've never even spoken to.

And I get some fern-green lace to go with it.

Back at Ryder Ranch, we finish up chores and lock the barns. Andy goes to his house with Ginny, and I'm alone again, rattling around in this big house with nobody.

I have a drink and then I have a smoke on the back porch. Then, it's time for bed, but instead, I go up to the third floor to stand in the attic room for a while. There are a set of four skylights covered by panels. I hit the button that slides them back and stand there, staring up at the sky.

This whole acquiring a woman thing takes longer than I expected.

My eyes run over the fern-green walls I painted and think about Freya and every time I've seen her in the last few weeks. She does the same things every day, the way any person does, but there's something about her every move that has me infatuated.

When I designed the house, I'd hoped this could be a playroom—of the adult variety—in addition to whatever my future wife wanted it to be. Probably for reading or something by day. Up until now, I never had the motivation to finish it.

But now, I do.

I stand in the center of the room, looking up at the sturdy central beam. I enjoy power plays, aspects of BDSM, and I prefer being in a

Dominant role during sex. I wanted a private place to play with my future wife. This beam was supposed to be an anchor point for a ring or two. The idea was, the submissive could be suspended with her head hanging upside down so only the sky and stars were visible— a kind of sensory deprivation.

I tilt my head back. The Milky Way spills overhead.

Maybe that's the root of why I haven't talked to her yet.

She's sweet, she goes to church, she works at a café where she makes pastries all day. I'm not her kind of man. Yet, here I am, thinking about what she'd look like suspended naked from my ceiling.

Thinking hard, I go downstairs and make a coffee while I find the blueprints for the attic room.

I think it's time to get back to work.

# CHAPTER FIVE
# FREYA

## AUTUMN

There's an odd feeling in Montana that I can't name, and I don't get used to it. It's like somebody's watching me. It comes and goes. One moment, I'm hopping out of Bittern's truck and heading down the street to work, feeling fine. The next, I'm unlocking the café door and looking over my shoulder, scalp prickling.

I consider asking Tracy if this is normal for Knifely, but when I think through the conversation, it sounds silly. So, I keep my mouth shut, because how am I supposed to explain I feel like I'm being stalked?

Maybe I'm stressed out being in a new place. Aiden is as horrible as usual. I'm lonely, and maybe I'm starting to imagine things.

Usually, Bittern comes to get me after work. He works up on the McClaine Ranch because he can't hold down an official job. Every night, he leaves around six and swings by the old gas station, about two miles from the café, before picking me up.

Then, one night, he doesn't come.

Tracy is gone in the city for a business conference. I spend the day prepping trays for a catering order. Everything is ready for Tracy in the morning, all wrapped in plastic and put in the fridge. I eat a leftover croissant as I sweep and wipe everything down. Then, I put my coat on over my skirt, thick tights, boots, and sweater and lock up.

Overhead, buffered from my view at the counter, gray clouds roil on the horizon. Everything smells ominous. The leaves on the maple at the street corner are flipping.

There's that feeling, the one I hate. Like I'm not alone.

I lock the café and push the key into my pocket with my wallet. The street is cleared out, save for a few people at the bar a few blocks down. I consider going there and calling Bittern to come get me. But no, I don't want to cause him extra trouble.

If I hurry, I can get to the drop-off point before the rain hits.

The wind picks up. The further I get from town, the more that feeling fades. My body relaxes as I push my hands in my pockets and walk fast, head down. I'm not scared of rain. I *am* scared of being stranded, easy prey for anyone passing by.

The drop-off is a patch of gravel where the state route meets the back road up to the McClaine Ranch. Bittern's truck isn't there; he's a few minutes late. But that's not uncommon.

I stand, waiting.

Overhead, the clouds churn. An icy raindrop hits the back of my neck and trickles down. Shivering, I wipe it away, but they keep coming, hitting the pavement with loud splats. I'll be soaked by the time Bittern shows up.

A cold, lonely wind whips through, tugging my curls. There's a heavy rush to my left, and I turn, expecting to see a car. Instead, a thick gray mist rolls over the hills, heading right for me.

My heart drops. It's a solid wall of rain.

It hits me before I can move, and I'm soaked in seconds. Breathless, I rip off my coat and hold it over my head. Rain pelts me from all angles as the wind tears at my skin and clothes.

I wait, miserable and scared. I don't like standing at the edge of the road on a good day. In a storm, it makes my heart pound in my throat.

The wind is getting stronger. I manage to look at my phone, which has no service on this part of the road, and see Bittern is almost thirty minutes late.

Something must have held him up at work.

Pit in my stomach, I start walking, because I don't know what else to do. There's no one else to call. Aiden and Ryland are in the city today—not that they would pick up if I called. Tracy is miles away at her conference. There's nobody else to call, and I have no place to go.

The road blurs in my vision. The rain is so heavy, it's dripping into my eyes, even with my coat pulled over my head.

My body is numb with fear. My feet pump, taking me further from town. The state route is empty, or I might be desperate enough to try hitchhiking. So, I keep my eyes on the white line at the edge of the pavement and keep moving.

There's no other option.

About three miles in, the road narrows and becomes gravel for a while before widening again. Here, I feel a little safer. I can move through the grass ditch at the edge, the woods on my left side for cover. At least, if I need to run, I won't be out in the open.

It poses a different problem—the bridge.

I see it up ahead and, right away, my stomach sinks. Sputtering and wet, I climb out of the ditch and move down the road until I can't get any further. The creek is swollen, red-brown water roaring over the bridge. It's a one-lane without guardrails, and the water surging over it is moving treacherously fast.

I can't get through that.

The only thing stronger than the disappointment is the panic. Right then, the wind gusts so hard, I stumble. My jacket rips from my hands and disappears into the creek to my left.

Fear settles in like ice.

Real fear.

I should have gone back to the café and slept on the floor until the storm broke. Now, I'm miles from town, the storm only strengthening, the temperature dropping. If I walk back, it'll be pitch black by the time I get to the drop-off point, so I'll have to walk two miles in the dark on the state route. If I go forward, I'm likely to drown. If I try to wait it out in the woods, I could die from exposure.

I turn, taking in my surroundings.

All around me, Ponderosa Pines stretch up to the sky. The woods are unforgiving, and if life has taught me anything, it's that I'm vulnerable. I can be hurt.

A faint rush reaches my ears. I blink, squinting up at the road. Through the rain, two lights appear, pale white, about the level of a truck.

I don't know what to feel. Maybe I'll die of exposure in the woods, but I would rather do that than meet the wrong kind of man. Falling asleep and never waking up is preferable to torture.

My brain tells me to move.

My feet stay planted.

The lights get closer until I can see the vehicle clearly. It's a huge, dark gray truck with a tire strapped to the roof. It pulls up and around to my right and stops. I'm rooted to the ground. My body is frozen, even though a scream claws its way up my throat.

The passenger door is pushed open.

There's a man sitting in the driver's seat. He's tall, larger than Aiden by a few inches, and he's broad without being bulky. His dark hair is shaved and fades up to a little length on top. It's the same deep shade as his hooded eyes. He's in work pants and a charcoal Henley that clings to his broad shoulders.

My pulse flutters so hard, I feel it on my tongue.

He leans over. "You need help, sweetheart?"

His voice is low with an undertone of gravel. It doesn't sound like he raises it much.

I shake my head, speechless with fear.

"Let me take you home," he says. "I can bring my truck over the bridge."

Again, I shake my head. Why won't my legs work?

He sighs, one hand resting on the wheel. It's then I notice all the dark tattoos over his exposed skin. There are even some going up his neck to his strong jawline.

"Are you Freya Hatfield?" he says.

That catches me off guard. I clear my throat twice.

"How did you know that?" I ask, my voice cracking.

"Deacon Ryder," he says. "I live on the ranch next to your farm."

A trickle of relief goes through me. The people who come into the café talk about the surrounding ranches all the time. Ryder Ranch comes up in conversation the most. I've never seen Deacon, but I know he runs it, and he's rumored to be one the best horse trainers around. I just didn't realize he looked like that.

"I won't bite," he says. "Get in the truck, sweetheart."

I look at the water, rising by the second. It does make me feel better that he's a prominent person in the community. It feels like the chances of him hurting me are somehow lower.

Heart pounding, I reach for the handle and try to pull myself up. My foot slips. A warm hand wraps around my wrist and pulls me into the passenger side. He reaches past me and pulls the door shut, cutting off the raging storm.

"There's a blanket behind you," he says, spinning the wheel to reposition the truck. He backs up and squints. "That water might be too high."

My body is shaking so hard, I can barely pull the blanket over it. He flips the heat on full blast and spins the wheel again, turning the truck all the way around.

"I think we'll have to take the back way," he says. "The highway is closed for an accident. Semi jackknifed."

"This is the back way," I whisper.

He shakes his head, accelerating. The truck speeds down the road, spraying mud. It eats up the distance I stumbled through with ease. In seconds, we're back on the state route.

"What are you doing out here? You don't have a car?" he asks.

I look sideways, studying him. He's handsome, despite his face having brutally cut angles. There's a bump in the middle of his nose. He glances at me, and I'm taken aback by seeing his eyes up close. They're dark, but there's a softness to them I didn't expect. In the middle of such a rough face, it's startling.

He's like Aiden but not like Aiden.

I shiver.

"You okay?" he says.

I nod. "Sorry, what did you say?"

"I asked why you were out here," he says. "You don't have a car?"

I shake my head, still feeling like a deer in headlights. "I can't drive, really. I don't have a license."

His forehead creases. "Why not?"

"Nobody taught me to drive," I say. "I don't have a car."

He doesn't answer, but I notice his jaw muscle flickers. I turn, and through the window, I see we're almost at the drop off. There's no sign of Bittern waiting for me. I check my phone, which is stuffed in my pocket.

My stomach sinks. It's soaked. I hit the button and nothing happens.

I have to fight back tears. It took me a month of saving to get this cheap phone. Now, it's ruined.

Deacon turns the truck onto the gravel route that veers up the mountain. My muscles tense up. I've never been this way before.

I wet my dry lips. "Please don't hurt me," I whisper.

He swings his head around, like he's surprised.

"I'm not gonna hurt you, sweetheart," he says.

I shift, pushing my back against the door. "That's what somebody who was going to hurt me would say," I manage.

He lets out a quiet sigh. "Open the glove box," he says. "There's a gun in there. Shoot me if I try to hurt you."

That shuts me up. It takes me a moment to recover from the image of shooting him. Then, I shake my head.

"No," I say. "Just don't hurt me."

He keeps his eyes on the road, but there's a ghost of a smile on his harsh mouth.

"I won't," he says.

We're both quiet then. The windshield wipers are loud. I don't know how he can see, even with them. The rain is coming down so hard, it's difficult to make out anything past the hood of the truck.

I'm warming slowly with the blanket wrapped up to my chin and the heat blasting. Now that I'm not shivering, I can think more clearly. Yes, I'm afraid, but I also have to be reasonable about this. He's our neighbor, not a stranger. If he was going to hurt me, he would have done it on the back road by the creek.

I can reasonably conclude he doesn't intend to.

My eyes keep drifting over to him.

He has a dark magnetic energy, a raw sexuality. Maybe it's confidence. I follow the curve of his broad shoulder down his forearm to where the sleeve is rolled. His thick arm is wrapped in ink to the tips of his fingers. I let my gaze linger, going further down to his belt.

Heat curls in my lower belly, shocking me.

Am I turned on by him?

I shake my head once, forgetting he can see, but he doesn't turn his head. He just keeps driving with a slight frown set on his face. My stare goes right back where it left off—right to the bend of his wrist, his fingers hanging loose over the top of the steering wheel.

His hands are very...attractive. I've never taken the time to think about hands as something erotic, but now, despite everything, I'm having a physical reaction.

I'm just stressed out.

We come to a quick halt, snapping me out of my daydream. I blink, and the windshield wipers swish.

My jaw drops.

There's a tree across the road, broad and long, barely illuminated by his headlights. There's no getting around it or dragging it out of the way. The trunk alone comes up to the grill of his truck.

"Goddamn," he says under his breath.

I sit up straighter. "What's that mean? Is there another way back?"

He shakes his head, jaw set. "Not until the water drops.."

I shake my head. "What... Can we just cut it back?"

He smiles, one corner of his mouth jerking up. "No, I don't have anything to cut it back with. You got one option, sweetheart, and you're not gonna like it."

My stomach sinks.

"Walk," I whisper.

"No, you're not walking home in the dark in a storm," he says. "You come back with me. You can take one of the guest rooms. In the morning, I'll come down, assess the damage."

A heavy gust of wind shakes the car. It's so dark, I can't see anything out of my window. He shifts in his seat, and my mind goes to the gun in the glove box. I take a deep, shivery breath.

"Are you the only one who lives there?" I whisper.

"Not on site. I'm the only one in the house, but I have live-in employees next door," he says.

I chew my lips. He shifts the truck in reverse and spins the wheel with his palm until we're facing back where we came. He accelerates without waiting for my reply. At this point, I don't think it matters what my answer is. He's asking me as a courtesy.

We're going to Ryder Ranch whether I want to or not.

"So what do you do, huh?"

He's talking casually, like he's got no other mode. I clear my throat, trying to match how unbothered he is, and failing.

"I work at the café," I say, my voice squeaking.

"With Tracy?"

"You know Tracy?" I ask, surprised.

"Yeah, I know Tracy," he says, making another turn. We're on a smooth road now, driving on a gentle incline. The rain is still pouring down, and the wind beats on the truck. "We do city meetings together sometimes."

A little tension eases from my shoulders.

"She's never mentioned you," I say.

"We're more business friends," he says. "You like what you do?"

He has such a strange way of making small talk. His voice is casual, but it feels like he's really listening and wants my answer. Nobody listens to me, but this man is listening with his whole concentration.

It's intimidating.

"Yeah, it's nice," I say.

Before he can speak, an overhead sign that says Ryder Ranch looms out of the darkness. He pivots the truck to the right, and we're heading up a long driveway. Through the rain, I think I see lights.

He rumbles to a halt and puts the truck in park. "I'm gonna get you inside. Then I need to check the barn."

I nod, wordless. He leans in, and for a second, I think he's reaching for me. Then, he pulls a black cowboy hat from the backseat. Before I can move, he puts it on my head. There's a second where he looks at me too long, like this means something.

"Keep the rain off your face," he says.

I nod, wordless. He disappears, and I hear his boots crunch for a second before my door yanks open. He holds out his hand. I hesitate, then put mine into it. Everything is cold in that second, but where our skin touches, that's bright hot.

It travels up my arm.

And down to my lower belly.

Down between my thighs.

Shocked, I let him lift me out and usher me through the dark. We go up some porch steps, and he taps the keypad on the door. Then, his broad arm wraps around my waist and guides me into the front hall.

I don't know what to do but go along. He pushes the inner door shut, abruptly cutting off the storm's raging.

My eyes adjust. His house is beautiful. The wooden walls are stained until they're almost black. The hall floor is rich oak, shining with a deep blue rug rolled over it. On the walls hang black and white photographs of different horses, probably prize studs from Ryder Ranch.

Someone cared a lot about this house when it was built. I wonder if it was him.

"You're shivering again, sweetheart," he says.

He steps closer and takes his hat off, hanging it by the door. Our eyes meet, and something crackles in the air, like a spark. There, then gone. I look down, aware our bodies are inches apart.

He's enormous, bigger than he was in the truck. The Henley over his torso is soaked, sticking to every ridge of his stomach. My eyes drop lower. There's a slight rise under his zipper.

Oh, God—I jerk my eyes up to meet his dark gaze. There's that off-kilter smile again.

"You good?"

I shake my head. There's something wrong with me, or I wouldn't be ogling him. "I think I'm shocked," I whisper. "I don't know... I was really scared when I had to walk alone and I lost my coat at the river."

My body shivers harder in response. He clears his throat.

"You need to get those wet clothes off," he says, voice husky.

I look down. My fern-green sweater is suctioned onto my body, showing my curves and the clear outline of my bra underneath. My skirt clings to my tights, which now have a run down the right leg.

"I don't have any other clothes," I whisper.

"You can wear one of my flannels," he says. "But you need to get warm first. You want a bath?"

Just talking about wet clothes and baths has a raw heartbeat thumping between my legs.

What's wrong with me?

He's the opposite of who I want. I know better than to look twice, but here I am, staring up at him without a thought in my head. I know just by looking at him that he's a scarred-up, knuckles-in-the-drywall son of a gun. I should walk away right now.

The problem is...he's got such pretty dark eyes.

And he's talking to me real slow and deep, calling me sweetheart. It's like warm water trickling through my veins, all the way to my guarded heart.

"Head down the hall," he says, not waiting for an answer. "You're clearly shocked, so you're going to listen to me until you feel better."

He puts a hand on my lower back, ushering me down the hall. From the back of the couch, he takes a blanket and wraps it around my shoulders. Then, he helps me sit on one of the couches and heads up a flight of stairs that winds over the back wall of the living room.

I hear his boots upstairs. The room is dimly lit, but I can see the walls are all painted deep navy blue. There's a broad beam running down the ceiling. It leads all the way to a gas fireplace that's easily as tall as me. The stone is shiny white, and the orange flame reflects off it in a dizzying pattern.

He lives in the most beautiful house I've ever seen. Everything feels purposeful, like he knows how to take care of it. It's confusing, because he looks like the men I know who do nothing but destroy. I've never met a man who cared about his home.

His boots sound on the stairs, and he comes into view.

"Come here," he says.

There's no room in his voice to refuse. I set the blanket down and head to the stairs, pausing at the bottom.

"Should I take my boots off?" I whisper.

He nods. "You can."

I slip them off and pad up to him in my wet socks. He goes on ahead, leading the way through a hallway painted like the downstairs. There's a nightlight glimmering at the far end, but otherwise, the hall is dark. It's not ominous, but it's not comfortable either.

He pushes open the door, second to the last. Inside, I can see a large room with wall-to-wall windows on the far end. My jaw drops, and I forget about him for a second. My feet carry me through the doorway. I barely hear him shut it behind us.

The lamp is on and the fireplace crackles, shedding enough light for me to see. The floor is dark wood, the walls deep blue. The hearth is black stone, and there's a set of panels on the wall above it. Below that are two mirrors on hinges. They're turned away from the bed, but if it moved, they'd reflect it back.

I turn my head, creeping closer.

The panels are four rectangular paintings that make up a scene. It's of some kind of beast, hunting, and there's a woman fleeing from it. She's running, but up ahead is a lake.

She has nowhere to go.

Cold trickles through my body. I turn slowly to find him standing in the bathroom doorway. Warm light spills out around him.

"You need to call somebody, sweetheart?"

Everything floods back. "Yeah, but my phone is dead. I think it got wet."

"I got a spare flip phone you can have if you want to switch the card," he says.

I hate accepting charity, but I've been forced into it for years. I'm in no position to pretend I can do without his help tonight. So, I just nod, offering a weak smile.

"I got a bath running for you. There's a flannel shirt on the chair," he says. "You can lock the door. I'll go do the barn chores and get the guestroom ready. Okay?"

He's looking at me in that way, eyes fixed on me like there's nothing else in the room—all that heavy attention focused right on me.

"Okay," I whisper.

He doesn't move. Head down, I dip past him into the bathroom and turn, my hand on the door.

"Thank you for helping me," I whisper.

"Just being neighborly." He gives me a long look with his dark puppy eyes.

My breath quickens. Is this shock or something else? He's standing so close, and I'm so cold. My body must be starving for heat. That has to be all it is. Avoiding his eyes, I shut the door and sink against it.

What have I gotten myself into?

# CHAPTER SIX
# DEACON

She's here. After months of wanting.

I have a deep hunger. Now that she's here, it aches in my marrow. She's in my house, flesh and blood, all soft curves, soaked clothes barely clinging to her perfect body.

The light under the bathroom door burns in my vision, leaving light spots behind my eyelids. I take a step back. I've already watched her for months.

What does it hurt to watch her a little more?

Silently, I open the closet door and step back into it. There's a section where the wall isn't fully finished. I used to keep a dresser in front of it, but a few weeks ago, I moved it with the intent to finish the seam.

Now I'm glad I didn't, because where the wall and the doorway meet, there's a sliver of an opening. It looks directly across the bathroom, to the tub at the back left corner. Steam rises from the dark copper basin, surrounding her in a fine mist.

She lifts the hem of her sweater and pulls it over her head with difficulty. It sticks to her skin then peels away.

My groin tightens.

She's so beautiful. Curvy, her waist dipping in and blossoming out, the fine line of her spine going up to her drenched hair. She looks like one of those women in old paintings, where they're always naked and languishing on something. Classically beautiful in her softness.

She undoes her skirt and tugs it down along with her tights. That makes her bend, but I don't see her ass until she kicks them off and stands again.

*Goddamn.*

It's better than I imagined, and I spent a lot of time fantasizing about it. My breath catches. She hooks her panties and peels them down, kicking them off her ankle. Then, to my disappointment, she sinks into the tub without turning around.

I tilt my head. That's alright. I'll have plenty of time to see the rest of her body later.

My dick is so hard, it hurts. Silently, my hand finds its way to the ridge and palms it.

I can't do this here, not now.

But God, I want to.

There's something so sensual about her. Maybe it's her dark curls, the color of the woods. Or her velvety skin. Or her big pale blue eyes that remind me of ice on the deep river that runs down the mountain.

Or it's the aura around her that I don't know how to explain. It's like she was made for a different world.

I don't know, but I do know that she was made to be mine.

Moving on the sides of my boots, I leave the closet and go back into the hall. By the time I have my coat and hat back on, my dick has gone down, but my head is still rolling the image of her naked body around, fixating on every tiny detail. The mole by her shoulder blade. The single dimple above her ass.

When the barn is secured against the storm, I go back inside and change in the guestroom. She's here, so I put a shirt on with my sweatpants before going down to the kitchen.

Downstairs, I take the phone from my office and lay it on the kitchen table. It doesn't have a tracker in it. That felt invasive, so I just cloned it so I can see her texts if I need. I have an uneasy feeling about her situation, like sooner rather than later, she's going to need help.

My hands move of their own accord as I make toast and coffee, but my head is in that bathroom with her. My whole attention is concentrated on it.

Over the summer, it occurred to me that this is more than attraction. I have an obsession. It started with soft fern-green. It escalated to watching her daily in the café, to watching her in the church parking lot, and went all the way to seeing her undress through the crack in my closet and giving her a phone so I can keep tabs on her.

I have a problem.

But I don't have a problem with it.

She clears her throat. I turn. Right away, my dick twitches. She fills out my flannel perfectly. The top button is open, showing her cleavage. The hem comes to the middle of her thighs, leaving those curvy legs bare.

"You hungry?" I manage.

She nods, eyes huge. "I didn't get dinner."

"Sit at the table," I say. "I'll make something."

She obeys, but her eyes follow my every move, wary like an animal. I set the coffee and toast down in front of her.

"You like fried eggs?" I ask. "Bacon?"

She nods.

"Not a big talker, huh?"

She shakes her head. I smile, and I think I see a flicker of one in return. I take a cast iron skillet and set it to warm up while I get the eggs and leftover bacon from this morning. Her gaze follows my every move, even when she takes a sip from her mug.

"So, tell me about yourself," I say.

She clears her throat. "There's nothing much to say. What do you do?"

"I own the place and I train the horses and sell them. We also do some cattle out here."

"I don't do anything that interesting," she says thoughtfully. "I work at the café. At night, I go home and do the cooking."

"You don't have nothing you like?"

She tilts her head. "I collect moths and butterflies. Some beetles."

That catches me completely off guard. I stare at her for a minute, the grease in the pan crackling as the bacon reheats.

"Like, you keep them in a bucket or something?" I ask.

She laughs, and my head goes empty. It's a soft, pretty sound, barely bubbling from her throat. A blush fills out her cold cheeks.

"No, I collect them when they're dead and keep them preserved," she says.

"Why?"

I don't mean it in a bad way, I've just never met anybody with a strong interest in bugs and moths.

"Because they're beautiful," she says. "And interesting."

I lean on the counter, crossing my arms. "Huh. How many do you have?"

"Hundreds, near about."

"That's a lot of bugs."

She tilts her head, and her guard goes up again. "You think it's silly."

"I think it's respectable and unusual," I say. "Not silly."

She giggles again, and this time, she bites her lower lip for a second. I get a flash of her teeth, and when she lets it go, I see the tip of her tongue. Then it's gone, and I'm turning around under the guise of cracking eggs, but really, I've got a half-boner pushing at the front of my pants.

God, she's perfect. I think I'll keep her.

"Do you mean that?" she asks.

I turn back around. She's watching me intensely.

"Yeah. Why wouldn't I?"

Her eyes drop. "Everybody makes fun of it. Except Bittern."

There's a raw note in her voice, a little bit of pain.

"It's as good as any other interest," I say, flicking the stove off. I plate the eggs and bacon and set them in front of her. She looks down but doesn't move. "That alright?"

She nods. "I've just never had anybody cook for me."

I sit down opposite her with my own plate. "Yeah? Why's that?"

"I live with my stepfather and his two sons," she says. "None of them cook."

"So you did it?"

She nods, taking a bite of bacon. "This is good. Thank you."

We eat in silence for a while. The storm rages against the house, making the windows rattle. Inside, it's warm and the walls are thick. This is the way I like to live close to the wilderness but not quite in it. Like an animal, deep in a winter cave.

It lets me live free but still keeps the door open for a home.

"So...what do you like to do?" she asks quietly.

I lean back in my chair, wiping my hands on my napkin. "When I'm not training the horses? I run the ranch with Andy, my manager. I do a bit of carpentry, did the interiors of this house. Blacksmithing, barrel racing when the fair comes around."

She turns her head in a slow circle. "You built this house?"

"I had a friend do the blueprint with me and get the bones up," I say. "But I put in the walls, flooring, and all the little details."

"It's beautiful," she says. "The pictures of horses in the hall—are those ones you trained?"

I nod. "All my prizewinners."

"Do you have a horse?"

Pausing, I notice she's leaning in, her elbows on the table, interested for the first time. I've seen her simulate being animated to customers. I've also seen her face fall as soon as they turn away. This expression is different.

Her shell is crumbling. I'm doing something right.

"Yeah, I got a stallion," I say. "He's called Bones And All, but he goes by Bones now that he's just for riding and work."

"Do you have a dog?" She cocks her head.

"No. I had a cattle dog for a while, but he passed. He was old," I say. "I like dogs a lot, like to get another one, but I just haven't found the right fit."

She's quiet, mulling this over.

"You like dogs?" I ask.

She nods. "I always wanted one, but Aiden said no pets."

There's a trail of sadness through her words. I watch her for a second as she sips her coffee. Her soft, full mouth purses. Then, the tip of her tongue flicks out again. My dick jerks in response.

I've jerked off a lot to the scent of her ribbon, but that doesn't compare to seeing her in person, feeling the heat of her presence or catching the vanilla scent that came off her when I lifted her from my truck.

"You like living with your stepfather and his sons?" I ask.

She shakes her head. Then, her pupils blow, like she made a mistake. "I mean, they're fine. I like Bittern."

"Bittern?"

"He's Aiden's youngest son," she says.

"And you like him? Do the others hurt you?" I try to bite back the thinly veiled threat in my tone, but it comes out anyway.

She squirms. "No, not really. Bittern is nice, but he's quiet from his accident in the mines."

She hesitates, like she's expecting me to cut her off. I wait for her to continue.

"Aiden had three sons," she says. "His oldest, Wayland, died in a work accident. Bittern was with him, but he lived. He's been off ever since, and he coughs a lot."

Sadness tinges her voice, and it occurs to me Freya Hatfield has a lot of sadness in her. I wonder if she loves the butterflies and bugs, or if she never had any companionship to replace them. I met people like that in foster care, kids who bonded to animals, even insects, because they were loners in an unstable world.

"What are your favorite things?" I ask. "In the whole world."

She stares at me like she's startled. "I like outside," she whispers. "I like the woods. I like the stars more than anything. I have notebooks where I track them. When I was little, I used to pretend I could live up there, like it was its own universe."

I listen, entranced. My mind goes up to the attic, where I installed four skylights so I could suspend my submissive beneath them, so I could put her in the stars. The woman I love will fit right into the place I've built.

Freya is the perfect fit. She doesn't know it yet, but she will.

"I dissociated a lot as a kid," she says. "Things got rough. You know how it is. But I don't do that as much now."

"Why?"

She considers it. "Montana is different. This part of it feels so wild. Dark. Some parts of growing up were...hard. But I miss the Appalachian Mountains."

"You don't like our mountains?"

"I've just never met them."

That takes me aback. It doesn't make sense, but somehow, it makes perfect sense. We're both quiet for a moment. Then, she gets up and starts to pick up the dishes. I rise, towering over her body, and take them from her hands.

"You're a guest," I say. "No work. You tired?"

She backs up, edging out of my space. She does that a lot.

"Pretty tired," she says. "Is that the phone?"

We both look down at the flip phone I laid there earlier. I nod, giving it over. She offers me a nervous smile and disappears into the hall with it. Her voice rises and falls for a minute. Then, she comes back in, a crease between her brows.

"Bittern says his truck got four flat tires while he was at the gas station," she says. "That's really strange."

I keep quiet. It's not that strange, considering I was the one who took a nail gun and shot the tires out while he was inside paying for gas and a six-pack. My only regret is that it took me longer than I anticipated. I'd planned on picking her up at the drop-off, not the middle of the woods.

"He had to get Ryland to come get him. I told him I was staying with Tracy," she says.

"He can't know you're with the neighbor?" I ask.

She shakes her head hard. "No, Aiden would lose it if he knew I was with...a man."

She has a reaction to speaking his name. It's so subtle, I almost miss it. But I lived with Phil and Amie, so I learned to tune in to the little details. I hear the caginess in her tone. The tiny contracting of her pupils. The slight increase in her breathing.

She's scared, deep down. Anger floods my veins.

"Is Aiden a problem that needs handling?" I blurt out.

She sets the phone down. "Why?"

I shrug. "If Aiden's a problem for you, I can handle that problem."

Her tongue darts out, wetting her lips. If I weren't fired up about Aiden being a potential abuser, I'd have a reaction to that. But inside, I'm angry the way I was when I saw what Amie went through. There's something about injustice against people who can't fight that flips my switch, makes me do insane things.

"What are you saying?" she whispers.

I set the mugs in the sink and turn, wiping my hands dry on the towel.

"I mean, if he's putting his hands on you, I don't mind putting a fence stake in his head."

That came out a lot stronger than intended. Her jaw drops.

"What?" she whispers.

I smile. "I'm just joking, sweetheart. But if you got somebody putting their hands on you, I'm happy to do the neighborly thing and have a word with him."

I half expected her to go pale. Instead, the prettiest blush creeps over her face and slips down to the swell of her cleavage. I'll bet she blushes like that when she comes, all laid out on her back with her hand between her legs.

I've thought about that a lot too—what Freya looks like when she touches herself. It's a bit of an obsession at this point.

She tucks a curl behind her ear. "I'm kind of tired. Could I go to bed now?"

"Of course," I say. "You want anything else? Shot of whiskey?"

She hesitates by the door. "Sure. I'm still a little cold"

I take out a bottle of honey whiskey and pour two shot glasses. She picks it up in her delicate fingers and shoots it, like she does it a lot. She shivers. The glass clinks on the counter.

"Thank you for letting me stay," she says.

"The storm should be calmed by the end of the day tomorrow," I say. "I can't promise it'll be done by the morning."

She nods.

"Alright, let's get you to the guestroom."

# CHAPTER SEVEN
## FREYA

He shows me to a room at the start of the hall, by the stairs. There's an attic door, but it's locked. He stands by it while I say goodnight, says if I need anything, I should call for him.

I shut my door, lock it, and stand in the middle of the room.

It's beautiful, like the rest of the house. The walls are the same dark wood. The furnishings are blue. The fireplace is pale stone, and it flickers a soothing orange. Between the two windows is a preserved coyote. I don't like the thought that he killed it. I know they're a nuisance, but it's so pretty.

Maybe he didn't. Even with his scars and blurry tattoos, he's surprisingly gentle.

My skin prickles as I cross the room. I pull back the covers and climb in. The bed is so soft, I sink down. My body is tired, strung out from being so afraid. The shot of whiskey helps unwind my nerves.

Something catches my eye above the fireplace. I lean in—it's a series of the same panels from his bedroom but different scenes. This time, the woman is wading into the water, almost to the other side. The bear nips at her heels.

I shudder, sliding back so I don't have to look at it.

It's probably nothing. A collectible.

My mind drifts to him downstairs. He sat at the head of the table, knees spread, body relaxed. Everything he does is big but not overwhelming. He takes up so much space, but he stays out of mine.

There's a dark side to him. Something came out when he said he'd kill Aiden. Maybe it was a joke, but something flickered in his eyes that made me feel like…maybe it was serious.

He would protect me?

My head fills with him. Bits and pieces of his body. The stretch of his t-shirt over his broad chest and shoulders. The tattoos over his forearms that ripple when he clenches his hand on his coffee mug.

His lean fingers and broad palms…. Shame moves through me at the feeling gathering between my thighs.

I shouldn't. I rarely do this.

But God, he makes me want to.

Quietly, as if he could hear me all the way down the hall, I slip my hand under my flannel. My pussy is wet, and I dip my finger inside.

My eyelids flutter.

I wonder what the tip of his finger would feel like inside me. Bigger than mine, the perfect amount of roughness. Touch wet, I bring it back to my clit and start circling. A little spark of heat starts deep in my hips.

The floor creaks.

I snap back to reality. There's a single word in my head as I pull my hand up and flip to my side.

*Whore.*

Shame creeps over me like a shadow. I shouldn't want men like him. They're the kind who have made my life hell from the start—inked up, brutal, trigger-happy. They consume until there's nothing left but dust and bruises.

And yet, when he looked at me like that from across the table, he seemed…different.

Undomesticated, yes. Like a gentle beast capable of damage but doesn't commit it. The idea is alluring—strength without destruction.

I close my eyes. I'm alone, so it's alright to let my feelings show, but too many years of stuffing them down makes that hard. I just lay there until my body relaxes. I've fallen asleep terrified and sad so many times. Falling asleep well-fed in a house with an unknown man isn't as hard as I thought.

For the first time since leaving Kentucky, I'm anchored.

My eyes flutter and shut. My body releases all the tension it's carrying, and I find myself melting into soft flannel. The comforter over me is heavy. My breathing slows, and the last thing I remember is giving in.

I'm on my back in the forest. The river rushes by a few feet to my right. It's night, the moon caught in the tangled branches overhead. My body is so heavy, I can't move an inch.

There's something between my thighs. My hands slide down my body and slip through short hair. There's a man down there, face buried in my pussy.

With effort, I lift my head.

*Deacon Ryder.*

My body jolts me wide awake, sending me gasping, upright in bed.

It's lighter than I expected outside. The digital clock says it's two. Heart thudding, mouth parched, I slide from bed and go to the window.

The storm has let up, and the sky's ablaze with northern lights. Shades of pink, blue, and green waver over the horizon. Down in the yard, his arms crossed and his feet planted, is Deacon. He wears his hat, but I can tell he's watching the sky, soaking it all in.

I've never seen the northern lights before. It might be the most beautiful sight I've ever witnessed.

Without thinking, I cross the room and pull the latch down. In the hall, I go as fast as I can without tripping. Feeling my way along the wall, I make it down the stairs. My heart thuds in time with my feet as I dash along the hall and tear the door open.

He turns, but I run right past him and come to a halt.

The sky is astounding. Everything is bathed in a pink glow, tinged with the suggestion of green and deep blue, so vast it takes my breath away.

I turn. He's a shadow against the house.

The world feels upside down, like the sky is on fire. I don't feel like Freya Hatfield. There's no Aiden to remind me I'm a whore like my mother. My first time feels light years away. It's all because he's looking at me like I'm the most beautiful thing he's ever seen.

I am alive. Fire roars in my bones.

Right now, I know desire without shame. It's an animal hunger that doesn't care about my past or future. All it knows is right now. All it wants is his hard, hot body against mine. He's no Braxton Whitaker. He won't leave me used. No, I think this man will eat me whole with nothing left to feel when he's done.

My chest heaves as I creep closer. He towers over me, not moving.

"Why are you looking at me like...that?" I breathe.

He swallows, sweat etching down his neck. "I want you," he says.

It's so straightforward. There's no trying to trick me, no lying about what he wants.

My hands ball. I'm fighting between the desire to protect myself and this need. It's a losing battle. This is all new. I've never felt lust for another person before tonight.

It's shocking. I don't know how to control this.

"Why?" My voice cracks.

He doesn't speak. His boots crunch on the driveway. His body comes so close, I feel his heat at my front. Around us, the northern lights swirl. He takes off his hat and runs a hand over his hair.

I see him in profile for a second. Harsh, broken nose. Face like it was carved from stone. Eyes that flip from predator to something I've never seen in a man's face—softness.

"Deacon," I whisper.

His name hangs between us. Intimate. His rough palm cradles my face. He smells good, feels good. Tonight, I'm desperate for pleasure. The thought of touching him, of letting him touch me, is spine tingling.

His body curves over mine, my skin tingling with his warmth. His presence is coal on fire, black as night and hot as the sun.

"Freya," he says, his voice cracking.

Boldly, I lift my hand and lay my fingers over his lips. "I don't want to think," I whisper. "I just...want."

His mouth is firm and warm. Distracted, I trace it with my middle finger, from one end to the other. My heart flutters so fast, it reminds me of a butterfly encased in my prison of ribs.

I skim my touch down his chin, over the rough hair of his short beard. Down his throat where his pulse thrums. Between the collar of his shirt.

Down to where it's bare skin and dark hair.

His hand encircles my wrist. A shock moves along my arm. With his other hand, he pulls me close. His mouth comes down on mine. A moan bursts from me at the same moment a groan rumbles in his chest.

His kiss is so brilliant, it makes the northern lights go quiet. He's rough and hungry, consuming me with his mouth. It isn't the first time I've been kissed, but it feels like it.

I'm reeling, just letting him have his way. Dimly, I feel his hand on the back of my neck.

My fingers grip the front of his shirt. The world spins. I'm a limp mess in his arms. There's no need for me to shift my thighs together—I can tell how shamefully wet I am.

He forces my lips apart, swiping his tongue over them. I let him in, and his tongue touches mine for a second before he withdraws.

Our eyes meet. He's tousled, the front of his shirt halfway open. At some point, I ripped those top buttons. My palms are pressed to the messy ink beneath his bare skin.

I'm burning. I want to rake my nails down his chest, to rip his clothes off. His eyes are feverish as he grips my wrist, dragging my hand from his chest to his groin.

I gasp as he presses my palm to the front of his pants.

I can feel him under the fabric. Big, thick. Instinctively, I try to wrap my hand around it through the front of his work pants. I can't, but I can feel he's bigger than I can hold properly. His heartbeat thumps beneath my palm.

I shudder but don't let go. Flushed, I drag my gaze over his big body. It's clear now. He's going to fuck me. It's going to hurt.

"Take me upstairs," I gasp, before I can lose my nerve.

I don't have to ask him twice. He picks me up in his arms and carries me with quick strides up the walkway and through the front door. His boot kicks the door shut and the bar falls. Then, we're going up the stairs, the dark wood ceiling circling overhead. My arms wrap around his neck.

He smells so good, so real, like a man—sweat, skin, soap.

At the end of the hall, he elbows the door open. I turn my head, taking everything in.

Through the floor-to-ceiling windows, the northern lights ripple in shades of pink and green. The outline of the mountains runs like ink through them.

He lets me fall onto the bed. It's soft flannel, and everything smells like him. Then, his big body is against mine. It's glorious, but I need more.

I've been so sad for so long. Tonight, I'm free.

His mouth works its way down my neck. Hot, slow. His hips work mindlessly against my leg. His body is so big, I don't know how this is going to work.

That doesn't matter, it turns out. He's already shifting me up the bed and sliding between my thighs. My flannel shirt hitches up. A groan sounds in his chest as he kisses over my mouth, biting my lower lip and chin.

"Fuck," he breathes, voice low and raspy.

My mouth trembles, wanting to say his name. It feels too personal, but there's nothing impersonal about the way he's grinding his hips against my leg.

"Deacon," I whisper, head back.

The word rises to the ceiling, smoke in the wind. That wind is nothing in comparison to the mountain shifting as his body moves against mine. His hands unfasten the flannel covering my breasts, pushing it aside to bare them.

My nipples prickle, going hard.

There's a second where he doesn't react. Then, his dark eyes glint and his mouth parts. Reverently, he cups my left breast, though there's more than he can hold.

I'm not lonely. No, I'm moored to his shoreline.

He bends and kisses between my breasts. My spine arches. He moves an inch lower and kisses me again. God, I can't bite back my whimpers. His mouth is soft, passionate. Gentle. I didn't know it was possible for a man to be this gentle.

He goes lower. Down over my naval. Down to—

Everything comes to a halt. I want to be fucked, but the thought of letting him pleasure me fills me with familiar shame. No, I need this to be about him. I'm not ready to be in the spotlight. Just the thought triggers that voice in my head Aiden planted there.

*Whore.*

"I need to taste you," he says, voice thick with a guttural rasp.

I shake my head. "That's not what I need now. Please."

He glances up, dark gaze locking on mine. "What do you need, sweetheart?"

My hips roll up against his groin. One hand grips my thigh, right above my knee, and drags it up. Calluses are rough on my skin. My eyelids flutter when he takes the edge of my panties and pulls them down. They tangle on my right ankle, and I give a frustrated kick to get them free.

Cool air grazes my aching pussy.

He's still wearing his shirt and pants. His boots must have ended up on the floor. My thighs spread wide as he pushes his knee up and reaches down between our bodies.

He's undoing his belt, and it clinks at his hips. I catch my breath, biting my lip. The hiss of his zipper cuts the darkness. He lets out a harsh breath, like it's a relief to let the monster in his pants out of its cage.

My pussy throbs. Do I ache for pain, to be punished for what I'm about to do?

My hands come up and grip his shoulders. His skin burns hot through his shirt. Our eyes meet, and he leans in, brushing his mouth against mine, nuzzling me with his crooked nose.

My head falls to the side. Through my hazy vision, I see the waves of pink and green around us like a dream.

I think, even if we never do this again, I'll remember this forever.

His arm shifts. Rough, hard fingers graze my bare pussy. A whimper slips free as my hips lift from the bed. I can't control it, this lust. It burns and burns.

"You're soaked," he groans.

That's the final piece of permission I need to give in completely. He pushes, and I feel him, enormous, as the head of his cock forces itself into my pussy.

At least, it tries to, but he meets resistance right away. We both gasp. He's notched just inside, stretching me until it burns. My thighs twitch. My nails rake at his shirt. I'm not sure if I want to cry or come.

Slowly, I become aware of something I didn't expect. Something hard, warm, smooth.

"What is that?" I gasp.

He glances down. "It's pierced."

Confused, I stare. The corner of his mouth twitches.

"Lost a bet, pierced my dick," he says. "You don't like it?"

I'm so turned on, I don't care about anything but getting him inside me. Frantically, I shake my head. Then nod. "Just put it in."

His hand goes down to where the final button of my shirt is fastened and releases it. A bare palm drags across my stomach and grips my hip, stroking me like he's trying to get me to ease up.

"Relax and I will," he says. "Open up for me, sweetheart."

His voice, deep and hoarse, sends another surge of lust through me. The muscles in my lower body loosen a little—enough that he slips in another inch.

Hard, thick—God, oh God.

It's stretching me where I'm so sensitive. The clawing desire deep inside me purrs as he fills me. I'm shattering into a thousand pieces, and yet, he's at the center, holding me together. Our eyes connect. Sweat drags down his jaw in the dark.

I love this forcefulness. It's violent, but somehow, it's not violent at all. I can just taste what he's capable of on the edge of my tongue.

And I want more.

"Please," I burst out.

His mouth meets mine. It's as good as it was the first time. Warm, real, rough. Visceral in the way I've always thought sex should be. My hips rise, he pushes back.

"Sweetheart, you're fucking tight. We're going slow," he says.

"I don't care," I gasp.

I'm not sure of that, but I'm so desperate, I can deal with the consequences as they come. He laughs softly and shifts his body, bracing his weight on his knees. Then, in one, even stroke, he pushes himself all the way in.

Stars pop behind my eyes. I arch up into him and my claws come out. They tear down his arms. There's a split second of pain. Then, it ebbs to a throb, replaced by pleasure that makes me want to writhe.

Instead, I keep perfectly still. He twitches—God, that feels good.

He's heavy—I didn't expect that. He shifts his hips and his cock moves. Soft tingles of warmth spread through my belly. My eyes flutter shut, and I release all the air in my lungs.

"Do that again," I whisper.

"Do what?"

"Move, but just a little."

He obliges. The smooth, hard head of his cock strokes my deepest point. It makes me want to whimper and curl my toes all at once.

"Oh God," I gasp out.

He nuzzles my neck, beard rough. "Does that feel good, sweetheart?"

My lips tremble, and I can't get anything past them. He pushes deep, holding it for a second, grinding gently against my clit and sparking that burning heat that makes me go wild. I hear myself moan, my hips shaking hard.

"Fuck, that's so sweet," he breathes. "All out of words."

My cheeks burn. "Do it again," I manage. "Please."

He obliges, grinding on my clit. I shudder, letting myself moan again so he knows how good it feels. A glitter of sweat drags down his neck. His body ripples as he moves back, disengaging his cock from me. My hips twinge, from want more than pain. He sits back, and my eyes fall to his lap.

God, he's big. It's hard to tear my gaze away.

"Want you to sit on my face, sweetheart," he says.

My stomach drops. I clamp my thighs shut and push up on my elbows. "What?"

He shakes his head once. "Been thinking about it. I want you to put that pretty cunt on my face, suffocate me. I see you riding your hips and thighs up on me, so do it with my head in between them."

My lips part. I'm locking up, and shame trickles in.

"No," I whisper.

His forehead creases in thought. "You think it won't feel good?" he asks.

Shame is strong again. It was gone for a second, but now it's back. And with it is that word—*whore*. I hear it in Aiden's voice, an echo in my head. I'm a whore for wanting to be touched. Selfish, a slut without trying to be. He taught me that, ground it into my head. Now, even alone with Deacon, I can't get away.

"I just want you to fuck me," I whisper. "Hard."

He doesn't argue. I appreciate that. I don't want to think anymore. I want every confusing, conflicting thought fucked from my head.

I spread my thighs, hoping I can tempt him into pushing his cock back in. He leans in, and his hard hand wraps around my neck as his mouth brushes mine.

*Yes, please. Turn my brain off. Don't let me think about this.*

"I will eat your pussy if I have to tie your legs open," he says, voice harsh. "Not tonight, but I swear, I will."

My shame disappears as he takes control from my hands. This isn't my fault, after all. He's the one in charge.

"You want to be fucked dirty?" he presses.

Flushed, wet, my pussy spread for him, I nod hard. The corner of his mouth turns up and, in one movement, he slides an arm under me and flips me onto my hands and knees.

The wind knocks from me. I don't have time to recover before his hand goes to the back of my head. His fingers fist in my hair, dragging my head back. I see myself reflected a dozen times in the mirrors inlaid in the headboard.

I've never seen myself so desperate.

"Let's fuck then, sweetheart."

# CHAPTER EIGHT
## DEACON

When I brought her home, I knew we would end up in my bed, deep down. I just thought I'd try to make it sweet. Soft, like a girl like Freya deserves. I didn't expect her to want it rough.

She looks so good on her hands and knees. Her spine is arched. She's naked, her skin glowing in the firelight. Her waist narrows down and her hips blossom out, her ass full and round. She's the prettiest woman I've ever seen, much less touched.

My hand looks wrong on her waist. She's better than I deserve, but I'm just fucked up enough to go through with this, from beginning to end.

She has me, hook, line, and sinker.

"Put your hand on the headboard," I order.

She obeys. Her knuckles are white with tension. The angle arches her spine and spreads her ass, giving me the first view of her pussy in this position.

Goddamn, it's perfect.

Soft, full, a dusky pink. I spit on my fingers and flip my hand facing down, pushing my middle finger inside to watch her stretch around it. The sound that comes out of her is...well, it's been a long time in my imagination, and it's even better in reality.

"Hold still," I order.

She obeys, but her thighs tremble. Inside, she's better than I imagined. And I imagined it a lot, all soft, tight, slick with arousal. I felt it on my dick, but it's different exploring it with my finger.

This feels like pussy I won't be able to give up.

Not that I mean to. No, I already got a room in my house waiting for her. This is just the first step in making her stay.

I move my fingers until I find that little swollen place inside and stroke it. She gasps, back arching hard. A glitter of wetness slips between my knuckles. I have to resist the urge to bend down and lick it.

I want to taste her so badly.

"Look at you," I murmur, transfixed. "Look at that fucking pussy."

She clenches down on me. My head goes blank, and I slip my fingers free and move up behind her ass. One hand goes into her hair, the other sliding between us to guide my cock to her soaked cunt. The head slips inside, piercings and all.

We both gasp, her louder than me. My eyes fall to where my cock meets her pussy. She's fluttering, gripping me. Then, in one, even stroke, I force her to take every inch, all the way until I feel the resistance of her cervix, smooth against the tip of my cock.

"I can feel the...piercings," she breathes.

I work my hips. "You like it?"

She nods hard, moaning. I slide my hand up, gripping her throat, and pull her back against my abdomen. In the fracture-inlaid mirrors across my headboard, her dusky pink nipples and full breasts are reflected a dozen times.

Slowly, I drag out and slam back in.

She cries out and her tits shake. My hips work, my cock stroking into her hot, velvety cunt.

She'd make a perfect submissive.

My mind flashes with that image. Freya, bound on her knees with her arms tucked behind her back, hair falling down her back, full mouth open, eyes big and fixed up at me. Dark ropes snaked around her curves, binding her until she's fully helpless.

My brain buzzes.

Maybe it goes too blank.

She's so beautiful in the darkness of my bedroom. Curvy, soft, too pretty for a man like me. I need her to stay this way forever. It's been weeks of waiting. Now, I finally have her in my bed.

I'm falling hard. The ground is inviting.

Gently, I pull out halfway just to feel her grip me like she's trying to keep me in. Then, I fuck into her, rutting my hips hard. The sounds of our bodies meeting, her wet cunt wrapped around my cock, fill the bedroom.

I thought I could make this romantic for her.

But it's just dirty, visceral.

She takes it as I slam into her, ass shaking. Little whines, low moans, fall from her lips. My hand leaves her hair and grips her at the waist. Her curves are the prettiest thing I've ever touched—supple in some places, soft and round in others. I want to bite them hard enough to leave marks.

The bed hits the wall, over and over.

I catch flashes of her in the mirrors. Open mouth, pink tongue. Bright blue eyes, dark lashes like feathers. The pale underbelly of her throat, faint fingerprints on it. Full tits, the little curve of her lower stomach.

And when I look down, the way that perfect ass shakes and that pussy just takes me as I use it... It's too much.

There's nothing left in my head. I'm just pounding blood and desire.

I push her down onto her belly, lifting her hips until she's on her knees so she's spread with her spine arched. From this angle, I'm so fucking deep. I bend, kissing her shoulder. My hips pump. I swear, I'm up in this girl's throat. By the sounds she's making, she feels it too.

"Deacon," she whimpers.

Oh God, she's saying my name. A tingle shoots down my spine. I grip her hair, shoving her to the bed with her cheek against the quilt. Her eyes are wet, her lips swollen. I fuck harder, faster. Pleasure is a roaring inferno, but I can still stop it if I want.

I should ask if she wants me to pull out.

But I don't.

Instead, I shove my cock so deep inside her, I can feel her cervix push back, and I come hard. The feeling is euphoric. Not once have I fucked a woman without a condom. Now, here I am, balls deep with nothing between us, emptying every drop of cum into her cunt.

I waited so long for this.

We both go still. Physically, I'm satisfied, but the rest of me is already wondering how I can get my mouth on her pussy. Slowly, I push myself upright. She sniffs, lifting her head. My cock is still hard, and she winces as I pull it out. A bit of my cum drips down her swollen pussy and hits the bed.

I swipe it with my finger and put it back inside.

"Are you alright?" I ask.

She nods, sitting back on her heels. Her ass is so beautiful at this angle, round, soft. I'm distracted by it, and I don't notice she's looking at herself in the fractured mirrors.

She sniffs again. I catch her gaze in my reflection.

Her eyes are wet—does she regret me?

"Don't move, sweetheart," I say.

I go into the bathroom, not bothering to turn the light on, and run a washcloth under warm water. When I return, she's sitting against the headboard, forearm over her breasts. Her brows are creased. Her mouth is pressed together in a worried pout.

I zip my pants and sit on the edge of the bed.

"Can you open up for me?" I ask gently.

She bites her lip. A pink stain spreads over her nose and cheeks. For a moment, I think she'll refuse. But then, her thighs part, and I ache in my pants at the sight of her battered little pussy, dripping cum onto my bed. She winces as I wipe her clean and set the rag aside.

I lean in, brushing her tangled curls back.

"I know you don't want me putting my mouth on your pussy, but I want to touch it," I say. "All you have to do is lay back and spread those perfect legs."

Her breath hitches, eyes glittering.

"It should feel good for you too," I say, keeping my voice low.

"I've never done that," she says finally.

"Never been touched? Or you've never come?"

"Never been touched like this."

I take hold of her thigh and ease her onto her back. She slides down, her hair a dark cloud around her face. She gasps as I lay my body alongside hers, one hand resting on her lower belly.

Our eyes meet, inches apart.

I kiss her, so softly. She moans, and some of the tension in her body eases. I pull back. Our noses touch, and I can taste her sweetness.

"You like kissing?" I ask.

"Yes," she breathes.

I kiss her again, taking my time, being gentle the way someone like her deserves. All the while, I keep my hand rubbing over her skin, down to the mound above her pussy, down until my fingertips find her clit.

I pull back. Her eyes are wide, glazed like she's drunk off sex.

"You like that, sweetheart?" I murmur. "You want me to touch this pretty pussy?"

Her lids flicker. "You're so dirty."

Her voice is faint, probably because I'm dipping my fingers into her and taking the slickness of our cum to rub over her clit. Her thighs tense. Her hips lift an inch off the bed and come back down, her spine locking.

"Good fucking girl," I praise.

She's in profile, and I'm stretched out beside her. A little huff of breath escapes her lips. If I had to guess, she's close. It won't take her long to tumble over the edge. I see it in the tightening of her stomach. I feel it in her swollen clit between my fingers.

I pinch it, rubbing. She whimpers aloud. I bend in and kiss the side of her neck, pushing her head to the side so I can access the slope of her shoulder.

She pants. My fingers move faster, back and forth.

"Let it out, sweetheart," I tell her.

Her spine locks, her thighs spread. I'm aware I need to soak this all in—the first time she comes for me. It's perfect. A ripple of pleasure moves through her soft curves. Her thighs tremble. Her toes curl and her feet arch. A little cry slips out, her hands moving up to grip the pillow. I slip my hand down, pushing my middle finger inside and pressing the heel of my hand against her clit.

She grinds and explodes.

Shaking around my finger until she's a spent mess on the bed.

I kiss her forehead. "Good girl."

I need a stiff drink after that. She peels herself off the quilt and we both sit up. Her face is pink, her hair tousled. She looks thoroughly fucked and satisfied.

God, I'm proud of that.

"You go use the bathroom," I say. "I'll go down and get you some water."

She nods, watching me closely as I rise to pull my shirt off. Then, she stands up and promptly falls over. I catch her in time, wrapping an arm around her waist.

"My legs are...shaking," she gasps.

I can't keep the self-satisfied smirk off my face. "Need me to carry you to the bathroom?"

She shakes her head, pushing my hand off. Her steps are unsteady, but she makes it to the bathroom. I get the fleeting impression of her pout, her flashing eyes, and then the door shuts.

I'm alone, standing by the bed stained with what we did.

All I can think is...I need more.

My eyes fall on the floor, where her flannel shirt and panties lie. Head blank, I pick up her panties, flip them over to the strip of fabric where her pussy sits, and push them against my face.

That's what I need more of.

My brain buzzes, and I'm rock hard again. I push the panties in my pocket and go downstairs. When I return with a glass of cold water for her and a shot of whiskey for me, she's back in bed. The sheets are pulled over her breasts, her curls tumbling around her naked shoulders.

She drinks. I nurse my whiskey and watch.

I don't want her to go home, but I can't scare her off by asking her to stay the first night we spend together.

She doesn't know I've been planning on getting her into my bed for months. That can't come out until I've got her locked down. She needs time. Maybe a little space.

Then, she'll come back to me.

She burrows into the bed. I stretch out beside her. Gently, I stroke her neck and back, the dip above the curve of her ass. She's exhausted, so it takes less than five minutes for her eyes to start flickering. Then, her body goes limp, and she's out.

I rise and go into the bathroom to clean up. When I step out of my pants, I pause. My eyes drop down at my halfway hard cock.

She bled. I spit on my fingers and rub the pink streaked up my length. I put my finger in my mouth, just to make sure it really is blood. Metal and something intoxicatingly sweet fills my mouth.

Was she a virgin? If she was, I wish she'd told me. I wouldn't have been so rough.

These questions will have to wait until the morning. I get in the shower and jerk off, trying to get my dick to calm down so I can sleep. Seeing her come got me all hot and bothered again. Afterward, I dry off and put on sweatpants before getting back into bed with her.

This is all I've ever wanted—the little sigh she lets out in her sleep as I pull her into my arms, the feeling of peace as her curves fit perfectly against my body.

There's no going back for me.

She's worth everything I'm going to do to make her mine.

# CHAPTER NINE
## FREYA

I sleep hard and wake to something rough brushing my shoulder. The pillow smells good—soap, skin, aftershave. Eyes shut, I inhale as warm breath and stubble drag over the nape of my neck.

For the first time in my life, I slept with a man in my bed.

He kisses me at the top of my spine. I'm deliciously warm beneath the heavy covers, his bare skin against my naked back. Light kisses feather down my upper spine.

"Open your legs for me, sweetheart."

His voice is rough from sleep. It goes right down and centers in my pussy. Eyes still shut, I moan in my throat, and he spits in his hand and lifts my thigh. His fingers work over my sex. Then, he shifts until I feel his hard stomach and the short hair at his groin.

He pushes the tip of his cock into me, swearing under his breath. Pain ripples as he sheathes himself, but there's something so softly erotic about what he's doing that it turns to pleasure at the first thrust.

Why is this so intimate? I don't really know him.

He takes my hip, lifting my thigh back over his leg, and starts fucking slow and deep. My eyes flutter open. The pale gray light from the not risen sun spills through the windows. The hills stretch out, dark and beautiful.

He groans, pulling me back. Hot breath fans over my nape.

"You feel so good," he breathes. "Let's get you on top. I want to see you like that."

Before I can react, he pulls me off his cock, flips onto his back, and sets me back on it. My eyes widen as I sink down onto him—big, thick, four rounded points.

He's big, I'm tender from last night. His gaze runs over my body. Unsure, I wrap my arms around my breasts, but he grips my wrists.

"You're so beautiful," he murmurs.

I believe him—I've never seen anybody say so much with just his eyes. He releases my wrists and wraps his hands around my waist, thumbs brushing the undersides of my breasts. I feel so small in Deacon's lap. He's a behemoth of a man, his hands almost touching at my spine.

"Ride me," he rasps.

I shift my hips, and the final inch pushes in. My body fights him. I've never felt this full. The veins, the ridges, the heat—it takes over my senses, until all I feel is where our bodies join.

My hips move, guided by his hands. I take him even though it aches because I'm starving. I'm so starved for something I've only fantasized about—a man who touches without harming.

He looks at me like I'm the most beautiful thing he's ever laid eyes on. I've never been worshiped like this, with this perfect mix of hunger and gentleness.

I didn't expect this from him. Shy, my hips stutter, and I close my eyes.

"No, no, sweetheart, you look at me," he says.

Face hot, I obey. He keeps moving my hips, back and forth with little strokes. My pussy is soaked—I can hear it between us. He's so deep inside me, I know when he pulls out, I'll feel him for days. Slowly, I pick up the rhythm. He lets one hip go and puts his fingers between our bodies. His touch finds my clit and circles it.

Oh God, I'm going to come.

It hits me so fast, I can't do anything but gasp. He presses his thumb against my clit, triumphant. I'm flushed, pleasure pumping through me in slow strokes. There's something so good about coming with him inside my pussy. It scratches an itch deep inside and it goes for so much longer.

I glance away, overwhelmed.

"You look me in the eyes when you're on my cock," he says.

He's demanding, but his voice is so low and rough, it doesn't intimidate me. Burning up, I shake, defeated, on top of him. It moves through me in waves, far more intense than what I felt last night. Finally, it ebbs, and I'm limp, barely able to sit up.

"Fuck," he murmurs. "That's my girl."

I'm not his anything, but there's no time to protest, because he pulls me off him and flips me back into the position he fucked me in last night: on my knees, ass up, with my cheek against the bed. With one inked hand, he grips the headboard. With the other, he holds my hips and pushes back inside.

"God, that's a tight little pussy," he groans.

He's so filthy. It's a good thing I can bury my burning face in the bed. Bracing me in his grip, he ruts hard, like he did last night. His pierced cock hits up against my cervix, making my toes curl. It turns out, I like a little pain.

I'm dripping down my thigh.

He speeds up, panting, and I feel like I'm going to shatter for a second. Then, he pushes in and shudders. It goes on longer than last night, like it's better. His body goes still as he thrusts one last time and pulls out.

I stay where I am. I can feel his eyes on my sex.

He clears his throat. "Do you need a morning after pill?"

Taken aback, I slip onto my belly and roll to my side to face him. He's got sweat etching down his neck. There's creamy arousal and cum smeared on his cock. I can't tell if it disgusts or turns me on. All I know is I did that, I met this man yesterday, and now he's covered with what we did together.

Now, there could be consequences.

Mentally, I start calculating my cycle with my heart pounding in my ears like a drum. I'm four days out from my period. I ovulated two weeks ago, so there shouldn't be much of a chance of me getting pregnant.

I glance up, suddenly aware that I'm naked and I barely know this man. His eyes are alert, watching me. I tug the flannel sheet up over my breasts, holding it there.

"I'm due for my period in a few days," I whisper.

He shakes his head, like he doesn't understand.

"I track my cycle. I'm not fertile," I say. "But I'll take it if you want me to."

It's not foolproof, but I've been tracking my cycle carefully for the last couple of years. I've never had the money or access to the pill, so it was my only option.

He shakes his head, almost like he's relieved.

"No," he says. "I believe you."

There's an awkward silence. In the light of day, I don't know what to do with myself. The northern lights are gone. The sun is up, and last night feels like a distant memory.

And he's looking at me like I mean something to him.

"I'll get breakfast going," he says in that rough voice that makes my toes curl. "Clean you up first."

Breakfast? He wants to fuck me like that, ask me about my period, and then feed me breakfast. My stomach swoops. Why is he acting like this is something more than a night where he gets to use me, no strings attached?

"It's Sunday," I whisper. "Church day."

He goes into the bathroom. I hear the water running, and he returns with a wet washcloth. "The storm is back. I'll drive you wherever you want to go after it breaks. Church can wait."

I glance over and find he's right. There's gray rain whipping over the hills. Warmth slips between my legs, jerking my attention back. He wipes me off, uses the same rag to clean himself, and tosses it into the laundry basket. Blushing, I look away as he pulls on a pair of sweats.

He has a powerful, raw sexuality. It doesn't turn off. It's not intentional. It's just there, potent in every move he makes.

He goes to the dresser, rummaging in the top drawer and coming back with a flannel. I can smell his scent on it as I pull it shyly over my body.

Getting dressed in front of each other feels more intimate than what we did last night.

He leads me downstairs, hand engulfing mine. In the kitchen, the rain thunders against the windows. There's bacon crackling and grits bubbling on the stove. He sets a cup of coffee before me. I wrap my hands around the warm mug and lean back in my chair to watch him cook.

My eyes linger on his shoulders. He wears a charcoal gray Henley, a clean one today. It fits his body well, hugging his shoulders and biceps. The collar is a little frayed, the top button open. The tattoos go up his neck to his jaw. His hair is buzzed short, but it's thick enough to cover most of the ink that extends under it.

He's trouble. I know his type. He's got those dark puppy eyes that'll have me forgiving him for everything he does—bar fights, rap sheets, and everything in between. I thought I'd learned my lesson about men like him. And Lord, do I know better than letting him do what he did last night.

At least, I thought I knew better.

"Coffee alright?"

I offer a small smile. "It's good. Thank you," I say.

He gives me a look that reminds me of all the filthy things he said to me in his bedroom. It's followed by a slow drag of his eyes, a little flick at the end so he can look at my breasts. He's not trying to be subtle.

"I want to ask you something," he says, crossing his arms and leaning against the counter.

"Okay," I say, guard rising.

"When I went to clean up last night, there was blood on my dick," he says.

I stare, mortified beyond words.

"I'm not a virgin," I whisper.

His brow creases. There's a faint tattoo, barely visible on his upper cheekbone. I didn't notice it until now.

"Did I hurt you?"

"Maybe a little, but not enough to worry about." I shrug, squirming. "The other man...he was...wasn't you."

A muscle ripples in his jaw. Those eyes are like coal, black and simmering hot. "Did he hurt you?"

I don't want to get into my one and only sexual experience before I've even had breakfast. It was disappointing enough when it happened. I don't need to recount it in front of this six-five slab of muscle who's far more sexually experienced.

"He wasn't small. It just wasn't an extra limb," I say curtly.

The corner of his mouth twitches but not in a smile. It takes me a second of staring at his hard face to realize what's going on.

My stomach flutters—all full of butterflies again.

He's *jealous*.

That's almost...flattering. If only he knew the underwhelming circumstances of losing my virginity. But he doesn't push it, and I'm grateful. He puts two plates down, and we eat in silence. Finally, he leans back, his knees spread.

"I'm gonna ask you another question, sweetheart," he says.

There's a serious note to his voice. I nod, bracing myself.

"You go to church and shit," he says slowly. "But...last night, that was a little more than I was expecting from you."

I blink, not speaking.

"I've never been religious, but I thought there were some rules about fucking," he says.

It's a reasonable question. I think hard.

"I'm not really that kind of religious," I say finally. "I'm just doing my best. I've always figured, if God made me, he knows me better than anybody and gets why I do what I do. You know, as long as I'm not hurting anybody."

For a second, I expect him to laugh. Instead, Deacon nods thoughtfully. "Makes sense to me."

"I started going to church to get away from the house," I said. "Aiden thought it was a waste of time, but Bittern stepped in. I went on my own. I could cut through the woods and get there pretty easily, be back home to make lunch."

He looks at me like he wants to say something. A muscle in his jaw flickers. Then, he reaches out and puts his hand on my knee under the table. With the other hand, he drains his coffee and sets the mug aside.

I stare down at my lap. I've never been touched like this—casual intimacy. My heart thuds, speeding up. Maybe this is all too fast.

"I think I'd better go home," I say.

He leans back and flicks open the curtain. "It's letting up."

I go to get my things before he changes his mind. It's clear he doesn't want me to go, but I'm risking making Aiden angry if I'm not there to make Sunday dinner. I put my dry clothes on, although I can't find my panties, and get my boots in the hall.

When I step onto the porch, Deacon is by his enormous truck with wheels higher than my waist. There are boards poking out of the bed, a bandana tied around one. He has a rack on the roof with a tire and some random tools strapped to it.

"Come here, sweetheart," he says.

My stomach swoops. I go, and he lifts me up and deposits me inside, waiting for me to scramble to the passenger side before he swings in. He turns the key and leans back, glancing over his shoulder as he guides the truck around and heads toward the road.

My heart thumps in the back of my throat. I slept with this man. I just went home with him because he asked. I let him take my clothes off and fuck me like it wasn't anything at all.

I don't know why I did that, the same way I just caved with Braxton. Maybe because, deep inside, I was hoping I'd find something different. It terrifies me that, last night, I did.

I glance sideways. He reaches out and lays his hand on my knee, like I'm somebody that means something to him. His eyes are still on the road. He just holds me and drives, knees spread and body relaxed in the seat.

I clear my throat.

"Can I ask you something too?" I say.

The corner of his mouth jerks up.

"I like that little drawl you've got there," he says. "And yeah, go ahead."

Heat creeps over my cheeks, but I stay the course.

"How old are you?" I force out.

His jaw works. "Probably a little too old to be fucking you, sweetheart."

My mind fills with images of last night—up close, glaring snippets of sweat, gasps, the sound he made when he came.

I clear my throat. "That didn't stop you, sir."

He doesn't answer right away. Instead, he shifts, and I glance over just in time to see him adjust himself.

"I just turned forty," he says.

*Oh.*

All the tattoos and scars make more sense now. He's lived my lifetime almost twice over. This isn't his first rodeo. I should've guessed that from last night.

I swallow past my dry throat. My eyes swing around and fix out the window. He tightens his grip on my thigh.

"That scare you, sweetheart?" he asks, his voice a soft rumble.

"Do you usually go after women like me?" I burst out.

There's a long silence.

"No," he says finally. "You're the first woman I've slept with who wasn't my own age. I usually go for...more experience."

Maybe I should be offended that he's calling me inexperienced, but I'm just relieved he's not going after me because he thinks I'm young enough to be manipulated.

I clear my throat again, wishing I'd had more than coffee to drink this morning. We keep going until we're around the other side of the property, at the end of the long driveway that leads to Aiden's house. It's newly hewn and the gravel is still fresh gray.

Deacon parks but leaves the engine running. He leans over, one hand on the back of my neck, and kisses me deeply. He tastes like coffee and...Deacon Ryder.

When we break apart, his eyes are heavy.

"I won't tell anybody," he says, his voice all low and husky.

"Thank you," I whisper.

His dark eyes are captivating. I look up and fall over the edge. He kisses me one more time but doesn't pull back right away.

"Open," he breathes against my lips.

I part them. His tongue flicks out, touching past my teeth and grazing my tongue. My nipples prickle against my bra. Boldly, I slide my hand over the thigh of his worn work pants to his groin. He's hard underneath, pushing against the zipper.

His breath catches. I pull back.

"Goddamn," he breathes, head dipping.

The way he says that word, low and raspy in his chest, turns me on more than anything else.

"I got something." He leans across the seat to the glove box. I watch as he takes out a flat box and puts it in my lap. It's about the size of my hand.

"Found that early this morning," he says. "For your collection."

My heart starts pattering. I can't bite back my smile as I lift the lid and gasp. It's a fully intact Polyphemus Moth, the brown shades almost luminescent. The two eyes on its spread wings are brilliant.

"Found it by the barn," he says. "I guess the cold got it."

"Thank you," I say breathlessly.

He leans in and kisses me again. I climb out, giving him one last look, and start up the drive. He sits there in his truck until I'm out of sight. Then, I hear the engine fade away.

My feet are heavy as I climb up the front porch. It looks like Ryland's truck is in the driveway, but Bittern's is gone. I don't mind Bittern. He's not too mean to me, but Ryland is just awful some days.

I lean back and scan the gravel, looking for Aiden's truck, but it's nowhere to be seen. Inside, I creep upstairs and offload my bag and boots and get changed. While I'm upstairs, I put the moth in my display case. It's so beautiful, and it makes me smile. Deacon saw that moth and he thought of me.

I go downstairs and tie an apron over my dress. Yesterday, I put a chicken into the fridge to thaw, and it's ready to go into the oven. I take it out and start cleaning it in the sink.

The back door slams open. Ryland appears, cigarette in his lip.

I look up. "Hey," I say nervously.

He jerks his head. "Where were you?"

"I got caught in the storm," I say. "I stayed at Tracy's house."

His eyes narrow, like he's trying to figure out what I did that's got him pissed. But there's nothing wrong with me staying with my boss to keep out of the storm.

"What's for dinner?" he asks, opening the fridge.

"Chicken," I say. "Greens and potatoes."

He shuts the fridge. "What time?"

"Same time as usual," I say.

I don't say it mean. I say it nice and soft, the way I taught myself to speak to my brothers. But he gives me a dark glare and shoves open the kitchen window so he can have a cigarette. It irks me to no end that he smokes inside. Aiden built this nice house, and they don't care for it the way they should.

Deacon would never smoke inside.

"There's a couple guys from over the hill coming for dinner," he says. "And a man from the city government."

I glance at the chicken. "I don't know if I have enough."

He looks coolly over my shoulder. "Well, if you'd been here last night, you'd have known about it. Better go come up with something else."

I hear the rumble of Aiden's truck coming up the drive. Ryland shuts the window and takes a beer out of the fridge. He pops the cap in a sharp movement on the edge of the counter and leaves.

I get up and throw the cap in the trash. There's a little mark on the countertop where they use it as a bottle opener. It irks me to no end.

Through the window, I see Aiden and Ryland standing at the bottom of the steps. Aiden waves his arm, and Ryland sits on the open tailgate of his truck. They both laugh. Then, Aiden moves up the steps and the door opens. I dip my head and start picking the remaining feathers from the chicken. Bittern culled it for me; he doesn't do a very good job at the plucking part.

Boots sound. I feel my stepfather glance at me before he opens the fridge.

*Pop.*

*Hiss.*

He's got a beer out. I look up, and he's leaning against the counter, one arm crossed over his chest. Why is he staring at me?

"You stayed at Tracy's, huh?" he says.

I nod. "Yes, sir, I did."

He lifts the beer to his mouth. He's acting like he's not trying to pinpoint what I did wrong. Finally, he shrugs and pushes off the counter.

"We've got some men from town for dinner," he says. "Make sure there's enough for everybody."

He goes upstairs. My stomach is a cold knot.

In the daylight, I can't deny a horrible fact. He and Deacon are the same type, tatted up and rough-hewn. Aiden is only eight years his senior. They even walk the same, all big and casual, like they own the world.

Disturbed, I start cutting the chicken into pieces. There's one thing I know, and that's how to turn a little food into a lot. I pour oil and batter the chicken twice and fry it. The bag of potatoes under the sink are boiled and whipped with heavy cream.

By the time I see two trucks coming up the drive, there's enough food to feed a dozen men. I pile it on the table as Aiden comes downstairs. He's showered, his hair still wet, and he's got a good shirt on.

These men must be important.

I take off my apron and head to the hall, intending to make myself scarce. He clears his throat, and I freeze.

"You stay for dinner," he says.

"I don't want to get in the way," I whisper.

He points two fingers at me and then at the table. "You'll sit and be quiet for the meal. No backtalk."

I nod, throat tight. "Can I get cleaned up first?"

He jerks his head at the stairs. "Hurry up."

Eyes down, I go upstairs and get in the shower. I used the little money I have to make mine pretty. The bathroom has two soft towels and a scented soap bar, but it's not anywhere near as big and fine as Deacon's house or the bathroom adjoining his bedroom with a tub so big, I could have sunk to my chin in warm water.

I scrub up and put on a dress. My hair is braided and wrapped in a knot at the nape of my neck. I'm trying to look modest because I don't know these men and I don't want them looking at me like vultures.

Downstairs, there are three new men in the dining room. Two are young, maybe early thirties, and the last is older, streaks of gray in his hair.

They're at the table, talking. Their voices are loud, punctuated by laughter. I go to the kitchen and start bringing out the food. One young man, with brown hair that just reaches his shoulders, looks me up and down as I set the platter of chicken down.

"Who's this?" he drawls.

Aiden glances up. "My stepdaughter, Freya."

The man holds out his hand. Confused, I shake it. "Kasey McClaine. Pleasure to meet you, sweetheart."

I don't like that he's using the same word Deacon used. It makes my eye twitch.

"Pleasure," I say, voice cracking.

Kasey points to my other side. The other man, who looks pretty similar sits there, watching us. His hair is buzzed, and he has a tattoo of a skull on his forearm with a big scar through it.

"That's my brother, Elijah," he says.

Elijah leans over and shakes my hand too. I'm not sure why I'm getting so much attention, but it's making me uncomfortable.

"Pleasure to meet you," I say politely, knowing one wrong move could upset Aiden. "Let me just go get the food, and y'all can get to eating."

Kasey gives me a smile that feels patronizing. Skin crawling, I go to the kitchen and bring back the mashed potatoes, broccoli greens, and bread I whipped up last minute.

Then, I awkwardly take the last seat beside Aiden, and everybody fills their plates.

I don't know why I'm here, but it's like being put on display. I'm painfully aware that it's impossible to hide my curves in this dress. I wonder if Aiden is using me somehow. My cheeks are hot the entire dinner. Kasey keeps looking at me like he's got every right to stare.

I keep my mouth shut and play dumb. The men eat, and I listen to them, piecing together what they're doing.

The McClaines own the land above Ryder Ranch. Their property and my stepfather's new land are separated only by the furthermost corner. I'm unsure what a lot of the words they use mean, but it sounds a bit like they're making a deal with a builder or a company for the land on the other side of Ryder Ranch.

I wonder if Deacon knows. It doesn't sound like something he'd like.

They wind down. Silently, I make the empty plates disappear and bring out drinks. Aiden has cigarillos in a wooden box; I set those on the table, even though I hate the smell. Pretty soon, the dining room is hazy and the conversation is loud. I clean the kitchen, relieved Aiden isn't making me stay.

Around ten, the men get up. I'm still wiping the countertops as they go down the hall. My neck prickles, and I turn. Kasey walks in, giving me that look that says he's hungry, but not for what I just made.

He opens his mouth to speak. Mentally, I cringe back. Out of nowhere, Aiden appears at his elbow. He's boozed up but cognizant. A vein pumps in his flushed neck.

"Goodnight," he says firmly.

Kasey veers off, touching his hat, and disappears. Aiden's pale stare swings and fixes on me.

"And you can go on to bed," he says.

I nod, setting the rag aside and wiping my hands on my skirt. His lip curls.

"You're just like her," he says hoarsely. "Just sitting there, eating all that attention up. Makes me sick."

Here it comes. I drop my head, picking my thumbnail. I'm raw from being on edge all night. A tear is already sliding down my cheek and hanging on my chin. I can't look up, or he'll see it.

He clears his throat. "Just go to bed."

Relieved, I duck past him and run up the stairs. I got off easy tonight. I didn't have to sit there while he called me a whore like my mother—the whole damn speech. Pushing the lock down, I sag against the door.

I made it through another day.

After I'm in my nightgown and on my side, staring at the moon, it starts to fall into place.

The realization that Deacon is the same type as the rest of them is disturbing. After Braxton, I told myself never again. I swore I wouldn't end up with a man like that...a man like Aiden, who burned through his wives like they were nothing.

He ruined them both. Lady Hatfield was Aiden's first wife by common law, his high school sweetheart he got pregnant before she was fifteen. My mother, Laurel Rose, was his next victim, pulled into his life after Lady fled. She was young too, on the run from her father with a toddler in tow. I'm sure it was easy to manipulate her into thinking Aiden was a safe place to land.

Those two women are strangers to me, despite me living in their shadow, but I know their pain, know what they went through. Bittern told me a lot of it.

And yet...I think maybe Deacon is different underneath.

My eyes are tired. I'm ready to fall asleep, but they snap open when I realize there was a lump in Deacon's pocket on the drive home. I remember glancing down when he was adjusting himself and seeing it.

That son of a gun took my panties.

# CHAPTER TEN
# FREYA

I'm so disappointed and conflicted.

During the day, I'm disgusted that I couldn't keep my legs closed. At night, I toss and turn, my body hot like I have a fever. In the morning, I wonder if this is what got Lady Hatfield into her horrible marriage or made my mother think Aiden was safe. He probably seemed so charming, just the way Deacon is, at first.

I know all these things in my head.

But my body is a traitor.

I go into work, and it feels like somebody's watching me all over again. People pass by on the street, in their flannels and cowboy hats. Customers come and go. Tracy arrives during the afternoon and asks me to go to the farmer's market to get pumpkin for the pastries.

I go, but I can't keep from looking over my shoulder every step of the way.

When I return, Tracy takes the pumpkins to boil them down at her house, leaving me to close up. It's late in the afternoon by that time. Everything is soaked, but the rain has let up. I clean up and drag the trash out the back.

I'm putting it in the bin when I freeze.

Something squeaks. No, it's more of a whine.

Turning, I run my eyes over the narrow alley. There's a furry black puppy tied to the air conditioning unit with a string. Horrified, I drop the bin lid and run to it, holding out my hand. It yaps, rolling its head in a circle at me.

It looks well fed. I frown, staring down at it. It licks my hand and yaps twice.

Who would just dump their puppy like that?

Angrily, I untie the puppy and carry it back into the café. It fits in one of Tracy's tote bags, its little head poking over the edge. Then, I put on my coat and lock up, stepping out onto the street.

"You got a dog in that?"

I jump out of my skin. There's a tall man wearing a Carhartt and a cowboy hat standing at the curb.

"It's not mine," I say, glancing around. The street is still populated, so I'm not alone. "Somebody abandoned him in the alley."

He steps closer, leaning in to look. He's got a nice face, rough like the rest of the men in Knifley. I can't get a good look at it because he's focused on the puppy, but he doesn't give me a bad feeling.

"You gonna keep him?" he asks.

I shake my head. "I can't. I'll take it to the shelter."

"There's no shelter," he says. "Take him to one of the local ranches. They've always got space for one more."

He touches the brim of his hat, and then he's gone, crossing the street. I stare after him, realizing that's not a bad idea. The other night, Deacon said he wanted one, he just hadn't found the right dog yet.

Maybe this is too perfect not to be a sign.

Bittern picks me up and promises not to say a word about the puppy. I feed it and put it in the barn. The next morning, I don't have work, but he doesn't know that. I ask him to take me to the bottom of the road that leads to Ryder Ranch, spinning a story about Tracy needing me to pick something up. His eyes are dull, as usual, and he doesn't ask questions. He just gives me a pale smile and drives off.

I'm in one of my moods where I don't regret what I did with Deacon. When the night comes, I'll probably sink into depression, but for now, I feel fine as I head up the hill and around the corner to the gate of Ryder Ranch.

I pick up the puppy, letting it sit on my shoulder. It yaps all the way up the driveway to the front porch.

The yard is empty, but I can hear a commotion in the barn. Quietly, I walk over the driveway to the attached paddock.

Through the open end, a big, dark gray stallion, likely Bones And All, enters the paddock with Deacon astride him, riding at an easy posting trot. The puppy whips its head around and starts yapping again.

The stallion spins on a dime and pricks his ears forward. Deacon's dark gaze settles on me, and his brows rise. He comes to the fence, looming overhead. Suddenly, I feel incredibly small.

He clears his throat. "What're you doing here, sweetheart?"

Right away, my knees go weak. I'm not sure I remember why I'm here in the first place. Am I delivering a dog or wanting something else?

"I found a puppy," I say, but it comes out in a whisper.

He dismounts, steel tipped boots hitting the ground in a spray of mud. His horse shakes its head, bridle jingling. He comes to the fence, leaning his inked forearms over it.

"What is it?" he asks.

"It's a dog," I say.

The side of his mouth jerks up. "I mean, any idea what the breed is?"

I shake my head, feeling silly. He drags his eyes from the dog to me, and they linger there, hotter than fire. My neck is burning up, and all I can think about is how he felt inside me. Big, overwhelming, intensely perfect.

"You walk here alone?" he asks.

I shake my head, then nod. "Bittern dropped me a few miles back on his way to work."

A crease appears on his forehead. "I'll bring you back. Don't be walking on the roads alone. It's not safe. Come on into the barn for a minute, sweetheart."

That word is like a hook in my heart. I circle the barn, and he heads through the paddock entrance. We meet inside, and he takes the dog from my arms, flipping it on its back and holding it up.

"I'd say a Heinz fifty seven," he says. "It's a boy. You got a name for it?"

I shake my head. He turns over a milk crate and puts the dog in it. Then, before I can react, he picks me up and carries me to the tack room and kicks the door shut with his boot.

He doesn't waste any time setting me on a wooden trunk and pushing between my knees. His mouth grazes below my ear. His hand slides up my waist and cups my breast. My palm comes up, pushing at his chest.

"Deacon, I just came to give you the dog," I gasp.

"You gave me a boner too," he murmurs. "Need to fix that before I take you home."

His mouth is so hot, and it feels so good. I keep pushing but not very hard. He pulls the neckline of my sweater to the side. Teeth and hot tongue graze my shoulder. In my boots, my toes curl.

I need to say no.

I know better than to let this happen again.

"Deacon, please."

He bites me again. My heart is going fast, unsure what's happening. He reaches up and takes my face gently in his fingers, turning it to make me look into his eyes.

"What does please mean?" he asks, voice low. "Please stop? Please bend you over and fuck your pussy?"

My eyes widen. He kisses me, inked fingers still firm on my face. My body melts into him, my thighs tightening around his waist. Dimly, I feel him reach between us, and his belt clinks as he undoes it.

I'm in one of my woolen skirts, halfway down to my knees. His mouth moves over mine, giving me his tongue. My ears roar, desire surging in waves. Roughly, he pushes my skirt up over my hips. This morning, all my tights were dirty, so I put on a pair of winter socks.

He looks down. "Fuck."

"What?" I gasp.

"Goddamn thigh highs," he says.

He pushes the front of his pants open and pulls me to the edge of the trunk. My eyes widen as his cock comes free. Has it always been so big? And the piercings on the head fascinate me. Four silver bulbs on each side.

A desperate throb moves through my pussy.

He reaches between us and pushes inside me. I'm soaked, so he slides in, but not without a burning sensation that takes a few thrusts to turn to pleasure. My nails become claws and dig into his upper arms.

Our eyes meet. Fire crackles. I'm either terrified or the most aroused I've ever been.

He braces his boot and starts fucking. This is pure animal instinct, like we'll both die if we don't do it. I never imagined lust like this was possible. I'm just mindless with him, starving every time he looks at me.

He touches my clit with one hand, rubbing in quick circles with his thumb. The trunk hits the wall. The tack room is filled with the soaked sounds of him rutting into me, again and again, making the ceiling spin overhead.

My orgasm hits, spreading through me like hot water, blossoming from my pussy, washing through my thighs and lower belly.

"Oh God," I whisper, shuddering hard.

He kisses my open mouth. "That's right, sweetheart, you come on my cock."

He gets harder, his pace picks up and his eyelids flicker.

"Pull out," I gasp.

Too late. He looks me dead in the eyes and comes, jaw gritted. This time, I feel it better than I did last night. He jerks, deep inside. His lids flicker as he lets out a low moan. Then, he goes still, breathing hard.

I want to tell him he can't just do that, but no words come.

"You want something to eat?" he asks.

"What?"

He pulls out of me and puts his cock back in his pants, fastening his belt. Then, he puts my panties over my pussy, covered in his cum, and lifts me to pat my skirt back down. The world spins. I grip his arm.

"You hungry?"

I shake my head. I ate breakfast before I left the house. He picks his hat up off the trunk and puts it back on, winding his fingers through mine. I follow him, confused and still panting.

He leads me back out into the barn. My eyes adjust to the bright light coming from outside, and when they do, I realize there's a wiry man with gray hair walking toward us. I tug my hand out of Deacon's and tuck it behind my back.

The man looks up. Then, he looks at Bones, still standing with his saddle and bridle on, and at the swinging door to the tack room.

"Who's this?" His voice is gruff but pleasant. He takes his hat off and offers his hand.

"Freya Hatfield," Deacon says. "This is Andy."

I shake his hand, giving him a shy smile.

"You're one of Aiden Hatfield's kids?" Andy asks, eyes narrowing but a smile still on his face.

"He's my stepfather," I say.

"Huh," says Andy. "Well, I see."

Deacon's hand settles on my lower back, like he's saying something without words.

"You mind if I take Bones out to check that gate? He's already saddled up," Andy says.

"Fine by me," says Deacon. "Take this puppy with you. When you get back, put him in a kennel in the living room."

"Puppy?"

Deacon points to the milk crate. "Freya found a stray."

He nods and swings on Bones. Deacon hands him the puppy, and he tucks it in his front pocket. Its front paws and head hang out, eyes big. For a moment, I think Andy doesn't like me, but then he gives me a grandfatherly wink as he turns Bones and heads out. Deacon's hand tightens on my waist.

"Let's go inside," he says.

I turn, shaking my head. "I have to go home. Aiden will wonder where I went."

He looks like he wants to say something, but he just nods and heads out the front side of the barn. I follow him as he heads to the truck, opening the passenger door. I can't get in by myself, and my boot slips. He picks me up one handed and drops me into the passenger seat. The look he gives me from his heavy lidded eyes goes right to my pussy.

He gets in and the engine purrs. I forgot in the last few days how powerful his presence is—big and raw, openly sexual. My eyes are glued to his inked hand as he uses his flat palm to spin the wheel and back the truck around to head to the road.

We drive, both silent.

My entire body prickles. I swear, I can still feel him inside me. I twist my hands in my lap. I don't know how he did it again. I came up here to give him a dog and, within minutes, he had my legs wide open.

I don't know what this is. Something real? Or another turn in the cycle of every woman before me?

The mountains rush by, the dark kind I don't know. They aren't the Appalachian Mountains, soft like a blanket pulled around me. It occurs to me that when I'm with him, I forget how unanchored I feel.

"I want to see you again," he says.

I glance at him just as he reaches over and puts his hand on my thigh. Heat erupts and pours through my body. I can't stop staring at it, the scarred knuckles, the ink blurred from the sun. He's moving his middle finger in slow circles, the way he does on my clit.

"Did you take my panties?" I burst out.

The corner of his mouth goes up.

"Yeah, I did," he drawls. "You want them back, you can come get them from my room."

I gasp, staring straight ahead. I'm so flustered, it takes me a moment to realize he's not heading back to my house—he's turning off on a dirt road. He drives a few miles down, then pulls off.

"Come here," he says, unlatching his seat and pushing it back.

I stare, heart pounding. "What are you doing?"

Unceremoniously, he picks me up and hauls me into his lap, wrapping my knees around his waist. His hand slides up my spine, and he pulls the band from the end of my braid and shakes my curls free.

"What are you doing?" I repeat.

"Just touching you, looking at you," he says, voice dropping. I notice it gets husky when he's turned on.

He digs his fingers in my hair, gathering it in his fist. Then, he leans in, curving my spine back, and kisses me. Arousal bursts out like water from a dam. We both moan, and my fingers dig into him.

He tastes so good, and he knows what he's doing. The few kisses I've had before him weren't very pleasant or skilled. Deacon takes his time with it, starting slow before kissing me with passion. One hand grips my hair while the other slides up under my skirt and digs into my ass. I kiss him back, unable to keep from grinding my pussy on the ridge of his cock under his pants.

The truck windows steam over. His hands are all over me. I'm dry humping, gasping against his lips every time his belt buckle hits my clit.

I know better.

I really do.

But I can't fucking stop. I don't know why, after all those years of promising myself I wouldn't end up with a man like him, I fell right into his lap.

Time blurs. I forget where we are and that I need to get home. We make out, bodies grinding frantically, for what feels like a few minutes. But when we break apart, I glance at the clock on the dashboard; it's been almost thirty minutes.

"You have to take me home," I gasp.

"I want to see you overnight," he says. "Had you in my bed once. I need it again."

I open my mouth and words I didn't approve come out.

"This weekend," I say. "Pick me up on Friday. All the men are going into the city overnight, so you can come after seven."

The corner of his mouth jerks up. "Good girl."

I'm so turned around, I can't respond. He lifts me out of his lap, adjusting himself before putting the truck in drive. I sit there, trying to get my curls under control, as he drives back out to the main road.

We pull up at the bottom of my driveway, out of sight of the front porch.

"I'll see you at seven-thirty, Friday night," he says.

I nod, pushing open the door and jumping out before he can confuse me again. I feel his eyes on me as I run up the driveway until I'm out of sight.

That night, I toss and turn. It's hot, so I crack the window. Then, my feet get cold even though my pussy is so hot and restless, I can't close my eyes. It doesn't do any good to touch myself. My fingers don't feel like his.

So, I sit at my desk, surrounded by all the remnants of my childhood, aware for the first time I've stepped out of the final threshold of it. I gaze down at the butterflies, the rare insects, the books, the flowers I painted on my bed frame. Part of me wants to go back to them, to sit in my usual state of disassociation and wish for the stars.

But for the first time in my life, something real makes me feel alive.

Maybe it's not forever.

But it could be for now.

# CHAPTER ELEVEN
# FREYA

※

The trucks pull away after dinner on Friday night. I go to my room at the back of the house and shut the door.

The sun is setting, and a single golden ray cuts through the window. My collection is neatly stacked on the desk and above it, my butterfly specimens glittering in an array of colors. My bed is neatly made, the red flannel quilt tucked beneath the mattress. My clothes hang in the open closet. The rug I braided from rags lays like a coat of many colors over the floor.

I stand in the center, hands folded.

Maybe he won't come.

Or maybe he will—that's more nerve-wracking.

I think back to the night I spent with him. We started as strangers. But when we woke up, I think we became something else I can't name. And I liked it. I felt safe in his arms.

That's unexpected.

My eyes follow the vines and flowers I painted on my bed frame, over the dried flowers, cedar, and lavender, the jars full of rocks and shells.

The Appalachian Mountains, the soft green hills, the snakelike rivers, were my safe place. Now, my safe place is boxed and painted onto my furniture. I'm roaming in my heart, ready to let the wind pull me up and blow me away.

Somehow, instead, I ended up in the bed of a man who looks just like the men I've been running from all my life.

I turn on the radio so the house isn't dead quiet. Then, I wash up in the bathroom and braid my hair down my back. The air has a little chill to it, so I pick out jeans, boots, and my fern-green sweater.

Something crunches on the driveway. I frown, freezing.

That doesn't sound like a truck.

I put my boots on and go downstairs. Through the front window, I see Deacon Ryder on his dark horse, so tall, he's a shadow against the sunset.

My stomach swoops. He's rough but so damn handsome. And he didn't forget he was coming for me.

Heart thumping, I push open the front door. He dismounts and heads toward the porch, stopping at the bottom step. He takes off his hat and slaps it on his thigh. A puff of dirt comes off it. He looks good, windswept, like he was riding hard. They were probably working all day up at Ryder Ranch.

I slip out onto the porch. I should be afraid of being alone with him, but I'm not, and I'm worried that means something. Things are moving fast.

"You look pretty," he says.

"Thank you," I whisper. "I didn't realize you were going to pick me up on a horse."

"That a problem?" He turns to look at Bones. "I can hold you right up here in front of me."

"It's fine," I say quickly. "I'll go get an overnight bag."

"Pack light," he says.

It doesn't occur to me what that means until I'm heading back downstairs with my messenger bag over my shoulder. Was the implication that I shouldn't bother to pack many clothes because I'll be naked?

He's standing by Bones, waiting. I let him lift me up, and then he's behind me, holding me against his warm chest. He clicks his tongue, and Bones prances sideways before turning to head up the hill where our property lines touch.

I'm glad for his iron arm over my body, because Bones runs like the devil is on his tail. He seems to love it, but I'm shaken, especially when he scales the low portion of the fence easily and gallops down the hill on the other side.

I swear, my teeth are chattering from fear when we pull up in the driveway of Ryder Ranch. Deacon slides down, unbothered. He glances up and sees my face, and a line appears on his forehead.

"You alright there, sweetheart?" he asks.

I nod. "Just a little cold."

He lifts me down effortlessly. I feel him, a warm, thick slab of muscle against my body. Then, I'm on my feet, and he's hollering for someone in the barn to come get his horse. Andy appears. His eyes glint as they run over me, but he doesn't seem surprised. I stand awkwardly while they confer in the overhead light.

The man takes Bones' reins and disappears into the barn. Deacon comes back to me, his hand on my waist, and ushers me up the stairs and into the house.

I'm swept off my feet. One minute, he's showing up to my house on a horse called Bones. The next, he's got me in his house and he's taking my jacket. I look down at him, on one knee, pulling my boot off, and realize I like this.

Nobody has ever taken care of me before.

He sets my boots aside, but he doesn't get up. One hand, blue from ink, touches the inside of my knee. Our eyes lock in the dim hall.

"You hungry?" he says, voice husky.

I shake my head. My mouth is dry as dust. "I ate," I manage.

He's probably hoping to take me up to his bedroom, but right then, the puppy cries in the living room. I dart around him to look in. He has a wire pen by the hearth, and the puppy is rolling on newspaper, kicking a toy in its back legs. It sees me from the corner of its eye and flips, lifting its fuzzy head.

I get blinders, forgetting all about Deacon, and go right for the puppy.

"Oh, he's so sweet," I whisper, picking him up.

He nuzzles my neck, chirruping in his throat. Deacon appears at my elbow, hands on his hips. He gives the puppy a stern look, as if he's jealous.

"I better not hear any bullshit tonight," he says.

The puppy ignores him, writhing in my arms. I look up at Deacon, all the tension gone from my body. Maybe it's the puppy, or maybe it's being out of my house and back at Ryder Ranch, but here, I feel like I can let my body relax.

"What's his name?" I ask.

Deacon shrugs. "Doesn't have one yet."

"Can I name him?"

My voice is higher than usual. Am I being...bubbly? I haven't been bubbly since I was a little girl, and it feels...so good. Deacon looks at me, and his brows lift.

"Yeah, whatever you like," he says. "You want a drink? I got wine."

I nod. "I don't drink wine, but I'll do moonshine if you have it."

The corner of his mouth turns up. "Yeah, I think I do."

He disappears into the kitchen. I kiss the puppy on the head and set it back down, letting him go back to attacking his toy. I follow Deacon around the corner and find the closet door behind the fridge open. There's a soft crash, some cursing, and then he appears with a jug of moonshine in his hand.

He shuts the door and sets it on the counter.

"No getting drunk," he says.

I lean on the counter next to him.

"Why's that?" I say.

He fills a shot glass and sets it down. "Because I brought you here to talk," he says. "Get to know each other."

"And?" I press.

He pours a second shot and hands it over. "I'm gonna fuck you good and hard, sweetheart, so keep your head on straight for it."

Heat explodes. The way he says it, all intense, takes my breath away. I shoot the moonshine to cover up my blush. A smirk flashes over his face as he bolts his shot.

He looks at me, I look up at him. All I have in my head is the memory of him flipping me onto my hands and knees and telling me to hold the headboard.

"It tastes like apples," I say.

"Supposed to be apple pie," he says. "Ginny made it."

"It's good. I'll have another shot."

There's a little sass to my voice, and my accent is coming through harder than usual. Maybe it's because I'm nervous. He pours me a splash more. I bolt it, flipping my glass and pushing it next to his. He leans in, and I shudder as his mouth brushes the side of my neck. His body shifts against mine, pinning me into the counter.

My stomach swoops and my pussy tightens, like it remembers him and wants more.

He tilts his head and his mouth finds mine, as hungry as the first time. He tastes like apples and Deacon—familiar, sweet, with an edge of something masculine. There's desperation on his tongue as it swipes against mine.

He pulls back and pushes his head against my neck insistently. His short beard is rough on my skin. His mouth burns, hot as a fireplace in winter. A tingle shoots down as my body remembers how it felt between my legs.

My thighs clench. His gaze drops.

God, I want him again.

"Can't get you out of my head," he says, voice hoarse. "Spread your legs for me."

His eyes lock on mine. They're a bed of coals, simmering beneath darkness. My nerves tingle. With trepidation, I lift my hand and touch the bare skin above his collar.

He tenses, like he feels it all through his big body, but he keeps still. I trace down until my finger hits cloth, and then I undo his top button. He's warm. I felt his body in the dark before. I crave the feeling again.

I didn't want to fall for one of these rough Montana men with their hard hands, their windswept faces, and their cold eyes that feel like November. I never wanted a hellraiser, a heartbreaker, like Deacon Ryder.

But he's different, at least I want to believe he can be.

Holding my breath, I run my finger from the hair on his chest up his tattooed neck to his chin and lower lip. He looks at me like he can't tear his eyes away, and that makes me uneasy. If he decides he wants more than pleasure, I think he'll be hard to get rid of.

But right now, with the cold creeping in from outside, I can't refuse. He's everything I swore I wouldn't fall for—from the soles of his boots to the tip of his head, from his lifted truck to the ink up to his jawline to the way he walks like he's got somewhere to be and damn anybody who gets in his way.

The problem is, I never realized how intoxicating that getup could be on the right man. Mouth dry, I start unfastening his shirt.

One button at a time, until it falls open.

I study his chest. The ink on his skin covers everything, dark blue and black. Scars disrupt it and tug the lines here and there. I pick out a few things I recognize—a bird, leaves, chains, mountains, bones. They're all jumbled up, like he didn't have a rhyme or reason in selecting them.

I graze my fingertips over them. He keeps still, like he's worried I'll shy away. Maybe that's a quality he learned from training his horses. He clears his throat. I glance down. There's a rise beneath his zipper—he likes me touching him.

"Where did you get these?" I whisper.

"Around," he says. "Most I got when I was underage. I'm lucky I'm not dead from infection."

"Do you like them?"

His jaw works. "I don't know if liking them factors into it. It's a long story, sweetheart."

"Well, I got all night," I say.

He cocks his head, the corner of his mouth turning up. "No, you got all night for other things. We can talk later."

There's a distant buzz in the back of my head. and I know the moonshine is hitting. I've got a good resistance to it at this point, with my stepbrothers making it in the tobacco shed all the time. I've been skimming it since I was a kid. It takes a lot of moonshine to make me dead drunk, but buzzed is a different story.

I need the liquid courage right now. Maybe that intimidates me more than I realized.

My fingers move down, undoing the final buttons of his shirt. A tremor shivers down his stomach as I touch the trail of hair leading to the belt. He's watching me, lips parted, eyelids so heavy, I can't read his expression.

He wants me, but tonight, I need something different than what we did. If I'm going to sleep with this man again, I want to see every detail this time. My fingers ache to run over him and explore his hard, inked-up muscle. I'm so curious about his body.

My fingers stop on the buckle of his belt. I glance up, the question in my eyes, and he nods once. His throat bobs.

Carefully, I pull the leftover end of his belt free and press it back until the tine slips from the hole. I tug the opposite side of his belt free, feeling like I'm unwrapping a present. There's an intimidating button underneath. I pause, my fingers hovering.

"Go on, sweetheart," he says, voice hoarse, like he might die if I don't.

Against my plain cotton panties, my pussy gives a deep pulse. There's an itch in me, and I know he knows how to take care of it. I tense my inner muscles, achingly empty.

In one quick movement, I undo the button and tug down his zipper. The tension releases as the front of his boxer-briefs stretch to accommodate what's underneath. My fingers falter.

"Don't stop," he says.

I glance up at him, and a rush moves up my spine. I'm soaked between my legs, my heart thumping at the base of my throat. He's on the verge of panting, and I haven't even touched him where he's most sensitive.

My fingers curl on his waistband. He inhales sharply. I tug it down and he snaps free, hitting against his hard, lower abdominals.

I let the band go and cover my mouth with both hands.

He's big and fully hard. The hair over his tattooed groin is cut short, neatly kept. That's something I'm realizing about Deacon. He might look rough, but he's meticulous, his house in order. Even when he sweats, it smells good, like clean salt.

The house is completely silent. I know his blood is going hard; I see it in the thick vein running up his heavy length. I have to touch him. Lips parted, I trace the underside, and he twitches.

His head goes back. "Fuck," he breathes.

He's strong, like a bull. But when I wrap my hand around his cock, I swear, his knees buckle just a bit. Before I can let my nerves get the best of me, I slip from the counter, drop to my knees, and take the head of his cock into my mouth.

I don't know how to do this, but I have a pretty good idea I can figure it out.

He groans, his thighs stiffening. My eyes flutter shut as his hard, hot length slides between my lips. Salt and clean skin fills my senses. He's leaking into my mouth, and it's good—so good, I suck to get more.

His palm slides against the back of my head. Not holding me in, just cradling me. Like I mean something to him.

His gentleness brings down my walls faster than anything else. My jaw aches a little as I push down. I'm halfway, and there's nowhere else for him to go.

Wriggling my tongue beneath him, I work it against the vein and the little lip beneath the head. A harsh moan sounds from up above. More salt spills out, slipping down my throat.

My head is empty for the first time in my life. There's no danger. My body isn't tensed to react. He strokes my nape, gripping it. I moan around him.

"Goddamn it, girl," he rasps.

Out of nowhere, he's pulling me off his dick by the scruff of the neck. He picks me up, and the living room falls away below us as he carries me upstairs.

His dark room is lit by the fireplace. Through the window, black and gray clouds writhe in the sky, stretching for miles around Ryder Ranch.

Then, he's got me in his bed. His fingers undo my clothes, leaving me naked on my back.

He sits up on his knees and pulls his shirt free. My heart beats in my mouth that still tastes like him. His pants come down, revealing more tattooed skin. Then, he's naked, his body like a solid wall of warm muscle and ink.

In my desperation, aided by the little buzz in my head, I sit up and push him until he falls onto his back, stretched out, taking up so much of his bed.

Hungry, I clamber up his body and straddle him. His cock is pressed beneath us. His heartbeat pulses through it. His rough chest burns beneath my palms.

We pause, gasping. I don't know where I got the courage to get on top. He makes me wild. Fearless.

His hand grips the back of my neck, pulling me down. I lean in, and he kisses me the way he did under the northern lights.

I come alive. Everything prickles with magic.

Deep inside, my body tells me to be careful. He's like a wild animal, hiding in his beautiful house with nobody to fill it. Winter is coming fast, and he'll spend it alone, his nights surrounded by starlight in his shadowy room.

Unless he intends to spend it with me.

Deacon breaks away, bringing me back down to Earth with a thump. His dark eyes, up close, aren't frightening. They're beautiful, warm pools I want to dive into. I touch his face, relishing the rasp of his beard, and kiss his mouth. Slowly, I let the tip of my tongue touch his lips.

He follows my mouth with his as I pull back.

"What do you want from me?" I whisper.

He sits up, his arms wrapping around my body, holding me in his lap. Skin on tattooed skin. Hard against soft.

"You," he says.

The way his voice is just a rasp when he whispers is so soothing, like waking up scared and hearing someone safe coming for me.

"Why?" I breathe.

He nuzzles his nose under my chin. His lips run over my collarbone.

"You're something," he says. "Something I shouldn't be allowed to have, but I want anyway."

I understand that to my core.

"I don't know," he continues. "I'm not like you, sweetheart, I don't have nice words. But I know you stopped me with one look. That has to mean something."

My head falls back. He's kissing me, licking me, biting my skin.

Up until now, I've only experienced male attention as a negative. I've been called a whore plenty. I've been touched by someone who didn't like me but wanted to get all the pleasure he could from my body.

But I've never had anybody touch me the way Deacon does.

I'm not sure knowing better has got anything to do with what we do in his bed. It's a pull I can't resist, I couldn't fight it from the moment we met. And I'm scared I'll just keep coming back for more.

He brushes my chin with his mouth. "I need you, sweetheart."

Breathless, I nod. He flips me to my back and pulls me beneath the quilt. The world is just heat and darkness and him. Insistently, he shoves my thighs apart and sinks between them. He spits into his hand, and his palm runs over my sex. Then, the head of his cock pushes against my entrance, and I wince.

"That hurt?" he asks.

I nod again. "A little bit. You're big."

The corner of his mouth turns up. "Thank you."

"It's not a compliment. You've got an extra limb down there," I whisper, surprised I have it in me to tease him.

He reaches up and takes a pillow, lifting my lower body and setting it down onto it. It's a flat pillow, so there's only a slight tilt to my body.

His lips brush my forehead.

"Sometimes, I can be rough," he says. "But I don't mean to be."

"It's okay," I whisper. "I like it."

"Tell me if it hurts and you don't like it," he says, giving me a piercing stare.

I nod. He spits on his fingers again, and they slip between us. This time, they find my clit and move in slow circles—not right on it, just barely grazing where the nerves are most sensitive. Heat tingles up my thighs and centers in my core.

His fingers go faster, getting closer. My eyes flutter shut for a second, and I let myself moan because I want him to keep doing that. He shifts his thumb to cover my clit, moving it back and forth. Pleasure tightens inside, rising until it's an itch he has to scratch. My hips undulate. His fingers keep going.

Then, he stops.

My eyes snap open. He's lifting me, rolling to his back, and settling me astride his body.

"Changed my mind," he grunts. "Need to feel that tight pussy wrapped around my dick."

I tense as he lifts me with one hand, reaching between us, and guides himself into me. Slowly, holding his wrist for balance, I let him slide into my pussy. It's as heavy and thick as it was the first time around. I bite back a groan as our bodies connect.

He has this look about him when he's caught up in lust. It's a hungry stare, with heavy lids, a little red at the corners of his eyes. A vein pulses in his neck. Sweat glitters in the hair down his stomach.

A shudder runs along my spine.

I could fall hard for this man.

"Start riding, sweetheart," he orders.

He puts his hands on my thighs and rocks them. I lay my palms on his warm chest and slowly undulate my hips. A shock of pleasure hits me as his cock moves deep in my lower belly. Experimentally, I flex my pussy, and he groans, eyelids flickering.

"Fuck, you've got a tight little cunt," he breathes.

There's something about seeing such a big man on his back, breathing hard because of something I'm doing, that drives me wild. I brace my knees and let him move me, rolling my hips as he does.

This is why all men ever talk about is getting laid. It really can be that good.

I'm jerked from my thoughts by a sharp slap on my upper thigh. It stings, but in the most delicious way as he grips me, squeezes, and slaps again. I ride faster, nails digging into his chest.

"That's my girl," he drawls.

He fucks and talks so dirty. All my defenses are down. The ceiling spins overhead as I let my head fall back, still riding him hard. It's not lost on me that, tonight, I'm not ashamed. Of anything. What we do is as instinctual and shameless as eating or sleeping.

Our bodies know only carnal satisfaction. Our minds, we can figure those out tomorrow.

Our hearts…those might take longer than a day to learn.

We fuck until there's nothing left. This time, he pulls out and comes on my stomach. We're both too tired to clean up. Instead, we fall asleep, wound up in each other.

# CHAPTER TWELVE
# FREYA

It's barely an hour later when I jerk upright with a start. My body aches, but it's so sweet. Rolling to my back, I push myself up in bed. It's the middle of the night, and he's gone. The place where he slept is cool.

There's a neatly folded flannel shirt by the bed. I pull it on and pad across the floor to the window. Down below, I see the barn, the driveway, the gates in the distance. To my left, I see a rectangular shed that's halfway built into the side of the hill. The door is open and light spills out. Smoke rises from the chimney.

My toes curl, cold on the floor. I should go back to bed and leave him to his own devices, but part of me wants to see who he is when he's alone. I press my hand to the window glass, checking the temperature. It's cool but not cold.

Downstairs, the puppy sleeps by the glimmering fireplace. I push my boots on and step onto the porch. The wind is cool and it smells like autumn. My stomach flips as I hurry past the shadows creeping beneath the pale half-moon. The grass is drenched in dew. I leave wet boot prints up the path to the shed.

Silently, I slip into the doorway and pause.

My stomach swoops. It's a blacksmith shop, bigger on the inside because it's built into the hill. The ground is made of huge, square stone blocks. The walls are red brick. At the back is a forge, burning bright. On the other end, to the left of the forge, is a long table with an assortment of iron tools. At the center of the room is an anvil. Working at the anvil, soaked in sweat, forehead creased in concentration, is Deacon Ryder.

The firelight glints. It cuts a dark shadow down one side of his body. There's a pile of what look like large nails, almost like a smooth tipped railroad spike, on the floor below the anvil. I recognize them—they're stakes used for fence repair.

The thick walls of the shop buffer the sound from outside, but once I'm in the doorway, I hear it: the heavy crackle of the fire, the clang of his hammer, the heavy scrape as he draws a thick, iron rod from the furnace.

Sparks shower in the dark. He's lost in what his hands are doing, like a meditative practice.

I wonder why he's here, why he isn't asleep.

He freezes, and the hammer goes still. He lifts his head and his black eyes fix on me, so intense, I feel myself shrink back. There's a short silence. He sets the hammer and iron down on the table and holds out his palm.

"Come here," he says.

My heart picks up. Feeling like a field mouse approaching a cat, I duck into the shop and go to him. He slides his hand around my waist. It covers almost the entire right side below my ribs.

"What are you doing?" I ask, voice husky.

"Working," he says.

I look down at his tools. "On what?"

"Stakes. I use them to repair and hold down the fencing," he says.

"Why tonight?"

He sighs, running a hand over his forehead, but doesn't answer. Finally, he beckons me and sits down by the table, spreading his knees so I can stand between them. Both hands go around my waist, fingers knitting over my spine. He looks up at me, and I sink into his chest.

I can't help but trust him. His gaze is a different shade of darkness at night. During the day, it glitters like obsidian. At night, it's soft like velvet.

He makes me wonder about so many things. How did he end up here? Why build a big house with nobody to live in it? Why does he wake and go out to look up at the sky? Why is he soaked in sweat, pounding iron at three in the morning on a cold night?

I reach up and touch his temple where he has a scribble of faded ink.

"Why aren't you sleeping, sir?" I whisper.

"Because you're here," he says simply. "Don't want you to go, sweetheart."

My heart flutters faster. My mouth tastes dry, a bit like fear, but not the kind I'm used to. Not the kind that I feel from my stepfather and brothers, or the men who whistle at me in the street.

The fear Deacon sparks in me is sweet, almost like desire, but dark. If I crushed it between my teeth, it would spill into my veins like a drug, addictive enough to get me high and keep me coming back.

"I haven't stopped thinking about you since I met you," he says. "Can't stop thinking about tasting you."

I'm breathing hard. I know he feels it. He has me in his arms.

"I don't know you," I whisper. "I'm scared to know you."

His grip tightens. "Why?"

Into my head pours a stream of memories: unsavory ones, holes in drywall, nights spent curled up in a fetal position trying to cry silently. I know men and what they are capable of when angry. I've conditioned myself to survive them.

But I don't know men like Deacon. He's uncharted territory.

"I don't know how to explain it," I gasp out.

"Sweetheart," he says, voice guttural, "I want everything."

His words break with desperation. I squirm in his arms, but he wraps one iron forearm around my body and holds me tight. I press against his chest, twisting. He takes my wrists and holds them tight in one fist. My stomach sinks—I don't even have a fraction of his strength.

Our eyes lock, and the tension is thicker than the heat from the forge.

"Trust me, sweetheart," he says, voice low and grating like iron on iron.

God, I think I might.

# CHAPTER THIRTEEN
# DEACON

There's darkness in me, hidden deep down, beneath the humor I use to cope. It grew there a long time ago and never died.

It was the fuel that made me pull that fence stake from my shoulder, walk bleeding out to the house, and sink it into Henderson. Amie's picture was still on the mantle, blank eyes watching as I killed her son. I never felt shame like that before, never felt it again.

Darkness and shame made me light a match and burn it all.

Tonight, it's back. Despite how I fought to be a different man for her, it's part of me. Keeping hold of her, I sink down to my knee. Her eyes are huge, breasts heaving beneath my flannel. I swear, I can smell how wet her cunt is. I bend my head, and she tries to pull back as I push my face into the apex of her thighs and inhale.

Sweet, potent. God, that makes me feral.

My dick presses against my zipper, my head empty. I've held back. I've been patient. Tonight, I'm getting what's mine.

Deftly, I rise and flip her so she's bent over the table and pull her hands behind her back. Before she can speak, I grip her shirt and tear the buttons open with my free hand. It slides down her arms, and I let it fall around her ankles.

Her naked body writhes, spine arching. Her curves are breathtaking in the half-orange light. I release her hands and gather her hair, pinning it against the nape of her neck and pushing her cheek against the table.

"I'm going to eat you out, sweetheart," I say.

She jerks, trying to turn her head, but she doesn't tell me no. Entranced, I run my palm down her spine, over the curves of her ass, down to the little wet valley between her legs, until I find what I've spent the last several months jerking myself off to—the soft heat of her cunt.

I love giving oral, more than anything. I'd do anything to lay back and let her fuck my face until she soaks it. It's killing me that I haven't tasted her yet.

That ends tonight.

My heart pounds. I flip her around, lifting her into my arms. Her legs curl, and I grip her thigh, falling back against the wall.

Our mouths meet, and she moans on my tongue. My hand slides between her legs and my fingers delve into her pussy, hard enough that she cries out against my mouth. I break away, breathless.

"Take it," I urge, fucking hard with my hand.

Her eyes roll back. She has the sweetest expression when I'm ruining her, a mix of pleasure and pain. Her full mouth parts, flashing the pink of her tongue. Her throat bends, exposing her soft skin.

"Deacon," she whimpers.

Bracing her on the table, I take her by the throat with my free hand and fuck her pussy with my fingers. Our eyes meet. All I see is clear innocence. Pale blue like the sky, big, thick lashes. God, she's something else.

"Yeah?" I grit out, still fucking her on my hand. "You got something to say?"

Her throat bobs as she shakes her head.

"Good," I say, releasing the last bit of my conscience. "Because I'm eating your cunt, and you're gonna wrap those legs around my head and come on my face."

Ruthlessly, I draw my fingers free and flip her onto her back on the table. She squirms, and I gather her wrists, holding her down. Our eyes lock. She bites her lip, brows creasing. I'm walking a fine line, I know that. I have to remember that if she can't trust me, she can't trust anyone.

But she hasn't said no.

I bend in, kissing her mouth hard. Her breasts heave as I trail those kisses down her breasts, her stomach, to the soft, naked mound over her cunt. That scent hits me again. It feels like snorting something. My veins open, blood pouring to my groin. I'm not the same as I was when I fell asleep. She does things to me. She makes me better and so much worse.

I bury my face between her legs, drowning in her taste, in the sweet wetness in her cunt.

Distantly, she gives a little cry and pulls against my grip. I find her clit and run my tongue over it, sucking it into my mouth and working it with rhythmic pulses. Her body fights me, and it triggers something deep inside that makes me want more.

I'm so fucked up. I hoped she wouldn't see this side, but God, I want to chase her, to drag her down and fuck her on the stone floor. I want her to beg me to stop while she comes around my cock.

I never meant to be aggressive with her, but I can't help myself.

She clearly can't help herself either, because she gives a defeated wail and shudders. My cock aches somewhere below. I shove my face against her cunt, pushing my tongue inside her wet opening so she can come on it. And it's the best thing I've ever felt—softness pulsing strong on my mouth.

I'm in a heaven I don't deserve.

The moment her orgasm ebbs, I pick her up and carry her panting body to the forge. By the window, her skin was cold. I lay her over the anvil, letting her torso hang upside down. All that hair falls to the stone ground. Balancing her thigh in my grip, I start to unzip my pants with the other hand.

"Deacon," she gasps.

"It's just my cock, sweetheart. You know how to take it," I say.

My eyes fall on something else, the fence spike I was halfway finished with when she arrived. It's sharpened on one end, the steel blunt on the other side. I haven't pounded it down, so it's still round. It looks a lot like the stake I put in Henderson that night.

It looks a lot like the worst thing I've ever done.

One handed, I take it up, wrapping the fingers soaked in her arousal around it. She's helpless at this angle. The anvil is below her lower back, her upper body hangs helplessly. Her thighs are spread, inches from my groin.

"You want fucked?" I breathe.

"Yes," she whimpers.

Arousal slips out, glittering in the forge light. Deftly, I flip the stake around to the blunt end and spit on it. I touch it to her clit, and she jerks, moaning.

"What...is that?" her voice cracks.

I want to see this thing that's haunted me slip into the soft heat of her cunt. The worst and best things in the world, intertwined. Slowly, I drag it down to her opening and press it in. Her body responds, shuddering, but keeping still. There's nowhere for her to go at this angle. I have all the power.

"Is that—"

"A fence stake? Yeah," I murmur, fascinated by how she takes it.

Inch by inch. Soft, pink pussy on hard metal. She's so wet, it slides right in. The cry that breaks from her lips sends blood pouring through my veins, pooling in my groin. Ruthlessly, I fuck her cunt with it, the wet sounds echoing in the blacksmith shop. She cries out. I push her to the limits.

Arousal drips over the ink on my knuckles. I crouch over her, pressing my mouth to her swollen clit. Her hips shake, jerking beneath me. She's more beautiful than anything I've ever seen, her curvy body bent over the anvil and her pussy taking the steel. A tremor goes through it, one I feel up my arm. And she comes again, this time squirting around the stake.

Heat shoots down my spine, erupting.

God-fucking-damnit. I meant to fuck her, but it's too late. My cock jerks against my zipper. Pleasure throbs, and I withdraw the stake so I can lean my forehead against her thigh and let myself come in my pants. We both shudder, our breath harsh. Then, everything is still.

"Deacon," she whimpers.

I drop the stake on the anvil block and pick her up, letting her tumble into my arms. We're on the floor, she's in my lap. Her lower lip is swollen with a hint of blood.

"What was that?" she whispers.

I run my lips over her forehead, pushing my face into her hair. "You."

"What?"

My grip intensifies, digging into her soft curves. "You. You fuck me up, sweetheart."

I pull back, brushing her hair from her face. Her pale eyes are enormous.

"You didn't fuck me," she whispers. "Why not?"

I can't bite back a laugh as I press my forehead to hers. "Give me a few minutes and I can."

She's already flushed, but she goes red as the realization sinks in. She glances down then up again.

"Did you...come in your pants?"

"Yeah," I say, pulling her closer. "You make me crazy, sweetheart. I'm trying not to scare you, but God, you're fucking up my head."

She hiccups, and I wonder if she's going to cry. Instead, she curls up in a ball in my lap and presses her face into my shoulder. Reverently, I hold her, stroking over her tangled curls. Inside, I'm relieved.

I showed her a flash of my true colors, and she didn't run.

"Take me back to bed," she whispers.

I carry her all the way there. She lies still while I clean her body, while I kiss it and touch the delicate opening of her pussy to make sure I didn't hurt her. Her eyelids are heavy. Gently, I pull her against my bare chest.

Skin on skin, better than I ever imagined it could be. I close my eyes and, for the first time, I think I see a way forward for us.

Darkness and all.

# CHAPTER FOURTEEN
# DEACON

She sleeps, curled up with her cheek pressed to the back of her hand. Before I leave for chores the next morning, I kneel beside the bed. Her hair, which she usually braids down her back, is loose. The voluminous curls are a tangle around her head. I brush them back, and she stirs but doesn't wake.

I'm so aware of how fragile her presence is.

She's afraid of me sometimes. Maybe I would be too if I were her size.

And yet, she didn't run.

Out of nowhere, I flashback hard. One second, all I see is her angelic face. Then, I'm drenched in hot blood, dragging my body down the hill toward the farmhouse with a metal stake sticky in my fist.

A monster.

I stand so fast, I see stars. I've worked hard to erase everything that happened here all those years ago. I burned the house to the ground, tore out the foundation. I made a ghost of what I did.

The home I built in its place is the complete opposite of Phil and Amie's farmhouse. The people who work here are happy, well paid. We have a strong sense of camaraderie. No man or woman works without proper compensation. Not the way I did, breaking my back with those horses so Phil could cash out.

I thought I could mask who I am, but after last night, I'm done with that. She doesn't know what I'm doing to get her. But she saw me clearly last night, and she didn't leave. Maybe once she's finally mine for good, I can admit everything I've done.

The truck door slams in the yard. It takes me a second to come down to Earth and remember I was expecting company. Silently, I put my work boots on, fasten my belt, and grab my jacket and hat. She's still asleep as I shut the door and head down the stairs, through the front hallway, and out onto the porch.

It's colder than I expected today. Everything smells like wet leaves.

In the driveway is a silver truck with double tires in the back and a horse trailer hitched to it. I put my hat on and pull my coat over my shoulders, making a circle around it to find Jack Russell digging through the back seat.

"You forgot I was coming," he says, stepping out and slamming it shut.

"I didn't." I shrug. "Took your sweet time, though."

His dark green eyes narrow as he fits his hat on. "I've been busy over the summer. There's shit going on all the damn time."

"Ain't one thing, it's another."

"Let's get the horses out," Jack says, heading toward the barn. "I can't stay longer than a few hours."

We go into the barn. Luckily, I already had Apocalypse in Exile pulled from the barn where we keep the studs the other day for a checkup. He's at the far end, pale head hanging over the stall door. Jack makes a beeline for him, standing while the stallion sniffs his shoulder.

"You want to take them out?" I ask.

He nods, unlatching the door. I take Bones out and saddle him up. Jack takes his sweet time getting the saddle on Exile, but I don't mind. He's letting him sniff over his shoulders and every piece of tack before he puts it on. Exile seems to like him, not shying away.

"Is he usually this calm?" Jack swings astride him, adjusting in the stirrups.

I shift my weight, and Bones heads out the door, Exile at his heels.

"Exile's one of my calmest stallions," I say. "Never scares, doesn't stir up shit."

We head east to the flat area by a group of trees. Here, there's a paddock and a course set up for barrel racing. I do most of the training in this space, and it's small enough to keep the horses from getting distracted. We ride past it, and I shift to a posting trot, Jack following my lead. Exile's got the smoothest trot I've ever seen, next to Bones.

"You got problems," Jack says.

I don't bother to ask how he knows, I just nod. We ride through the valley and crest the hill on the other end. From here, the upper east side of Ryder Ranch is fully visible. Jack slows to a walk and Bones falls into step beside him.

"Gonna ask you something," I say.

"Shoot," says Jack.

"You know I want to settle down," I say, squinting over the horizon. "Why do you think that hasn't happened for me yet?"

He stares at me for a long second. Then, he shrugs.

"Possibly because you live in the middle of fucking nowhere," he says.

"That's a legitimate point," I agree. "That'll do it."

Jack's eyes sweep over me. "If you're worried about all the ink and broken nose, don't be. Women don't pick men for surface-level shit, not when it gets down to it. They like it when you notice things they like and make them orgasm consistently. That's about it."

That's good news for me, because I can do both things.

"What about all the...you know."

Jack glances over, shaking his head. "No, I don't."

"The murder."

Jack knows how I got Ryder Ranch, knows the rest of the shady things I've done for myself and others, including him. It's part of the reason we're such close friends. We both know far too much about each other.

"If you're worried about the Hatfield girl not liking you, I wouldn't," he says. "I looked into that family, and every man in it has a mugshot or twelve."

We turn back, starting at a slow walk toward the ranch house.

"That's what I'm afraid of," I say.

Jack's jaw works. "I can't help you there. That's a whole other conversation."

We don't speak. My mind is fixated on the idea of Freya just living in my house. Rising in the morning and humming in the kitchen while she makes her coffee. Falling asleep on the couch in the afternoon, surrounded by books about insects and butterflies. Having dinner with me after the sun is down and the chores are done.

I want the small business of living more than anything. I want her time, every minute of it. The boring parts, the hard parts, the difficult parts.

She was so easy to fall for, and I fell hard. Now, I just have to pinpoint what's holding her back.

We head to the barn, and Jack pulls to a halt outside the door, stacking his hands on the saddle horn.

"I should have guessed you had company," he says. "I can tell when you just got laid."

"Shut up. You can't."

He jerks his head at my hat. "You sleep on your right side when you sleep alone. The other side is flat."

I touch the side of my head. The corner of Jack's mouth curls.

"She's on the porch," he says. "I'm just fucking with you."

We both turn. Freya stands there, a dark figure with her arms wrapped around her body. She's dressed in a black turtleneck sweater and a close fitted skirt that comes to the middle of her thigh, tights, and brown leather boots. Soft dark curls are piled on her head, highlighting her elegant neck.

We both look at her for a long moment. She looks like something from a book. Pretty, whimsical, and homey.

"Yeah, she's out of your league," says Jack.

"I'm aware. Come on, let's get the horses fed and put away," I say. "Then we can talk about whether you want Exile."

He nods, and we head into the barn. The entire time I'm putting Bones away and pouring out his grain, I have the image of Freya on the porch dancing in my mind.

I got a taste of her last night and, God, was it good. I love animalistic sex, the same way I like kink. Last night proved she gets off on it too. If she hadn't gotten tired, I could have spent all night with her thighs around my head and her pussy on my mouth.

Somebody flicks the rim of my hat. Jack swims into focus.

"Light's on, Ryder, but nobody's home," he says.

I shut the stall door. "I'm just thinking."

"She's got you whipped."

I don't respond. Everybody I've ever talked to about Freya has said the same thing—that I'm well and truly whipped for her, even before we officially met. It seems like Freya's the only one who doesn't know we're supposed to be together.

We head to the porch. Freya stands by the door, weight on one hip. Her arms are wrapped around her body. She looks from me to Jack shyly. He takes off his hat and holds out his hand.

"Jack Russell," he says.

She steps forward and shakes it. "Freya Hatfield."

"Pleasure to meet you," he says. "I won't ask you if you're related to the Hatfield family if you don't ask if it's Jack Russell like the dog."

She smiles, the ice melting. "I'd be rich if I had a dime for every time it happens," she drawls in that sweet accent.

"Oh, I'd be a millionaire," Jack says, putting his hat back on his head.

She's so pretty, I barely hear what he says. Then, my attention is pulled elsewhere as a smell so good, it makes my mouth water, hits my nose.

"You cooking, sweetheart?" I ask.

She nods, pulling the door open. "Y'all want breakfast?"

We both nod, climbing the porch. She slips into the house and disappears into the kitchen while we kick the mud off our boots and follow her inside. In the kitchen, Freya has a plate in her hand and she's piling it with food.

"Go sit," she says.

We both sink down, not a thought in our heads. She sets two plates in front of us and pours coffee.

"Eat before it gets cold," she says.

As stereotypical as it is, I'm trying to figure out how soon is too soon to propose the minute I put the fork in my mouth. It's no slight to Ginny. She's good at her job, but there's something about the meal Freya makes that turns my brain off until my plate is clean. Everything is creamy, crumbly, and perfectly fried, seasoned to perfection, and drenched in brown sausage gravy so rich, it makes my head sweat.

We sit in silence for a second. I think Jack is speechless.

Freya gets up and starts clearing plates. I take her elbow.

"Don't worry about that," I say.

She shakes her head. "You said I could cook, so for right now, it's my kitchen," she drawls softly.

My head spins. I wish Jack wasn't here, because I'd have this girl up in my bedroom right now. As if he's reading my mind, Jack stands and reaches for his hat.

"I should head out," he says.

"I'll walk you." I get up.

We leave through the front. Jack stands by his truck and takes out a cigarette. He gives me one, and we smoke for a second. Finally, he gestures back at the house.

"You'd better put a ring on that girl," he says.

My brain doesn't catch up with my mouth before I answer.

"I plan on it," I say.

Jack shakes his head. "I don't blame you. I think I need to sleep for the next few days to recover from that." He stubs out his cigarette and swings into the truck. "I'll be back with the trailer and a check for Exile next week. There'd better be a meal in there somewhere."

I shake my head, watching him back down the drive and disappear. Then, I go back inside to find her wiping everything clean. She yelps when I come up behind her and spin her around to kiss her mouth. The taste of Freya and coffee melt on my tongue. Her face is pink when I pull back.

"Stay," I say.

Her smile fades. "I'm sorry," she whispers.

"Too soon?"

She nods, not speaking. I go to let her go and accept my fate, but she holds me near. Her arms come up around my neck.

"Dance with me," she whispers.

I don't dance. I always assumed I had two left feet. But I can't tell her no to anything, so I reach past her to the radio in the kitchen window and turn the dial. It crackles, and the beginning of a slow song that feels like I've heard it somewhere starts.

"I don't know this one," I say.

She presses her temple to my chest. "I do. It's from a movie."

I hold her waist, and we sway. I think that's all she expects from me. When I look down, her lashes are lowered. I dip my head and breathe in her sweet hair. It smells like something familiar, something I've ached for.

There's nothing poetic about loneliness.

It just fucking hurts.

Now that I have her in my heart, in my bed, and my loneliness is gone, I know how much I hurt before. I'll let her go home this time. Then, I'll make all the right moves to get her to come back and make this house into her home. We have time. She can take all of it that she needs.

But when all is said and done, she'll stay.

"Tell me about home," I say.

She lets out a little sigh. "What do you want to know?"

"Everything. Tell me what you miss the most."

There's a short silence.

"In the morning, before anybody else woke up, I'd go out and walk down the road," she says, voice fragile like a spider's web. "We lived on a dirt road when I was little. Then, they poured gravel. After a while, they paved it. But I'd walk down the side to where it met the state route. In the summer, it was too hot, but in the fall, I'd get up early and walk all the way to the end. There was a creek that ran alongside it with raspberry bushes all around it. I'd take the ripe ones and put them in my pocket. When everyone was gone at work, I'd crush them and use them to paint."

"Do you still have the paintings?"

"No, they didn't keep," she sighs.

"How old were you then?"

"Around nine, maybe ten," she says. "Aiden took Wayland, Ryland, and Bittern to work in the factory. They made cabinets. When they came home, they smelled sweet like cherry wood."

"Did anybody stay with you?" My stomach has a pit in it. It sounds a lot like my childhood, trying to survive without anybody to look after me.

"No, but I knew better than to go far from the house," she says. "What about you?"

"I was in a foster home when I was that age," I say. "Between seven and ten was one of the better ones. I felt bad for the woman who ran it. She was trying to do right by us, but we were a bunch of fucking unruly boys with nobody to keep an eye on us. I got pulled and placed with another family at eleven."

She turns her head. Her blue eyes pierce right to my heart.

"That's hard," she whispers.

"I was tough, always have been," I say. "We were like *Lord of the Flies* in there sometimes, and I was the ringleader. Poor Carrie. She was a good woman, but she had a hole in her heart."

"What kind?"

I shrug, still holding her tight. "The kind somebody else put there and not even giving out all the kindness in the world could fix."

"What happened after?" Her voice is as fragile as her gaze.

"Stayed in one of the worst homes I ever got placed in for six months," I say. "Protective services pulled me from that, and I ended up at a ranch. Those foster parents ended up adopting me."

"Oh," she says, a faint smile on her lips. "That's some kind of happy ending."

I lean in and kiss her forehead. Her hair smells so good, like vanilla. Like home.

"Yeah," I say. There's no way I'm getting any deeper into my past right now. "So, what did you do all day? All alone with yourself like that?"

"I went to school most of the time. But a lot of times, I missed the bus because I had to get breakfast ready and on the table before I could go. Then, there were a few years where the road collapsed and I couldn't get to the bus stop," she says. "The school was ten miles from home, so I couldn't walk. And part of that was highway."

"So who taught you all the stuff you know, like the bugs and shit?" I ask.

She smiles, rolling her eyes at my words. "I had a library card, and that was only three miles from the house. When I wasn't there or at school, we had a moonshine still in the tobacco barn."

I feel my brows lift. "You made moonshine instead of going to school?"

"What about it? I stayed legal," she says. "Bittern grew weed, but not for very long, because he wasn't any good at it. But I needed the moonshine so I could trade it for groceries, the things I didn't want anybody to know about."

"Like what?"

She blushes, a little. "Pads, bras. Sometimes, I could get those from the nurse at school, but not always."

The song ends, and she stops swaying. I look into her eyes, clear blue like a pale morning sky. She's so beautiful. She sees me looking, unable to keep my gaze from her face.

"I should go home," she whispers. "I don't think I'm comfortable staying another night. I worry about Aiden coming back early."

I don't push her. I had my doubts she'd stay the weekend. Every time I reel her back down from wherever she lives in her head—up in the sky, sitting on the edge of the moon—she feels fragile in my hand.

Like if the winds change, she'll blow away.

"I'm sorry," she says.

"Don't apologize," I say. "I understand."

We don't speak on the drive home, but when I drop her at the end of the drive, I tell her I'll see her soon. She cocks her head at me like she's going to say something but then shuts the door. For the third time, I watch her disappear over the hill toward her stepfather's house.

God, I wish she'd just stay.

# CHAPTER FIFTEEN
# FREYA

I can't stop thinking about how he danced with me in the kitchen.

Yes, the sex is unbelievable, but that dance shook me up.

The house is as tense as it always is under Aiden's dictatorship. There's something going on that I don't know about. Aiden makes Bittern take his land surveying equipment out and work on something from dawn until dusk. That strikes me as strange. Bittern got his surveyor's certification years ago but never did anything with it. Now, all of a sudden, Aiden's got him putting in for lost time.

I watch them from the corner of my eyes.

Aiden can't be trusted. If he's not being outwardly horrible, he's got something cooking up in his head to be horrible for later.

At least he's gone a lot. Ryland goes with him, and I see their trucks disappear toward the road that leads up to the McClaine ranch. He has to head west and double back to avoid trespassing on Deacon's land. I know that grinds his gears. I silently enjoy his annoyance.

I spend most of my time at work. Autumn brings the fall festivals, the farmer's markets, and the auctions to the towns and cities. It's good for Tracy's businesses, and she's often pulled away, leaving me in charge of the café. I don't mind working alone. The townspeople are curious about me. I make up better stories to tell them about my past than the truth.

Most of them call me church girl. I'm not sure why.

The men never write their numbers on napkins and leave them. That's confusing. Back at home, I had boys hanging on my window at the ice cream shop now and then. Here, the men from Knifley are respectful when they order, and they don't flirt with me much.

The days slip by. It feels like dozens, but it's been less than a week since I saw Deacon.

I wonder why it feels so long.

The café keeps me company. I sell coffee and chat with people I know but not well enough to say we're friends. It's late afternoon, one day that feels like fall and the pumpkin pastries are flying off the shelves, when I've got a few customers left and I'm thinking about closing thirty minutes early. There's a young man talking to me, leaning on the counter. He's a cowboy from one of the neighboring farms. They like to stand around and shoot the shit so they don't have to get back to work.

I smile and nod where it's appropriate.

The door swings open. The little café is filled with a strong presence that makes me lift my head.

My stomach flutters. I tuck a curl behind my ear.

Deacon Ryder walks in, the bell ringing in his wake. He's as tall as the door and more than half as broad. As usual, he's in that charcoal gray Henley that clings to his shoulders, frayed at the collar where it touches his neck. Over it is his Carhartt jacket, and on his feet are his work boots.

My mind is filled with images of what he did to me that night in the blacksmith shop. The fire flickering, his dark eyes on me, lids heavy with desire. The dizzying and exhilarating experience of being bent backward over the anvil. The fence stake was a little...unexpected. It woke me up to the fact that I think Deacon is a little wilder in the bedroom than he's been letting on.

My face flames just thinking about it.

Deacon crosses the room, boots loud on the wooden floor. The man looks up, shifting over a few steps. Deacon sends him a sideways glance.

"You flirting with my girl?" he asks.

The cowboy shakes his head. "Nope, just leaving."

Alright, it makes more sense as to why no man in Knifley gives me more than a polite nod. The man leaves, and it's just Deacon and me in the café. He takes his hat off and sets it on the counter.

"That wasn't very nice," I say.

"Have to establish my territory."

Heat creeps up my neck. "What's got you so full of it today?"

"I've just got a whole lot of something," he says, "and now I got somewhere for it to be."

"What does that mean?"

He shrugs. "Nothing. Can I get a coffee, sweetheart?"

I turn to fill a paper cup, and he lets out a low whistle. Startled, I let the carafe go and turn on my heel. "Don't whistle at me."

"Why?" His eyes glint with a smile. "You look pretty good in that short little skirt."

I pull at the hem of my skirt. It's new. Tracy gave me a bag of her grown daughter's clothes. This morning, I was feeling a little bolder than usual, so I put on a plaid skirt that hugs my hips and upper thighs and tucked in a black sweater with a dipped neckline. Nothing's showing, and I'm wearing a thick pair of black tights underneath, but it's still a little sassier than what I'm used to.

His eyes run up and down.

"You look pretty good," he says again.

That look steals over his face, the one that makes his head cock and his lips part.

I turn back around to fill his cup, but knowing he's looking me up and down, probably hard under his zipper, has me flustered. I take my time getting a lid and fitting it on. Then, I hand it to him.

He gives me two dollars. Our fingers brush. The sensation tingles up my arm.

"Don't you close up soon?" he says.

"In a few minutes," I say.

He glances over the empty room. "Can't you close up early?"

I lean over the counter, looking up at him through my lashes. The part of me that tells me not to get involved with him has been quiet lately. Or I'm ignoring it on purpose.

Truthfully, I'm horny for him. He did something to my brain when he ate me out in the blacksmith shop. It hasn't been the same since.

It keeps me awake, my hand tucked between my thighs, trying to rub out the same feeling and failing. Deep down, it gets me a little pissed that it's this man who pulled it out of me.

"What are you asking?" I say.

He bends in, kissing me briefly. "Lock up the shop, sweetheart. I want to fuck you before I head home."

My brows shoot to my hairline. "You really know how to romance me."

The corner of his mouth jerks up.

"I'm not trying to romance you," he says. "I'm trying to fuck you up against the wall in the back alley so I don't have to jerk off too many times before I can fall asleep."

My jaw is on the floor.

"Is that how you get all your women?" I ask.

He leans in and gives me those big, dark puppy eyes. "I don't have women, sweetheart. I just got you."

That goes right down my spine like warm water. If I hadn't spent the whole week thinking about him and all the dirty things he's done to me, I would know better. I would, and I'd say no, I'm not letting him have a quickie in an alley with me.

I forget that I should know better.

I take the key from under the counter and lock the front door and pull the shades. He sets his coffee down, watching me as I turn off the sign and walk right by him to the back door. Then, he snaps into action and follows me into the narrow alleyway.

It's colder than it was this morning. I wrap my arms around myself.

"Someone will see," I whisper.

He takes my hand, pulling me to the dead end by the big air conditioning unit that comes to the middle of my thigh. His jaw is hard. There's a visible pulse in the vein in his neck.

"Nobody's walking down here at this time," he says.

"What happens if they see us?"

He shrugs. "They get a show, I guess, but they won't see you. Turn around, put your hands on the wall."

This is the riskiest thing I've ever done. There's a rushing in my ears as I turn and spread my palms on the brick wall. It's a little dirty, smudged with soot, and cold. There are leaves gathered on the concrete at our feet. I glance down, distracted, as he moves up behind me.

His mouth touches my neck, heat on cold skin.

"God," I whisper, my body coming alive.

My hair is loose today. He buries a hand in it and fists it at the roots, holding me still. I close my eyes, focusing on his other hand dragging down my hip and pushing my skirt up over my ass. He gives me a little spank that stings deliciously.

"So pretty," he murmurs.

I open my eyes as he tugs down my tights and panties. The brick wavers in front of me, and cold air stings my bare skin. His belt clinks before he spits in his hand and dips it between my legs.

"That's a little bit wet, sweetheart," he says.

I nod, unable to speak. There's a fever coming over me, wiping my mind clean. He rubs the wetness into my sex, dipping his middle finger in briefly. Then, he braces his boot on the concrete, and the tip of his cock notches against my opening.

He pushes, giving a frustrated grunt.

"Arch your back," he murmurs. "Like that... Good girl. Relax. Let me in."

I'm doing my best not to clamp down on him, but it's difficult. He pushes, and I start panting as the first inch slides in. It hits right on that sensitive spot he touches with his fingers.

"Fuck, you're a tight little thing," he says under his breath.

He says these things like they're nothing, like they don't have my pussy fluttering around him. All I can do is moan as he presses all the way inside, deep enough that I get that sweet ache again. He thrusts, and I cry out, loud enough that he lets my hair go and covers my mouth.

"You need to adjust?"

I nod, eyes rolling back to look at him. He's hovering over me, body pressing hard and hot against mine. With his other hand, he pushes under the front of my skirt and into my panties. His fingers find my clit, and he pulls out an inch and fucks back in.

"Better?"

I nod, unable to speak through his grip. He groans in his chest, and I know he's hungry. I feel it in his next thrust; it's rough, almost bruising.

"Fuck," he groans from between his teeth. "Goddamn, that's good."

I shut my eyes again, just letting my body feel pleasure in waves. His fingers circle my clit fast, wet from my pussy. His cock thrusts in deep and holds for a half beat. I can feel his piercings as he drags out, teasing me deep inside.

Everything falls away.

I'm not Freya, scared and unsure. I'm beautiful, desirable, wanted so badly that I bring this man to his knees, all two hundred and fifty plus tattooed pounds of him.

That's powerful.

Heat bursts between my thighs. My eyes fly open, and I can't keep from crying out into his hand. He makes a rough sound in his throat. His hips speed up, taking me harshly through my orgasm.

"Good girl," he pants. "You come on my cock, sweetheart."

Once again, there's no shame, just breathless pleasure throbbing where our bodies meet. I should tell him to pull out. Now, before it's too late.

I might not have been taught much about birth control, but I know we can't do this anymore. He needs to start wearing a condom, or come on something that isn't the inside of my pussy. Otherwise, I'm going to be in over my head in trouble. There's no way Aiden will let me stay if I wind up pregnant. He's been clear on that account.

I twist my head. He lets my mouth go.

"Don't come in me," I gasp.

He groans through his teeth and pulls out. His knuckles go white against the brick. I press my legs together and feel him between them, jerking and spilling his cum over my naked thighs. The wind picks up, cold. The faint soapy scent of his pleasure hits my nose.

God, there's something so raw and easy about fucking him.

I can't let it go. It's the complete opposite of the feeling I get when I look up at the sky and want to be anywhere else. Like being whole, like being in love with being alive and everything my body feels because of it.

I've never loved being alive. It's usually just bearable.

Being alive has always consisted of just getting through the day, for me and everyone around me. But not Deacon, no. He eats up life the way he does my cooking. He lives big and confident in a way I can only dream of.

Buried beneath him, I taste the raw pleasure of living, and it makes me want to cave the next time he begs me to stay.

"Jesus, I made a mess of you, sweetheart," he says.

He zips up and turns me around, kneeling. From his coat pocket, he takes a creased bandana and wipes my thighs. Then, he leans in, and I tense. But all he does is kiss my clit and pull my panties and tights up and my skirt down.

Oh, I'm a goner.

He gets up, belt still hanging open. "I think I need a smoke."

Sex like that has me considering acquiring a few vices too. I lean against the wall, arms crossed over my chest. He takes a bent cigarette out of his pants pocket, puts it straight, and lights up. There's a long silence before he exhales and gives me a stare that makes my stomach flutter.

"I don't want to go, but I got to," he says.

"Where are you going?" I ask softly.

"To see your stepfather."

All the butterflies in my belly go cold and die out. "Why're you talking to Aiden?"

He sighs. "I haven't really brought it up, but I think we got a land dispute coming down the pipes and heading straight for us."

I wrack my mind. Is this the reason Bittern's been out surveying the land? Is there some kind of property line issue with the farm?

"Why?" I say.

He studies me for a second. Then, he takes a drag.

"Nothing you need to worry about. I got it handled," he says. "But given that I'm being summoned to some kind of mediation with him and I got to have my lawyer there, I'd say it's good he doesn't know I'm coming in his stepdaughter on the regular."

"Deacon," I gasp.

He gives me that halfway grin. "What? Like it isn't true."

I narrow my eyes. "What does summoned mean in this context?"

"It means I got a letter from his fuckass lawyer with a date I have to show up," he says, like it doesn't matter much to him.

"When is that?"

He flips his hand, showing his worn leather watch. "About forty minutes from now."

It scares me that he's talking to Aiden. He doesn't know my family, and I don't want him to. Arms still around my body, I turn and walk up the alley and go inside. It takes a second, but he comes in through the back door.

"What's the matter, sweetheart?" he says.

I turn, chewing my lip. "Aiden's not...nice. You shouldn't be talking to him."

"I know he's not nice," he says. "We're talking legal shit, not trying to be friends. What's really wrong?"

I go behind the cash register and start counting out the money for the night. He thinks I'm ignoring him, I know, but I just need a second to figure out what I feel. He leans on the countertop, his eyes searing the top of my head.

"Come on, talk to me," he says, voice low.

"I just...I've never known Aiden to go up against somebody and lose," I say.

I stack the ones in a pile next to the fives. I wish he wasn't so damn charming. It might make staying away easier. The last thing I need is to get tangled up with a man Aiden's got it out for.

"Hey, hey, sweetheart, look at me." His voice is all gentle and rumbly, and it's making it hard to keep a wall up.

Reluctantly, I obey, looking right into those dark eyes, a crease through his forehead. It occurs to me that if anybody can take on Aiden, it's probably Deacon. He's got an inch or two on him, and he's broader in the shoulders.

"Don't you worry about me," he says.

I stare at him, gears turning in my head.

Maybe the reason my mother married Aiden was because he had some muscle on her drunk of a father. There's a practicality in getting with a man who, no matter his character, can punch an asshole in the jaw, especially if there's an asshole around who needs it.

I have a couple of them, but I have no desire to be so involved as to see Deacon give Aiden or Ryland a beat down.

I just want out of this mess. I need everybody to go back to ignoring me. Getting noticed all the time is stressing me too much. The problem is, Deacon won't go away. And I don't want him to.

"You'd better go," I say quietly.

He sighs. "Give me a kiss before I do."

Obediently, I offer my mouth, and he kisses it. It's just as nice as it was the first time—the right amount of pressure, a little heat, a hint of tongue. But my stomach is all twisted up in knots, and I can't enjoy it.

He puts on his hat and goes. I stand in the door, arms crossed tightly, and watch him swing into his truck.

Part of me is so wrapped up in him that I don't want to think too hard about this. The other part wonders if I'm just another turn in a cycle I never wanted to be part of.

# CHAPTER SIXTEEN
# DEACON

I go into South Platte to see my lawyer before I show up at the mediation. Jay Reed's office is dark and cool, located in the lower level of a house turned into an office in South Platte. It smells like the coffee he's got in his Styrofoam cup, on his desk by his boots. When I walk through the door, a bell chimes, and he looks up.

"Speak of the devil," he says.

"Who was?" I say, taking my hat off and sinking into the chair opposite his desk.

"Me," he says. "You're the devil, and I'm speaking of you."

"Alright. Coffee, and let's hit the road."

He stands, going to the coffeemaker in the corner. "We're having this meeting in city hall. I proposed that location because I can't have you throwing punches."

I look down at my knuckles. They've got too many telltale scars to pretend I don't like a good bar fight. I rise, and he hands me a foam cup and gets his briefcase. We step outside, and I stand under the overhang while he locks up.

"Let's go," Jay says, putting his hat on. "Before the rain hits."

The sky roils. City hall is just across the street, so it doesn't take long to duck into the front room. The floors are plain brown, glazed, and the walls are rustic wood. There's a bull's head over the front desk and a police officer playing on his phone behind it.

"We're here for a meeting with Aiden Hatfield," Jay says.

I throw my cup away, my mind going back to what I just did to Freya. I should be ashamed of myself for feeling so smug about it.

But I'm not sorry. Not even a little.

The door opens behind me. Aiden Hatfield comes through the door, followed by his oldest son, Ryland. The quiet one is nowhere to be seen. They're both in suits, hair brushed back, but no hats. Maybe they don't wear hats back in Kentucky. I take mine off, cross the glossed floor, and hold out my hand.

"Nice to see you," I say.

If he's taken aback, he hides it. We shake hands. I wonder if part of him knows I'm putting his stepdaughter through the mattress every opportunity I get, but I doubt he does. He'd be livid. I know men like him. In his eyes, everything and everyone who depends on him is property.

"This must be your son, Ryland," I say.

Ryland shakes my hand, and I release him quickly. His father is built like me—big, tall, but lean, with tattoos and rough edges. The son is similar but lacks his confidence. Out of all the Hatfields, Aiden is the one I need to watch closely.

He's smart, confident. That makes him dangerous.

"Thanks for coming in," he says, offering a tight lipped smile.

"Oh, my pleasure," I say, turning and beckoning to Jay. He comes over, taking off his hat, and extends his hand. "This is my lawyer, Jay Reed."

That gives Aiden some pause. Clearly, he took a look at me and made the assessment that I don't keep my ass covered. There's a hair less confidence in the handshake he gives Jay. Ryland doesn't offer his hand.

The officer shows us to a meeting room. There's a table in the middle, big, round and made of wood. I sink down at one end, spreading my knees, and lean back. Jay sets his things down and puts his palms together.

"Anybody want a coffee before we start?" he asks.

I shake my head. Aiden gets one from the table on the far end. Ryland sits, his chin in his fingers, and watches me, like he thinks he can intimidate me by staring.

I'm not intimidated by much. I think all that got scared out of me before I turned ten. What I can't get with my lawyer, I'll get with my fists.

"Alright, you want to tell me what this is about?" I say.

Jay clears his throat. "I have the papers you sent over with a plan for the zoning council and city government. Before we get into it, this is an informal meeting. We're just talking, seeing if this can get resolved before it needs to be kicked somewhere more serious."

Aiden jerks his head. His smugness makes me hate him. I'm silent because I know it's what Jay wants from me, but inside, as I listen to what they want, deep anger sparks. As it sinks in, the flames climb high.

My suspicions were correct.

They plan on getting an easement across the strip of land that separates the Hatfield farm from the McClaine's property line, across the western point of Ryder Ranch. Then, they'll run a road up through Aiden's land and sell out the entire southern side of the McClaine's land to real estate developers.

Over my dead body.

I grew up with one truth being ground into my head, day in, day out—I came from nothing and I deserved to die with nothing. No parents, no money in my pockets. Dropped on a doorstep, made to work for every meal. Ryder Ranch is the result of years of hard work, determination, and the willingness to do the unspeakable.

Nobody is going to take a square foot of that land from me. I keep my eyes on the table. Not for their sake, but for Jay's. He's handling them. There's a reason he's the best lawyer in the area.

But fuck, I want to put my fist through Aiden's face.

Aiden has a bunch of business jargon he pulled out of his ass, probably. But the upshot of what comes out of his mouth is, he's planning on getting rich. And all he wants from me is that easement. He says that all casual, minimizing it, like I don't know what that really means.

Because it means I'm about to get fucked.

To my credit, I keep it together all the way to the end, but I let Jay be the one to shake hands and close the meeting. I'm silent, blood thumping like a fast-approaching war drum as we stride from the room.

# CHAPTER SEVENTEEN
## DEACON

We step out onto the street and stand there, completely silent. The storm hit while we were inside. Rain lashes the buildings and pours into the gutters. I stare out, not seeing, just trying to wrestle with the anger raging through my chest.

My land is the only thing I've ever had.

It's where I fantasized about bringing Freya. Figuring out what makes her tick, what makes her fall for me. Coaxing her into marrying me, having babies with her, filling the empty house with a world we make together.

I know, on a surface level, an easement won't ruin that. It's whatever comes next when they start bringing trucks through, when I hear the trees fall and the rocks are blown from the ground.

Smoke, dust, and worse: civilization.

Slowly, I become aware that Jay is talking to me. I put my hat on.

"What?"

"Do not go after the Hatfields," he says.

I jerk my head in a sharp nod, looking past him.

"Deacon, look at me," he says, pointing two fingers toward his eyes. "You keep your hands off them. No fighting, no shooting, no talking to them. Got it? Any communication goes through me."

I work my jaw.

"So help me God, I will kick your ass myself if I hear you've done otherwise," Jay says, as if he's not half my body weight. "You get in your truck and head home. I'll call you tomorrow."

"You got any cigarettes?" I ask.

He takes a pack from his pocket and hands me one. "I need to hear the words from you."

I light up. "Alright, I can keep away."

"I'll fucking hold you to that," Jay says. "I've got another meeting, so I'm heading out. You drive right home. Don't stop or go anywhere else."

He crosses the street, his good suit soaked. I watch him disappear back into his office before stepping out into the rain. Water sprays up around my boots as I head a few blocks down to my truck.

Inside, I take off my hat and lean back.

My eyes fall to my hand on the steering wheel, knuckles white. I've got a knife in my pocket and a gun hanging on the holster behind my headrest, but I'm craving the crunch of cartilage under my fist.

I think, before Jay ever said a word, my mind was made up.

Jaw gritted, I pull off the curb and head to the more expensive part of town. There's a boutique there, and I ordered something a few weeks ago. I got a text this morning saying it was ready to pick up. Before I give somebody a beat down, I need to get it.

I go inside, the bell ringing as I walk in. The woman behind the counter balks at me for a second. She's new, wasn't here the last time.

"I got an order to pick up," I say.

She glances behind me at the only escape route. "Um...what's the name?"

"Ryder," I say. "Deacon."

She nods, dipping into the back. She returns with a flat gift box tied with a black ribbon. There's a fabric gift receipt pinned to it with my name on it. I'll take that off before I give it to Freya. Maybe it'll make up for whatever I did earlier that had her upset.

"Was it already paid?" she asks, flipping through the receipts by the desk.

I take my card out. "No, I ordered in a hurry."

She runs my card and puts the box in a plastic bag to protect it. When I step back outside, the rain is letting up. In my truck, I undo the ribbon and lift the lid.

Inside, on the top layer of tissue paper, sits a blue silk lingerie set. Nicer than anything she's ever had in her life, likely, but not half as fine as she deserves.

I'm not sure there's anything pretty enough to be on Freya.

I stare down at it, entranced by how different it is than anything I'm used to. The details are incredible. White stitching all along the edges in a complex pattern. Little gussets of some variety over the cups. I make sure my hand is clean and lift the bra to look at the panties.

*Goddamn.*

I probably shouldn't have looked in the box because, on top of being livid at Aiden Hatfield, I'm now horny for his stepdaughter. Both of those things get my blood pumping in two different ways.

I take a beat. Then, I close the box, put it in the back seat, and turn the truck around. I'm not heading to the Hatfield's anymore. I'm going to go see Jack and have a drink in the bar. Or a coffee. Jay would approve of that.

The rain has let up by the time I'm in West Lancaster. I park around the side, in the alley, like I usually do. I've got the door open, and I'm stepping into the wet street when I realize the truck in front of mine belongs to Aiden Hatfield. He's in the bar right now. I slam my door shut.

The anger that rises isn't violent.

It's hard, like heated iron, and it burns so hot, I can't keep it inside anymore.

Without missing a beat, I take a switchblade out of my pocket, pop it out with a metallic hiss, and stick it into his left rear tire as I walk by. The feeling is so satisfying that I wrench it out and sink it into the front tire for good measure.

Then, I go inside and the door shuts behind me.

The bar is halfway full. Jack stands against the back counter, arms crossed. There's a blonde woman with a harshly cut bob, his sister, getting ready to head out. She puts a purse over her shoulder, hugs him, and slips through the back exit. That's probably for the best. Jack would be pissed if I started a fight in front of Lisbeth.

I swing my eyes over the room. Aiden sits by himself in the corner. A few paces away, Ryland is trying to talk on his phone over the noise.

I see red. I shouldn't do this. Jack is going to be pissed off if I fuck up his bar on a weekday afternoon. But right now, I don't care. From the corner of my eye, I see a flash of Jack, his eyes widening. Then, I cross the room and drop down directly across from Aiden.

He jerks his head up, brows rising.

There's a second where the tension vibrates between us. Then, the corner of his mouth curls.

"You really want to do this, Ryder?" he says, voice cool.

I should trade words to work this out. Instead, I pick up the table and flip it. He's thrown back against the wall, the chairs spill out. The crash shakes the room and sends customers scurrying for the door. It's too early to get involved in a bar fight for most people.

Not for me. I'm ready to go.

Aiden's eyes flash like an animal as he pushes off the wall, reaching for the chair closest to him. I duck, last second, as it flies over my head and hits the floor behind me, skidding and colliding with the wall.

"Jesus Christ," I hear Jack snap.

He's fine. I'll write him a blank check before I go. I'd pay a heavy price for beating the shit out of Aiden.

Recklessly, I lunge at him. He skirts around me and his fists come up. I straighten, waiting. I'm not here to fistfight this asshole for encroaching on my land. I'm here to humiliate him for the way Freya goes pale when she hears his name.

I don't think he hits her—there's no evidence of it—but he terrorizes her, that's clear.

And that's enough.

I lift my palms. "Come on, motherfucker," I say. "Hit me."

He cocks his head, eyes flashing. I move aside as his fist comes right at me, but not quick enough. He catches me in the corner of the jaw, and

I reel, shocked. Goddamn, this asshole can punch. I shake my head once to clear it and then go for him, swinging and hitting him in the shoulder.

He stumbles, tripping over the table. We both fall like a sack of bricks, me straddling him. I take the opportunity to put him in a chokehold and flip him onto his stomach. For a second, I have him. Then, he uses brute strength to buck me off and strikes me hard in the face. Stunned, I spit, blood spraying across the floor.

We both roll, crashing into the rubble, fighting like dogs to get the upper hand.

We get some hefty hits in. There's something wet and metallic on my thigh, but it doesn't hurt. Or, at least, I can't tell through the bruises that Aiden's beating into my body.

The blood takes everything up a notch. I whirl, and we're both on our feet again. This time, when my fist hits his jaw, he feels it. He hits the wall, gasping. From the corner of my eye, something swings. I duck, scrambling back. Ryland is a foot away. My blood surges, my lips pulling back to bare my bloody teeth.

I'm not worried about Ryland—he's a pussy. I expel air through my clenched teeth, spraying him with blood. Shocked, he reels back.

I go after him, swinging and hitting, beating him back relentlessly until he falls against a table. It splinters. His leg swings, taking me out.

I fall over him and don't waste any time beating him to shit while I've got him pinned. His face is bloody when I finally see Aiden coming at me from behind.

Aiden swings. I'm on my feet, ducking, hitting him in the chest with both arms, throwing him back. He stumbles. I swing, hitting him in the face. One, twice, three times. His head jerks, wobbling.

A gun clicks.

"Get the fuck out," Jack says, voice hard.

Everybody freezes. Jack is on our side of the bar now, his shotgun pointed at Aiden and his handgun trained on Ryland. The chaos of a second ago vanishes, replaced by utter silence.

"Get. Out."

Jack's dark eyes flash. Painfully, Aiden pushes off the wall. Ryland doesn't stick around. He scrambles like an animal through the smashed furniture and blood before getting his footing and bolting. The door swings, a gust of cold air stinging my skin.

Aiden and I lock eyes. His chest heaves. Neither of us move.

Finally, he spits blood, wiping his face with his palm. "If you thought I was coming for you before, I will fucking wipe the floor with you when this is done."

God, if it didn't put Freya in danger, I'd tell him what I'm doing with his stepdaughter. I'd love to see the look on his face. But I keep my mouth shut. He strides past me, back straight, shoulders back. I have to admit, I underestimated the toughness of Aiden Hatfield. Most bullies are weak, crumbling the minute someone their own size appears. But to his credit, Aiden didn't back down. I believe he's going to come back swinging.

That doesn't scare me. Bring it on. It's been a while since I had anyone serious to fuck with.

Shaking out my bruised hands, I move past Jack and reach for my hat. I don't remember it, but I must have laid it on the bar when I walked in.

"You," says Jack, shoving his handgun into its holster.

"Yeah, yeah, I'm leaving," I say.

"No, you give me a blank check for the tables," he says. "Help me put this shit back together."

We've been here before a few times. He circles the counter and goes to the back closet. When he returns, he's got a broom and a trash can. We both know the drill and get to work. Jack doesn't criticize me for what I did, never has. As far as I can tell, he thinks that would be like telling a fish not to swim.

We clean up, and then I write him a check. Then, we both have a shot and I leave. Maybe that wasn't the smartest choice, but, fuck, do I feel so much better getting it out of my system.

It's dark outside as I walk through the damp alley and get in my truck. I'm halfway home when my foot hits the brake so hard, the wheels leave rubber burned behind it. My heart picks up. For the first time today, I'm scared.

Without thinking, I turn the truck around and head right for the Hatfield's house.

# CHAPTER EIGHTEEN
# FREYA

I hear the truck before I see the headlights. My stomach aches, the way it always does before something bad happens. In just my night slip with my dressing gown tied tightly over it, I creep down the stairs on bare feet.

Doors slam. Angry boots crunch on gravel. The doorknob turns, but it's locked. I was here all alone, so I locked it. Aiden curses on the other side of the door, his keys jingling, and then the door is kicked open hard enough that it slams open and hits the wall.

My jaw goes slack as they burst through.

Aiden's all beat up, a black eye and blood on his chin. His shirt is torn, stained red. Behind him comes Ryland, bruises on his face and blood on his knuckles. Bittern is the last one through, but I don't think he was part of the fight, because he looks fine. Just sweaty, a little drunk.

I shrink back against the wall. Aiden hits me with a piercing glance as he goes to the kitchen and takes the whiskey from the top cabinet. He slams it on the counter, and Ryland slides over three shot glasses. I shiver, trying to make myself small.

"I'm gonna kill that motherfucker," Ryland spits.

I whirl to run, so scared, I can't see straight. This isn't their normal drunk and angry. This is the gray area where I might get hurt. I need to get out of here now.

"Freya," Aiden barks. "Get your ass in here."

My heart drops. They used to get drunk more back home, but it's been so much better the last few months. The timbre of his voice activates my flight instincts that have saved me time and time again. But I don't have a choice. I have to obey or risk escalation.

I slip into the doorway, hands behind my back.

"Yes, sir," I say, voice shaking.

Aiden's jaw works as he swallows his next shot. I glance at Ryland leaning against the sink with his bloody shirt crumpled in his hand. Bittern sits at the table, eyes down, neck flushed.

I'm sick to my stomach. Aiden's got a couple different kinds of rage, and this is the worst one. Somebody humiliated him.

"You know people in Knifley," Aiden says. He takes another shot. "You know them up at Ryder Ranch too?"

I shake my head hard. "No, sir, I don't."

He lifts a hand, pointing. "Why do you look like you're lying, girl?"

"I swear," I say, voice shaking. "I swear, I don't know anybody from up there."

He slams the glass down on the table. "You come here and sit down."

This isn't the first time he's made me sit while he rages. I take a step, but Bittern stands abruptly, head down. He shoves his chair back and circles the table before he grabs me by the elbow. My feet barely touch the ground as he drags me down the hall and out onto the front porch.

"Bittern—"

"They got all fucked up by Deacon Ryder," he says, voice low. "You go on and get out of here, Frey. Go on, run to Tracy's house."

With my free hand, I pull my dressing gown around my body. "I can't run to Tracy's. It's ten miles through the fields. It's dark."

He drags his gaze up. It's haunted by whatever was burned into his head in the mines. It's times like this when I wonder if they dug right down into hell and he looked the devil himself in the eyes.

"Don't stay," he says. "They're gonna get fucked up. Aiden's angry, and he'll take it out on you. Go to Tracy's. Take my truck."

"I can barely drive," I whisper.

He reaches out and grabs my arm clumsily, looking me earnestly in the eyes. "I seen things, Frey, when they get angry. You take my truck and drive to Tracy's tonight, and I'll call you when it's safe to come home."

My mouth is dust dry. I wonder what he's seen Aiden do.

"Okay," I whisper.

He takes his keys out, pulls the one for his truck off the ring, and puts it in my hand. I close my fingers around it.

"Will you be okay?" I ask.

He nods. "I'm fine. I know how to fight."

That's not true. Bittern doesn't hit back—he just takes it. Without another word, he turns on his heel and goes into the house. The lock clicks, and I'm standing in the darkness, my feet bare. I have a bra and panties on, but nothing over it except my slip and thin dressing gown.

I wrap my arms around myself, and my fingers graze something hard at my hip.

My phone—it's in my pocket.

Something smashes inside the house. I whirl and run down the stairs, across the frosty lawn in my bare feet. I don't go to Bittern's truck—I run down the strip of grass between the fence and the driveway all the way to the road, to the little rise over the mailbox where my flip phone has signal.

My hands shake. I go to Deacon's number—the one he must have put in there before he gave it to me, but I've never used before—and hit the call button. My heart thumps, off beat.

*Please pick up.*

*Please.*

My silent prayer pounds in my veins like a drum. The phone crackles. I think it goes dead for a second, but then I hear him.

"Hey, sweetheart," he rumbles.

"Deacon," I gasp, hot tears erupting. "Please come get me. Aiden's all messed up. Bittern told me to run because I wasn't safe at home. Please come get me. I don't even have shoes."

"I'm coming, sweetheart," he says. "I'm already on my way."

There's something calming in the way he says it, like there was never any world where he wasn't coming for me. I hiccup, taking a deep breath. Overhead, the stars hang heavy and bright white. It's chilly, but I'm so scared, I barely feel it.

"How—how far are you?" I whisper.

"About a mile out," he says. "You stay on the line. You just keep talking to me, okay?"

I gulp hard, wiping my face. "Okay, I'm fine. I'm just scared. Bittern dragged me out of the house, said it wasn't safe. Aiden's so angry. Bittern said you beat him up."

"I'm so fucking sorry," he rasps. "I got on the road as soon as I put two and two together."

"Why'd you beat him up?" I whisper.

He gives a short laugh. "Because I'm a fucking asshole."

Lights glimmer far off, where the road curves up.

"I think I see you," I say.

"I'm almost there," he says. "But don't hang up."

Warmth steals into my veins. I stay on the line, not speaking, until he pulls over in front of me and opens the door. I take his outstretched hand, and he draws me into the truck without a word. His foot hits the gas, he backs up, and then we're heading back to Ryder Ranch.

"I'm sorry," he says.

He's just a shadow. I can't see his face, but I can tell he's upset.

"It's okay."

"I've been in enough homes where men beat their women to know better," he says, voice like steel. "I should have realized they'd take it out on you."

"They didn't," I say. "Bittern got me out."

He clears his throat, one hand on the steering wheel, the other on my thigh. "I'll take him off my shit list."

I look down at his hands, bloody but not cut up as badly as Aiden's. His knuckles are smashed in, the messy ink scraped back from the center finger. My stomach turns. The blood is caked, dried dark on his skin.

"You're hurt," I whisper.

He flexes his hand, tearing it open enough that a drop of red trickles out. "Not much," he says. "I'm not worried about me. I'm worried about getting you home safe."

Home—he says the word like it's my home too, like he can somehow take his big, empty house and make it the place my heart aches for. I didn't believe it, but here in the truck, with his warm presence beside me, I wonder if it's possible. Someday, somehow.

I don't know if that's what I want.

He grips my thigh so hard, his knuckles start bleeding in earnest. I watch the crimson drip down my skin, so raw inside, but I don't have it in me to move.

We're parked in his driveway when he notices he's dripping blood onto my bare thigh. He pulls his hand back and gets out of the truck. I see his body move in the dark, circling to open my door. He picks me up, lifting me.

My stomach swoops. My numb toes curl.

He carries me up the stairs and into the warm house. A wave of relief washes over me. A low whine comes from the living room as he sets me down. It's Stu—I'd named him something simple. He's loose, and he comes toddling down the hall and sniffs my foot.

"Sweetheart."

I turn. Deacon has his coat off, bloodstains stark on his shirt. He's got a bruise on his cheekbone, a trace of red on his chin, but otherwise, he's unharmed. The beating his knuckles took is a testament to who won that fight.

I underestimated him. He went up against Aiden and Ryland and came out on top.

"I'm going to run a bath," he says. "Did anybody put their hands on you?"

I shake my head, wrapping my arms around myself. Something is shifting in me now that he's in the light. His broad shoulders tower over me. His jaw is set so hard that it's square. I can't tell if his nose is broken like usual, or if it has a new break in it.

It probably doesn't matter to him at this point.

Coils of heat spark in my limbs. They reach the cold ends of my fingers and toes. I've lived for years under Aiden's tyrannical thumb. He was always the biggest, baddest man in the room with the meanest punch—until now.

Until Deacon walked in.

Maybe I misjudged Deacon. Maybe I misjudged myself. I don't know—I'm too messed up inside right now to know. Tonight, I hurt, and there's one man who can take that away.

"Deacon," I whisper.

He turns his head, inches from me. His body gives off so much heat and, God, I'm chilled to the bone. I reach up and grip his shirt. His mouth parts as he bends, and his nose brushes mine.

"Fuck," he says, eyes flicking up and down. "I got...I got a lot of adrenaline pumping through me."

"Fuck me," I whisper, nipping his broken bottom lip. He tastes like he's wounded, not just plain blood.

He shakes his head. "No, sweetheart. Not now."

"Deacon—"

His simmering, coal black eyes flash. "Not now."

Since that day he took me home in the storm, he's been open and gentle. But tonight, drenched in red, I can feel steel bars scraping up like gates, like a barrier between something dark that I tasted in the blacksmith shop but haven't sunk my teeth into yet.

I think he might be different, deep down.

"Please," I whisper. "Don't leave me alone."

He shakes his head—he keeps doing that, like he can shake off the frost creeping over his dark eyes. He turns on his heel, scooping up Stu, and disappears into the living room.

Unsure, I follow him. He sets the puppy in its pen and turns on me. I stumble back, but he scoops me up, holding me in both arms the way he carried me inside. He goes up the stairs, down the hall, and into his bedroom before I can react.

He kicks the door shut with his boot. I expect him to set me down, but he brings me into the bathroom and puts me on the sink. When he draws back, his brows are lowered.

"I don't want to hurt you, sweetheart," he says. "No fucking tonight."

I wet my dry lips. "You won't hurt me."

"You don't know me."

The words come out forcefully. This time, I get the message.

He touches me like I'm breakable, like it matters if he hurts me. But he's also violent, rough—I was so afraid he might be. He knows that all I know is violence, and he's standing between me and himself right now so I don't have to see what that side of him is like.

It's heartbreaking.

I was foolish to think he was gentle with everyone the way he is with me. He's a man, and he walks like one with all that confidence I'll never have. Boots on his feet, gun on his belt, shoved up under his shirt. The hitch in his step is more a swagger, and there's something else that's been there all along but I haven't noticed until tonight—he takes on the world like he doesn't have backup.

Just him and his fists.

I don't think people end up like that by accident. He's carrying a lot of violence and darkness inside.

I stare up at him. For years, I looked out into my small world and I understood it. I sorted men into neat categories to keep them from hurting me.

Like Aiden.

*Not* like Aiden.

Deacon doesn't fit into either category, and that hurts my head and heart. He can be violent the way Aiden can, but I'd never have called him, scared and freezing in the driveway, if I didn't know he would protect me. My body knows something my head hasn't realized yet.

It's all too much. I'm scared. I don't know where the train of me and him, which is now firmly hitched together, is headed.

"What is this?" I blurt out.

He sobers. He puts his hand on my cheek, holding it. His lids are low, and he's got a faraway expression. "This is just me making sure you're alright."

"I'm alright," I whisper.

"I want you to get some sleep," he says. "I have to clean up."

There's no use arguing. There's a little warning in his eyes, like he can be gentle if he wants, but he's got enough edge to make me sit up and listen this time.

He turns the shower on, and I think he's limping but I can't tell. He might just be tired. Then, he comes back to the sink and kisses me. Soft, sweet. A tremor goes through my body.

He pulls back. There's a second where I think he's going to say something. His jaw works. His forehead creases. Then, he taps my chin and walks out.

# CHAPTER NINETEEN
# DEACON

I'm breathing hard in the guest bathroom.

There's a shard of wood, a half an inch thick, sticking out of my upper thigh. It must have happened when I fell into the shattered table with Ryland. I didn't notice it until I was sitting in the truck beside her. It doesn't hurt. It's more of a dull pain and tingling shock.

It's not bleeding, but the wound is swollen around the wood. It just hurts like a motherfucker.

I strip my shirt and unfasten my belt. Pain ripples as I peel the fabric of my work pants off the wound, letting them fall to mid-thigh.

Jesus, it looks fucked up.

The skin is traumatized, puffy around the puncture. Blood laces the edges, crusted. Maybe it's longer than I think it is, because every time I take a step, it feels like I'm being stabbed.

I take the first aid kit from under the sink and pop it open. Working quickly, I set the alcohol and gauze up and wash my hands. Then, I take a rubber handled toothbrush and put it between my back molars. There's metallic phlegm seeping from my sinuses that tells me I need to check my nose for breaks when I'm done.

I take a breath, bite down, and wriggle the wood from the soft flesh. My vision flashes red and yellow.

Fuck, that's a shot of adrenaline.

I take the toothbrush out, spit blood and snot into the sink, and put it back in. Working quickly, I push the tip of my finger into the outer edges of the wound, searching for splinters. I should take myself to the quick clinic, but I don't have time tonight. Maybe I won't go anyway. It wouldn't be the first time I've put myself back together.

My entire body aches as I turn on the shower and step in. Hot water pours over me, making the nicks and bruises sting as I wash up. I'm slow to turn off the faucet and limp back to the sink to dry off.

Rubber between my teeth, I clean the wound and sew it back together with two stitches. Normally, I wouldn't sew a puncture wound, but it's ragged at the edges. The wood tore me up going in and out. Finally, I pack gauze over it and tape it down.

Good enough.

There's a man in the mirror, looking back at me, kicked to shit. The corner of my mouth turns up. I really threw Freya into the deep end. It wouldn't surprise me if, once she's had a night to sleep on it, she decides she wants nothing to do with me.

Not that it will keep me away.

Aching inside and out, I pull on sweatpants. My nose doesn't feel broken. I think it's just beat up, so I leave it alone. In the dark, I go down to the kitchen and take a couple of Tylenol and wash it down with a shot of moonshine. The sharp taste, a bit like apple flavored paint remover, puts some life back in my veins.

What am I so afraid of showing her?

The kinky shit? Or the ugly, self-destructive shit?

Maybe both.

The house is so quiet. The weight of everything that happened settles on my shoulders. Today was one of those days there's no coming back from. Jay might have been able to negotiate his way out of the easement, but not now. I'm not worried about assault charges. I know men like Aiden, and he won't hide behind the law.

That's all I can say for him—he'll throw down before he whines about it.

All this leads right back to the woman in my bed. She knows what I did today. I can't hide who I am anymore.

Maybe all this pretending I'm not a fucked up asshole isn't worth it. I think I want her to see me for who I am—my violence, my recklessness, how my brain struggles to produce the fear chemicals I need to keep me from doing stupid shit. Even what I did to get Ryder Ranch.

The floor creaks up above. She's not sleeping.

My mind goes back to her curvy body hanging over the anvil in the blacksmith shop. My hands grip the counter edge. In my pants, my cock goes rock hard, despite the beating my body took today.

Something cold that I don't let out unless the proper barriers are in place rises in me.

She wanted me. She *begged* to have me tonight. Maybe I'm not as good of a man as I hoped.

I'm halfway up the stairs before I realize what I'm doing, but I don't stop myself because I've done this dozens of times. I know I can control myself. I'm an expert at dipping into the worst parts of myself and using that to meet my submissive's needs but never going over the line.

I open the bedroom door.

She pulled the armchair from the hearth to the window, and she's curled in it, cheek resting on her hand. Her pale eyes are fixed on the sky.

"Freya," I say.

She looks up. Her dressing gown is gone—she's in just her slip with nothing underneath. I'd get kicked to shit all over again for a night with a body like hers. And yet, somehow, for some reason, she's offering it to me for nothing.

"Deacon," she whispers.

"Come here."

She comes, and I gather her hair up, wrapping it once around my hand. She gasps as I draw her head back.

"You wanted me," I say.

Her throat bobs, her lips part. Her mouth is full, so soft, like a pale pink flower. I bend and kiss it—vanilla and velvet petals, hard, harsh, open. I want to drink her down, to breathe only the air from her body.

"All of me?" I say hoarsely.

She nods, not hesitating. Something is different. Her walls are down and she's vulnerable.

"If I do anything you don't want, you say red," I say.

Her brows knit together. "You mean...like a safe word?"

I nod. "Exactly. Like a safe word. We'll pick a different one later. For now, say red. And if you can't speak, tap my side. You got that?"

She backs up a step. Her throat bobs. My eyes trail down over her full breasts and the swell they make over her hourglass waist. Her hips flare out, her smooth legs tapering down to delicate feet. She's the whole goddamn package.

She lifts a hand and pushes the straps of her slip down until it hits the floor.

God, I'm *dying*.

"I'm gonna go hard on you, sweetheart," I say, my voice rough. "You have to use your words if you want it to stop."

She nods, eyes huge.

"I can say red," she whispers.

Stepping close, I wrap my hand around the back of her neck and drag her against me. "Good girl."

Her spine arches, her lips part. She offers them to me, and I kiss her hard enough that our teeth clash. My head goes empty. My cock throbs, sensitive against the inside of my sweatpants. I lift her easily, spreading her thighs to wrap them around my waist. Her arms slip around my neck, her curls spilling around us.

We fall to the bed. She looks up at me with wide eyes.

"You're hurt," she says.

I glance down at the gauze coming up over the waistband of my pants. "It's nothing I can't handle," I say.

"Maybe you should rest."

I almost shake my head, but something flickers over her face. It looks like...a little bit of fear. That stops me in my tracks. I don't want Freya to be afraid of me. She's clearly aroused. Her nipples are hard and I can smell how wet she is between her legs, but that doesn't negate the fear.

"What's going on in your head, sweetheart?" I say.

She shakes it. "Nothing."

I place my hand on her throat, holding it so she can't turn away. "Talk to me."

She swallows beneath my palm. "Aiden fights like you. I have a lot of feelings inside me right now… I'm grateful you saved me, but I don't like what you did. It was violent."

She spits out that last word like it's poison.

"Aiden had that coming," I say.

"I know," she sighs. "But I don't like it."

I open my mouth to answer, but she clears her throat. Her eyes meet mine, and her lashes glitter.

"Do you know how terrifying it is to be a woman in a house with a man who can't keep his temper?" she whispers.

My mind goes back to Phil and Amie, and I almost say that I do, but I realize at the last minute that's not right. I take a beat and think it over.

"No," I say. "I don't."

I release her. She takes a shuddering breath. "Aiden hit the tables, the walls, broke the glasses until I gave up and we drank out of red plastic cups. When the factory closed, he put a chair through the window. Bittern fixed it, but we had plastic over the window all winter."

My stomach sinks.

"But you're sure he never tried to hit you?"

She shakes her head. "He didn't need to. I've seen what his fists can do. He hit Ryland, Bittern, and Wayland—Bittern more than the others."

"What do you mean? Like beat them?"

"No, he'd fight with them," she says. "He said he needed his sons to be able to take a punch."

I'm quiet. It's no wonder she's frightened by what I did tonight.

"I didn't mean to scare you, sweetheart," I say. "As much as I'm happy to give another man a beat down, I've never raised my voice to a woman."

Her lips part. "What stops you?"

"Never had any desire to," I say honestly. "And I never hit a motherfucker who didn't deserve it."

She fixes her eyes on the ceiling. There's a long silence. Then, she clears her throat again.

"Sometimes, I feel like I'm in a washing machine, just churning through the same cycle over and over again," she whispers. A tear etches out and slides into her hair. "Aiden hits people because his father hit people. My mother ran from a drunk and ended up with somebody worse. Lady did the same thing."

"Who's Lady again?" I ask.

"Aiden's first wife. Bittern, Ryland, and Wayland's mother," she whispers. "Well, he never married her officially, but he called her Lady Hatfield. I didn't meet her, but Bittern talked about her a lot. Aiden ran her off when she threatened to take his sons and split up. It wasn't too much later that my mother came along. She was...really young. She didn't stand a chance with Aiden."

Her voice is flat, like everything is just trickling out of her mouth and she can't stop it. I clear my throat, because it's time for me to be honest.

"The people who adopted me had similar problems. I saw him, and I swore up and down I'd never make any woman's life hell the way he did," I say.

She turns to look at me, her big eyes glimmering with tears.

"And that just...fixed you?"

"Sometimes, all it takes is for one person to make that choice," I say. "I want a family. A wife who's happy, kids who aren't scared of me. Turns out, it's pretty easy to not hurt your girl if you never fucking started in the first place."

"But...did you ever get hit as a kid?"

I nod. "Yeah, sometimes. Not by women."

"And you just never hit anyone back?"

"No, if I'm being honest, I fought a lot. I learned pretty quick that if you're being abused, one good punch can shut that shit down forever. But I have the privilege of being six and a half feet tall. And a man. Not everybody can protect themselves."

She's quiet. I stroke her hair, wiping the tears from her temples.

"Sorry, I didn't mean to cry," she whispers.

"Cry all you want, sweetheart," I say. "I'll just sit here if that's what you need."

Her hand darts up to wipe her eyes. "Did you get in that one good hit that shut it down?"

"I did."

"Can I know what happened?"

I shake my head. "Not tonight."

She doesn't protest. Instead, she shuts her eyes, chest heaving as she takes a deep breath. There's a long silence. I let her take all the time she wants, because I don't have anywhere to be but here with her.

"I just... I lived on eggshells my entire life. I don't know how to get off them," she whispers. "Even when I'm with you, it takes so much for me to forget and feel comfortable."

"Look at me," I say gently.

She drags her eyes to mine. There's so much hurt in there. Deep down, there's no doubt in me that I'll make Aiden pay for what he's done to her. She won't have to know about it. All she has to know is that, if she stays with me, she never has to be afraid again.

"Stay here, with me," I say.

"I want to, but it's more complicated," she whispers.

"Why?"

Her lips tremble. "Bittern got hurt in the coal mines. He's not ever been the same since. He coughs and he can't do much. Sometimes, he feels like a little baby animal. I can't just leave him."

I should shut the hell up, but I can't bite my words back.

"Bittern is a thirty year old man," I say. "He doesn't need his little sister looking after him."

She blinks, tears welling up again. "Bittern looked after me when nobody else did. As well as he could...considering how bad off the accident left him."

The last thing I want to do is make her cry. I wipe her cheek with my thumb.

"I get it, sweetheart," I say. "I get it."

Her lip trembles. "Part of me can't blame Aiden for some of it. What's the point of even trying to be anything when there's nothing to try for?"

"What do you mean?"

"I mean, there was nowhere for men to work but the factory. No step up, nothing to look forward to. It hurt everybody. Aiden's father prepared him for it by being the first person to hurt him—before life could, I guess. So he did the same to his sons. He was never into wearing rose colored glasses. He told me he didn't want a daughter because I could get pregnant and he'd be stuck with another mouth to feed. I think Aiden was sick of feeding people. But he did keep food on the table no matter what. Aiden's awful, but he's never been a deadbeat."

She sounds so guilty and desperate. I release her, pushing my body up to sit against the headboard, and lift her to sit under my arm. She lets her cheek rest on my shoulder.

"I want more," she says brokenly. "Maybe that's selfish, but I want more than just food on my table."

I curl my arm around her, pressing my lips to the top of her head.

"I know," I say. "And it isn't selfish."

She closes her eyes. The mounting emotions of just a few moments ago are gone. Gently, I stretch my throbbing leg out and lean back. She's in my arms for tonight. Tomorrow, I don't know what that brings, but I know I'll keep trying until, one day, she doesn't want to leave.

At first, I thought I was the one dragging my past in like dirt on my boots, but it's Freya I needed to be worried about. She has pain clinging to her, seeping from her skin.

And yet, in her pain, I see a path forward.

I'm a rough man. I've done my time in a holding cell and thrown enough fists to last most men a lifetime, but I've never raised my voice like that in my home. I've never put holes into the walls or broken dishes out of rage.

It took me a while, but I have the dark parts of me bridled.

I know what I want. She knows what she doesn't. Right here is the place where we can meet in the middle.

"Look," she whispers.

I raise my head to where she's pointing through the windows. The clouds have parted, and the Milky Way is a glimmering river across the sky. Sometimes, I forget to look up. I've lived on this ranch so long, but there's nothing like viewing it with her fresh eyes.

"You ever seen anything like that before coming here, sweetheart?" I ask.

She nestles down, her head on my stomach. Her eyes are so heavy, they're barely open.

"No," she whispers. "I've never had anything like this."

I stroke her hair until her breathing deepens. Her body slumps. I pull the sheet over her and rest my hand on the swell of her hip. There's a lot more I need to say to her. I have a feeling she's got a lot more to talk through with me. That can wait.

Every time she comes here, I pry her open a bit wider, and out spills pain with a little starlight to keep it company. I don't mind; I think she just wants somebody to see it too, maybe to tell her it's alright to feel hurt.

I do, I see her clearly, and because of that, I can't let her go.

# CHAPTER TWENTY
# FREYA

The next morning, I'm surprised to find I don't regret being so honest with him. I'm shaken by everything, but when I get up and go to the bathroom, there's peace in my chest.

That's new for me.

I'm reaching for the faucet when I stop short, a little prickle going over my body. Turning slowly, my eyes fall on the chair in the corner. Sitting on it is a pale pink box with a black ribbon tied around it.

Right away, I know it's for me. I pick it up and set it on the sink. My fingers untie the ribbon and set it aside. Butterflies erupt in my stomach. I slide open the lid, and my breath catches.

It's a bra and panties set.

Blue silk, clearly expensive. My fingertips skim over the fabric, cool and soft. The edges have white lace, so fine, I have to lean in to inspect it. He spent money on this, a lot. No doubt, he wants to see me in it.

My mouth is dry as I turn on the shower. There's a little bag of toiletries, rose scented, including some lotion and a razor, in the box. I lock the bathroom door and take a shower without worrying about running the hot water tank out. I just scrub and shave and wash my hair. When I get out, I'm so clean, I tingle as I work the tangles from my wet curls.

I'm not brave enough to go downstairs in these clothes, but I want to try them. So I do, pulling the silky underwear over my body. Turning in a slow circle to see how perfectly the bra and panties fit me. I've never looked so feminine, so soft, before. My face is practically glowing.

Up until this moment, I've never felt beautiful. I can be pretty, but I'm not the kind of woman who makes men stop and turn around.

I get it now. I see why Deacon stares at me.

I can't stop staring either.

Pretty for the sake of being pretty has only existed in the context of natural things for me. Flowers, birds, sunsets. I've never thought about it for myself. It's frivolous and exciting.

Hands unsteady, I take off the bra, and the panties and put them back in the box. I tie the bow shut and lay it on the chair. There's no world where I'll put that on in front of him without being prompted. I keep my head down as I put on my old bra and panties beneath the flannel shirt hanging behind the door and head downstairs.

The kitchen is empty. I slip inside and get a mug down. The coffee is dripping when I hear keys jiggle at the side door. I freeze, turning around just as a woman with cropped brown hair walks into the kitchen.

We both freeze. Her eyes widen as she sets her tote bag on the table.

"What—oh my," she says.

"I'm so sorry," I whisper, cheeks burning. "You must be Ginny."

She covers her mouth with one hand for a second. When she takes it away, she's smiling.

"I'm sorry, I just... Deacon doesn't have...um—"

"Sleepovers?" I manage.

"Well," she says, "yes."

There's no point in pretending I'm not with Deacon like that.

"I'm sorry, I'll go back upstairs," I say, reaching for my coffee.

"Oh, no, no," she says, bustling into the kitchen. She steers me to the table, pulling out a chair and pushing me down. "You sit, dear. Let me make you something to eat."

She's over the moon, which is unexpected. She sets my coffee down and puts a swirl of creamer in it. The caramel scent is welcome on a morning like this, when I can see frost patterns on the window.

"I thought I noticed somebody who wasn't Deacon was in my kitchen," she says, still smiling like it's Christmas morning.

"I'm sorry. I tried to leave everything spotless," I say.

"Oh, you're sweet. It was perfect," she says. "Oh, I'm so sorry. I should have introduced myself. I'm Ginny, my husband Andy is the manager out here on the ranch. I just do the cooking and make sure the house is clean."

"I'm Freya," I say. "It's nice to meet you."

"Oh, I'm thrilled," she says.

She actually is thrilled. I'm not sure why. I sip my coffee while she gets eggs going on the stove. In a few minutes, she's sinking down beside me with two plates of breakfast.

"Now, you tell me about yourself," she says, sitting back like I'm about to tell her something exciting.

"Um...I just moved to Montana in the winter," I say.

"Where from?" She has a sip of coffee, watching me owlishly over the top.

"Eastern Kentucky," I say.

"Oh, that's where the accent is from," she says. "I like it. It's cute. Why'd you move here?"

"My stepfather bought some land," I say. "He had a huge family farm and he sold it for a lot, so he just picked somewhere and went. At least, I think that's why. He never gave me a good reason for it."

"So how'd you meet Deacon?" she asks.

"We ran into each other during that big storm, and he gave me a ride," I say.

She looks at me like something is dawning on her.

"Oh," she says. "You're the church girl." She says it like it holds a lot of weight, and her expression backs that up.

"I don't know," I stutter. "I didn't know he knew much about where I go to church. I mean, we talked about it a bit, but...not before we met."

Ginny is looking at me like everything makes sense. I'm uncomfortable under her scrutiny, so I take a bite of toast. Butter and crisp bread melt on my tongue.

There's a peacefulness in the morning here at Ryder Ranch, that I'm not used to. Mornings are usually my least favorite time. Everyone in my house is in a bad mood, most of them hungover. It's a race to get food on the table before someone snaps at me.

But here, nobody raises their voice at me.

Nobody is angry at me for existing. In fact, Ginny is looking at me like I just made her whole week.

"So how long have you worked for Deacon?" I ask, eager to fill the silence.

"About fifteen years," she says.

"And...you like it?"

"Oh, Deacon's a sweetheart," she says. "Andy and I will work here until we retire."

My mind goes back to his face in the truck: jaw set, nose broken, bleeding hand on my thigh. I'm not sure I'd ever call Deacon Ryder a sweetheart, not after he beat Aiden bloody.

"You alright?" Ginny asks.

I rearrange my face and nod. "Sorry, it was an eventful night."

Ginny's brows go to her hairline. I blush, unable to help myself.

"It's not that—"

"It's alright. I understand."

"No, no," I stammer. "My stepfather, he got really angry and drunk, and Deacon came and got me. That's why I'm here."

Ginny's face goes from flustered to concerned. Her brows knit, and she gives me a look that stares right into my soul.

"Do you need to stay up here with us, dear?" she asks.

"If Deacon wouldn't have beat my family up in a bar, it wouldn't have happened," I say, unable to stifle the little bite in my voice.

That's not really fair. This isn't the first time something like this has happened. Ginny lets out a tired sigh. Her eyes drift to the window that, from her chair, looks out over the barn and yard.

"He does that sort of thing," she says, shaking her head.

"Is he safe?" I blurt out.

She swings her head back around. "Safe?"

My throat is dry. I'm hoping I can trust her judgment, woman to woman.

"Is he safe, or does he get angry?" I whisper. "Like my stepfather does."

Ginny's face softens, her eyes getting a faraway look. She picks up my hand and squeezes it. My chest aches.

"He's safe for you. Your stepfather, probably not," she says.

My lips part. "I don't want him getting involved with my family."

She pats my hand and stands, taking away our empty plates. "I suggest your stepfather not use his fists on you, because I can't vouch for what Deacon will do if he catches him doing that."

"He doesn't," I say, shaking my head.

Ginny starts the coffeemaker on a second cup and goes into the back room, behind the kitchen for a minute. When she comes back out, she has a plastic grocery bag in her hand that she sets on the table.

"I keep a few changes of clothes up here at the house in case of spills," she says. "I reckon you didn't bring nothing but your nightgown on you last night."

"I was in a hurry," I say.

"Well, take that upstairs and see if anything fits," she says.

Obediently, I carry the bag upstairs. There's a pair of jeans that fit alright. The only sweater is a pretty Icelandic print, and it compliments my hair and eyes. I pull it on and tie my hair up before going back downstairs to the kitchen. When Ginny sees me, she cocks her head.

"Oh, you keep that sweater," she says. "It's pretty on you."

"Oh, I can't," I protest.

"Not worth arguing with her."

I turn to find the kitchen door leading to the four season porch is open. Deacon stands on the stoop, screen door jammed open with his elbow. He's in his work pants and boots, a charcoal gray Henley over his broad torso. It's rolled up to his forearms, all his chaotic tattoos on display. He's got a cigarette between his lips and a cup of coffee in his hand. There are two thick bandages over his knuckles.

We make eye contact. A tingle moves through the vicinity of my heart.

"Morning, sweetheart," he says, taking the cigarette out.

He has an odd way of holding them, almost like a pen between his first finger and thumb.

"Hi," I say, barely audible.

Deacon steps to the side, and my eyes fall on another man standing in the yard, smoking. There's something familiar about him. He's tall, lean, and broad in the shoulders. There's an easy, open way about him. His eyes are bright gray-blue, his hair dusky brown. He's got a handsome face, like a film star, just worn around the edges.

I think all these western men are a little rough at their edges.

The man takes his hat off. "Jensen Childress, miss," he says.

"Freya," I say, keeping back. "I know you, I think. You were standing outside the café when I found Deacon's puppy."

Deacon's staring, like he's afraid Jensen's about to embarrass him. There's a heavy bark, like a big dog, and the owner of that sound careens around the corner. It's a big hound with drooping jowls and black dapples down its back. Distracted, I step onto the four season porch to get a better look. I love animals, and I can't resist trying to pet any dog I can get my hands on.

"That's Chicken," Jensen says.

I swing my gaze around. "That's his name?"

"It's the only word he responds to, anyway," says Jensen. "Ain't worth shit except for hunting raccoons and keeping the foxes off my property."

Deacon's eyes follow me as I circle him and Jensen, unable to resist the urge to pet Chicken. The hound smells like a barnyard, but he pushes his nose into my hand and nuzzles it. He's got big brown eyes, droopy and sweet.

"Oh, he's nice," I say, scratching his ears. "I love hounds."

Deacon clears his throat. I glance past him and see Ginny's gone and the dishwasher is running. Jensen puts his hands on his hips.

"Let's finish talking later, Ryder," he says. "I got a job up at Sovereign Mountain, but I'll be back around in a few days."

Deacon jerks his head in a nod. Jensen starts around the house, heading for a big white truck parked by the barn. He whistles, opening the door. Chicken is sitting at my feet, staring into the middle distance, eyes unfocused.

"Chicken," Jensen yells.

I nudge the hound, and he stares up at me. "You better go."

Jensen slaps his thigh. "Jesus Christ, get in this truck."

Chicken heaves himself up and takes his sweet time crossing the yard. He doesn't get in the truck. Instead, he just stares up at Jensen until he snaps and lifts him into the passenger side. He's grumbling under his breath as he gets inside and pulls the truck out, heading down the drive.

Then, it's just Deacon and me, standing on the stoop with the chilly autumn air settled around us.

He flicks his cigarette in an empty pot. "You feeling alright, sweetheart?"

"About what?" I say, not backing down from his midnight stare.

"About me having to pick you up from your stepfather's house so he didn't fuck you up," he says bluntly.

"I'm fine," I say.

"You okay to hang out here with Ginny today? I got slammed with shit around here, and Andy's pissed because I'm not pulling my share," he says.

I nod. After our discussions last night, it might do me some good to have some time to myself to digest.

He reaches up and taps my chin. "Good girl. I'll see you tonight for dinner."

He's so full of it, and I just eat it up when he says things like that. I watch him head to the barn and disappear inside. Ginny isn't anywhere in sight when I go into the kitchen to make another coffee, but I find her on the back porch, shaking out a rug.

"Can I do something?" I ask.

She turns around. "Oh no, this is my job, and I get paid well for it."

I fidget. I need something to do.

"Alright, you want to grab a broom and clean off the porches and walkways?" she says. "Then we can get to dusting. It's cleaning day."

That sounds perfect to me. She finishes shaking out all the rugs from the living room, and when she's done, I start sweeping up. On the front porch, I can see Deacon on the hill behind the barn. He's on Bones while Andy sits beside him on a gray horse. They're doing something that involves a lot of gesticulating. Deacon gets down and slaps a fence post, and Andy gets down to slap it too. I think they're doing repair work, because the post falls over.

A cold wind gusts in, smelling of winter and horses.

I could get used to Ryder Ranch.

It's so quiet. It's so safe, just like him.

We eat together in the kitchen. Deacon comes in a few minutes before Ginny gets ready to leave and goes upstairs to shower. I help her with the dishes, and then she leaves to have dinner with Andy. I go upstairs, but there's nothing to change into but one of his flannels. The bathroom door is shut, the shower running.

I stand outside for a second.

His presence is strong. I inhale, catching the sharp scent of his soap.

Why do I feel like I'm at the entrance of a cave, looking into the dark, knowing there's a big animal just out of sight?

A shiver runs down my spine.

Silently, I go downstairs and curl up on the rug before the fireplace in the living room. Stu whimpers, crawling from his bed, and I lift him out to play. He tugs at my sleeve and growls softly. I think he's growing.

The house is quiet. Deacon moves about upstairs. He's a big man, so he moves heavily, but not with anger. I wonder briefly if Bittern could have been like him.

A twinge of guilt moves through me.

I left him with Aiden and Ryland.

"You hungry, sweetheart?"

My eyes focus as I lift my head. Deacon's at the bottom of the stairs, standing behind the couch. All the blood in my head rushes down and culminates between my thighs.

He looks so good, big body still dotted with water from his shower. I get up and scoop Stu back into his bed. Deacon watches me as I circle the couch and come up to him.

Boldly, I put my palm flat on his lower belly, on that delicious, tattooed V disappearing beneath his waistband. His body tenses. Beneath the fabric, he lengthens in response. Transfixed, I drag my palm down to cup him, warm and heavy.

Our eyes meet. The air snaps with tension.

"Can dinner wait?" I whisper.

He nods once. "Dinner can wait."

The expression I saw in his eyes the other night flickers. It didn't disappear. It laid in wait, like a beast in the shadows. Deep inside, I wanted it back.

His hand comes up and cradles my face. "You're a desperate whore when you want it," he says.

The bottom falls out of my stomach, and at the same time, my body is flooded with arousal so strong, I want to whimper.

"What...did you call me?" I whisper.

He digs his fingers into my hair. "Whore. My whore."

Quick as a flash, I whirl and make for the stairs. One moment, I was peaceful by the fire. The next, my head is spinning, and shame washes over me in a wave at my body's response to that word. Deacon's footfalls follow me as I move down the hall and disappear into his room.

I don't know what the plan is. Maybe lock myself in the bathroom until I can get my breath?

He follows me, forehead creased, eyes unreadable.

"What's that word to you?" His voice is hushed.

We're on either side of the bed. For the first time, we're at odds. I'm alone with him, and I can't tell what he's feeling. But instead of wanting to run, I want something else I don't have a name for. It's violent but hot and exciting.

It centers in the pit of my belly, right below where I feel him when I'm on top. He takes a step closer. I take a step back.

My heart thumps.

Is this part of a game?

If it is, the ache in me wants to play it. He cocks his head, studying me closely. I shift to the side, coming around the corner of the bed, pausing to study him.

"You like being my whore?" he asks quietly.

I wet my lips. "I don't know," I manage.

He takes a step closer. I snap, making a dash for the door. His arm comes out, and I slam into it, the wind knocking from my lungs. The ground falls away as he picks me up and I hit the bed on my stomach. There's a sharp tearing sound. Cold air hits my skin as he strips me naked.

"Open your fucking legs," he orders, "you pretty, filthy whore."

Arousal is so much stronger than shame this time. I hesitate, trying to turn my head, but he grips my hair and holds it facing away. His zipper hisses. I hear the groan he always releases when he lets his cock out of his pants.

"Deacon," I gasp.

He drags my head up, leaning over to look at my face. "You say *red* if you want it to stop. That's your safeword for now. Understood?"

The same lust that flooded me before our first time is back. This is a game and, deep down, I want to play it. Maybe I don't understand very much about it, but he's giving me a safety lever I can pull if I want. That's all the permission I need.

"Yes," I gasp.

His mouth drops to my temple, hot, insistent. His hard cock drags over the backs of my thighs.

"What is it about being called a whore?" he murmurs. "You like it? Or hate it?"

"It's what he calls me," I whisper, face burning.

He tenses. "Who?"

"Aiden."

The word gasps out. My lashes are wet, but I don't want to stop this game. There's a raw, hungry ache deeper than I've ever known in me, between my thighs and in my chest. For the first time in my life, I don't want to hide for safety.

I want to be known. Deeply. I want him to know how that makes me feel.

There's a short, heavy silence. He releases my hair and wraps his fingers around my throat, cradling it. I hear him spit, and his other hand rubs over my pussy. My clit throbs, desperate for a touch that only grazes it. Then, he pushes himself into me in one stroke, making stars burst behind my eyes.

"You going to be a good girl for me and take it like a whore?" he asks.

My body buzzes.

"Yes, sir," I gasp.

He rumbles, I feel it against my back. He grips my right breast, circling it with his thumb. Then, he spanks it, a little slap that goes right down to my pussy.

"You call me daddy, sweetheart," he says. "At least when I've got my cock this far up your cunt."

Lust flashes, igniting a hot, insatiable itch in my pussy. He pulls out and thrusts hard, sending a jolt of pain and pleasure through my hips. God, that hits the perfect spot.

"Go on," he says.

I can't get that word past my teeth. It's stuck, mired somewhere in my humiliation. I've never said that word in my life. The man who got my mother pregnant is a ghost, having left without so much as a name. The man who raised me is a villain, hellbent on punishing me because his ego is bruised.

I've never felt safe with a man before, never safe enough to call him anything but his name.

Until now.

But the part of me that should know how to speak that word is broken. And in that brokenness, I hit a wall.

"I can't," I blurt out.

It's too vulnerable.

"Yes, you can," he says, voice firm.

There's a note in it that tells me I can't disobey. My head is completely empty—it can't compete with what I'm feeling in my body. I don't know what this is, but it lights me up. There's no desire to run from the shame that word makes me feel. It's just there, and that's alright.

"Yes, daddy," I whisper.

"Good girl," he breathes. "Now, I'm going to fuck you like the dirty whore you are, and you're going to take it."

He ruts his hips against my ass, hard. My fingers dig into the bed, knuckles white. He grips my shoulder and hip and starts fucking hard. The bedframe scrapes on the floor. The sound of our bodies meeting fills the room.

I clench my teeth, afraid if I don't, I'll bite my tongue.

He's like a force of nature, pounding relentlessly through me. There's nothing I can do but lay there, held up by his hands, and take it.

There's no pain.

No anxiety.

No fear.

Just this endless pounding drum.

I have no desire to be anywhere but here. The stars hang in the sky, blurry in my vision, but I don't long for them. The hole in my heart, the disjointed piece of me, is whole for tonight.

I'm jerked back to my physical body as he pulls out and flips me on my back, pushing me up on the pillows. My thighs flop open, my body exhausted. His hand grips the sheet by my head. He pushes his cock into me, and a groan reverberates in his throat.

I can only gaze up at him, because for the first time, I've found something brighter than the stars.

His life force is the strongest I've ever felt. Like a rushing river, a roaring fire, when he's inside me, I feel it pour through my veins.

That's what I felt the first time he fucked me. Not the beauty of the northern lights—him.

His face comes into focus, the tattoos running down to his chest. I reach up with a shaking hand and run my fingertips down his throat. Over his collarbones. To his pectorals. His thrusts slow, going from short and shallow to deep and long.

"You're soaked," he murmurs.

We can both hear it between our bodies. I nod, still breathing hard.

"Call me that again," I beg.

He leans in, mouth just brushing mine. "What? A whore?"

I nod. He kisses me, open mouth, giving me the familiar taste of him. When he pulls back, he nips my neck. My spine arches, letting him go even deeper.

"Tell me you're my whore," he orders.

"I'm your whore," I gasp.

"What do you call me?"

That gives me pause. His hips are going so slow now, just a drawling thump, a second of reprieve, then another thump that makes my stomach swoop. I swallow. His dark eyes are glowing coals, a warning in them.

"I'm your whore, daddy," I whisper.

"Say it out loud, or I'll put you on your knees and fuck it out of you," he says.

He ruts his hips, and there's a hint of cruelty in them.

"I'm your whore, daddy," I gasp out.

"Good fucking girl."

He pulls out and flips me on my stomach, lifting my lower body before entering me again. I gasp, rubbing my face into the bed. Pain explodes over my ass, and I hear the crack of his palm. Stars pop in my eyes. Then, I hear him spit, and it hits my lower back.

He grips my hair and starts fucking again. I'm spent, I have nothing left. He leveled on me, aimed, fired, and I'm flat on my back, completely done for tonight. At least, until I can get my head on straight in the morning.

I'm barely aware of when he comes, but I feel it hit my inner thigh.

And I'm faintly disappointed.

# CHAPTER TWENTY-ONE
# DEACON

I hold her, play with her hair, stroking her body for a long time. I tell her she's beautiful, that she's a good girl. She smiles up at me weakly, eyes hazy. I tore open a wound and let some of the poison drip out. Now, she needs aftercare.

I kiss her temple, breathing in vanilla.

"We never ate dinner," I say.

She shakes her head, giving me a shaky smile. "I'm a bit hungry."

"You shower, and I'll find a couple trays and bring the food up," I say, disentangling myself.

She nods, peeling herself off the bed. The last thing I see as I close the bedroom door is her naked body with my handprints on her ass disappearing into the bathroom. I can't help but smile as I descend the stairs. I did that—that's mine.

I bring up the food. We eat, and I think over what I want from her. It's time to talk to her about what I'm into and what I want from a relationship with her. We need to have an open discussion.

She finishes her food. I set aside the trays, pushing myself back against the pillows.

"Come sit in my lap," I say.

There's no room for disobedience in my voice. She hears it and crawls naked up the bed to straddle me. I touch her curls falling over her naked breasts. She's the prettiest thing, and I'm on my knees for it.

"Let's talk," I say.

"About what you just did?" Her brows arch.

"I'm into some kinky shit," I say. "It's not bad shit, not if you do it right."

She bites her lip, chewing hard on it.

"Okay," she says finally.

She isn't rejecting me outright, but it's impossible to read her face. Her pale blue eyes are soft, narrowed on me like she's trying to figure me out.

"I'm going to lay some things out for you," I say. We're in the territory where my background in BDSM is a strength. "I want you to understand what I want from you. Then, we'll talk about what you're willing to give and what you want to give."

She stays perfectly still, blinking, watching me like a wary deer.

"I want you to stay with me. You don't have to decide what this is, what we are, but stay," I say. "We'll have a contract you can get out of if you choose. It'll outline how you want to be treated. Your needs, my needs, and we'll work through those differences."

She wets her lips. "Like a kink contract?"

I'm impressed that she knows what I'm talking about. "Just like that."

"So you can tie me up?" she says.

"So I can care for you," I say firmly. "So both of our needs are met."

"And you need to tie me up."

"I'd like to."

"Is it negotiable?"

"I'm happy to negotiate."

She's quiet for a long time. Then, she sits up straight and folds her hands in her lap. "Alright, explain."

Before now, I would have walked away from anyone who didn't want this as badly as I do. I never engaged in anything but vanilla sex with women who hadn't signed a contract.

But with Freya, nothing is simple. Everything has a hundred different layers, and I'm clearly willing to do things I didn't think I was capable of to make her mine.

"I'd like to have you as my submissive," I say, as if this is just another negotiation and not a conversation I've turned over and over in my head for months.

She purses her lips. "Why?"

"Because I want you," I say. "And I want you like that."

"How?"

She's so forceful in her curiosity. I take a drag from my cigarette.

"I want to care for you. I want you to belong to me," I say. "That's what I meant by what I said last night. Give me everything, and I'll keep you safe."

Her lids lower as she digs at her thumbnail. "So you'd be in control?"

I nod. "It's more complex than that, but yes."

"How can I trust you not to...abuse that?"

She has every right to ask that question after everything she's been through. I've thought about this part of BDSM so many times before. This is what can make it dangerous, why it's important to be careful entering into contracts or doing scenes with people I don't know well. The only thing that separates what I do with her from the unthinkable is a single word.

And therein lies the weak point.

She can submit to me. She can put her life in my hands. But her safety is completely built upon the trust that if she safewords me, I'll listen.

"Have I ever hurt you?" I ask.

Her face goes still, her eyes are far away. There's an expectant pause. Then, she shakes her head.

"No," she admits.

"Look at me, sweetheart."

She lifts her chin. I wrap my hands around her waist, absently entranced by the soft curve of her waist.

"Kink doesn't have to be about extreme lengths. For me, it's about the...connection. With you," I say, trying hard to articulate this clearly.

"The main thing I want from you is for you to let me be the caretaker. We can talk about the kinky shit on a case-by-case basis."

The corner of her mouth turns up.

"That's hard for me to...process," she whispers.

"Why?"

"Because...nobody has taken care of me," she says. "My mother left when I was so young, I barely remember her. Growing up, I dressed myself, I fed myself, and when I cried, I comforted myself."

My chest aches. I pull her near, and her arms slip around my neck.

"Not anymore," I say firmly. "From here on out, that's my job."

Her hands come up and trace the lines of my face. I'm still, barely breathing. She's always been like a wary animal. When she's close, I hold my breath for fear of scaring her away.

"I need to think about this," she says.

"We'll talk tomorrow."

She bends in and kisses me, slow and deep. It's slow fire, all the way down to my groin. Then, she lays her head on my chest, and I settle back against the pillows and hold her until she falls asleep.

The moon is up, the sky clear for once. The stars are so thick, they cast everything in a pale white glow. Through the center of it spills the Milky Way. I've looked up at the sky over Ryder Ranch time and time again, but it's different with her, knowing how badly I need her to stay and watch the stars with me. Forever.

My eyes shut. She's snoring a little, her hair fluttering over her face.

This is peace like I've never known.

It feels like a second later when I'm wide awake, my arms empty. I blink hard, fixing my gaze out the window. The sun is rising over the inky mountains. The fireplace still glimmers. Her side of the bed is a lump of blankets.

My body hurts worse today than it did yesterday. I swing my legs off the bed and pull on my sweats, being mindful of the gauze on my thigh. Then, I limp into the bathroom.

My heart stops.

There's a note stuck to the mirror with medical tape.

The world screeches to a halt. I rip it down and open it.

*Bittern said it was safe to go home. He said Aiden hit him. I have to go make sure he's alright.*

*Please don't be angry with me.*

My stomach sinks that she thinks I'd ever be angry with her. I'm angry, but never at Freya, never at the woman I'm in love with. No, Aiden is the problem here. I crumple the paper and toss it in the trash.

My heart is pounding. My mouth is dry.

Did she run because of Bittern? Or because of our conversation last night?

Working quickly, I put on my clothes and head downstairs. Ginny is in the kitchen, and she sends me a concerned look, but I keep walking. Gravel crunches under my boots as I stride down the driveway and into the barn.

*Goddamn.*

She took my horse.

I'm impressed but also planning on spanking her ass the second I catch it. Bones' stall is open, but his saddle is still on its bar. I run a hand over my face, unsure how to handle this. She's in a sensitive situation. I can't break into her house and demand to see her, can't put a gun to Aiden's head and order him to hand her over. The minute he realizes he can use her against me, he will.

And I can't outright kill him, at least not without a plan so I don't get caught.

But I can get her back.

I saddle up Silver Phantom and burst out of the barn into the mist still gathered on the hills of Ryder Ranch. I don't urge her. She loves to run, and her long legs eat up the distance to the fence line.

My heart pounds with Silver Phantom's hooves. I'm moving up the hill that leads to the spot where we met, coming at it from the south, when I stop short. The woods open to the clearing before the creek. Thick mist darkens the shadows of the Ponderosa pines in hazy trails.

Something moves in those shadows.

Silver Phantom throws her head, prancing. Then, a dark shape appears and my heart sinks.

It's Bones.

He's riderless, his bridle hanging on either side of his neck as he trots in the direction of the ranch house. I slide to my feet and whistle. He jerks his head and pivots, coming down the hill and halting beside me. Tied to his forelock is one of her green ribbons.

My throat is dry. She put it there so I would know she made it back safe.

Jaw set, I untie it, push it in my pocket, and sling the reins over his shoulder, taking Silver Phantom's as well. Then, we start walking back. I don't want to ride. I need time to think through everything before I have to pretend I'm fine.

Silently, I promise myself this is the last time she leaves.

# CHAPTER TWENTY-TWO
# FREYA

I'm on my knees, a cardboard box at my side. Glass litters the floor in the kitchen. The blue willow plate Bittern said belonged to my mother, the only thing of value I've owned, is smashed. It wasn't enough to drop it, so it had to be ground to nothing.

A tear hangs off my chin. I keep my head down, being mindful not to cut myself on the glass.

There's a step in the hall. I look up to find Ryland leaning in the doorway.

"Are you making breakfast?" he asks.

He looks hungover. There's a heavy darkness in his eyes, blue shadows beneath. He's in a pair of beat up sweats, no shirt, and the bruises Deacon left on him are in full view. They make me wince.

"Yeah, in one second," I say, forcing my voice into that low, sweet tone that keeps me safe.

He stares at me, only to snort and leave. The sound of his steps are quickly replaced by the shuffling walk I know to be Bittern. He appears around the corner. I get up quickly, edging closer so I can get a look at his face. It doesn't look bad, and a faint black eye is all I see.

"You alright?" I ask.

He nods, his eyes unfocused. "Gonna have a smoke."

I hear his voice catch, the guttural sound of his lungs dying echoing in my ears.

"Bittern," I blurt out.

He stops, looking up. Another tear seeps out.

"Don't," I whisper.

He swallows. He's in his sweats too, his undershirt stained. Slowly, he runs a hand over his face and lets out a sigh.

"I'm fucked already," he says.

All at once, it's too much. The smashed kitchen, the rattle of Bittern's chest, the venom in Ryland's eyes, the unspoken fear of when Aiden will wake up. The house closes in around me, squashing me until I'm heaving for a breath.

I turn, my boots crunching on the glass, and burst out the side door. Bittern follows. I feel him hover over my body as I sink down on the stoop.

"Hey, Frey, don't worry about me," he says, almost sheepishly.

I wipe my face with my palm. "How can I not?" I whisper. "Aiden shouldn't be buying land out here with all that money. He should be sending you to the doctor. We shouldn't even be here, Bittern."

He's quiet. I look over my shoulder, and he's squinting out over the hills. The mountains sprawl out, the same ones in the far off distance that I can see from Deacon's bedroom. I turn back around and close my eyes, squeezing them shut.

I want to go back to Ryder Ranch.

But I'm so afraid.

I'm paralyzed that, under everything, Deacon's the same kind of man I swore I'd never touch. And yet, I think it's slowly dawning on me that he's not. He's only ever touched me gently. He listens to me, he holds me, he says all the words I want to hear.

I want to trust him.

And yet...if I do, I'm trusting that, in twenty years, I won't have a daughter who sits on her back porch, biting back tears.

It's all happening so fast, I'm struggling to process how I feel about Deacon after the last few conversations we've had. But something changed when he came to get me. I saw the stark difference between him and Aiden. Now, I have to grapple with my misjudgment and wonder if there's a path forward.

He thinks there is—that's clear. I might not think I'm his woman, but he thinks he's my man.

Bittern clears his throat, jerking me out of my thoughts. "You want me to clean up the kitchen?" he asks.

I shake my head. "No, I'll do it and make breakfast before Aiden gets up."

"He doesn't hate you," Bittern says.

I push myself to my feet, looking up at him. "What?"

"Aiden doesn't hate you," he says, not looking me in the eye. "He hates her, and you look just like her, you know. I don't know if anybody ever told you that, but you look just like your mama."

I know this, but today, the unfairness of it all hits deep. I can barely nod my head before dropping it to hide my frustrated tears.

He walks down the steps and goes past me. I see him digging in his pockets, but he left the cigarettes on the porch railing. Quick as a flash, I go and grab them, pushing them in my pocket.

"I'll let you have one after breakfast," I say.

He sighs. I go inside and get back on my knees and pick up every damn piece of glass and porcelain. When everything is in a bucket and hauled to the trash, I sweep so I don't wake Aiden and mop until the floor sparkles. Then, I put everything back together, load the dishwasher, and set the table. By the time Ryland walks back through the front door, the bacon is done, and I'm finishing up the eggs.

Bittern comes in and leans in the side door. He looks down a lot. I think it started when he worked in the mines.

He used to be so easy-going and happy. Now, he doesn't look above anybody's shoes. Deacon was right in saying he's thirty and he should be able to take care of himself, but he doesn't understand Bittern like I do. He doesn't know that Bittern is gentle and that life was brutal to him.

I want him to live, but I'm scared because I think he's just waiting to die.

"I'm gonna go wash up," I say.

Bittern nods. Ryland walks past me without a word and starts washing his hands in the kitchen sink. I bite my tongue and leave, going up the back stairwell to my room.

Everything is as I left it. Nobody bothers to come in here, thank goodness. I run my fingertips over my glass cases. The sunlight catches the earthy orange of the monarch's wings, the swallowtail's brilliant yellow and black.

This is my jewelry box, my most prized possession. The little part of the world where my heart is happy.

My beetles are some of my favorite. I have two rare beetles here, one I could probably sell for a little bit of money. But they're so pretty, and they're all I have to show for my twenty-two years on this Earth. I think if I ever sold them, it would tear a piece of my heart out.

The floor creaks downstairs. I shake myself and wash up, braiding my hair and putting on a sweater and skirt. I don't have my belt. It's with Deacon now.

I hope he'll return it.

I take a second to look myself over. I'm neat and modest, wearing the armor that gets me through the day. I tuck my hair behind my ear, turn my lights off, and close the door to my sanctuary.

Downstairs, Aiden, Ryland, and Bittern sit at the table. They're talking, but when I start filling their plates, they go quiet. Aiden leans back, spreading his knees with his boots planted.

I glance over as I take my seat near the end, on the other side of Bittern. Aiden's eyes are on me, but I can't read them.

"Where'd you go?" he asks.

I keep my eyes on the table. "To Tracy's."

He takes a sip of his coffee. Ryland starts eating and Bittern does the same. There's a long silence. My nose starts running, and I can't keep from sniffing.

"God, girl, just eat your fucking food," Aiden snaps.

When I was little, I learned quickly that crying in front of Aiden didn't soften him. It only makes him angrier, so I taught myself to take a breath and hold it until I couldn't physically cry to avoid getting in trouble.

For some reason, my body betrays me today. A tear slips from my lashes and etches hot down my cheek. I swipe it away fast, but he sees it.

"Get out," he says, voice soft.

I haven't eaten since last night, but hunger is preferable to this. I stand and flee the kitchen. As I go, I hear Bittern say something. It takes me a moment to work out what.

"Don't make Freya cry," he says, voice rough.

My chest aches. I hurry back upstairs and shut my door. Then, I think better of it, because I don't want to run the risk of Aiden walking in and entrapping me. He's never done that before, but it's a fear that lurks in the back of my mind.

I take my jacket and go outside. Chickens scatter as I go across the yard to the woods. I don't want to run back to Deacon. I need time to think about him. I can't leave Bittern.

But I can't stay in that suffocating house.

My heart aches for a place to run from my problems. I need the soft arms of the Appalachian Mountains to rest in, the sheltering trees, the forests dappled with sunlight.

For the first time, when I think of home, the vision doesn't stop there. It morphs into the dark living room of Deacon's house. In my mind's eye, I'm lying on the couch on my side, watching snow drift past the window. My cheek is against the rough fabric of Deacon's work pants over his thigh.

His hands stroke my hair.

For a split second, I long for that with everything I have. A fantasy where I can put all my trust in him. Where there isn't a voice in the back of my head telling me he could be just like Aiden, I just don't know it yet.

The clouds scud over the sky, thickening the further I go from the farm. I'm at the edge of the forest when the rain hits. I'm so tired of rain at this point. I huddle in the roots of the Ponderosa Pines and wrap my arms around my knees.

I turn up my face. The rain etches down it.

I ran from Deacon because I was afraid of him, but now, I'm so afraid of being just another turn in a vicious, endless cycle. Now, I need him. I want him not just to save me, but to silence my doubt about him.

"Come find me," I whisper.

For a second, I imagine the wind takes my voice, that my words ride the storm through the woods, down the hills, across the fence line, carried by some benevolent forest spirit, all the way to him.

# CHAPTER TWENTY-THREE
## DEACON

There's only one person more useful than Jack Russell in a pinch, and that's Jensen Childress. He can tell me everything about everyone. I swear, he's got everyone locked down, owing him favors. He knows all their friends, their families, where they eat, who they talk to. His business is technically a construction company, but I know it's a lot more than that.

Not many people know he lives not too far from Ryder Ranch. I pull up his driveway to the sweeping ranch house at the end and put the truck in park. The screen door is shut, but the other door is open. Chicken lays on his side on the porch. When I get out and move up from the front barn to the steps of the two story house, he lifts his head and barks.

"It's alright," I call.

He heaves himself up and stares at me as I approach. Footsteps ring out from inside, and the screen door opens. Jensen appears in a white undershirt, work pants, and boots. He's got a beer hanging in his fingers.

"Not a great time," he says.

"I need help," I say.

He sighs, running a hand over his face. "Alright, what do you need?"

"I'm getting Freya back."

Jensen's face stays the same. "She lost or something?"

"No, she's at Aiden's house," I say. "I'm thinking I might acquire her from there."

"Like kidnap her or something?"

I nod. Jensen sighs, jerking his head inside. I follow him, Chicken at my heels. The kitchen is pretty clean, although there's some kind of project going on in the hallway. Two by fours are stacked on the floor, and sawdust crunches under my feet. Jensen kicks out a chair and leans against the counter, crossing his arms.

"What can I do you for? I don't know how I'm any help," he says.

"You know the Hatfields."

"I'm a fair weather friend to everybody."

"Do you talk to Aiden much?" I say, sinking down and stretching my legs out.

"Here and there."

"Does he leave town a lot?"

Jensen shifts his weight, giving me a look. "Did she run off on you?"

I nod. "She's worried about her brother."

"The addict one?"

That lifts my head. "How do you know he's an addict?"

Jensen shrugs. "It's pretty clear he's got something going on. I heard he was in an accident. Could be for pain from it."

I'm quiet, remembering how upset she was before she disappeared. I checked the phone her text messages were sent to and there was nothing. Bittern must have called her. I wonder if she heard desperation in his voice.

She didn't stand a chance.

"I want to know what Aiden's doing," I say. "I need a chance to get Freya out in the open, away from her house, so I can just go in there and get her."

Jensen's brows lift briefly. "That's your plan? Just…grab her?"

"It's a good plan," I say.

The sigh that comes out of Jensen is from deep down. "Alright, I'll see what I can do. It's probably to your benefit that I stay friendly with the Hatfields."

"It'd be helpful to have somebody who knows their comings and goings."

"Fine, I'll keep a general eye out." He shrugs. "Consider it a favor I can use later. I'll pull a Jack Russell on you but in reverse."

"One Jack Russell is one too many."

Jensen laughs then sobers quickly. Truthfully, we both know we'll just keep trading favors back and forth without keeping count. The last person who posed a real threat to my land is dead at the bottom of a ravine. I owe Jensen a bit for helping with that one, and the boys up at Sovereign Mountain. None of us keep count too good.

My phone rings. This is the second time it's gone off in the last five minutes. I've been ignoring the vibration against my leg, but this time, I take it out of my pocket.

"Alright, here's my ass beating now," I say, turning to head down the hall.

"Jay?" Jensen follows me to the door and holds it open.

I step out. "Yeah, honestly, I thought he'd be on my case before now. Wish me luck."

"Good luck. You're gonna need it." Jensen shuts the screen door and lifts a hand as I head down the steps to my truck.

I wait until I'm back in Knifley before checking my phone again. There's a text from Jay saying he's heading my way, that he wants to meet in his secondary office. I park the truck at the curb and decide to walk, hoping I can walk by the café and see Freya, although I'm not sure she wants to see me.

She did leave while I was sleeping.

I mull that over, like I have been for a few days. Freya's a hard woman to understand. One day, she's smiling, eyes bright. The next, she's all closed up with the saddest eyes I've ever seen. One second, she's shy, and the next she's naked and riding my dick like there's no tomorrow.

I shake my head. I can't get hard walking down the curb.

The door to Jay's office is shut. It's a storefront with a wooden door, like something out of a western. I check the knob, and it's locked. But the minute I let go, it swivels and opens, revealing Jay.

"You son of a bitch," he says, striding back down the hall.

I shut the door and follow him to his office in the back. It's one of those low rooms with fake wooden walls and carpets that remind me of the ones in the methodist church. He circles the desk and sinks down, staring up at me with a crackle in his eyes.

"You look like shit," he says.

I laugh. Jay is usually the picture of a gentleman lawyer, in his nice suits tucked over his cowboy boots. But today, his suit and tie are traded for jeans and a flannel, and he's not hiding his annoyance.

"Yeah, I got hit in the face and stabbed in the leg," I say. "But I'm fine, thanks for asking."

"Fuck yourself," he says.

I sink down in the seat across from him, stretching my legs out and leaning back. "Look, I pay for that nice house and truck. Just patch this up the way you always do, what you're draining my bank account for."

His eyes narrow. "I can't bail you out of everything. You assaulted two men and defaced their property."

"Defaced? I didn't deface anything."

"You slashed their tires, Deacon," he snaps. "You beat the shit out of two people. Not just any people, but the one's getting ready to drag your ass to court if you won't lie down and take that easement."

"What? They can't change a tire so they have to cry about it?"

Jay's eyes flash, the vein in his forehead standing out as he tries to gather himself. There's a pen on his desk. I pick it up, clicking it absently, waiting.

*Click.*

*Click.*

*Click.*

"Set that fucking thing down," Jay snaps.

I stop clicking. "I won't lie down and take it," I say, my voice dropping. "No easement. I don't want that development going in on my property line. Do you know what that does to my property value?"

Jay stands, hands on hips. He starts pacing, and I keep quiet and let him think. Finally, he stops and lets out a sigh, like all the air is let out of his tires.

"Do you know how hard it is to fight an easement?" he says quietly.

I shake my head.

He lifts a finger. "I've won one easement case in my entire career, and it was due to there being endangered turtles in a pond directly in the path of the road. One of my paralegals had a zoology degree, and he'd done a paper on it. That was it, a couple turtles."

His point is sinking in. I stare down at the desk.

"I'm already fucked on this case. Don't go making it harder by beating the shit out of the people dragging you to court," he says. "It's a little strip of land. That's all they see."

It's not a little strip of land. It's Aiden Hatfield selling off his land to let the highway come through, right by mine. It's the houses they'll build and all the people who will come flocking in. It's the way I won't be able to stand on my back porch and see the land rolling out for miles without a soul in sight.

It's the way I have to save the home I built for Freya before we even met.

I lift my hands. "What do you want me to do?"

He stops, giving me a hard stare. "Put your fists away," he says. "No fighting. No fucking Aiden's stepdaughter. No antagonizing anybody."

I shake my head. "I can quit fighting. Can't quit the stepdaughter."

Jay runs a hand over his face. "You're lucky I don't fire you. Get out of my office and keep your hands to yourself."

He's actually mad, I can tell. Jay and I go way back, and there's not a lot we can't resolve, but I can tell he needs some time to cool off. I get up, turning to speak, but he just points to the door.

"I'll do my best," he says. "You do yours."

"I can do that."

I leave him there, shoulders bowed. Outside, the wind has picked up. I cross the street and get in my truck, sinking back. If this had all happened a few years ago, I would have handled my frustration differently. I'd have gone down to the city and found something stronger than whiskey and a woman who knew what she was doing to make me forget about it for a few hours.

Not now.

Not now, when all I want is to wake up to Freya's curly head on the pillow next to me. Not now that I know what she tastes like, the way she lets out a little gasp when she comes, how her nails feel digging into my skin. I want to be in the kitchen with her, doing my best to dance with her to the radio. That's all I want anymore. I'm done. I've already made my choice.

A slow realization settles over me.

Freya didn't change me. I got older, a little wiser, and that version of me wants the gentleness of a woman like her. My tires are riding lower than they used to be. I've got enough stories to last me.

I'm ready to settle down, have been for a while.

I just got one more fight to finish.

# CHAPTER TWENTY-FOUR
# FREYA

It feels like it's been years since I left Ryder Ranch, even though it's only been a week.

I wake up disoriented. It takes everything I have to drag myself through the morning. Aiden and Ryland snap at me in the distance, but I respond only insofar as I have to and keep to myself. Bittern is doing something up on the north end of the farm. I don't know what, but it keeps him occupied.

They go into town on the fourth day. Bittern says something about how they have a meeting with Deacon. Hearing his name feels like a little stab below my ribs.

I think, if I just went to see him, it might help. But deep down, I know that if I go to Ryder Ranch, I'll never come home. He won't let me go back to living under Aiden's roof after what happened the night of the fight. I'm surprised Deacon hasn't come knocking on the door, except he has to know that will only make things worse for me.

I watch the sunrise while the men get ready. They come downstairs in their good shirts. Apparently, Aiden has a hotshot lawyer now, someone from the city. Ryland gives me a slow stare as I wipe down the countertops and load the dishwasher, but he doesn't speak. Everyone but Aiden goes outside. He's upstairs, his boots moving back and forth.

The kitchen is spotless. I take off my apron and hang it up.

Aiden's boots come down the stairs. He pauses in the doorway, his coat over his arm.

"We'll be back by dinner," he says. "We'll have the McClaines with us, and Mitch Silvers, the man from city government, so make sure you can feed them all."

I nod, not meeting his eyes.

He clears his throat. "You've been going somewhere."

I freeze, staring down at my hands on the countertop. They're worn, a scar on the back from catching myself on a nail as a child. I shake my head.

"You're not going to Tracy's," he says, voice curling.

My teeth cut into the tip of my tongue.

He takes a step into the kitchen, leaning in the doorway. "Just know if you drag your ass back here pregnant, you're out," he says. "You're lucky I let you stay here now."

My cheeks burn. "I pay rent," I whisper.

I should have stayed quiet. I know better, but my tongue got the best of me. His boots come closer until he's right beside me. I glance up and freeze.

My body wants to shut down. My brain knows what he's like and it's trying to protect me. Aiden's first wife was his high school sweetheart. She had three babies by him before she turned twenty. Then, she tried to divorce him, and he put a gun to her head and told her to leave the boys and run.

So, she ran. I hope she's so happy now. I hope she found someone who loves her, who only speaks softly.

My mother did the same thing, but she had the disadvantage of being very young while Aiden was older. He knew she'd developed a drug problem. There was no chance in hell she could take his children. So, she left too.

Bittern saw her obituary in the paper a few months later. She couldn't keep the needle out of her arm after all the mental abuse Aiden put her through. When I was nine, Bittern told me. I don't remember crying because I'd never had hope she'd come back. I never had hope that someone would step in and save me.

Until now.

My mind goes back to when I ran into the woods, when I wished the rain and the forest would carry my words all the way to Deacon. Maybe Aiden's first wife had a man like that waiting on the other side.

Maybe I should trust that Deacon could be that man.

"I know your type," he says, voice low. "I married your type. Twice."

My breath catches. My pulse is racing.

"But you wouldn't know," he says, voice caged between his teeth. "Because she left you. Not just me. She left you too."

Anger flows through me, clear like water. My fingers dig into the counter and my mouth is dust dry.

"She left you."

The words force themselves out before I can clench my jaw. I glance up at him and freeze. His dark eyes fix on me without expression. His mouth is set. The longer I look, the more I realize I can read a single emotion on the edges of his face—triumph.

He wants me to talk back, wants an excuse.

I hunker down. He lifts his hand and flicks me, across the cheekbone to my earlobe. It's not hard enough to do damage, but it's enough to sting. I wince, my hand going to my face. It's been a while since he's done that.

"You're lucky you have Bittern," he says softly. "Because I would throw you out tonight if he wasn't pleading your goddamn case."

My eyes flutter shut. If he touches me again, I don't want to see it. Into my mind's eyes comes the memory of being a little girl. Bittern knew Aiden didn't like me. He's not brave enough for full defiance, but he was kind to me when we were alone. He'd knock on the barn door while I was cleaning out the chicken coop, tears overflowing my eyes from whatever Aiden said to me earlier.

"Hey, Frey," he'd say. "I found you one of them beetles you like."

A tear slips out. I know Aiden can see it, but he'll be angrier if I wipe it.

"Jesus," he says.

His boots fade away. I force my eyes open as the truck revs outside and gravel crackles until it fades away. I wipe my face now that it's safe and slowly climb the stairs.

My clothes are laid out on the bed. I wash and braid my wet hair down my back. I have to go to work for a few hours. Tracy's expecting a little crowd because it's the last day of the fall festival in Knifley. She's stopping to pick me up in thirty minutes.

I pat my face with cold water until the pink is gone. My face is pale, my bright blue eyes taking it up.

The same color as the lingerie he bought me.

I turn my head back and forth. I've stood in front of the drug store makeup and wondered what I'd look like wearing some, but it always seemed like such a frivolous purchase.

It's not like anybody ever taught me how to use it anyway.

I tear myself away from the mirror. It's chilly out, with fall finally settling in. I put my leggings under my skirt and tuck in my sweater. Under my boots, I'm wearing woolen socks. Then, I head downstairs just as I hear Tracy laying on her truck's horn.

It's a pleasant day at work. We chat, fill orders, and clean up the shop before locking up. Tracy and I get a deep fried pie from one of the vendors, and she takes me home, dropping me at the end of the drive. I eat while I walk to the house and hope the men aren't home yet.

They aren't. I go straight to taking food out of the fridge and heating up the oven. The kitchen is warm, even though frost has started making patterns on the windows. I make the same meal I made the first time because it seemed like it went over well with the McClaines. The last thing I want is Aiden complaining.

Trucks pull up the drive. Men's voices fill the chilly air.

The door opens and Ryland comes in, followed by Kasey and Elijah. Bittern is talking with Mitch Silvers, the older gentleman from the city council. Aiden comes in at their heels with a group of men as loud and rough as he is. My stomach is a pit. I didn't realize there were going to be more of them.

There's enough food. I just don't like strange men in the house, especially in groups.

I should be used to it by now, but the last several months in Montana, with just Aiden and my stepbrothers in the house, made me too comfortable.

They fill the house with chaos. Loud voices. Laughter. Jokes that make my stomach turn even though I've heard them all before.

My mouth tastes bitter.

Nobody says anything to me. I fill all ten plates around the table and go into the kitchen to have my plate. Thankfully, Aiden doesn't pursue me and demand I eat with our guests.

My heart hurts. More than anything in the world, I want to go home.

The problem is, I don't know where that is anymore.

The wind is picking up outside. I slip through the side door and stand on the edge of the porch. Gusts of chilly air tease my skirt and hair. I look up and see the dark strands swirl before my eyes. I wish I could fly with them, up and up.

Floating into space, home to the stars.

A hot tear escapes. My lips part.

"Come find me."

The words tumble out, a little whisper, and the wind takes them with hungry hands and carries them away—up over the roof and the chimney, up over the hills and the dark mountains.

All the way to him.

If I could go back, I would be a brave little girl who went out into the world like the heroines from my books. I'd have taken Bittern's hand before he had a chance to go into the mines and we'd have run. Surely, there's somewhere in the world where we could have been safe.

Maybe if I had run, Bittern wouldn't cough. Maybe he would have a wife who loved me like a sister and babies for me to hold.

Maybe is a heavy word.

It haunts me.

A leaf blows over my face, and I catch it in my fingers. It feels heavier than usual, so I turn it over. Inside is a silk cocoon. I know buried in the soft depths is a little insect, waiting for the spring to come. The wind picks up again, and I step out into the yard and lift the leaf.

The next gust takes it. It tugs that little life into the sky, and I hope with everything I have that it goes to a better place.

Inside, the house glows gold. The voices in the dining room remind me I have to face them. Nobody is going to drop from the sky and save me.

There's just harsh reality.

And a future I can't differentiate from my past.

Heavy as lead, I drag myself into the house. The men are up and heading to the front porch to smoke. Head down, I clean the table and wipe everything down. The dishwasher is humming and everything smells of cleaner when I'm finished. I hang up my apron and go upstairs.

My room is so quiet. I slip my boots off and turn on the little light over my desk.

My collection glitters. The natural jewelry of the wings and shells gleams. My heart hurts less as I sink down on my chair and lift the lids.

I don't touch anything. It's not preserved correctly since I don't have the money for the right materials, so the little wings and legs are so fragile. One wrong move, and they'll be dust.

Boots sound on the stairs below me. They're moving fast, like they know where they're going.

My heart patters on my tongue.

They come down the hall. By the long stride with the slight hitch, I know they belong to Aiden. He walks like Deacon, but somehow, not like Deacon at all. Maybe because I'm not scared when I hear Deacon's boots ring out on the floor.

I have a half second to jump to my feet and turn before the door is shoved open.

He's not drunk, but he's not sober. In the shadows, his face is so harsh. His eyes are shadowed, but there's a glitter to them that makes me want to curl up and cover my head.

"You fucking liar," he drawls.

I take a step back. Aiden has never hit me, not really. He'll clip my ear, throw things past me, hit the wall behind my head. He's never beat me, but I'd be shocked if he never put his hands on his wives.

I'm not so sure he won't now.

"I—don't know what you mean?" I stammer.

He strides closer. I back up against the chair.

"You went to Ryder Ranch," he says. "You traitor. You little fucking whore."

The fear tastes sharp in the back of my throat, but worse is having him here, in my sanctuary. He's big, everything I've spent my life trying to shut out, yet here he is, angry and frightening in my doorway. I can't even run because he's blocking my only exit.

"I didn't," I whisper.

A muscle in his jaw ripples.

"Elijah saw you," he says. "His property is right up by the Ryder Ranch property line."

"I was just walking." I can barely get the words out.

He surges forward, bending over me. The back of the chair cuts into the center of my spine.

"On his horse? On Deacon Ryder's fucking horse, with him? You were just walking, huh?"

Those words put the nails right in my coffin. I put my palm up, trying to push him back. His hand comes up, shoving me so hard, I fall to the ground with a hard thump. My elbow takes the brunt of the fall. Shocked, I roll to my side, and Aiden towers over me.

"You fucking whore," he seethes. "You're just like her, nothing but a drain on me and my money. You don't do anything but fuck around with these...all this shit."

I see his arm rise. The entire world slows.

He picks up the case of butterflies and brings it down hard. I lurch forward, but he's too quick. My hands close on air, and the case splinters. Of course it does. I made it from milk crates and plastic sheeting. The fragile wood disintegrates as it hits the back of the chair, and a shower of jewels fly up and fill the air.

Little wings.

Rainbow shells.

Velvet antennas.

All the pieces of my heart. I hear my own scream. It sounds like somebody dying, like raw anguish.

He snatches up the case with the beetles and throws it down hard. Frozen, I watch it burst into a million pieces. His boot comes down, grinding, and my beloved beetles are nothing but dust.

I can't stop screaming, it just pours out of me like I'm possessed, all years and years of pain and hurt I can't hold back anymore.

Dropping to my knees, I start frantically trying to take the fragments back. My nails scrape at the wood, grabbing at the biggest pieces. Everything is so fragile from not being stored properly that the minute it hit the chair, the parts of each insect exploded. My floor is a mess under Aiden's boots, all dust and carnage.

He picks up the last case. I see it for a second, in the air. My hand goes up, trying to take it back. The corner of his lip curls. His forehead is flushed, a vein pumping through it.

"No." The word falls from my lips.

He throws it hard against the wall, and it shatters. Then, he turns and heads for the hall, stopping in the doorway to look back.

In the center of the room, everything falls like snow.

Little wings, so delicate they could belong to fairies, flutter to the ground in a soft flurry around me. I catch one in my hand, staring down at it.

This is all I have. All I've ever had. It was beautiful, and it never hurt anybody.

And he took it from me.

Rage floods my veins. My vision goes red, and I scramble to my feet.

"I hate you." The words burst out in a feral scream. "It's no fucking wonder they left you, you horrible, awful man."

His eyes blaze. I've never stood up to him before.

"Talk to me like that, girl, and I'll snap your neck."

"Do it," I scream, my voice breaking from the force. "You fucking kill me, Aiden Hatfield. It's better than living with you and watching Bittern die from black lung because you can't spend the fucking land money on your son."

It all pours out of me, everything I've kept dammed up. I hope it hurts, hope it stabs right into what's left of his heart.

Distantly, I become aware of boots pouring up the stairs. They're like thunder rolling over the hills. Bittern bursts into the room and sees me, my fists full of smashed wings.

There's a second of shocked silence. Then, he turns on Aiden.

"You go," he says, voice low. His brow is knotted.

"Get back," Aiden roars, shoving his chest.

Bittern snaps. His head goes down, and he barrels into Aiden, head-butting him through the doorway and into the hallway wall so hard, the house shudders. The voices downstairs fall silent. I rush to the doorway and see Ryland on the far end, clearly unsure what to do as his father and brother fall to the floor, limbs flying, cursing under their breath.

"Ryland," I gasp. "Please do something."

He's staring at them, frozen. Two big bodies push past him—the McClaine brothers—and dive onto the hall floor. It takes a second, but they get them pulled apart. Seeing Aiden panting, hair messed, with a bruise on his face seems to snap Ryland into action.

"Get them downstairs," he says.

For a second there, Ryland looks like a bullied child, but then the hard angles in his face, the ones he inherited from his father, come back in full force.

"You," he says, turning on me. "You stay in your room."

Cowed, I stumble through my doorway. He shuts the door, and I hear something get dragged close and jammed against it. Probably a chair from one of the other bedrooms. Then, all the boots make their way downstairs.

I sink back down my hands and knees.

My heart is in pieces all over the floor. Every good memory I have was tied to these little insects, butterflies, and moths. I kept every beetle Bittern brought me. I glance over and my stomach twists.

The Polyphemus Moth that Deacon gave me is crushed, nothing left but one of the golden and black eyes from its underwing.

Sickness passes through me like a wave.

I used to pity Aiden. He was all fucked up when Wayland died. I remember standing there in the kitchen, watching him outside. We had a beehive when I was little, but a late frost took all the bees. Aiden stood by the empty hive with his hands in his pockets for an hour. There were no bees to hear the news of Wayland's death. So, it just sat on him, like sickness.

But then, Bittern came back haunted. At first, we had no means to help him. Aiden got him medicine, but it didn't fix him. Sometimes, I think it made him worse off. He sat on the porch with a cigarette hanging from his lips and the light gone from his eyes.

When Aiden sold the land, I thought he would try to fix Bittern, but he didn't. He was too eaten up with anger, and Bittern never played along, he never joined in when Aiden railed against my mother. He always looked out the window and kept his mouth shut. Wayland and Ryland were mean like Aiden, reflected him back. But Bittern never did.

The older I got, the meaner Aiden became.

It's my fault for looking like her, for rubbing his face in it every single day. But my face isn't something I can change.

Mouth dry and body aching with grief, I pick up every single wing and put them back into what's left of the box. It feels like my lifeline is weakening. Maybe I'll just put my things in a bag and run until the hills of Montana are nothing but a smear in the distance.

Maybe I have to accept that Bittern can't be saved.

The problem is, tonight, he saved me.

It's hard to sort through the dust when my tears keep falling on it and turning it into paste. I do my best, putting everything into piles. All the pins I used to hold the exoskeletons down are put into my sewing kit.

There's a little brush in my closet I use for dusting. With it, I clean the floorboards and all the cracks in between.

Then, heartbroken, I go to bed. Tomorrow is another spin in the cycle. One thing I can always count on is the silent day after Aiden has a violent meltdown. Everyone will sit for breakfast, bruises on display, and act like nothing happened.

No one will acknowledge the carnage, so it'll just keep going.

Rinse, repeat.

# CHAPTER TWENTY-FIVE
# FREYA

Aiden doesn't let me out of the house. I don't know how he expects me to pay rent without a job. When I don't show up for work, Tracy comes to the front door, but he turns her away. I see her, staring up at the upper windows from her truck. I wave, but she doesn't see me.

Part of me knows he won't kick me out of the house even if I can't make rent. He's too sadistic for a solution that simple, or he'd have done it already.

Something holds him back.

So, I keep my head down. I cook, I clean, I avoid the men he brings to the house. I sort through the remnants of my collection and put the few insects that survived into a shoebox and hide it under my bed.

I had over two hundred specimens. Now, I only have thirteen left.

My only companions are the books under my bed, stacked up and covered with a sheet. I have twenty-three of them, worn by my hands and annotated with blue ink. Aiden knows I have them, but if I keep them hidden, he won't touch them. The only reason my collection is gone was because it was within easy reach during his temper tantrum.

In a week, my room is put back to rights, but it will never be the same again. My rainbow of colors is gone. Now, I sit alone on the bed with my book in my lap and stare out the window.

I wonder every night if Deacon looks at the same horizon.

One morning, I try to leave the yard and walk up the fence line. Aiden stops me, standing on the porch. He gives a sharp whistle and jerks his head toward the door. Flushed, I come back and walk past him up the porch steps.

"I can't trust you," he says. "Ryder Ranch is no friend of ours. I can't have you sneaking off to fuck around with that asshole."

I sink back into misery. My books get another reread. I paint ferns in the front and along the margins. Then, I go downstairs and make dinner and sit there like a wooden doll while the men eat.

The next morning, Aiden is already in the kitchen. He has a cup of coffee in one hand, leaning against the counter.

"You can go back to work," he says.

I nod, eyes down.

"Good. Get you out of the fucking house," he says, as if he didn't just lock me in for the last week. That's what Aiden does. He tells me one thing then does another. Sometimes, I think he likes giving me whiplash.

I take eggs out of the laundry room and start cracking them into a bowl. His eyes are on me, following my every move. I'm sure disgust is churning inside him.

"I don't want to fucking support you anymore," he says. "You're not my daughter."

He's blowing off steam. Every day since I turned eighteen, he's had the opportunity to kick me out, and he hasn't done it. Something holds him back. I beat the eggs, folding them to keep them fluffy. I have no option to leave anyway. Any job that would hire me won't pay enough for me to have an apartment and buy my own groceries.

I'm trapped in this endless cycle, and I don't see any way out of it. Nobody thought ahead for me when I was little. I was left to grow up without a plan for my future. Now, that future is here.

Aiden's thumb flicks the lighter, the same way Deacon does. Absently back, forth.

"You owe me rent for this month," he says.

My lips crack. I wet them.

"I can't pay you if you won't let me work," I say, keeping my voice steady.

"I didn't say you couldn't work," he snaps. "But you needed some kind of punishment for whoring around with Deacon Ryder."

I turn, trying to bite back my anger.

"Why do you care?"

It's a daring question. Aiden's eyes narrow. He takes a slow drag, smoking curling from his nose.

"Because Deacon Ryder is fucking us," he says coolly. "I'm trying to set this family up for good. He's standing between me and millions in development rights because that fucker's got some idea about pride."

His reaction makes a little more sense. I turn back around and pick up the spatula, turning it over in my fingers so I have something to do. It takes me a second, but I realize Aiden is talking again.

"You hearing me?"

"Sorry," I say.

"I said, you get me that rent," he says. "And have Bittern take you to Knifely to get the groceries this evening. Got it?"

I nod, keeping my eyes on the pan. The eggs cook slowly as I stir, scraping up from the bottom. His presence lingers, suffocating. Then, he strides from the room. The back door slams open and shut.

My shoulders sink. Hands shaky, I take out my phone and text Bittern.

*Aiden wants me to go grocery shopping in Knifley this evening. Please pick me up. I don't want Aiden to take me.*

He doesn't answer, but that's not unusual. He's working. Nobody bothers me for the rest of the day. I make dinner, but only Ryland and Aiden show up. That's not unusual either, but I do walk down to the part of the driveway where I have service and send Bittern another text. He answers back this time, saying he got another nail in his tire. He'll be too late to drive me.

I go back inside and sit at the table.

"Bittern's got a flat tire," I say. "I can't get the groceries tonight."

Aiden wipes his hands on his napkin and sits back. "I'll take you," he says. "I don't know what the fuck's going on with his tires. Jesus Christ."

I shrink back, glancing at Ryland. He cocks his head, smirking. He knows I don't want to be alone with Aiden, and he thinks it's funny. A little sick, I gather up the empty dishes and start the dishwasher.

Teeth gritted, I gather up the bags, change into a sweater, boots, and jeans, and meet Aiden by his truck. He doesn't help me in. Instead, he waits in the driver's seat until I scramble up and slam the door.

I press against the wall, trying to make him forget I'm here. He rolls down the window an inch and lights a cigarette.

I don't know why it disgusts me so much when Aiden smokes but not as much when Deacon does it. Maybe it's because Bittern is dying of black lung. He should know better, but he'll never pay for it the way Bittern will. Evil people like Aiden always live to be a hundred and five, probably dried to jerky from all their sins.

We get to the grocery store without speaking. Aiden says he'll be back and peels out of the parking lot after giving me two hundred dollars. Grateful he's gone, I take my time filling the cart with everything we'll need for the week.

He's outside, waiting with the engine on. For some reason, he helps me load the bags in the car. I don't like that. I'm more comfortable when he's mean. That's normal.

My mouth is dry when I get in. He holds out his hand.

"Change," he says.

I give him the ten dollars left over, and he pushes it into his pocket and puts the truck in gear. He pulls onto the road. I watch from the corner of my eye while the street lights flicker over his face. His jaw is flexed, one hand hanging over the steering wheel.

Just the way Deacon drives.

I shudder, not meaning to. He looks at me, eyes hidden by shadow.

"You cold or something?" he says.

"No, sir," I say.

He makes a noise in his throat but doesn't speak again. We head out onto the highway then turn off onto the state route when we see cop lights up ahead. It's clear there's some kind of accident. I lean forward as we turn away, frowning.

"Some of those fucking trucks can't drive," says Aiden.

I swallow past my dry throat. It seems like he wants me to answer.

"There was a semi jackknifed on the road during the storm in the same place," I say. "Tracy told me, right when the rain started."

His brows push together. "No, there wasn't. I drove right through that part of the highway coming home. It was clear."

I have to stay casual, but it hits me like a thunderclap that Deacon wasn't entirely truthful that day. But I'm not surprised. He wants me, and he's shown it through everything he's said and done since that night.

"Oh, I might have misunderstood," I say, keeping my voice quiet.

He flicks his attention back to the road. I sit there, fingers laced, and stare straight ahead. Why would Deacon have lied to me about the highway being shut down? Unless...he was just trying to get me home to Ryder Ranch?

I wouldn't put it past him.

My heart thumps as I press against the door and let my temple rest on the window. When we get back, I'll have to put the groceries away and clean up the kitchen again. I'm so tired, I can barely keep my eyes open. Then, I should get up early and see if Bittern will take me to see if Tracy will let me keep my job.

My eyelids flicker. I jerk my head up.

"What the fuck?"

I snap my eyes open. Aiden is leaning forward, eyes squinted. I follow his gaze, and my entire body tingles in fear.

There's a man standing in the middle of the road. He's got his back to us, but he's not visibly armed.

"Stay in the truck," says Aiden, taking a pistol out of the glove box.

He goes to open the door, but there's a colossal crash that shakes the entire truck. I scream and slam back against the seat. Something fell onto the hood of the truck, crushing it. For a second, I think it's an animal.

Then, I realize it's a man, crouched, a hat on his head and a rifle over his shoulder. He turns his head, revealing a face half covered in a black bandana.

Oh God, I'm going to die. Or worse.

Aiden lifts his pistol. Quick as a flash, the man stands and brings his boot down on Aiden's side of the windshield. The truck shudders from the enormous impact. It doesn't shatter, instead splintering like ice and bends in. I hear myself panting, pressing my body against the seat. Aiden is pushing open the door, getting out and lifting his gun.

"Hold," someone shouts.

The first man, face also covered, appears behind him. He's got a pistol, and he puts the barrel to Aiden's temple. Aiden goes still, sweat etching down his face.

The man in black jumps to the ground and circles the truck to my side. My ears ring, my blood roaring in my ears. Frantically, fingers shaking, I unlatch my seatbelt and start to crawl into the back seat. I know Aiden has another gun back there.

A hand closes around my ankle and pulls me back. It picks me up and swings me around, tossing me over the man's shoulder, knocking all the wind from my lungs.

My survival instincts kick in hard. I wrench my body hard from side to side, trying to hit him in the face with my hip. He swears, one hand gripping my upper thigh, clamping me down hard.

We're moving, and I see the pavement beneath him. I turn my head, trying to lift it, and he shifts me. The movement makes my face jolt into his back. Right then, I smell it: clean skin, salt, a familiar soap. I know this man intimately. I've spent enough time tangled up with his body, I should have known right away.

It's Deacon.

Relief and rage pour through my veins.

A truck door opens, and I'm dumped, albeit carefully, into the passenger side. The door shuts, but I can't see through the windows. I'm in Deacon's truck, I can tell even in the dark. Distantly, I hear another truck rev behind us, and Deacon swings into the truck, pulling his hat and bandana off. He has the truck in gear, and he's backing up, palm flat on the wheel and head turned.

Behind us, wheels screech. I glance back and make out Jensen's truck turning off onto a side road and disappearing. Deacon keeps going in reverse, at easily fifty miles an hour. My mouth is so dry, I couldn't speak if I tried.

He shoots out onto the state route, spins the truck in a circle, and takes off toward Ryder Ranch with his foot on the gas.

"Sorry about that, sweetheart," he says. "Didn't mean to scare you."

My jaw is on the floor. I look at him and then look straight ahead. We're speeding down the highway. My heart is still pounding from seeing him drop from the trees like a feral animal and land on Aiden's truck.

The only thing I can think is that there's no going back.

He made the choice for me. Now, I have no one but Deacon. That should scare me, and maybe it does, but I don't feel fear through my shock and indignation. Beneath it all is a strong, hot current of what he activates in me every time our bodies are near.

It makes my heart pound for a different reason entirely.

# CHAPTER TWENTY-SIX
## DEACON

I've been fucking around long enough. The time for that is over. Maybe she'll be pissed at me, but at this point, I don't mind. I can work this out with her all night if need be, but I won't be walking away.

And neither will she.

She has her hands clasped in her lap, eyes fixed on the road. God, does she look pretty, even ignoring me. Her hair is loose, tangled down her back. She's in a black sweater that hugs her body and a pair of jeans so tight, I could lick them off her thighs. I'd put my hand on her, but she might bite my head off.

We park, and I cut the engine.

"I can't believe you did that," she whispers.

I circle the car, pulling open her door. "Come on, sweetheart, jump in my arms and I'll carry you. Ground's muddy."

She turns, eyes flashing in a way that tells me she won't be jumping into my arms anytime soon. So, I scoop her out of the truck, put her over my shoulder, and carry her into the house. She's stunned, hanging limply. Taking advantage of that, I set her down and lock the door.

"Don't touch me," she snaps, backing up.

"Sweetheart—"

"And don't *sweetheart* me." She spins on her heel and makes a dash for the staircase.

I go after her. She's headed to the place I want her most anyway. I follow into my room and shut the door, kicking back against it so the lock falls. She makes a dash for the bathroom. I shoot my arm out, catch her around the waist, and pull her against me.

"Let me go," she pants.

"No chance," I say.

She wriggles violently, her hair falling over her face. I reach up to brush it away. She hauls her head back and bites down on my thumb—not hard enough to break the skin, but hard enough to be a warning I'm not in the mindset to mind.

"Jesus, fuck, girl," I say, spinning her to face me. "You need a rabies shot or something? Calm down."

"You kidnapped me," she hisses.

I take a beat. She's not wrong, but in my mind, I'd framed it as more of a heist. Or a stagecoach robbery. She wriggles again, both her hands clasped together in my grip. Her soft body pushes against mine, her stomach against my groin, waking my dick up.

Something dark I've felt since she ran from me lifts its head. It's possessive and angry. Not at her, but at the people who keep her from me. That anger has bubbled in me every second since she left.

She thinks she has a responsibility to them, but she doesn't. She has a right to be happy, to not be the pack mule for Aiden fucking Hatfield and his sons. She deserves to be loved the way only I can love her.

"Take your clothes off," I say quietly. "Or I'll take them off for you."

Her eyes widen. A slow flush creeps up her neck. I release her and go to where I put the harness and belt. It lays in shimmering, soft rings on the folded cloth, silvery and light, almost like chainmail. I haven't done metalworking this intricate in a while. I didn't have anyone to wear it.

Now, I do.

I return. She takes a step back, eyes wide.

"Go on," I say.

Her throat bobs as she swallows. Then, she pulls her sweater off, revealing her soft curves, her breasts overflowing her cotton bra. Jesus, she's so beautiful, it makes my chest hurt.

She hesitates. I nod.

Her fingers trip up, trying to get her jeans unbuttoned. I set the harness down on the belt and kneel in front of her, moving her hands away. She goes still, watching as I unfasten her jeans and work them down her thighs.

She's wearing a pair of pale blue panties. I bend, nipping at her clit through the fabric, inhaling the sweet scent of her pussy. She lets out a moan.

"I should say no," she whispers.

"Sweetheart, you were never going to tell me no," I say, pulling her panties free. She grips my shoulder while she steps out of them.

"Still," she gasps. "You don't deserve it."

"I know," I say. "But that won't stop me."

I look up into her eyes. There's something holding her back, something she's asking for but doesn't have the courage to say out loud.

"You remember what I said about safewords?" I say.

She nods, eyes huge. "Red?"

"Red," I say, rising. "Now, I'm going to fuck you, like it or not, and it'll be how I want it to be. When I'm done, I'm going to lock that pussy up so you don't forget who owns it."

Her jaw goes slack. Then, she nods, a soft, pretty blush seeping up her neck.

"You know how to address me," I say.

Her tongue darts out and in. "Yes, daddy."

"Good girl. Stand there, cross your arms."

She obeys. I pick up the harness, leaving the chastity strap. My cock is so hard, it hurts as I crouch before her and slip my hand between her legs. She's soaked, and it leaves a trail on my fingers. Gently, I apply pressure, and she shifts her legs apart.

It's been a while since I put a harness on anyone, but my muscle memory kicks into gear. One strap each goes around her upper thighs, another strap going all the way to her clit and attaches to them, creating tension.

Another hooks over her ass, a little ring in the middle to attach the chastity band onto. Without it, her pussy is exposed, surrounded by soft silver chainmail straps, almost like crotchless panties. Except this stays on her until I decide to unlock the lightweight padlock on her hip.

The upper part hooks right above her clit. This chain is so fine, it pools like liquid in my hand as I unravel it. The top loops loosely around her neck and clasps at the top of her spine.

I stand. "Go bend over the bed and tuck your hands behind your back."

She obeys, shifting experimentally. The metal will warm up, and she won't feel it anymore. The way I make my chastity equipment is different from other Doms I've met. Mine isn't made for discomfort. No, it's for soft ownership.

I want her to understand that she belongs to me, deep in her bones, but I never want her to hurt.

She's been hurt enough.

I lay the chastity strap on the dresser. I'll lock that on her in the morning. "I'm going to eat you out to warm you up. Then, I'll ride you harder than you're used to, sweetheart. Understood?"

She nods.

"Out loud," I say.

"Yes, daddy." The words slip out in a whispering breath. Her head is laid on the bed, eyes big, following my steps as I come back to her. Her spine is arched, her toes just touching the floor. It spreads her ass, showing her pussy tucked between the harness.

I kneel, lifting one leg and bracing her thigh on the edge of the bed. Her pussy is soaked, flushed pink.

"Can you be a good girl and keep quiet for me while I eat your pussy?" I ask, voice low.

"Yes," she gasps. "Daddy."

I bend in, dipping my tongue in the valley between her thighs and running it over the slick opening of her cunt. She whimpers, tensing. I dig my grip into her hip as my tongue drags all the way up to her asshole.

She twitches back. I bring my hand down on her ass, hard enough that she gets the message.

"My pussy," I say. "Mine."

She lifts her head, looking over her shoulder. "You're jealous," she breathes.

That catches me off guard. I stand, picking her up and turning her to face me. The defiance, the spirit I know, is bubbling back up. I should have known she wasn't giving into me that easily. I think all I did was make her shy back when I put the harness on her, but now, she's swinging back.

I touch her chin, turning it up. "I am jealous," I say. "I want your body, your time, and everything else."

"You can't keep me here," she says.

"I can and I will. That harness has a leash clip on it, and if need be, you'll sleep with it locked on the bed."

Her jaw drops. I swear, I can hear our hearts thump. I see it in the distance—the point of no return where she finds out what kind of man I am. But this time, it's different.

This time, she can't leave.

# CHAPTER TWENTY-SEVEN
# FREYA

Rage floods my veins. "How dare you!"

His hand shoots out and grips my wrist, pulling me against his body. "I've been patient, sweetheart," he says. "I have. But Aiden knows about us now, and he'll use you to get to me. I'm in charge now. I'll keep you safe."

I swallow—I'm the weak link.

"If I have to pick between my land and you...well, I'd rather not," he says. "I'm taking you out of this, so I can fight dirty."

My anger ebbs and flows. This isn't my fight. This is men doing what they do best. I'd have been just as happy with a shack in the woods, so long as I could be at peace. But no, they have to fight each other for money, for who's got a bigger metaphorical dick. And, of course, land.

"Look at me," he says.

I drag my eyes up. He's towering over me. His palm touches my elbow and drags up to my throat, wrapping around it. Thump, thump—my pulse flutters in his grip and between my thighs. My body understands what he's doing, even if my head doesn't.

He leans in, mouth brushing my hair. "Run again, and I won't be gentle."

I've learned that Deacon Ryder is gentle, but only until he chooses not to be. He has complete control over himself. But sometimes, he likes to unhook the leash and let whatever this dark shadow is out to play.

I go limp in his arms. The only way out is forward, but he won't let me go, won't let me leave until he reclaims what he thinks is his.

I squeeze my eyes shut.

I should have never let him pick me up in that storm. Maybe I never had a choice. He lied, said the highway was closed. He said so many things. Now, he has a lock on my pussy.

I underestimated Deacon Ryder.

"Get on your knees," he orders. "Hands behind your back."

I glance up, unsure if he wants me to kneel on the floor or the bed. He points at his feet, facing the fireplace. Shivering, I sink to my knees and tuck my hands back.

The fire dances before my eyes. Everything else is darkness, even him.

I think I've been hunted and captured.

The dresser drawer opens and shuts. He sinks down on the end of the bed so I'm kneeling, facing away, between his boots. Cool leather slips over my shoulders. I feel him securing a row of straps down both arms and pulling them snug. My arms are completely pinned in a sheath of leather.

"Sit up off your heels," he says.

His words are thick, sitting deep in his chest. I know beneath his work pants, he's hard.

I lift an inch, and he slides two thick bands of leather around my lower thighs. They secure with black buckles, like garters. Everything smells like real leather, and the inside is soft silk. I tilt my head, noticing there are words burnt into the leather, one for each thigh.

*Cum.*

*Slut.*

Oh God, I wasn't expecting that. He gets up again and returns, crouching behind me. His inked hand appears in my lap, holding a smooth rod with two clips at each end. I'm nervous, but I don't speak. I want to believe he won't hurt me. He hasn't yet, but he's never been like this before.

My spine tingles, warning me to be careful.

But my pussy is wet, like it's already been conquered.

He clips each end of the rod to the leather garters, shoving my legs further apart to make it fit. It clicks, and my legs are locked open. He rises and circles me, the front of his pants just above my head. I look up, and he looks down, touching my temple.

"You want out, you say your safeword. If you can't speak, you shake your head hard, side to side," he says. "Understood?"

"Yes," I whisper.

With his boot, he shoves my thighs further apart, and the rod clicks again, keeping me spread.

"No, you address me the way I taught you."

Cowed, I drop my head. His boots swim in my vision, heavy tread, steel toe.

"Yes, daddy," I manage.

His hand brushes my hair, petting me. "Good girl."

It's gentle. Without thinking, I press my cheek to his thigh and let him stroke me. Warmth and safety move through my body. I'm so tired of being strong. I want someone to share the weight sitting on my shoulders.

He lifts me from the floor and sets me on the bed, on my knees. Face burning, I lift my eyes to the mirror. My stomach twists. Arousal pours through me like fire. I've never seen myself like this, so softly erotic against the dark backdrop of his bed.

My nipples are hard, flushed deep rose. My eyes are glassy. I'm beautiful, curvy, punctuated by silver chains and black leather.

His pants and boots hit the ground. Then, he's behind me, his hard body naked. Our eyes lock in the mirror. He puts a hand over my throat, thumb against my jaw. His eyes have an edge of stern ice to them.

He's jealous, but I don't know why. He has no competition.

I wonder if he knows.

Or if he sees something I don't.

"Who do you belong to?" His voice is hoarse.

My lips part, but I don't know how to answer that. I've never belonged to anyone, and it feels good. He drags his hand up, gathering my hair in his fist. He guides my head back so I'm forced to watch him in the mirror.

"You belong to me," he says. "Mine. You don't leave."

Ice cold fingers trace down my spine. Between my thighs, I'm drenched. He shifts back less than an inch, reaching between us. I gasp as he notches his cock into me. From this angle, sitting on my heels with my legs locked open, my pussy is so tight. It fights him, but he forces himself in, jaw locked, eyes on me.

"Oh God," I gasp, vision flickering.

His chest heaves, ink glittering with sweat. "Is it too much? Or too little? Maybe I should fuck your ass."

I twist, shocked. "No, no, don't."

The corner of his mouth jerks up. He pumps his hips hard, pushing himself more than halfway into my pussy. A dull ache sparks in my belly. I don't understand how he can be so gentle, so amusing, so kind, but get him jealous, and he's an animal.

If he fucks me there, I don't think I can take that. He's already stretching me to the limit between my thighs.

He pushes me down, and I half expect to fall onto the bed on my face. But then, he slips his forearm through some kind of loop on the sheath that holds my arms locked behind my back.

Shocked, I hang from his arm, bound in place. His other hand grips the garter on my right thigh. He drags my head up again, hand fisted in my hair.

"This is my pussy," he breathes. "It stays right here."

My eyes water. I sniff, swallowing.

"Yes, daddy."

"Say it, tell me."

Heat burns from my head to my curled toes. "This is your pussy, daddy," I whisper. "It stays here."

He ruts his hips hard, slamming his cock up against my cervix.

"Good girl." The words force out from between his teeth. "You watch me fuck you. If I see your eyes leave the mirror, I will turn you over and fuck your ass. Understood?"

My breasts heave. The whites of my eyes flash.

"Yes," I gasp. "Yes, daddy."

He keeps his gaze on mine as he starts fucking in earnest. The bonds on my body, the rod between my thighs, keeps me at such an angle that I'm not taking any of my own weight. No, I hang from my arms, and he fucks me like I'm nothing but his toy.

Weakness, warm and welcome, pours into me. I don't have to do anything to please him but keep my eyes open and watch him ravage me. I never expect it, but tonight, I find myself slipping into submission.

My sense are wide awake. The heat of the fire is calming. The dull pain from the way he ravages me is a drug, burning me, tearing at my seams.

He takes, I give.

I see his lips move. I think he calls me his.

He pulls from me, pressing me onto my back, his inked body moving over me. The scent of our desire, mixed, is heady and raw. It makes my head spin.

One hand braces above me, the other reaching down to grip his length. I gasp, eyes darting down his tensed abdominals, down the trimmed hair above his groin to the hard cock in his hand. He jerks himself, his jaw gritted. There's something shocking about seeing such a powerful man so desperate.

"Say it," he groans. "Say you're mine."

I try to, but my mouth is so dry. I wet my lips.

"I'm yours," I whisper.

It's the first time I've given those words real thought.

Am I Deacon Ryder's woman?

His body tenses, his hips riding against his hand. Warmth hits my cheek, my breasts. The dip of my navel. He moans like he's satisfied but not satisfied at all. My eyes fly open and lock on his, glittering with sweat and lust.

"Deacon," I whisper.

I think I know what this is.

He bends over my helpless body, and his tongue drags over my navel, licking his cum up and shifting down. His rough fingers push apart the tender skin of my sex. My eyes roll back. I hear him spit his cum, hard. Then, those fingers are in me, plunging brutally, pushing his release deep into my body.

His teeth graze the inside of my thigh.

He's working his way back up. I moan, writhing. His strong, hot tongue curls in the pooled cum between my breasts. Then, he shoves my jaw with his hard head, forcing me to face him. His fingers push my mouth open, and he spits his cum onto my tongue.

My hips lift. Salt and Deacon.

"Swallow it," he orders.

Obediently, I swallow him. His eyes glint with satisfaction. He uses the tips of his fingers to rub the rest of his cum into my skin, into my neck, my face. His touch is harsh at first, but then it grows gentle, like the Deacon I know.

He picks me up, unclipping the rod keeping my legs apart. He tugs something behind my back, and the leather sheath falls to the bed. I flex my stiff shoulders and arms.

"Alright, sweetheart?"

He's back. I let him sit back against the headboard and set me in his lap, facing him. We're both breathing hard. The metal harness around my hips is still there, although it's warm and pliable enough that I barely notice it.

"Are you?" I whisper.

"I can handle my shit," he says. "Answer me."

I nod. "I'm alright, just shaken up."

He doesn't answer. His cock is still hard. I feel life thrum through him, beating against the underbelly of my thigh.

"Put my cock back inside," he says hoarsely.

I falter, but he gives me a look. Wincing, I take him by the base and push his cock back into my pussy. My body is learning his, all the ridges, the veins, and it welcomes him. He groans softly, fingers tracing my stomach. My brain buzzes with the pleasure of his skin on mine.

My body craves him. My fear is gone, dissipated. I wonder if this is what it feels like to hunt down a great beast like a wolf. The pulse racing pursuit. The clash. Then, the big warm body beneath mine felled to the ground.

Maybe it was me who got the best of him tonight.

I touch his face, the rough stubble of his jaw. He watches me, silent.

"Who are you?" I whisper.

The corner of his mouth turns up. "What's that mean?"

My touch runs over his mouth. It's beautiful, masculine and cleanly cut but full. It somehow fits perfectly with the brutal cut of his face. I don't know if I would call Deacon classically handsome, but he is wholeheartedly beautiful, like raw rock, like the gray landscape, like black mountains.

"I don't know," I whisper. "Would you like me to ride you?"

He shakes his head, reaching up to tap my chin. "Just keep me in that pretty little pussy while I have a smoke. You mind?"

I shake my head. I don't like cigarettes, but I'm used to them. There are a lot worse things he could be indulging in. He leans over and takes a cigarette and a lighter from the bedside table. Flame flares. He inhales and leans back against the headboard.

"Are you satisfied?" I whisper.

"That you're mine?" He looks at me through a haze of smoke. "You've been mine since I put you on your knees the night you got here. Just because you didn't know that doesn't make it not true."

My stomach twists.

"What happened to you?" The words slip out before I can stop them.

His brow rises. "Why? You mean, why am I an asshole?"

I nod. He laughs quietly.

"I've always been an asshole. That's why I got kicked from one family to another," he says. "I was adopted out and handed back. Ended up in the foster system until around twelve."

My lips part. "That's not your fault."

"No, that's not the fault of other kids. I've always been too much. The world made that pretty clear from day one. Some of it was dumb luck, some of it because I got a hard head and a personality problem."

He's smiling, but there's real pain in his voice.

"I can't figure you out," I say. "All the men I know are violent. You're like them, but you aren't like them at all."

His eyes soften. "I've been on the receiving end of violent men. The man I killed, he pushed me hard, and I let him because I knew if I hit back, he'd be done."

The bottom drops from my stomach. I should be horrified, but I grew up with Aiden. I'm hard to horrify.

"What did he do to you?"

He inhales, leaning back to release the smoke. "He got jealous and put a fence stake through my shoulder, stuck me right to the tree behind me."

*Oh.*

There's a distant roaring in my ears. I look, but he has so much ink on his shoulders, it's hard to see anything else from here.

"A fence stake?"

"The iron stakes I was making in the blacksmith shop," he says. "I use them to hold the bottom rung of the split rail fences in place."

My head spins, a chill slipping down my spine. He put one of those stakes inside me. He fucked me with a weapon.

"What did you do?"

He sighs, his jaw flexing. "I ripped it out, walked back to the house with blood just fucking soaking me. He was inside, so I went into the living room and shoved the stake into his temple."

Oh God, I might be sick.

"Why?" I whisper.

He shrugs. "Because I'd been kicked in the teeth from day one. I kicked back once, and that motherfucker never put a hand on me again. There's only so much beating a dog can take before it bites."

He has such an inelegant but effective way of describing his pain.

"That's how I got the ranch," he says, voice dropping until it's a soft rumble. "It belonged to that man's father. Now, it's mine."

The sickness in my chest is overwhelming. I wrench myself back, heart thumping for a different reason than before. His hands are still on me, hands capable of so much hurt.

And yet, hands that have never hurt me.

# BEFORE

I'm twelve. Not a woman, not a baby anymore.

But God, do I know about grief. It aches in my chest like a wound as I sit, hunched on the porch steps. Behind me, in the depths of the house, a door slams. Aiden is yelling, and I know I should make myself scarce. Bittern says something back. Somebody hits the tabletop, the coffee table that used to belong to my mother's mother.

I never met her, but I know she was young too.

A tear slips out. I wipe it back instantly.

The hot summer wind makes the goldenrod in the field ripple. I see it through the trees—a net of yellow, like a little bit of heaven just out of reach.

The screen door slams open, and Aiden appears. I turn, getting to my feet. I'm in one of Bittern's t-shirts, tied at my hip, and my feet are bare. My legs, bruised from God knows what, stick out like bird feet from under my shorts.

Lady Hatfield had big, tall children. Laurel Rose had me, short and inconspicuous. The advantage is, nobody would be tempted to send me to the factory or the mine. The disadvantage is, I'm no use to Aiden, and that makes me his favorite target.

He pauses in the doorway, glistening with sweat. His t-shirt is off, shoved into his belt. The beer swinging from his hand is empty. I don't know if he notices because he's so high, his pupils fill up his bright blue eyes.

For the first time, I can't blame him.

His son is down at the coroner's office. Not just any son, but Wayland, the big, strong firstborn.

Behind him, the door jiggles and swings open again. Aiden steps out of the way to let Bittern edge sideways around him. He slumps onto the bench, back against the house, and digs in his jeans for a pack of cigarettes.

I hope he's out. Then, I hope he isn't, because they'll send me down to the gas station for more. But maybe that would be better than being here.

He finds a wrinkled pack, takes one to give to his father and another for himself, and tries to light it. His hand shakes so bad, it hurts my heart.

I skirt around Aiden and take the lighter. Bittern gives me a soft look from the depths of his haunted russet eyes.

"Thanks, Frey," he says.

I flick the lighter, and he inhales. I wish he'd quit the cigarettes now that his lungs aren't working right, but I get it. He just spent a week trapped in a mine. I know he needs something to take the edge off.

Especially because they pulled him out of that prison with his heart still beating, but Wayland came out dead. The guilt from that must be eating him alive.

The days since we got the call about the collapse have been horrifying. Every night, I laid on my back in a cold sweat, thinking about Bittern down under the ground, all alone with nobody to hold his hand. When they let us know he'd been found, I went out into the goldenrod field and sobbed.

Aiden wishes it was Wayland who lived. I'm so grateful it was sweet Bittern, who doesn't say much but calls me Frey and brings me butterflies and beetles for my collection.

I glance over at him. He puts the cigarette to his lips, and his eyes focus through the trees. Smoke slips out. His eyes stay where they're at, locked into the distance.

He looks, but he doesn't see anymore.

"I'm gonna kill them both," Aiden says.

He keeps saying that about the two managers up at the mine who sent Bittern and Wayland underground that day. Maybe he's right and they were negligent. Maybe they were just doing their job and couldn't have predicted the collapse. It's hard to say, but it doesn't matter, because Aiden's made up his mind.

He'll go with the boys from the factory and kick somebody to shit for it either way. It's just the way of things.

Aiden puts the cigarette back to his lips. He blows smoke out.

Nobody says a word.

The next morning is Saturday. I hear boots on the floorboards. The doors smash, the truck fires up. I curl on my side in Wayland's old room. Aiden took my things off the couch and threw them on his empty bed yesterday.

"Might as well sleep here," he said. "Get you off the couch."

The bed smells like beer. I lay there, waiting until the truck engine dies away. Then I get up and strip the sheets and haul it out to the washing machine in the tobacco barn. I have breakfast, and while the sheets and quilt dry, I sweep the floor and scrub down every surface with bleach.

Wayland wasn't kind. He put his knuckles through the drywall the way Aiden does, tripped me with his big boots, and called me a whore. But I never wanted him to die, crushed beneath a ton of stone. At least, I hope it was quick.

Bittern comes out to where I'm sitting on the porch. He's in just his sweats. His ribs strain through his pale skin. He spent too long down there with nothing to eat and no sunshine. He looks like a cave cricket now, and I hate it.

"Let me make you breakfast," I say.

He nods and follows me into the kitchen. I make up leftover bacon, dip stale bread into eggs and fry it sprinkled with cinnamon and sugar. Then, I put it on the nice plate, the blue willow one, and set it in front of Bittern. He offers me the first smile I've seen from him in days.

"Thanks, Frey," he says.

We eat in the living room. After a while, Bittern gets up and turns on the TV. I sit with him and watch reruns and listen for the trucks in the driveway. It comes, around three in the afternoon, after Bittern falls asleep from his medication. I give it to him with a glass of water and a cup of applesauce so it won't hurt his stomach.

The trucks come to a halt. Aiden and Ryland's voices boom out, deep and loud, frightening because they're not sad right now. They sound like they got what they came for.

The back door kicks open. Aiden strides down the hall, knuckles bloody. Ryland comes in behind him with a shiner and a rip in his t-shirt. They go right for the liquor cabinet, probably in need of something to dull the pain from their bruises.

I stand in the doorway, pressed up against the wall. Aiden takes off his shirt and uses it to wipe his face and hands before shoving it in his back pocket and reaching for the moonshine. He's talking about something, but I can't hear through the roaring in my ears. Then, like he can sense my presence, he pauses and looks right at me.

"What do you want, girl?" he snaps.

I swallow hard. "Did you kill them?" I whisper.

He uses his teeth to take the cork out of the bottle and spits it into the sink. "Yeah," he says.

# NOW

"I—I can't," I gasp.

Deacon's eyes glint, soft black like the sky. "Revenge isn't wrong," he says. "It's just the balance of the world."

The pastor in my church back home taught us that an eye for an eye makes the world blind. Apparently, Deacon thinks differently. He stabs out the cigarette against the empty package. His hands come around my waist, almost touching over my spine.

Holding me tight.

I squirm, but I can't get free. His cock hardens, filling me once more. He's an animal. A gentle, brutal beast, and I'm afraid I'll fall for him.

"If you hit back hard enough, no one ever hits you again," he says. "And if you can't, find someone who can."

I go still. There's no point in fighting. His brow is creased, dark eyes fixed to mine. His cock twitches inside my pussy.

"Take it out," I whisper.

"No," he says.

I gasp. He spits into his hand and pushes it between us, finding my clit. Electricity hums between us. I could shake my head like he told me, but I don't. Maybe he'll listen if I do, maybe he won't.

But it's a comfort I have in the back of my mind, like a weak collar around a dog's neck. So long as the dog wants to be restrained, it's obedient.

He breathes out harshly. "Come on my cock, sweetheart."

I start riding him, my head falling to the side. He gathers my hair, bunching the curls in his fists. His eyes shift behind me. I turn and slow, entranced by the sight of us in the mirror.

My body is beautiful. My waist dips in, his hand on it, and my hips widen, full like an erotic painting.

"Lean into me," he orders.

Transfixed, I let him pull me against his chest. We both gaze at our tangled bodies. Flushed, I let my eyes slip down my arched spine to where my pussy is visible. It's wet, stretched around his cock. It's the prettiest, filthiest thing I've ever seen, and he can't tear his eyes from it.

The darkness of the room falls away.

The horror of his past melts.

It's just me and him, bodies fused together. The firelight sheds an orange glow over us. The chains on my hips glitter as I rise and fall, watching my body pull him in and let him slide out, glistening with my arousal.

My arms go around his neck. He circles my clit with his finger, and his other hand goes from my waist to my lower belly and applies pressure. A tight coil of need springs free. There's a hot ache that pushes right over the edge, and I cry out, my voice echoing in the room.

"God, girl, fucking come on me," he says, jaw tight.

I pump hard, pleasure twisting my spine. He holds me upright, hips still rutting into me. A vein stands out in the side of his neck. His collarbones are flushed as his body tenses. Then, he swears softly, and I feel him pump more cum into my pussy.

His lids flicker. My pleasure dies away, leaving me glowing.

"Pull off slowly," he murmurs. "I want to watch."

He's filthy, and he makes me want things I can't speak aloud. Humiliated, I let him lift me off his cock, and we both watch as he slips out. My pussy is flushed and swollen. His cock is drenched in what we did together.

I cling to him. "Kiss me?"

I didn't mean to voice that out loud, but now that my head is clear from orgasm and he's slowly softening, there's a cold dread in my chest. He flips me onto my side and pulls me against his chest.

His mouth finds mine. His kisses burn my lips and tongue. Reverent, generous. The same hands that know how to kill wind into my hair and hold my throat.

Dimly, I hear him tell me all the things I want to hear. That I'm beautiful, obedient, that I belong to him.

I don't know if those things are true, but after the way he fucked me, I need to hear them.

My heart is open.

He could break it if he wanted.

But I don't pull away because he knows what I need. He doesn't hold back his affection. My body is kissed, stroked, praised, and held until I forget everything. Until the stars flicker out as my eyes shut.

I don't want to float away in them tonight. For tonight, I'm safe down here on Earth.

# CHAPTER TWENTY-EIGHT
# DEACON

She's fast asleep when I get out of bed. It's the weekend, finally, and the ranch is quiet. The wranglers will have already taken care of chores—it's almost eight. I need to get my ass outside and pull my weight.

She doesn't stir when I roll her on her side and clip the leash to the hook above her clit. I'll leave the chastity strap off so she can shower and use the toilet, but when she's done, she gets it locked on for the rest of the day.

I kiss her forehead and clip the leash onto the bed and lock both ends. She can get to the bathroom easily but no further.

As I descend the stairs, I mull over yesterday night. I've always been careful when it comes to BDSM. I follow the rules because I like them, and they're there for a reason. But in a situation as complex as Freya's, they've become something of a shield. I'd rather she think I'm just being kinky than what I'm actually doing—keeping her safe.

Something is off with Aiden, beyond just being abusive. I can't put my finger on it.

He's fucking weird about Freya.

That's why I won't let her take her little bleeding heart back to his house. Whatever Bittern's got going on, he'll have to handle it himself. If I need to tie her up in the name of kink to keep her safe, I'm happy to do that.

It's a win-win situation.

In the barn, I saddle up Bones. My mind turns over the weird case of Aiden Hatfield the entire time I'm out working. When I get back, I let Bones out into the paddock on the east side and walk back to the house. When I open the door, I hear a faint yapping.

In the living room, Stu is awake. He's rolling around on the carpet in his kennel like he's got an itch. I scoop him up and bring the collapsable pen outside so he can grub around in the grass for a while. It's a little chilly but not too cold for him yet.

I wash my hands in the kitchen, knock the mud off my boots, and head upstairs. When I push open the door, she's awake.

And she's scowling.

Her hair is tousled, she's still naked, but she's got the blanket pulled up over her breasts. The silver chain trails up and disappears beneath it. I shut the door, and her eyes flick up, pale blue in the morning light pouring through the window.

"I can't believe you," she whispers.

"I said you weren't leaving this ranch, and I meant it," I say, crossing the room and sitting on the edge of the bed. "I need you to trust me on this one."

I lean in, meaning to kiss her. She tilts her head. The air crackles. I know we're both thinking about last night. I will be for a long time. It was the kind of intimacy I've only longed for but never experienced until now.

I kiss her. She lets me, parting her lips. We break apart.

"Fine," she whispers. "I'll do whatever this is, but you have to promise me something."

"Anything."

She dips her head, brow touching my chin. "Save Bittern."

I have no plan, no idea where I go from here with the Hatfields, but I can't deny her anything.

"I swear," I say. "In return, you be a good girl and listen to me."

She bites her lip, worrying it. "Fine."

I kiss her temple and pull back the sheets to unlock the chain. When I pick her up, she wraps her arms around my neck. It hurts my chest, but I don't know why. Maybe because it's the first time she's trusted anybody enough to wrap her arms around them unprompted.

We shower together. I get on my knees and wash the metal strands of the harness. It sits beautifully on her full hips, leaving no marks on her skin. She doesn't move away when I lift one knee over my shoulder and put my mouth on her pussy.

Instead, she welcomes it. She leans against the wall and runs her fingers through my hair.

She strokes my jaw, my neck. Little moans echo in the shower stall. I lick her pussy until I feel her thigh tighten against my jaw. Her knuckles go white, nails digging into my skin.

When she comes, I push my tongue inside her pussy to feel her pleasure like a heartbeat.

I don't fuck her. It's not the right time. Instead, I dry her off carefully and have her stand while I clip the strap between her thighs. To my surprise, she doesn't say a word about it. She likes this game.

I get her bra from the dresser and one of my flannels. It's warm inside, but I know she gets cold easily, so I pull a pair of tall socks up her legs. It's no burden for me—there's nothing sexier than seeing Freya in a pair of thigh highs. Before I get up, I have to think about the dumbest shit I can to make my dick calm down.

"You hungry?"

She doesn't move, arms wrapped around her body. My heart melts. She looks so lost and unsure.

"What's wrong?"

Her chin trembles. "My insects," she whispers. "My butterflies and moths."

I pick her up and lift her into my lap.

"What's wrong? You want them, I'll go get them for you," I say. "I'll break in and get them while Aiden's out."

She shakes her head, lashes wet. "No, it's all gone. Aiden got mad and smashed it. I know it's silly, but it took me so many years to build that."

I don't speak. There's an ugly, violent thing in my chest.

"I think that...broke my heart a little bit," she whispers. "I can't get over it."

Hand on her head, I hold her tight. Her body shakes, her tears bleeding through my shirt. I hope my heart sounds even to her, because inside, rage like I've never felt pours through me. It's not silly. It's devastating.

Some things are sacred. This innocent little thing that brought her so much joy is one of those things.

I can't fix this, but I can make sure Aiden pays.

I brush the hair from her temple. "You cry it out if you need to, sweetheart," I say. "Then, let's get dressed. I have something upstairs I want you to see."

She lifts her tear-stained face. "Upstairs? We are upstairs."

"There's an attic."

She wipes her face, brows creased, and sinks back against my chest. Her tears slow. Her body melts into me, and I feel her trust emerge. It's like an animal crawling out of a cave, blinking in the sun, ready to shoot back inside at any second.

Trust, love—these things take time, but we'll get there in the end.

# CHAPTER TWENTY-NINE
# FREYA

I'm shattered, but it puts a few pieces of my heart back together when he holds me and lets me cry into his chest. Nobody but Deacon has ever held me while I cried.

Outside, I hear the wind pick up. The weather is about to change. It flips the leaves the way it does back home, showing their pale undersides in a ripple. His heart beats faster than normal, beneath my ear. I count it, taking a breath every three beats until the tears slow.

He doesn't tell me it's silly to grieve for my collection.

I think I misjudged him. He's not like Aiden at all. Yes, he's big and strong and rough, but in Deacon's case, that's not a bad thing. He seems to have the darker side of himself under control.

I think that's alright. I think there are different kinds of men like him, and they're not all bad like Aiden.

Sticky from tears, I peel my face off his shirt. He clears his throat and turns me in his lap, shifting my legs apart to wrap around his waist. His hand comes up, and I don't flinch.

He wipes my face with the side of his tattooed finger. How many times has Aiden flicked me in that same spot? I don't know, but I do know now that Deacon would never ever use his hands to hurt me.

He lifts me to my feet. "Let's go," he says.

I nod, and he weaves his fingers through mine. We go into the hall, but instead of turning at the staircase, he opens the door to reveal a set of dark wooden steps leading up into an airy room. It's not like any attics I've been in before. The air smells faintly of fresh paint, and there's no mustiness.

My breath catches as we ascend into the attic. It's huge, with a tall, peaked ceiling with a heavy central beam. There are four panels of skylight on either side, letting in the gray sky overhead.

It's what's inside that drags me back down to Earth. At the far side of the room is a vast, plush couch, and behind it runs a wall of empty bookshelves. There's a desk to the right, huge and stacked with empty collection cases. Above it are rows of felt-bound journals.

I step into the center of the room, speechless. I'm dimly aware of the soft rug under my bare feet as I turn in circles.

Finally, I stop. There's a lump in my throat when I meet his eyes.

"Do you like it?" he asks.

My face crumples, and I nod, tears slipping out. He's beside me in a second. His arms go around me, pulling me into the safety of his broad chest.

His hand strokes down my hair. "This is your space," he says. "Just for you, sweetheart."

I can't conceptualize that kind of autonomy. I close my eyes and let him stroke my hair. We have such a long way to go, but I'm starting to think there's more to him than I thought.

Nobody but Deacon has ever given me anything, not unless I count the bugs Bittern brought me. Those were sweet, and they meant a lot, but it's not the same thing as Deacon learning what I enjoy and bringing it to life.

"I can't get back your collection," he says, tucking my hair behind my ear. "But when it's summer again, you can start a new one."

"Thank you." The word slips out, fragile.

He looks at me for a long time. Then, he taps my chin with the side of his finger. "I've got chores," he says. "I'll let you get to poking around."

He's gone, boots ringing down the stairs and hall. I cross the room and lean over the couch to look out the window. He walks down the driveway, his coat and hat on. I know it's cold, although it never seems to bother him.

While I long for the mild winters of the south, I think he likes the sharp cold of the winter out west.

He disappears into the barn. A moment later, he appears on Bones. They linger in the yard for a second as Andy appears. They both talk for a few moments, then Bones circles, and they head off to the western pasture.

Awed, I traipse around the room, inspecting everything—sanded and glossed framing, painted walls, dark wood flooring. A rug the same deep blue as the ones downstairs. A black stone mantel. The enormous oak wood desk that surely wasn't purchased in the last few days, stacked with empty collection cases. The right kind, to keep the moisture out and the specimens protected.

I turn. In the far corner sits a chest that comes to mid-thigh. Curious, I cross the room and unlatch it, dragging the heavy lid open.

My stomach swoops.

It's full to the brim. There are books, still tied up in gift wrapping. I pick one up and undo the ribbon, turning over a collection of fairy tales. Underneath it is a bolt of pink dotted fabric, the receipt still pinned to it. I set the book aside and pick it up, leaning in to look at the purchase date.

*Months* ago.

My stomach is tight, my heart fluttering. I set the pink dotted fabric down and tuck the receipt away, as if that will hide the realization I'm having.

He's been buying things for me since before we officially met. For weeks—months. When I piece that together with the knowledge that he lied the day we met and said the highway was closed...well, I can only draw one conclusion from that.

Deacon Ryder will do what it takes to get what he wants.

My eyes come back into focus, fixing on the opposite wall. My stomach turns over. I get up and walk across, laying my fingertips on the paint. It's the same exact shade as the fern-green I always wear. It's my favorite color, the same rich shade of the pines in the deepest parts of the Appalachian Mountains.

He has such an attention to detail. It's gentle, like his touch.

My hands are unsteady as I close the lid, not interested in going through the rest of the contents. I know two things for certain now.

One—Deacon Ryder is a damn psycho.

Two—I'm glad he's on my side.

I go downstairs. He's still outside, the yard empty. I check the clock—it's almost nine. I'm listless, shaken up by the attic room and unsure why I feel like I'm being pulled toward him like a magnet. I should run, but I can't.

Not after seeing that room.

So, I open the fridge and start taking stock of what I can make for dinner. It's absurd. He kidnapped me, and now he made it clear I can't leave. And here I am, cutting chicken into strips and heating oil on the stove, cooking for him like he's my man.

My brows crease in a frown. The golden oil starts to bubble on the bottom.

It's bothering me that I don't mind.

Maybe Deacon Ryder is my man, whether I like it or not.

Wrathfully, I batter the chicken and drop it into the oil. While it cooks, I dig under the cabinets until I find a waffle maker. My stomach craves comfort, so I make crispy waffles, fried chicken, and drag a jug of maple syrup up from the pantry.

He comes in as everything finishes cooking. It's almost twelve, later than usual, because it took me a while to locate the things I needed. The food is piled on a platter on the table and plates are set out.

Quickly so he doesn't notice, I give him a once-over. Right away, I have butterflies again. God, he looks good, all tall and sexy and dirty from being outside, sleeves pushed up, ink out, broad arms crossed over his chest.

He leans in the doorway. "You don't have to cook for me."

Wordlessly, I pull out his chair. His forehead creases, but he washes his hands and sits. I sink beside him, filling our plates before he can speak. When I look up, he's leaning back in his chair, eyes on me, like he'll wait all night for me to be ready to speak.

I fold my hands in my lap.

"How long have you been buying me things?" I ask.

My voice is fragile.

"Since I saw you," he says. "Outside the café, in the alley."

"When was that?"

He thinks about it for a moment. "Late winter."

"Why?"

A gust of wind whistles against the house. It rattles the bolted shutters. I don't need to look outside at the underbelly of the leaves to know there's a storm coming.

"You were always meant for me, no question," he says, voice a low rumble. He has a way of looking at me, head tilted down but eyes lifted. It helps me to not feel like I'm in his spotlight.

"You know my options are...limited," I manage.

He nods.

"And you took advantage of that." My tone isn't accusatory. I keep it plain, laying it all out.

"I know," he says.

"Is this what you do?" I burst out. "Just see women you like and stalk them until they have no other options?"

"Just you." His voice is firm. "Only you make me act this way, sweetheart."

My cheeks are hot. I stare down at the table.

"Hey, look at me for a minute," he says, voice dropping.

Slowly, I drag my eyes up. He's still looking at me with that patient expression.

"I won't lie and say I haven't been around," he says. "But I want you, bottom line. I have for months, and I'm tired of sitting on my ass about it. You're it for me, sweetheart."

He says it with total conviction. A chill moves down my spine and the shutters rattle outside. Inside, it's warm and I'm not afraid for the first time in my life. I don't know why. Annoyed, maybe, but not scared.

I should run from him again, but I won't, and the reason became clear to me today.

The attic.

Nobody has ever read me so well that they could put together a room of everything I love. Nobody else understands my need to have a space that's mine, where I don't have to listen for footsteps or angry voices.

My hands twist in my lap, knuckles white.

I'm safe now, but I need to know how much safety costs. That's the part we only just brushed on when we talked about contracts and kink and ownership before I ran. In part, I ran because of Bittern, but deep down, I know I also ran from him.

"Let's eat," he says.

Obediently, I cut my fried chicken, dip it in gravy, and take a bite. He gets to eating like he's not bothered by anything. The wind whistles, shrieking.

"Will it storm today?" I ask.

He shakes his head. "Not until tomorrow morning."

"How do you know?" I ask.

"I checked the weather."

For some reason, I thought he was going to say he'd lived in Montana all his life and knew it like the back of his hand. I've been so cut off with nothing but my flip phone and no access to a computer, I forgot the internet exists.

"Oh, that makes sense," I say.

His plate is clean before I'm five bites in. He sits back, wiping his hands on his napkin. "I've never had food as good as what you cook, sweetheart. Worth kidnapping you for."

I gasp. He gives me that lopsided smile as he gets up.

"I'm gonna work you over and work you out tonight," he says. "So you rest up today while I batten down the hatches for the storm tomorrow."

He doesn't give me time to reply. He just kisses the top of my head. His touch burns for a half second. A hand on my shoulder, his mouth on my hair. Then, he's gone, striding down the hall is his big, steel-toe boots that don't scare me anymore.

I stare at the wall for a long time. I'm not shaken up by what he's promised to do to me tonight. No, I'm shaken up because nobody has ever kissed me like that.

A brush of his lips as he passes by.

Casual…like maybe he loves me.

# CHAPTER THIRTY
## DEACON

After chores are done and the ranch is locked down for the night, I take her upstairs to the bedroom. She gets a cup of tea because I want her to think clearly. I have a splash of whiskey in the bottom of a glass.

I flick on the fire. "There are some clothes in our dresser."

Her eyes flick up, like she wants to call me out for saying *our* dresser instead of my dresser. But she sorts through the bottom drawer until she finds a slip and disappears into the bathroom to get undressed for bed. I strip and pull on my sweats and sink down into the chair before the fire.

The door opens. I glance up.

*Goddamn.*

Her dark hair flows down her back, the black silk slip dripping off her body. I hold out my hand, and she comes. Something shifted in the attic, as I hoped it would. There's an openness to her that wasn't there before.

I'm prying her walls apart.

Reeling her out of the world in her head.

Maybe I can give her a reality worth living in.

I set my drink aside and pull her between my knees. I run my palm up to the lace hem, brushing it just high enough to see the chastity belt glittering beneath.

I'm hard, but I can wait.

I run my palms down and up again. Her thighs curve so beautifully, tapering up above her waist. The rise and fall of her body beneath my hands makes my brain buzz.

She feels like something I'm too rough to own but too far gone to give up.

I've always lived in the real world. The violence, the pain. She feels like a breath of new air, like I caught a rare, beautiful bird in my trap, and I'm so in love, I can't give it up.

I am in love.

For a long time, I felt obsession and hunger. I think under it, there was always love. It's the only thing that explains what I feel. It burns like fire, like torture. It hurts too much to be just lust.

I run one hand to the inside of her thighs. Her head falls to the side, her lids closing. Lashes dark as coal rest against her cheeks.

I want her, forever. Nightly, daily. In every way, in every moment.

"Open your legs for me," I say, voice hushed.

She eases them apart, just enough so I can undo the strap. I set it aside and dip my fingers into her sex. Soft wetness envelopes my fingertips. A moan works its way out of her. I slide in deeper, to my middle knuckle.

And she drips. Fuck, she drips down my hand.

I bend in, drawing my wet hand from her body, and bite her thigh. It sinks beneath my teeth. She gasps, her hand falling on my hair and fisting. I grip her wrists, putting them both behind her back, and hold them there.

I release the soft flesh of her thigh. She whimpers. Head empty, I lick over the mark I left and give her another, biting into the silky skin. It's not hard enough to break it but hard enough to make my pupils blow and my head buzz. I drag my mouth away from her and pick her up, carrying her to the bed.

She gasps, hair spread out, as she falls back.

This is what I need from her tonight—hot, dark lust.

She cries out when my teeth sink into the delicate skin of her inner thigh. Her spine arches off the bed. I keep her down with a hand between her breasts.

"No, you take it," I breathe. "You wanted it, little whore, you take it."

She moans, whimpering.

I slap the curve of her ass. "What do you call me?"

Her lips part. "Yes, daddy."

I drag my tongue over the bite mark, up to her cunt. It's soaked. I run my nose over it, dipping my tongue into her cunt briefly. She's sweet, like nothing I've ever had before. I need her pussy all over my face, in my skin, running down the back of my throat.

"Take your clothes off and lay in the middle of the bed," I whisper, mouth still on her pussy. "On your stomach, arms behind your back."

My tongue drags over her soaked cunt, and I withdraw. I don't look over my shoulder to make sure she's obedient. I know she is.

In the dresser, I remove three lengths of soft black rope, shears, and a velvet bag. When I return to the bed, she's laid out in the center, her curvy ass on display. I take a step to the side, taking in the sight of her cunt tucked between her thighs. It's bare, lightly flushed, dewy with arousal.

My cock is heavy in my pants, so sensitive that I feel every step I take. When I woke up this morning, I got off in the shower, but seeing her in that slip makes me feel like I haven't come in weeks.

I brace my knee on the bed. She flips her head to the side, dark eyes wide.

"Will it hurt?" she whispers.

"No," I say. "Not this."

I take the rope and start binding her arms behind her back. This is a gentle tie, running up her arms with triple lengths at each anchor point. When it's done, it crisscrosses down her arms and stabilizes over her chest around her breasts. I slip my hand beneath and ease her up so she's sitting on her heels. Her soft curls fall down her back, warm in my hands as I gather them up and braid them down her back.

In the velvet bag is a handful of little black roses made of silk. One by one, I work them into her braid, tucking the last behind her ear. She keeps quiet, being such an obedient girl for me. When I'm done, I lean in to kiss her nape. A shiver goes down her spine.

"Why put flowers in my hair?" she whispers.

"Because I'm about to give you the most disrespectful fucking you've ever had, and I want you to feel beautiful for it," I say. "Remember when you're gasping for air and begging like a whore that I can be gentle."

A soft blush moves over her cheeks. I kiss the underside of her jaw, where her skin is like silk.

"Stay here," I say. "Don't move."

She nods once, breathless. I go to the fireplace and shut it off, turning the lamp beside it on. Then, I draw the metal cover over it and reach into the opening between it and the wall. When I built this house, my room was designed to turn into a playroom if needed. Tonight, I need it.

I draw the mirrors from both sides and latch them in the middle. They come up to my waist and go all the way to the floor, covering the entire hearth. From the closet, I take a kneeler and set it out.

On the bed, I pick her naked body up and carry her to the kneeler. Her brows rise, and her lips part as I set her down on it, facing the mirror.

Fuck—she's beautiful.

Arms are tucked behind her back, little curls brushing her neck, round breasts flushed with arousal. The chastity belt glitters on her full hips like starlight. I kneel behind her and take something from my pocket.

"Lean over," I tell her.

She nods. I shake my head.

"What do you call me?"

She squirms slightly. "Yes, daddy," she says, voice rasping.

"Good girl," I say, pressing on her nape and balancing her weight to help her lean over until her forehead is an inch over the floor. "Next time you forget, you'll be punished. Understood?"

I hear her gulp. "Yes, daddy."

"Good. You'll be rewarded for listening."

"Yes, daddy."

I leave her there, struggling to keep still. In the dresser, I take out a dildo, a plug, and a bottle of lube. Tonight, we're going to push limits. She has her safeword and she knows how to use it.

When I return, I kneel behind her. Her body shivers as I run my palm over her hip, stroking her curves. I set the items down, wet my fingers, and find her asshole.

She tightens. I think she's going to protest. Then, she moans, and her muscles relax enough that I can dip the very tip of my finger in. That surprises me. I didn't think Freya would be interested in anal, or I would have introduced it before tonight. But the longer I play with her ass, the more relaxed she gets.

I pour the lube over my fingers and stroke circles around her sensitive opening. With my other hand, I find her pussy. My cock throbs against my zipper. Her cunt is soft, soaked, and my fingers slip right in. She whimpers as I find her G-spot and start circling my finger, tapping gently.

"God," she bursts out.

I pick up the plug and start working it over her asshole.

"Tell me how good it feels, little cumslut," I pant.

She gasps, turning her head to the other side. Her dark eyes flash, dreamy with desire.

"It's so good," she moans, hips working.

"Tell me," I order, voice going harsh. "What feels good?"

She whines. "Your fingers...feel so good in my pussy, daddy."

"Ride back on them," I say, panting from how badly I want to just take my cock out and sink into her. She's soaked, slippery, and there's a faint sweet scent that has me feral.

She obeys, fucking back onto my fingers. The plug slips into her ass, and she shudders. A little burst of wetness drips down my hand, like she squirted without coming.

That scent hits me like a ton of bricks. My spine tingles. My head goes blank. When we had that conversation about her cycle, I did some independent research. I found out a lot of interesting things.

And right now, I'm pretty damn sure she's ovulating.

I pull my fingers out and put them in my mouth. My senses heighten. Her sweet taste spreads over my tongue, laced with something...some kind of feral signal I can read on a deeper level.

I want this.

God, I fucking need this.

Up until now, we've fucked and haphazardly tried to avoid pregnancy. Maybe that's a stretch, but I've never tried to get her pregnant.

That changes tonight.

My blood pounds. Feral need surges through my veins, making me so hard, it aches. My cock needs to be inside her, to feel her give in under me. I'm breathing hard, my fingers still circling the plug in her asshole. I want to be in her ass, but I *need* to be in her pussy.

I slide my wet fingers up her back and wrap her braid around my fist. It stabilizes her so I can unzip my pants and unleash my cock. I groan, the relief enormous.

"You gonna be a good girl and take daddy's cock?" I murmur.

"Yes," she gasps. "Please."

My eyes are glued to the plug glittering in her asshole. Below it, her pussy is soaked, swollen. Shifting my hips, I get closer. The flushed head of my cock touches her entrance.

God, she's like heaven. Hot, tight, inviting.

She bucks, but I keep her pinned. She's not going anywhere until this is done. I shift my hips in so she's sitting in my lap instead of on her heels. My cock slides in quickly, until I'm seated inside. Her inner muscles pulse, gripping me.

"Daddy," she gasps.

I tighten my fist in her hair, pressing her cheek to the floor. "Tell me what you feel," I grit out, pumping my hips.

"I feel full," she manages. "So tight."

"Good?"

"Yes, daddy," she says, voice broken.

I prop my free hand on the floor and start fucking deep. The smooth, roundness of her cervix touches the head of my cock as I do. I'm careful not to hurt her, but I don't back down. She likes pain, likes being helpless. I fuck her hard, knowing she's getting both.

My orgasm comes fast, tingling down my spine, erupting in my groin. I push my cock as deeply as I can into her, keeping the head on her cervix.

Just the thought of getting her pregnant is enough to push me over the edge.

My vision blurs. I see a flash of her bent over in front of me. I see myself crouched over her like an animal.

This is my wife. The mother of my babies.

The other half of my heart.

Tonight is the first night of our lives together. After the attic, she knows what I feel. She knows what I'll do to get her and keep her. My mask is off and so is hers. She might have been innocent when I met her, but I know she's filthy enough to match my needs and then some.

We're perfect together. Meant to be.

I come, pleasure making my vision flash. My hips pump in tiny movements, pushing my cum deeper as it spills into her body. I gasp, sweat trickling down my chest and falling onto her naked back.

"That's good," I murmur. "You're taking it so well for me, sweetheart."

She moans, the sound dreamy. I think she's slipping into subspace. That's perfect for what I want to do to her next.

Slowly, I drag my cock from her. "Stay where you are."

She doesn't move as I get to my feet and strip my clothes off. I glance at the mirror. My cock is still hard, stained with my cum and her arousal. It's different, almost slick. I swipe my finger down my cock and lick it clean.

She tastes so good, I can't do anything but grit my teeth so I don't get down and eat our cum out of her. No, that needs to stay put. Instead, I go to the dresser and get an attachment and the chastity strap. She's in the same position when I return.

Such a good fucking girl. I stroke her back and give her ass a little spank that makes her shiver.

I kneel behind her again. "Arch your back and spread your pussy for me."

She obeys, showing me her swollen cunt. I take out the short dildo and slide it into the strap. The strap clips into the harness, the dildo filling the entrance of her pussy, keeping my cum plugged inside her. I snap the strap into place. Now, the only part of her available to me is her asshole.

I'm gonna use it tonight. And she'll take it.

I lift her up, turning her around to face me. Her thighs wrap around my waist, her eyes enormous. I bend in, kissing her open mouth. She moans, her body limp and surrendered in my arms.

"What are you doing?" she gasps as we break apart.

I nuzzle her neck. "Making you mine."

# CHAPTER THIRTY-ONE
# FREYA

---

He strokes back a bit of flyaway hair. His inked up arms are so strong around my body. I'm safe, cherished. Degraded, but in the sweetest way possible.

I want more.

He clears his throat. "Let's talk your safeword. Do you want to keep using lights?"

"Lights?"

"Red, yellow, green," he says, hand drifting around my ass. My hips twitch as he touches the plug, circling it. "Green means keeping going. Yellow means you're reaching your limits. Red means everything stops."

I think it over. It's simple, easy to remember if I get overwhelmed.

"Yes," I say. His brow crooks. "Daddy."

He taps my chin. "Good girl. You're learning quickly. Alright, I want you back on the kneeler. Face the mirror."

He guides me to it, helping me sink back onto my knees. In the mirror, I'm beautiful. My face is flushed from pleasure, my hair braided with flowers. I'm not the scared girl I've always been.

Tonight, I'm safe, breathtaking, and pleasured.

He kneels behind me. Our eyes meet in the mirror. I exhale as he cups my right breast and runs his thumb over it, back and forth.

"How do you get me to stop?" he asks, voice rasping.

"Say red," I say.

"Good girl," he says. His hand leaves my breast, and he starts untying the ropes. They were firm, not cutting off my circulation, but it feels good to roll my shoulders as they fall away. He kisses my spine. My head lolls to the side.

I'm so ready to be his tonight.

He gets up to put the rope away. My pussy aches, clenching around the dildo. That makes me grip the one in my ass too. Pleasure rides through me in waves.

God, I want to come so badly.

I hear him open the dresser again. Then, he kneels behind me, easing me back to sit on his thighs. His body is warm and stable beneath mine. He's strong, he's fierce, but he's not cruel. I didn't know that combination was possible. It makes me fall into him, to trust him. He slides his palms over my waist, one hand resting on the chastity belt over my pussy.

"I want you to clean us off my cock with your mouth," he says.

My stomach flips.

"Yes, daddy," I whisper.

That word comes so easily now. Maybe because he's earning it. He puts his hand on my upper spine and bends me over again. The floor fills my vision. My spine arches so I'm spread open. The dildo plugging my pussy is snug from this angle.

He kisses down my spine. Then, I feel his hot mouth close over the plug in my ass as he pulls it from me with his teeth, spitting it to the side.

God, he's awful. Just filthy.

Palms to the floor, I keep still. He kisses the backs of my thighs, around the chastity strap covering my sex. Then, I hear the lube uncap. Something cold touches my asshole. I jump, turning my head.

"Eyes ahead, sweetheart," he murmurs. "Trust me."

I drag my eyes back, but my body blocks me from seeing what he's doing to me. Lube drizzles over my asshole, followed by an intense pressure that makes me bite my lip. God, I had no idea I'd love being touched there so much. It drives me crazy, especially because he hasn't let me come yet.

He pushes the tip of whatever he's holding into me. My eyes roll back and shut.

"Fuck, sweetheart, you're taking that so well," he rasps.

My pussy throbs. My head is completely empty. All I want is to please him. I keep still with my eyes shut as he eases the toy into me. My ass clenches down around it, and I can tell it's metal. For a second, I wonder if he put that fence stake in me, but then I remember this toy has a bulb on the tip.

"What is that?" I gasp.

"Anal hook," he says. "Shift on your hands and knees, lift your head, keep your back straight."

Wait...what?

Cowed, I do as he says, but my mouth is dry. He takes my braid in his hand, and it feels like he's fastening something to it.

"Shift to the side but keep your back straight," he says. "Look in the mirror."

He guides my body, keeping my chin up with his fingers. I'm three quarters turned from the mirror when he stops me. Carefully, he turns my head so I can see myself.

My toes curl. A deep red blush stains my face.

There's a steel hook in my ass with a handle that comes up to the middle of my back. Looped through the handle is a canvas strap anchored to my braid.

It makes sense that he's holding my head; if I dropped it, I'd feel the stretch.

I gulp. I think that's the point.

He brings his hand down on my ass, spanking hard enough to sting. I whimper, so wet, I feel myself drip around the chastity belt.

"Look at you," he breathes. "Daddy's little whore, plugged in every hole."

I'm blushing so hard, my ears roar. He rises, circling to stand in front of me. His cock hangs inches from my face, still soaked with our cum. He brushes a wisp of hair behind my ear. I look up, meeting his dark eyes.

"Do you want to come?" he asks.

"Yes, daddy," I gasp. "Please."

"Then put my cock in your mouth and suck it like you mean it," he orders.

God, I love it when he's harsh in the bedroom. It's not scary. No, it's like a secret between us, a little contract where he can let the animal inside out, and afterwards, I get spoiled when he's done.

Obediently, I open my mouth. He pushes his cock between my lips. Sweet and salt mingle on my tongue. He's a little higher than I can reach properly. I lean forward and freeze as the bulb in my ass stretches.

My pussy clenches.

That feels...amazing.

I bob my head again, taking him to the back of my throat. A moan escapes around his cock. He strokes my head.

"Eyes on me, sweetheart," he rumbles. "I want to watch you suck me and fuck your own ass."

I force my eyes to his. God, he's gorgeous. So big, broad, and covered in tattoos. Hungry, I roll my tongue around the head of his cock, playing with the piercings and the sensitive underside.

"You're such a slut," he gasps, vein standing out in his inked-up neck.

I suck, dipping my head. The bulb fucks me as my head bobs down and releases when I come back up. The sensation is overwhelming, but I can't stop. I don't want to escape it.

The warm skin of his cock and the smooth metal of his piercings push me closer to the edge. My thighs shudder with that hot itch that signals an orgasm is growing deep in my pussy, still filled with the dildo he locked there.

He looks back down. Our eyes meet.

I love being submissive to him in our bedroom. At first, this dynamic scared me, but now, I understand it's his way of caring for me and my way of being brave enough to let myself be cared for.

I'll never get enough of it.

Between the dildo filling my pussy, his pierced cock in my mouth, and the hook stretching my pussy every time I bob my head, I'm done for.

My orgasm hits me so hard, my mouth falls open. Heat ripples through me. Pleasure is a clear, strong force that rips me apart.

I shake, the bulb in my ass stretching me deliciously. When my orgasm ebbs, he's backing up a few steps. There's a dangerous glint in his dark eyes.

"Crawl to me," he says.

My limbs are unsteady, but I manage to make the few feet to him. He leans over me. "Put that tongue out," he orders.

My lips shake as they part, and I push my tongue out. I see a flicker of approval. Then, slowly, he spits from where he stands, and it falls onto my tongue. A ripple of shock starts, but it's not as strong as the arousal that follows. Without thinking, I swallow. He reaches down, wiping my lower lip. His fingers hover over my mouth.

"Good girl. Now, suck my fingers, cumslut," he orders.

I do as he says, sucking his two fingers like I sucked his cock. Then, he slides them out and circles my body. I feel him unstrap the hook from my braid. Dimly, I'm aware of him working the bulb from my ass. Then, a click, and cold wetness drizzles in its place.

He picks me up, turning me so we're sideways before the mirror. My orgasm left me so weak. His broad body sinks down, kneeling behind me. The hard, tattooed muscles of his arm and chest ripple as he jerks his cock with powerful strokes.

"Do you like fucking your own ass while you get me off with your mouth?" he rasps.

"Yes, daddy," I blurt out.

He spanks me again. I moan, and from the corner of my eye, I see him guide his cock to my ass. Should I beg for mercy? Or are we past that? I've taken a plug and a hook there tonight. I'm loose. If he's gentle, I can take him.

The head of his cock is warm and hard. It presses to my asshole, working inside. I can do this—I close my eyes and exhale. The head slips in, the piercings rubbing perfectly inside me. My eyes flutter open. God, that feels so perfect.

"Good girl, sweetheart," he soothes, stroking down my side. "Look at that pretty little asshole, taking my cock. What are you?"

I hesitate, unsure what he wants. What am I? Or what am I to him? Or what am I becoming with him?

Maybe I'm overthinking this. Maybe my mind is running away with me. He presses his cock in, and this time, it hurts. But that's over in a second as he seats himself halfway inside.

"I don't understand," I whisper.

He pumps in, out, dragging the veins and piercings. Pleasure and a hint of pain erupt.

"Tell me," he orders.

"I'm yours," I gasp out. "Your whore."

He starts fucking hard, sliding his cock in and out. My knees are so weak that I sway. He feels it, and his arm goes around me, picking me up with his cock still inside me, and carries me to the bed.

"Face down, ass up," he says.

I obey, and he fucks. That's all I want. Here, I'm limp, torn apart by pleasure, by this new experience of submission. My weakness doesn't put me in danger with him. Instead, it somehow pulls us closer and makes me trust him more.

I feel him groan, my face pressed into the bed. His hand grips my braid, pinning me down. He swears under his breath, and his cock twitches. My empty mind buzzes at the pleasure of him coming in such an intimate part of my body.

He can have it. I never had a choice.

If I am the girl who wanted to live in the stars, he's the mountains down below. Together, we feel like that place where the heavens and the Earth meet.

Beautiful, perfect. Meant to exist.

I sink into the bed as he pulls himself from my body. Dimly, I realize we took another step together tonight. First, he taught me sex could feel good. Then, that it could be safe. Now, he's shown me it can be so intimate, I feel it in my heart.

My heart... I feel him in my heart.

He rolls me onto my back, smoothing my hair. His mouth presses to mine, then down my neck.

"Good girl. You're so perfect," he praises. "Let's get you in the bath, clean you up, get you in bed. You deserve to rest."

I whimper, eyes heavy. His weight leaves the bed, and I hear the bath running and smell the flowery soap. Then, I'm in his arms, and he's letting me sink into the hot water. He gets in with me, pulling me into his lap.

"Are you satisfied?" he murmurs, face raspy on my neck.

"Yes, daddy," I whisper, eyes closing.

# CHAPTER THIRTY-TWO
# DEACON

"I want something from you," I say.

She's in my arms, cheek against my chest. Steam makes her hair curl and skin dewy. When I speak, her eyes flutter open. They still have the same dreamy expression, but I can tell she's out of subspace.

"What?" she murmurs.

"I'm taking care of you from here on out," I say. "You obey me, and I'll keep you safe."

Her barely open eyes are thoughtful.

"It doesn't mean I control you the way you're used to being controlled," I say. "Every morning, I choose your clothes, choose what you eat, how to sexually satisfy you."

Her brows rise.

"We'll talk every week, go over what you liked and didn't like," I continue. "You can always safeword me if you don't like what I'm doing."

I don't know what I expected, but it isn't for her to stretch up and kiss my mouth. My body tingles. I touch her face as she draws back.

"Yes," she whispers.

"Yes?"

"You can have me, take care of me."

I always knew I'd find a way to get her to say those words, but I didn't anticipate how good it would feel to hear them out loud. I'm the luckiest man in the world. My fingers trail suds over her breasts, her smooth arms, her throat. Just touching her.

She's precious to me.

I'll spend the rest of my life making sure she knows it.

# CHAPTER THIRTY-THREE
# FREYA

I wake slowly. Stretching around the suffocating warmth draped over me. My eyes flutter open, and then they widen as everything floods back: the ropes, the hook, the mirror over the fireplace, below the engravings of the bear.

The agreement we made.

Slowly, I turn over to face him. His thick, tattooed arm is laying across my body. I try to wriggle out, but he grips my waist in his sleep and doesn't let go. He rumbles in his chest. His eyes are closed, but I can tell by the sound that he's slowly waking. I nestle deeper into his chest.

There's something hard pressing into my thigh. I lift the cover and peer down and quickly pull it back up. He's rock hard.

Before I can react, he pushes me onto my back. His eyes are open now, dark and sleepy. His stubbly face scrapes up my neck as he kisses the little dip beneath my ear.

"Spread your legs," he says, voice husky.

I pulse twice, checking my soreness. The ache is sweet, remote. He doesn't wait. No, he pushes my legs open and slides inside me. Our bodies sink together. I'm crushed under the heat of his body, the firm curve of his bicep against my cheek.

It doesn't take long for either of us. He plays with my clit, and I orgasm silently, biting my lip. His body responds with deep, short thrusts. At the last minute, I shove him back, and he comes on my inner thigh.

"No coming inside," I murmur.

We lay still, letting our breathing even. He brushes a strand of hair from my cheekbone. "Look out the window, sweetheart."

I turn and my stomach swoops. Outside, the world is covered in a few inches of snow, thick flakes still whirling from the sky. It's the middle of October, the trees barren now. I can see the hills for miles, dusted in white, hunkered down.

"It's so pretty," I whisper.

I glance over. He's looking at me with a strange expression. Heavy lids, like he's longing for something, like he's a million miles away. I roll back over, even though I'm dying to go look out. He rumbles as I snuggle up against his chest.

He brushes a kiss across my forehead. There's that new feeling again—safety.

Slowly, I become aware of something else—something I thought he just took care of. It's wide awake again, pressing into the inside of my left thigh.

"You're still hard," I whisper. "When does that slow down?"

His head falls back. "Sweetheart, I'll be eighty and still ready to go the minute I see you naked in my bed."

He's laughing, I'm smiling, but inside, all I hear is that he intends to be eighty and still sleeping with me. Trying to square that away is too much.

My fingers trial over his shoulder, where there's clearly a scar under the ink. "What happened here?"

The smile melts off his face. Maybe I shouldn't have said anything. It's just...he's made me open up, knows all about me, but I don't know anything about him except for the shocking piece of information he chose to drop the other night.

"Is it about what you did to get the farm?"

"Are you asking to hear the whole story?" he says, voice rough.

I nod, my thumb tracing his scar. "I want to know you. All of you."

"I ended up in the system because nobody knew who my biological parents were. My mother dropped me at a hospital," he says, eyes lowered. "There was a ranch that took me on as a foster kid, and the guy...he was a piece of shit. He had a piece of shit son. His wife liked me, always wanted two boys, so it was her idea to foster."

He pauses. I can tell he doesn't like recalling his past, so I stay quiet.

"Her husband, Phil, he, uh...could have been worse," he says. "He was an asshole, but he did adopt me. Anyway...I was grateful to be out of the foster system, and I tried to show Phil and Amie that by working hard, making a shit ton of cash for them."

He pushes himself up, leaning against the headboard. I lay my cheek on his thigh, gazing up at him.

"Their son, Henderson, didn't like that," he says. "We butted heads. Fought at school, fought over girls, fought over attention. It escalated when Phil got sick and died. Amie was gone by then too. He left the land to me and Henderson."

My eyes trail over the scar, remembering the first time we talked about this. "So Henderson stabbed you with the fence stake."

His jaw is hard, his eyes fixed out the window. "Everything just came to a head one night when we were about nineteen. We fought over this girl he liked. She was sleeping with me. Sorry, I don't mean to talk about this shit in front of you."

"I'm not jealous," I say.

Truthfully, I am, a little. But I know it's ridiculous to pretend he hasn't slept with other women before me.

"Are you sure you want to hear all this?" he asks.

I nod. "I think it's only fair."

He clears his throat. "Alright. We got into it one night. Henderson and I had gone out to fix the fence line. We argued, and he took one of the fence stakes and fucking stabbed me with it. He put one through my shoulder and one in my thigh. I think he was going for an artery."

The room is blanketed in silence. Outside, the wind whistles. I glance over, watching as flakes start swirling in the pale blue light.

"You didn't die," I whisper.

He shakes his head once. "I ripped the spike out of my shoulder, walked back to the house, and put it in the side of Henderson's head. Then, I burnt the house down with him in it."

My stomach tightens. I'm a little sick, like the floor is tossing.

"That's how you got Ryder Ranch," I whisper.

He nods. "I got it by killing the son of the man who took me in."

My tongue darts out to wet my dry lips. I push myself into a sitting position. His dark eyes are dead, disconnected, like pulling back into his shell is the only way he can say those words out loud.

I don't know what to feel.

"Did you want to?" I whisper.

He shakes his head. "In the moment, yes. I thought I was in love with this girl. We fought over who had the real birthright to the land. He was so fucking angry that Phil left half to me."

"What was your name before?"

He shrugs. "On the hospital records, I was John Williamson. There was a nurse who named me. Guess she wasn't all that creative. Phil had this prize barrel racer called Deacon, and I was his rider. He changed my name to Deacon Ryder when they adopted me."

"Henderson was angry they adopted you?"

"That was just one brick in a whole wall," Deacon says. "When he stabbed me, he said I stole everything, his land, his future. And he wasn't wrong. But he was an asshole first."

There's a long silence. His story changes things, for better and for worse. I never wanted to fall for a man with blood on his hands, but I swear, every time I look at him, my heart goes weak.

Deacon runs a hand over his face.

"I think...maybe the reason I'm so angry about the easement is about this," he says. "I killed my brother. I hated him, but he was my brother. If I let that land be used like that...I'd think it was all for nothing."

"Deacon," I say gently. "It sounds like he tried to kill you first."

He nods once. "All I've ever wanted was a home. Phil gave me that, and I killed his son. They were both assholes, but the point stands."

"Do you regret it?" My voice is barely a whisper.

"No," he says.

His words hang heavy. It's obvious he doesn't like talking about this. He's cagey. Slowly, like I'm approaching a big animal, I crawl onto his lap and settle my thighs around his hips. He touches my naked waist, encircling it with his broad hands.

"You're so beautiful," he says, low, like he's marveling to himself. "I don't want to go out for chores."

I touch his temple, where he has a few graying hairs.

"You scared me," I whisper. "At first."

He releases a sigh. "I know, sweetheart. I tried not to."

The words I never meant to say slip out. I know they'll cut him like a knife. Maybe they're necessary. It's hard to tell.

"You reminded me of Aiden," I say, voice shaking. "I'm trying hard to break out of this cycle. I don't want to be my mother, running from a man like him. I want a good future."

He winces before he picks up my hand and weaves his big fingers through mine.

"I'm trying to show you I'm not," he says.

My lashes are wet. A tear etches out. I cry so easily nowadays.

"I know you're not," I whisper, touching my temple. My fingers graze down over my chest. "I know that now."

The wind picks up. I glance over my shoulder at the snow swirling. He leans in, breath spilling hot as he kisses the side of my neck. I'm back, out of the cold in my mind, in his arms with the fire warm against my skin.

"The horses are hungry," he says. "Fuck me one more time, sweetheart. I'll make it quick."

Just like that, the door is shut. We both said our piece and neither of us walked away. Instead, I slip between the sheets with him and we work our pain out without saying a word.

# CHAPTER THIRTY-FOUR
## DEACON

I start setting out her things right away. I enjoy the caretaking aspect of being in a Dominant and submissive dynamic more than masochism, although I wouldn't turn down putting her over my knee and spanking that beautiful ass. But outside of that, I'm grounded by giving her what she needs, even when she doesn't understand.

It's my job to know her heart. To keep it, to protect it.

My life has been so chaotic. I find so much peace in this exchange of power and care. It's the same with bondage. It feels like the eye of the hurricane—a place to rest, to breathe, to feel together.

I set her clothes on the chair by the fireplace. Then, I write a note for her and set it on the sink. She's still asleep when I leave the bathroom and step into the hallway, shutting the door behind me. Downstairs, I can hear Stu whimpering in his bed in the living room.

I take him outside with me, letting him stumble through the grass as I walk toward the barn. Inside, Bones is already awake and trying to get out of his stall. I feed him and turn him out into the paddock where he can get back inside if he gets too cold.

Then, I take Silver Phantom out because she's throwing her head and prancing. The ranch is quiet as I ride. I'm quiet too.

I think we've made a breakthrough in the last few days. The dynamic has shifted. Freya finally feels safe enough to let me take care of her. I found the key to her heart in that room in the attic. Now, everything has changed.

But we still have a long way to go yet.

After I get back to the barn and put Silver Phantom away, I head inside. The smell of coffee and something frying hits my nose, and my stomach rumbles. I kick off my boots and hang my hat and coat up, heading down the hall.

She's laying plates on the table. She's wearing exactly what I left out for her, but it fits her even better than in my imagination. That round ass looks so good in the short skirt that, suddenly, I'm across the room, bringing my palm down on it to watch it shake.

She whirls, eyes big. I bend and kiss her neck.

"Fuck, you look good," I murmur. "You smell good too."

She does, all warm vanilla and home. Mindlessly, I nuzzle her neck and inhale. My hips ride up on her ass, making her gasp.

"Deacon, it's breakfast time," she whispers.

"I know. I'm hungry." The firm curve of her ass feels so good against my dick, I can't stop.

She wriggles in my grip, turning to face me. "The food will get cold."

I kiss her until she's breathless. Then, she pushes me into my chair and fills the plates like her face isn't glowing pink. We eat in silence for a minute. As usual, her cooking is the best thing I've ever tasted, second only to her pussy.

"Did you read the note I left?" I ask.

She goes perfectly still. Her eyes swivel.

"I read it," she says.

"And?"

She sets her fork down primly. "I don't do that, really."

Taken aback, I put my utensils down too. "You don't touch yourself, sweetheart?"

Her cheeks are so pink now, they're glowing. She shakes her head.

"So when I fucked you the first time...was that the first time you came?"

"No," she says. "I didn't say I've never done it, I just don't do it much. Why? Do you?"

I shrug. "Yeah, a few times a week, maybe more. Less since you got here."

"Why?" Her wary gaze has a hint of curiosity.

"It's like an oil change. Out with the old, in with the new," I say. "Nothing wrong with it."

She squirms. It's killing her to have this conversation at the breakfast table.

"Do you like the way it feels?" I ask.

"Of course I do," she manages. "It's just…I think all the years of being called a whore made me think that if I did anything sexual at all, it would prove that right."

"I get called a whore," I say. "It's not a bad thing."

She turns a sharp stare on me. "You're a man. When people say that, it's a joke. When they say it to me, it's an insult."

"What about when I say it to you?" I ask, leaning in.

She bites her lip, releasing it, leaving a white mark.

"It's nice when you do it," she says, voice raspy. "It feels good, safe."

I study her. Inside, I'm imagining going into the blacksmith shop, picking up one of those fence spikes, and sticking it into the side of Aiden's head.

He's such an asshole.

And he's so weird about Freya, so deliberate in the way he tortured her.

Killing him would feel so good.

"In the morning, I want you to take the time that I'm in the barn and get yourself off," I say. "I'll get you a vibrator for it. When you're done, leave the vibrator on my pillow."

Her eyes widen.

"You want me to put a used vibrator on your pillow?" she asks, horrified.

"Yeah, I do."

"But why?"

"Because I like your cunt," I say. "I like the way it tastes, the way it smells, the way it feels."

Her eyes are wide, lips parted.

"You're...a lot," she says.

"Am I too much?" I ask.

She shakes her head. A smile, faint and soft, appears. "No. I think I like it."

I take her hand. She looks down and slowly curls her fingers through mine.

When we're done eating, she gets up to clear off the table. I get up to help, but she puts a hand on my chest and pushes me firmly into the seat. Her eyes flash. It takes a second to realize she's playing with me a little. I curl my forearm around her waist, pulling her against my side.

"Are you happier than you were?" I ask.

She nods, biting her lip.

"You can talk, sweetheart," I say gently.

"I know," she says.

"But you don't have to. I hear what you mean to say, even when you don't talk."

Her smile is so brilliant, all I can do is stare. I love this girl. She's not ready to hear it, but I would marry her tomorrow. I pick up her hand. Absently, I run my touch over her ring finger, wondering how soon is too soon for me to tell her I want to make this forever.

Maybe I should hold off until I figure out where I stand with her family and my land. It's been far too quiet since I took her from Aiden. I know men like him; he won't take this lying down.

He's going to hit back, and when he does, I have to take that hit and come back swinging.

Nobody will ever threaten her again.

It makes my chest ache to think about everything she's been through. She's so starved for love, and that's all Aiden fucking Hatfield's fault. Next chance I get, I'm going to beat him into a bloody pulp for what he's done, for what he's planning to do.

He shouldn't have fucked around with me or my woman. Fuck what my lawyer has to say about it. He can't get to me until the snow's melted and I don't have to answer his calls.

I'm about to be Aiden's worst nightmare.

"Deacon?"

I blink, her face coming into focus. "I thought you were supposed to call me daddy, sweetheart," I say.

"Daddy, then," she says, her drawl husky.

She's looking at me, like she's expecting me to say something.

"Are you going to be working all day?" she asks.

"Yeah, sweetheart, I run a ranch. Wish I could be with you, though."

A crease appears between her brows. I cup her face, stroking her cheek with my thumb. It travels down, running back and forth over her soft, full lower lip. Arousal thrums in my groin.

"You sure you're alright after last night?" I ask.

She blushes and nods. "Yes, it was intense. But I liked it. A lot."

"You're not a whore," I say abruptly. "You know that, right?"

"I'm not?" Her eyes are slightly unfocused.

"No, you're my whore," I say, reaching out to cup the back of her head. "Daddy's whore—it's a good thing, sweetheart. And it's different."

She swallows, eyes glittering. I take a moment to pull her into my arms, kissing her the way I did the first time we made out in the truck—slow, letting her know how badly I want every part of her. When we break apart, she's panting, some of the glassiness gone from her eyes.

"I'll see you tonight, sweetheart."

I leave her there, breathless. I think I got my point across.

# CHAPTER THIRTY-FIVE
# FREYA

It takes me a few minutes to get my head on straight after he's gone. Still burning up, I make some tea and climb up the stairs. In the hall, I peer out the window and see him taking Bones out, breaking into a trot as he heads toward the employee housing.

I don't know what tomorrow brings, but I'm happy to be here right now.

The house is peacefully silent as I start sorting through the things he bought for me. Journals, pens, bolts of the prettiest fabric I've ever seen, yarn, watercolors. I take it out and marvel silently over it.

Aiden hated that I liked my books, my insects. He taunted me for it every chance he got, and Ryland took his lead.

It was only sweet Bittern who understood. He sat on the porch steps after he got back from the mines and let me read to him. He liked the pictures in the fairy books. He'd watch as I colored them with a paint set he bought me from the dollar shop. He said it helped his head stay quiet.

My eyes are wet.

Poor Bittern. It's only now I'm older that I realize Bittern needs help, and not just for his lungs. He spent nine days in the dark, deep in the rock, and it broke him.

I don't know what Deacon plans to do to Aiden, but he can't hurt Bittern or it'll break my heart. He said he'd save him. I'll hold him to that.

A little yapping outside breaks me from my reverie a few hours later. I've been up here for hours, and it's well past noon. My knees ache as I get up and cross the room to look out the window.

My breath catches. There's snow falling from the gray sky, spiraling over the mountains, catching on the frozen ground.

It's beautiful.

Deacon appears in the yard. Stu hangs from the breast pocket of his coat, yapping his head off. He uses the side of his boot to clear the thin layer of snow and sets Stu down to do his business.

Warmth glows beneath my breastbone. I love how much Deacon cares for his animals. His horses are beautifully kept, even the ones he doesn't sell. I see the way they lift their heads when he walks by, hoping for his attention.

He's so good at taking care of things. I think he'll be good at caring for me if I can be brave enough to let him.

I go downstairs, and he comes in, briefly because he says he has a lot of work before nightfall. We eat sandwiches in the kitchen. He has a coffee and kisses my mouth before leaving Stu and me in the living room. We're both tired, so I curl up with a blanket over me, Stu in my arms, and let myself drift off.

I've never taken a nap during the day before. It's luxurious.

I dream of home, but not the same way I used to. This time, I'm staring up at the mountains, and they keep getting smaller and smaller until the smoky tops disappear into the horizon.

I cry, but I don't try to go back.

Warmth trickles down my back. I flutter my eyes open and roll my head to look around. He must have carried me upstairs. It's dark outside, the fireplace flickering. Deacon sits on his side of the bed, his rough palm running up and down my spine. A tingle of something I didn't expect—arousal, maybe—follows his touch.

"It's five," Deacon says. "Are you hungry?"

I sit up, realizing I'm still in my clothes. "A little, not a lot. Are you?"

He shrugs. "I could eat."

The way he says it sends a curl of heat down between my thighs.

"I set out your night clothes," he says. "You get undressed and come downstairs before we have dinner."

He bends, his lips brush my forehead. My body prickles from my head to my feet, and my nipples go tight under my bra. He gets up, and I listen as his boots go down the hall to the lower floor.

Curious, I rise and turn on the light. On the chair is a deep blue slip with a matching silk dressing gown. I lift it, my brows rising. He must have a stash of clothing he bought for me that I haven't seen yet. The idea is a little thrilling.

I put it on, leaving the belt undone. I want him to see the rise of my cleavage. The way it makes his eyes wander feels so good, so powerful. Then, I leave the bedroom and go downstairs to find him making dinner. There's only one place setting. I'm not sure what he wants or where I should sit, so I loiter by the door with my hands tucked behind my back.

He glances up and does that double take I'm starting to love. "Goddamn, girl. You look good," he says.

I smile without thinking about it.

His eyes linger on me. "You want coffee?"

I shake my head. He sets a plate on the table loaded with meat, potatoes, bread, and gravy. He's not a bad cook, but his food is different than what I'm used to—it's hearty, made for winters like this. He sinks down and spreads his knees, leaning back.

I look at him, unsure what's happening. He pats his leg once.

"Come here and sit," he says.

Momentarily, I think about refusing. Then, I remember our talk. This might be an odd arrangement, one I don't fully understand, but my word is my bond, and he's never asked me to do anything I haven't liked yet.

And I like the pleasure he gives me. After a lifetime of being ignored, it feels good to be desired.

I sit on his knee, and his firm arm wraps around my waist. My eyes follow his hands as he breaks the bread into smaller pieces and soaks them in gravy.

"Open," he says.

I do as he says, and he puts the food into my mouth. It's good, strong and thick. My brain buzzes, watching him lick the fingers that just touched my tongue. He eats some, then he feeds me some. It feels like some kind of ancient ritual. Like when he's done, we'll be bound forever.

The thought is a little frightening.

I look around while we eat, noticing there's only water and coffee on the table. That's different than what I'm used to. Aiden, Ryland, and Bittern drink in the morning, noon, and night. Occasionally, if his day at the factory was rough, Aiden would do a line off the kitchen counter. I'd clean up after him, always worried he'd somehow get in trouble, even though it was just me who saw it.

My childhood was littered with casual pain and the casual vices that patched it up.

I don't want that anymore.

I glance at him sideways. He's using the last bit of bread to mop up the scraps of gravy. The plate is empty, and I'm satisfied. He wipes his hands and shifts me to face him.

"Can I ask you something?" I say.

He reaches up and tucks a curl behind my ear. "You can just ask. No need to clear it with me first, sweetheart."

My cheeks go warm. "I see you drink and smoke, but not all the time."

"Yeah?"

"Like, you just have one here and there. You can go all day without anything. Do you not get addicted?"

He shrugs. "I've never been addicted. I smoke in the summer, not much in the winter. I like whiskey, but not enough to try to get drunk off it. I'm too big for it to have much effect on me anyway."

I consider this, unsure if I believe it. All I've known is men with problems on problems, men who were kicked down by life too many times to keep from turning somewhere for comfort. I can't say I blame them. The only thing that kept me from drinking to handle it was the thought it could make me like Aiden.

"So you just cope with life?" I ask.

He considers it. "I think sex is my outlet."

My stomach sinks, and it takes me a second to identify why.

"Can I ask—"

"Just ask, sweetheart," he says, dark eyes soft.

"Okay," I say, taking a breath. "How long had it been since you had sex when we slept together for the first time?"

He tilts his head like he's thinking hard again. "I saw you in the winter. I'd gotten laid a few months prior, so it's been almost a year from now."

Warmth settles in my lower belly. "You didn't sleep with anyone after you saw me in the winter?"

He shakes his head. "Why do that when I wanted you?"

He's very focused. I wonder if that's how he was able to keep this ranch running so well. It's beautifully kept, everything deliberate. From the things I heard while working at the café, he's known for having the best barrel racers in Montana. That takes dedication.

I drag my attention back. He's watching me, head tilted.

"The man you lost your virginity to," he says. "Tell me about him."

The warmth in my stomach disappears. "Do you really want to hear about it?"

"I do."

"Why?"

"Because it meant something to you," he says.

Truthfully, now that I've slept with Deacon, the memory of what Braxton did is faded, like a copy of a copy.

"I want you to tell me," he says, sitting up. "Run upstairs and sit in the chair by the fireplace."

I hesitate. He gives me a look that lets me know he's not fucking around. Ever since I agreed to be submissive to him, he's different. His energy is darker, more dominating. It's...secure.

I can turn my brain off.

Upstairs, I wait for him, pacing the room. I catch my own reflection in the mirrors by the fireplace. My feet go still; I look different.

All my life, I've had hungry eyes. Lean, like an animal.

But tonight, I'm soft.

The door opens, I turn. He comes in and locks the door. The click triggers an involuntary rush of arousal—my body knows his hands will be on it soon. He crosses the room, not looking at me, and drops the cushion on the ground before sinking into the chair on the hearth.

"Sit," he says, pointing to the pillow.

Cowed, I obey. He spreads his knees so I can fit between them. Then, he shifts my body so my feet are tucked beside me and my body is laid against his leg. Gently, palm on my chin, he rests my cheek against his thigh.

"Tell me," he says.

"He was one of Ryland's friends from Pike County on the border," I whisper. "I had just turned eighteen. I'd heard a lot of things from listening to my stepbrothers talk. I had it in my head that sex was this...amazing thing. All they did in their spare time was try to get laid, so of course I thought that."

He starts stroking my hair, up over my temple, behind my ear.

"Go on," he says.

"He came to get something while they were all at work. I was naïve. I thought I was so grown up. I was doing laundry in the tobacco barn out back. He came in... We had sex."

"That was it?"

I nod. His brows crease.

"That's not it. Tell me the truth."

I frown, staring into the fireplace. "He told me he wanted it. I asked him if it would feel good and he said yes. The ground was dirt. I remember I wore a pair of jeans that were so tight, he had trouble getting them off. But they looked good on me."

I falter, remembering that pair of jeans and how I never wore them again.

I sniff. "It hurt. A lot. Not the good kind. It was like sandpaper. I think I was too nervous to get wet. I remember telling him it hurt. He said it was supposed to because I'd never done it before. I figured I could just stick it out until he was done, but it took him forever. I didn't tell him to stop... I felt this pressure to let him finish."

I drag my eyes up to his, but they're unreadable.

"I don't feel that with you," I whisper.

He touches my cheek. "You can always tell me to stop."

I nod. "I could have told him to stop too, but I was just lost in the...disappointment. It was like I wasn't there. I think that's why I hate this memory so much. He just did what he wanted and left me there."

Something shifts in him.

"There? On the ground?"

I nod, rough fabric of his pants rubbing my cheek. "I bled, so I had to clean up with a rag. There was this pit in my stomach, like my whole chest was hollow. It made me feel so...used."

He's quiet—too quiet.

"It just made me feel bad," I say. "And I never had sex again, not until you. But you don't make me feel the way he did."

His palm runs up my spine. I can practically hear the gears in his head turning.

"I didn't know anything. No one taught me. I got lucky enough I didn't get pregnant. I didn't know to take a morning-after pill or even ask him to wear a condom," I whisper, embarrassed. "I wouldn't have had the money for either."

My mind goes to Aiden's first wife, Bittern's mother. I wonder if she was the same. Maybe nobody bothered to talk to her about preventing pregnancy. Maybe she didn't have a mother or a sister, just Aiden.

My heart aches—not just for myself, but for all the women who came before me.

The only difference between me and them is luck. I slept with a man not understanding the consequences. I could have gotten pregnant by one of Ryland's rough, older friends.

By some chance, I got out.

"What was his name?" he asks.

"Braxton Whitaker," I whisper.

His middle finger traces my jawline. It circles behind my ear and up through my hair. He strokes my hairline. The fireplace glimmers through my lashes.

Neither of us speaks. Something hangs in the air, a palpable feeling. The longer he strokes my hair and neck, the more it fades.

My lids are so heavy, and the fire is so warm.

I sink into him, draped in his lap. Dimly, I'm aware of him shifting, and I'm in his arms. He lays me down, and my eyes flutter open long enough to connect with his. Then, he's going down, and my spine is arching as his tongue drags over my pussy.

Four orgasms later, he's got me out like a light.

# CHAPTER THIRTY-SIX
## DEACON

She's sleeping. I get up and take my phone down to the kitchen. It's almost midnight, but I know Jensen will still be up. I'm tired, eyes burning. I call him, tucking the phone between my ear and shoulder so I can pour a shot of moonshine.

He picks up on the third ring. "Yeah?"

"Do you still talk to Brothers Boyd?"

There's a long silence.

"What the fuck do you want with Brothers?" Jensen asks.

"Kentucky, Tennessee. That's their territory," I say. "I want to call in a favor. I can pay."

Jensen clears his throat. There's a tightness to his voice he only gets when talking about back home. "I don't fuck around with Brothers Boyd, and neither should you."

"I know him."

"Yeah? How's that?"

"I sold a horse to him," I say. "It's been fifteen years, but I think he'll remember me. And this is serious."

There's a long silence.

"Fine, I'll text you the contact I have," he says. "Do not tell him it was me who gave you the number. Got it?"

"I got it," I say.

He hangs up. A minute later, a number with a Kentucky area code appears, along with a threat of what he'll do to me if I reveal it was him who sent it. Before I lose my nerve, I hit call and put the phone to my ear. It rings.

And rings.

There's no voicemail—it just keeps going. Just as I'm about to give up, the phone clicks. A smooth, low voice, thick with a southern drawl, breaks through the poor connection.

"Brothers Boyd," it drawls.

"This is Deacon Ryder," I say. "I sold a palomino mare to you over a decade ago."

There's a silence, then: "Well, fuck me, Deacon Ryder," he says. "You know, I could use another one of your fantastic horses sometime."

"I got a good crop clearing next year," I say.

"Well, I might just take you up on that," he says. I hear the scrape of a chair on hardwood flooring. "You've got good horses, Ryder, made of fine stock. Now, what can I do you for?"

"I need a hit," I say.

There's a slow laugh, thick as syrup. "Right to the point. I like that," he says. "What's the name?"

"Braxton Whitaker."

"That's not known to me."

"He's from the Kentucky-West Virginia border. He might not be alive, but he was five years ago."

"Hmm, got an address?"

"No, but he's from Pike County."

"Alright, let's see now." His voice is a low drawl that bubbles like a stream. Through his drawl, there's a thick vein of finery, not unlike the perfectly fitted checked blue suit he wore the day I delivered his horse.

"I can pay you," I say.

"You can pay in cash, or I can take out a favor on you," he says. "But I need to make sure this isn't against my best interests first. If not, I'll have one of my boys pay him a visit next time they're in the area."

"I'll pay cash."

"That's alright by me," Boyd says. "Now, what did this man do to you?'

I consider telling him the story, but only for a half second. My hand tightens on my phone. No, he needs it in plain language so he understands.

"He fucked my wife."

"I see," he says. "Well, I didn't know you were married, so congratulations on that account. Let me look into this, and I'll have one of my secretaries reach out with either an invoice or a denial."

"Thanks, I appreciate this."

"Oh, I don't mind it at all," he says. "And you tell Mr. Childress that the gentleman from Kentucky says hello. He still owes me a fucking horse."

"I don't see him much, but I will," I say.

He laughs. "Goodnight, Mr. Ryder. We'll be in touch."

He hangs up, and I stand over the sink, holding my phone. Before my eyes, through the window, the snow swirls in slow circles.

I thought I was different. I saw her at the café and I thought I could be a different man. I practiced it so hard, even I believed it for a little while. But the minute she told me about that man and how he made her feel, the old Deacon came back with vengeance.

I'm still the same person who put a spike into a man's temple and took his land.

I return to bed. She's on her back, all soft skin and fern-green silk. I lay down and tug the blanket. Her breasts rise and fall. A quiver goes through her belly as she sighs.

I spread my hand and lay it on her belly, between her hipbones. Hearing what that man did to her made my vision flash red.

She's so desperate to be loved. I see how she reaches out blindly, longing for something she never got growing up. I think it's the reason she fell into Braxton Whitaker's arms, why she fell into mine so easily.

All she ever wanted was to be loved gently. Instead, the men who should have been gentle left her heart bruised. That's why I don't feel bad about hiring Brothers to pop a bullet into Braxton.

He deserves it.

# CHAPTER THIRTY-SEVEN
# FREYA

I can barely drag myself out of bed the next day. My body feels heavy, my head full of static. It takes a second for my eyes to focus. Then, I see it—miles and miles of snow, so bright that I squint as I force myself to leave the warm nest I've made of pillows and quilts.

Deacon is gone, probably already clearing pathways to the animals. I stretch and my hips pop. That doesn't surprise me—with the amount of sex I'm having, I'd be surprised if they didn't.

He comes in while I'm frying eggs in the kitchen. I hear him stomp his boots on the porch and hang up his coat. Then, he's in the doorway, arms crossed over his charcoal Henley, watching me, his dark eyes soft in the harshness of his face.

He doesn't speak. I turn off the stove and fill the plates. When I turn, he's still watching me.

"What?" I whisper.

He shakes his head, a little smile on his mouth. It strikes me how strange it is that a man staring at me while I cook suddenly isn't something to be afraid of. Instead, it gives me butterflies.

We eat together, and he kisses me before he goes. It's casual, like he knows I'll be there when he gets back.

I stand at the sink and watch him go into the barn and come out a moment later on Silver Phantom. She's stunning in the snow. Watching her prance makes me wish I was out there with him.

I think about that for a while. When he comes in for lunch, I bring it up.

"You want to come with me?" His brows are raised.

I nod. "Unless I'm in the way."

He shakes his head. "I'm going to do some work in the horse barn. You can come along, sweetheart."

I've never been included in anything before, not anything important. It has me smiling as I gather up my clothes. He put the chastity belt on me in my sleep but not the strap that covers my pussy. It takes me a minute to work my jeans over it, but once they're on, I can barely feel the delicate metal.

I reach into the closet for my coat and pause. There's a crack where the molding wasn't installed. I rest my temple on the wall. From this vantage point, I can see right into the bathroom where the copper tub sits.

I frown.

It's probably nothing. I shake my head, pulling on my coat and leaving. At the end of the day, if he used that to look at me, it's not any worse than anything else he's done. In fact, it's pretty low on the list compared to dropping from a tree, kicking in Aiden's windshield, and kidnapping me.

I'm at a point now where I don't care anymore.

He's standing on the porch when I come out. Silently, I follow him to the barn, where he has Bones and Silver Phantom saddled up. I clamber up on the mounting block and get on. I've ridden a little, enough to take Bones back to Aiden's house that morning, but I'm no expert.

I can't ride the way Deacon does. He moves with his horse like water, his center of balance firmly rooted. The reins stay slack and I don't see him shift his feet. All he does is click his tongue, and Bones heads out of the barn. Silver Phantom goes on her own, following them out into the snow.

The air is so pure. I take a deep breath of it and release it in a frosty cloud.

"It's beautiful," I say.

"Winter is my favorite season," he says. "I like the quiet."

"It's always quiet here," I say.

He shakes his head. "Not in the summer when we have buyers coming every day for the horses. You'll see."

Neither of us speak. Those two words hang in the air. He intends for me to be here when summer comes. I don't rebel against the idea.

We move through the employee housing. Everything is still, and I assume the wranglers are out working. The houses are simple but well-built and comfortable. On the far side, about a half mile down, I see a portion of the ranch I've never encountered.

It's a flat space with several paddocks and a huge barn. Bones recognizes it, clearly, because he breaks into a trot, prompting Silver Phantom to do the same. It takes me a moment to get the rhythm. I'm envious of Deacon, who posts easily, like he doesn't have to think about it.

When we get to the barn, I feel like my brain is scrambled. He hits a button by the door and it rolls back. Inside is a fully heated barn with dozens of stalls. When we ride in, a few horses put their heads out and stare. Deacon dismounts and helps me down.

"These are all your horses?" I do a slow turn, taking in all the doors.

"I run a breeding and training operation," he says. "These are the mares."

"May I look at them?"

His dark eyes linger like a touch. "Sure, sweetheart. You look to your heart's content."

Every day, I like the way he calls me a sweetheart a little more. Butterflies in my stomach, I go to the nearest stall and look in. There's a Paint horse standing on the other side. She lifts her head and snorts.

"That's Mind Your Business," Deacon says, leaning on the door.

"Why?"

"Why is that her name?" He puts finger and thumb in his mouth and whistles. The mare gives him a stony look and twitches her ear. "She's got an attitude like she's telling me to fuck off and mind my business."

I laugh. "I like her."

"Over here, we've got one of my favorites, Envy of the Angels," Deacon says, crossing to the opposite end. I join him, peering under his arm.

There's a stunning white horse standing just inside. She comes right up and nuzzles Deacon's shoulder, knocking his hat askew. He rights it, taking something from his pocket and feeding it to her.

"What's that?" I ask.

"Dried apple," he says. He steps back, walking a few doors down.

I follow, frowning. "What happens to them when they retire?" I ask.

He shrugs. "Most I sell off for hobby horses. Others just retire here until they keel over from old age."

I lean over to look into the newest stall. Inside is a gangly chestnut horse, clearly not an adult yet. Deacon takes more dried apple out, and it comes over, nuzzling his palm.

"Who's this?" I ask, reaching in to pet its head.

"Whoopsie Baby," he says. "One of the stallions got out, didn't know the dam was in heat. Bam, Whoopsie Baby."

I laugh, unable to hold it back. Deacon is just so…well, he's himself through and through. There's a glitter in his eyes that tells me he likes it when he can make me laugh.

I love this, just being with him.

We get back to the house around five. I put a stew in the crock pot, and we eat it with bread. Then, Deacon says he has paperwork and disappears down the hall. I try to let him work, but after pacing the house for a while, a familiar restlessness seeps in.

I creep down the hall and peer into his office. He's at his desk, laptop open, a stack of folders next to it. I watch him silently. He has this habit of clicking his pen wildly, but he doesn't seem to notice.

I clear my throat. He looks up.

"Need something, sweetheart?"

The words catch in my throat. How can I tell him I'm addicted to him? I need to borrow his big body to bring me back down to Earth when I blow away.

"Just you," I whisper.

He clears his throat. "Run upstairs, change, and bring me the strap for your belt."

As I climb the stairs, I realize I'm starting to understand that nothing he does is by accident. It's all by design.

I drift. He grounds me.

Upstairs, I change into one of his big shirts and take the strap from his bedside table. He's back to typing on his laptop when I return. I knock on the doorway, and he beckons me without looking up. Heart pattering, I stand by his elbow and wait.

He takes his time. Then, eyes like hot coals rest on me.

"Lift your shirt," he says.

Obediently, I raise the hem, exposing my pussy and the metal around my hips. He's taken the strap on and off enough for me to know he needs me to shift my legs apart. When I do it without being told, he gives me an approving nod.

He sets the strap over my pussy and locks it.

"I've got to finish this up, sweetheart," he says. "Then I'll play with you for a while."

He guides my hips to set me on his knee. Then, he goes back to whatever boring thing he has on his screen—some kind of spreadsheet. Occasionally, he rubs my thigh and waist absently.

He doesn't have to tell me what this is for—his words were a deliberate choice. I'm his toy, locked up and obedient until he decides he wants to play with me.

I shift my hips. I'm soaked against the strap, and I'm anchored to him, no longer drifting into the dark parts of my mind. He keeps me there with his touch. Absent, lingering. Rough calluses, worn ink. Fingertips that dig into the soft swell of my hips around the harness.

After a while, he sits back.

"You wet for me?" he asks, closing his laptop.

"Yes," I whisper, face warm.

He turns my face up. "Yes...what?"

My tongue darts out to wet my lips. "Yes, daddy."

"Good girl," he says, lifting me from his lap. "You go on up to the attic and I'll be there in a minute."

My stomach flutters. How many times has he made it do that today? His eyes follow me as I leave the room and head up the attic stairs. I turn on the light and sink down on the reading chair and pull a blanket over me. Overhead, through the exposed skylights, I can see that the clouds have cleared.

The sky is breathtaking.

I've never seen the world the way I do from Ryder Ranch. It's a little closer to heaven than the rest. Here, I can keep both feet on the ground but still be in the stars.

He comes up in a while, carrying a length of rolled up rope and the box he left in the bathroom. I sit up, my heartbeat increasing. There's a familiar tingle between my legs.

"Get up and strip, sweetheart," he says.

Obediently, I stand and remove my shirt. It falls to the floor, and I put it on the chair. He opens the box and takes out the lingerie. His hands are rough, firm, when he pulls the panties over the harness. Before he settles them, he unlocks the strap and bends in to kiss my wet pussy.

Right then, I realize something I can't say aloud.

He loves me.

It's in the tremor of his mouth, hot over my clit for a fleeting second. It's in the depths of his eyes as he looks up at me. It's in how gently he clasps the bra over my spine before putting another kiss above my navel.

Do I love him?

And if I do, who speaks first?

He circles me. His mouth brushes my nape. "Do you trust me, sweetheart?"

I nod.

"Words." His voice is firm.

"Yes, daddy," I whisper.

Silk slips over my eyes, blocking everything out. My heart pumps. My fingers clench at my sides.

"That's my girl."

He picks me up and lays me on my back on the floor. I feel it creak as his weight shifts, and then the familiar softness of the ropes slip around my limbs.

I don't know what he's doing, but I trust him.

His hands leave my body. There's several minutes of him moving around me. Then, slowly, I feel myself lifted, and I'm no longer grounded.

I'm drifting through dark space.

"Deacon," I gasp.

"I've got you, sweetheart," he says. "You're safe."

I'm so helpless; he's in complete control. All I can do is hang from the ropes and let him lift me up. How high, it's impossible to tell.

Then, all movement stops. The pressure is pleasant. I don't think I could take it for longer than a half hour or so, but it feels stable, comforting. I'm weightless. My ankles are tied, my arms behind my back. The ropes cradle me without cutting into my skin.

My head falls back. His hand cups the back of my neck. I startle when his mouth meets mine, upside down. He kisses me deeply. Sparks go off in the darkness. Heat coils up, white hot, glimmering through my veins.

Slowly, my body relaxes.

He pulls back, his fingers brush my hair, and then the blindfold falls away. I blink, focusing my eyes.

Then, I gasp.

Overhead, all I see are a million stars through the skylights, softly pale, brightly glittering. Black, blue, and silver in a cascade. This is how I imagined it might be to float up into the sky, to leave the world behind.

No pain, no sadness.

Just floating, breathing, heart beating.

"You alright?"

I can't tear my eyes from the sky. He's near. I sense him.

"Yes," I whisper. "It's beautiful."

With difficulty, I stretch my neck back and see him standing over me, looking down. From this angle, the stars are behind his head. He's half shadowed, and I can't read his dark eyes, but I don't have to anymore.

I trust him.

"Breathe, Freya," he says. "Slow. Sink into the ropes."

He brings his hand up and cups the nape of my neck. His other hand slides down and pushes the cup of my bra aside. His thumb circles my nipples. I'm bound and suspended, and the sensation is so strong that I try to squirm, but I can't. There's nothing to do but take it and feel everything.

He eases my head back so I'm hanging again. His clothes brush my side, moving around to stand beside me. His rough palm moves over my left breast. Fingertips stroke down my stomach, under my panties, between my thighs.

God, I might die.

It's too much but not enough.

"You're soaked," he murmurs, dipping his fingertips into my pussy. "You want to come for me?"

"Yes," I gasp.

He brings two fingers up and finds my clit, circling it. "Tell me who makes you come."

"You make me come, daddy," I whisper without thinking.

The hot coil deep inside me burns brighter until it spreads through my body like electricity. He doesn't stop. His thumb circles my nipple. His fingers brush back and forth over my clit.

*Faster.*

*Faster.*

*Faster.*

I close my eyes, letting go of the stars for a moment. Here, my heart is raw, and it reaches out for him in the dark.

Pleasure blossoms, ink dripping into water. My muscles tighten and release in my bonds. Distantly, I hear him praise me as he slides his fingers inside so I can grip them. All the tension I've carried for so long pops like a bubble.

I'm spinning, falling slowly.

Pleasure is a warm, soft force, reminding me I still have a body. It flows, it ebbs. It leaves me shivering in the ropes as he pulls his fingers from inside me. Then, he's letting me down, unhooking the rope from somewhere I can't see and reeling me gently to the floor.

The ropes are worked off me, and then I'm in his arms. He's on his knees, my legs wrapping around his waist.

"Who am I?" he says.

My nails dig into his shoulders. "Mine," I whisper.

His chest rumbles. "That's right. What do you call me?"

I press my face into his shoulder. He smells like Deacon—solid, unyielding. My entire world. "Daddy," I manage.

He strokes up my back, taking me by the nape. "That's my girl."

He picks me up easily and carries me back to our bedroom. Neither of us speak as he lays me down. I know what he wants, and I obediently spread my legs so he can press inside me.

It feels like coming home after being gone for so, so long. I know him by touch now. All the ridges, the veins, the fullness.

I know him by scent. By heartbeat.

Our eyes connect, our foreheads brush. There's a warmth that could last forever in my veins. We're both broken in two, but together, I think the two halves could make up the whole world.

# CHAPTER THIRTY-EIGHT
## DEACON

The snow gives us a handful of days that blur into each other. I'm in paradise. Other than keeping the ranch running, all we do is eat, sleep, and fuck.

She made a breakthrough in the attic, maybe more important than any other breakthrough before.

The sex is raw, animalistic, straightforward. I've never felt so close to anyone in my life. It's like our bodies aren't whole unless they're connected. When I'm not with her, I ache. When I am, I want more. I want it deeper, harder, more frequently, if that's even possible.

The next several days become two weeks. I know by now that Aiden will have worked out where Freya is, even if he didn't immediately notice it was my truck. I wasn't exactly trying to hide it, but the snow holds the world at bay and gives me time with my girl.

Then it melts and lets everything back in.

The first mild day, after the roads clear, Jensen comes over. He pulls up on a Tuesday in his truck and lets his hound out. I'm standing in the bedroom by the windows, threading my belt. Freya's up, staring at the ceiling with a crease between her brows. She's been weirdly silent since she woke up.

"Looking pretty good, sweetheart," I say casually.

She glances sideways, lips thinning.

I reach for my jacket. "You okay?"

She nods, rolling on her side facing away. I circle the bed so I can look her in the face. "Feel bad?"

She huffs, throwing aside the covers. "I didn't realize I had to play twenty questions at seven in the morning," she snaps, going into the bathroom and shutting the door hard.

I stare, confused. Downstairs, Jensen beeps his horn, impatient. Reluctantly, I leave the bedroom and go out to meet him.

We stand in the driveway and shoot the shit, talking about nothing for a while. It's cold—not cold enough for winter, but cold enough our collars are turned up, our hats pulled low. I'm feeling a bit off from Freya snapping at me, but I'm trying to let it bounce. I don't think I did anything to make her mad.

"Freya here?" Jensen asks.

I nod, jerking my head back at the house. "She's been here since I took her from Aiden."

"She want to be here?" He blows thin gray smoke into the wind.

I think back to last night. I got in late and kissed her awake. She rolled onto her back, eyes barely open, and let me in.

She's sweet, submissive. I think she likes the little rituals we do together. Every morning, I find that vibrator on my pillow, wet with evidence she used it. I have my doubts I'll be getting that this morning, though, not with the mood she's in.

"Yeah, I think she does," I say.

"Has to be better than what she's used to," he drawls. "Did you talk to Brothers Boyd?"

I nod, stabbing out my cigarette. "Yeah, we're good."

"Can you tell me what you needed him for?"

I shake my head. "Better not. You want breakfast?"

"Jack says she cooks better than he's ever had, so that's a yes," Jensen says.

We go inside. Freya has the table set already, with a place for Jensen. We sit, and she plates the food, and pours coffee. She's still not speaking.

The meal is excellent, as usual. Jensen is trying to make small talk with Freya when I hear tires rumble up the drive.

I lift my hand. Jensen goes quiet.

"Somebody's here," I say.

Chicken starts baying on the porch. I get up and lean back to look out the window. I think I know who's approaching, but it still lights a fire in me when my gaze falls on Aiden's truck.

I glance back at Freya. Her eyes are wide, her hands clasped in her lap.

"You stay here, sweetheart," I say firmly.

I give Jensen a look, jerking my head at the hall. We step out, and I shut the kitchen door. Freya is already at the window, looking out. I can tell by her footsteps and the little gasp that sounds through the wall.

"Hatfields?" Jensen asks.

I nod. "Let me get my shotgun."

Jensen nods, reaching into the holster at his belt and taking out his pistol. He checks it, keeping it down. Inside, I'm deadly quiet as I go into the living room and take my shotgun down from above the mantel. There's an ammo case under the couch. I kick it out, pocketing a handful of slugs.

"Don't shoot," I say, walking past Jensen in the hall. "Not unless they shoot first."

"Never thought I'd hear those words from Deacon Ryder," Jensen mutters.

I elbow open the door and step onto the porch. Chicken is going crazy, his feet braced on the floorboards and his head thrown back. I put two bullets in my shotgun but let it hang open over the crook of my elbow.

Aiden gets out. He's got a pistol on his belt, but nothing bigger that I can see. Ryland jumps out the other side and circles the truck to stand by his father. I don't see Bittern, to my relief. If this escalates, I don't want to shoot the only brother Freya cares about.

I swing my gaze over to Aiden. I get what Freya was saying about us being similar. Aiden is me on the outside, just a meaner version. Maybe he'd be me if I hadn't had people like Andy, Jensen, and Jack to keep me in check.

"You got some kind of nerve standing on my ranch, Hatfield," I say.

He shifts his weight to one leg.

"You got some kind of nerve kidnapping my daughter," he says.

That gets me going, but I keep my composure. Freya isn't his daughter. To be that, he would be required to treat her like a human.

"Didn't seem like you wanted her around," I say.

"How'd you figure that?"

I snap the shotgun shut with a quick thrust. "How'd you figure getting a bullet between your eyes, motherfucker?"

"Alright now," Jensen says, holding up an arm. He sends me a look, warning me to calm down. I know he's right—we've been out here less than a minute, and I've already made a death threat. Honestly, I thought I'd snap in seconds having to look at Aiden's assbackwards face.

"The fuck you here for?" I ask. "Chicken, you quit."

For the first time in his life, Chicken listens and sits down. He's on high alert, the hair on his spine spiked. I swing my gaze back to Aiden.

"Better start talking," Jensen says.

"I came to give you these," Aiden says, taking an envelope from his pocket and tossing it onto the bottom step. Jensen leans down and picks it up, handing it to me.

I open it. Court summons.

I keep quiet—not for long, but long enough for everything Jay Reed told me to run through my head. Maybe those were more suggestions. I don't want to keep quiet. I want to put my shotgun down and give this man what he deserves.

I think that's probably his problem. Nobody's ever beaten him so bad that he thinks twice before bullying women a third his size.

My mind goes to the fence stakes in the blacksmith shop. I can't stop fantasizing about pinning this asshole to a wall like one of those bugs in Freya's collection.

He'd deserve it.

"If you don't appear in court for this, we will sue," Aiden says. "If you want to clear this up, you'll sign off on the easement."

I keep quiet. Jensen's watching me like he's waiting for a gunshot. Even Chicken is staring up at me, one jowl tucked in his teeth. Slowly, I fold the paper in half. My boots are the only sound in the damp, cold air as I descend the steps.

I stop a foot from Aiden. Behind him, Ryland is raring to go, shifting his weight back and forth.

He smells like some kind of soap with a hint of liquor. Up close, I can see his tattoos are just as fucked up as mine. We're both shaped by years of hard living on the outside, but that's where the similarities end.

"Does it bother you?" I ask quietly.

We're about the same height. He's looking me dead in the eye.

"That you won't give up that easement bullshit? Yeah, fucking bothers me," Aiden says.

I shake my head. "No, does it bother you that I fuck your stepdaughter?"

His face turns to stone. The only thing that moves are his pupils, blowing to fill his eyes. The thought that has poked at my subconscious for weeks resurfaces: Aiden cares a little too much about who's fucking Freya.

"Does it bother you that her mother left? That that one's mother left too?" I jerk my head at Ryland. "But my girl, she stays...enthusiastically."

Ryland surges forward. I whip up the shotgun and point it at him.

"Stay right there, you son of a bitch," I say, keeping my voice low.

Everybody freezes. A few stray bits of snow fall, and I swear, I can hear them drift down. Slowly, I take the envelope and tuck it into the front pocket of Aiden's coat.

"The problem with you is, you've never met your match," I say. "So nice to meet you. I'm not a little girl you can scare by breaking shit. Hit me, and I'll curb stomp your sons into the ground and bury them in my compost pile. Now, get off my land."

His jaw works. His hatred is so intense, it turns his eyes black.

"Alright," he says. "We're doing this the hard way."

He steps back, jerking his head at Ryland to get in the truck, and starts backing up. Behind me, the door slams open, and by the sound of stockinged feet, I know it's Freya. Chicken lets out a low growl.

Aiden's eyes fix behind me. I see it then: intense disgust. Quick as a flash, I lift the shotgun.

"Say a word to her, and I'll shoot you," I say.

It's eating him up not to get the last word in, but he gets into his vehicle. But not without hitting the side of my truck hard as he walks by—that makes my blood boil. They peel out, spraying mud and gravel behind them. I'm so fucking angry, I have to take a beat to compose myself before Freya sees my face.

She's standing by the door, arms wrapped around her body. The wind whips her hair around her pale face. Her eyes are wide and wet, a single tear etching down her cheek.

Chicken lets out one last bark and sits. Freya's eyes fall on him as another tear slips out.

"Chicken is a fucking stupid name for a dog," she snaps, yanking open the door. "You should name him something better."

She disappears into the house like a storm cloud. The door slams so hard, it echoes through the yard. Jensen's jaw hangs loose. He turns on his heel and throws his hands up.

"What the fuck did I do?" he says.

I hand him the shotgun, shaking my head, and follow her into the house. It's not Jensen she's mad at. I'm not positive it's me either, not unless she heard the comment about her staying with me. Still, that was barely risqué.

There's something else going on.

Her feet patter overhead. I follow her upstairs, turning the corner just in time to see her disappear behind the attic door. I cock my head, listening to her flip the deadbolt and patter up the steps.

She's feeling feisty this morning. I try the handle, and it's locked. Sighing, I go into our bedroom and take the jackknife from my bedside table. Back in the hall, I kneel and push the blade in the crack to pop it open.

Good. I'd rather not scare her by kicking the door in. As I climb the stairs, I hear Jensen's truck head down the drive. Apparently, he's not sticking around, and I don't blame him.

She's sitting in the reading chair, knees pulled up, arms wrapped around her legs. There's a pout on her lips and a crease between her brows. Tears glitter on her lashes. She glances up as I step into the room and looks away, fixing her eyes on the floor.

"No, thank you," she says.

"No, thank you...what?" I cross the room and crouch down to look up at her.

She tilts her chin, looking me dead in the eyes.

"No, thank you, daddy," she says coolly.

I'm speechless for a second. She appears to be pushing, trying to get some kind of reaction from me. Gently, I lean in and brush her hair back, lifting her chin so she can't turn away.

"Did Aiden scare you?" I ask.

"No," she whispers.

"What's wrong?"

Tears spill out in earnest. Quick as a flash, she wipes them away. I hold my hands out, palms up.

"Nothing," she says, bunching her fists.

I bite back a sigh. "Do you know what you want?"

Her throat bobs. It's several difficult minutes before she shakes her head. Another tear slips out. It's gone in a second, wiped on her skirt.

"Are you willing to talk about it?" I press gently.

She shrugs. I can see how she's at war with herself. Finally, she swallows hard, like she's pushing back a sob.

"I'm just stressed out," she sniffs.

"Why? Because of Aiden? He won't come up here again, I promise."

She shakes her head again. "Not really. I think that was just the last straw."

I try to take her fingers in mine again, but she closes them. Her whole body shudders.

"I need a test," she sobs. "I got up this morning, and I realized I'm late."

The entire world goes quieter than a fresh snowfall. My brain absorbs what she's saying, but slowly, the pieces click into place.

She might be pregnant.

I did this on purpose, but I think, deep down, I thought it wouldn't work. Now, here I am, realizing for the first time that maybe it did. She could be carrying my baby. I could have a family with the woman I love more than anything.

Dazed, I pick up her stiff body and sink onto the chair, turning her to face me in my lap.

"Hey, you look at me, sweetheart," I say.

I pry her face up. It's swollen, and her blue eyes are so scared, it hurts my chest.

"I'll go get a test from the gas station," I say.

She stares at me for a second. Then, she sniffs. "You're not…angry?"

My chest aches.

"No. Why would I be angry?" I say. "I'm the one who did it. Are you angry?"

She shakes her head. "No, just afraid. Aiden used to say if I got pregnant by somebody, he'd throw me out."

My mind flips through a dozen images of all the violent things I'd like to do to Aiden. I want to go after him right now, drag him out of that truck and enact some vigilante justice. Instead, I bring her hand to my mouth and kiss the backs of her fingers.

"Aiden is not your problem anymore."

"I know," she whispers.

I brush her hair back, wiping her puffy face. "Is this what you want?"

Her lips part before the tip of her tongue wets them. Her eyes are bright for the first time in a long while.

"All my life, I thought this wasn't what I wanted," she whispers. "But now… I think that I wanted a family…just not the kind I had growing up. And you…you're not like that. And I…want you. I want to have a baby with you."

My heart stops. The world slips away.

Her lower lip trembles. "I'm trusting you," she whispers. "Please, please don't break my heart."

"I love you, sweetheart," I say, the words tumbling out. "You can trust me. I swear, I won't hurt you or let you down."

A hesitant smile tries to shine through her tears. "Like...what kind of love me?"

"Like can't live without you kind of I love you."

She doesn't say it back. She falls apart instead. Her body shakes with sobs, so hard that I pull her against my chest and they soak my shirt. She doesn't need to say the words until she's ready.

She's scared of being hopeful, tired of being scared.

I let her cry it out. When she lifts her head, I wipe her tears. It means a lot that she lets me see her vulnerable.

"I'm going to put you to bed," I say. "You'll stay there and rest while I get a test."

She nods, wiping her nose. I pick her up, holding her close, and carry her down to our room. She lets me undress her and work her slip over her head. Then, she snuggles onto her side. I smooth back her hair.

"Thank you for not being mad," she whispers.

I crouch down. "If you're pregnant, I'll be the happiest I've ever been."

Her eyes are sleepy. "Really?"

I nod, stroking her cheek. "This is what I've been waiting on, sweetheart. You, me, and a little guy."

"Or girl." Her lips curve.

"I'll take whatever comes."

Her eyelids flicker. I press a kiss to her temple and lock up all the doors and windows before leaving the truck. Before I go, I send Andy a text to let him know to keep an eye on the house.

Then, knuckles white on the steering wheel, I drive to the gas station. If she's not pregnant, I want to keep trying. I've wanted a family for a while now. But that's changed. I don't want just any family—I need Freya to be my wife. I want to have babies with her, to raise our kids on Ryder Ranch together.

I want to hold her hand when I'm gray and there's no more tread on my tires.

My heart has never gone so hard just buying something from the gas station. I put it on the counter. The clerk, who's worked there for ten years, gives me a look, but she doesn't say anything as she rings up the test.

I put it in my pocket, walk across the muddy parking lot, and swing into the truck. The road is crowded, which is strange for this time of day. I'm halfway down the bypass when I realize there's a truck stalled out in one of the intersections and police cars parked around it. I stare at it for a minute, thinking I recognize the person standing by the truck, but it's hard to see what's going on.

I grit my teeth, the impatience killing me.

Of course, today of all days, there has to be a traffic jam. I do a U-turn and go back the way I came, my foot sinking down on the gas pedal. There's a state route that takes a little longer, but it's usually pretty clear.

I'm distracted. My thumb hits the wheel.

*Tap.*

*Tap.*

*Tap.*

The gray trees fly by. My truck bounces over the rough concrete. If she's pregnant, she'll be starting to show by springtime. I could be a father by the summer.

I can't keep from smiling. If she says yes to me, I'll make sure she never regrets it. By rights, she shouldn't even be a possibility for me. She's smart, beautiful, and she's got the sweetest soul that shines through her bright, clear eyes.

My truck lurches, and right away, I can tell there's something wrong. The wheel, which I was barely holding, spins. The world blurs, but I keep my composure enough to keep my hand loose so the truck can do a full circle and come to a halt halfway in the shallow ditch.

What the fuck?

Heart thumping, I take the rifle from the backseat and kick open the door. I'm in a wooded area, less than a mile from the entrance of Ryder

Ranch. Up ahead, the trees thin, and the road cuts through a field. Just over that hill is the gate.

I jump out, water and mud coming up over my boots. The woods are empty, but the birds are still singing. That's a good sign. It means nobody is around.

Slowly, I check overhead, then in the tree line, which is mercifully sparse. There's no disturbance. Treading carefully on the sides of my boots, I circle the truck and walk back to the place where I spun out.

There's a spike strip a dozen yards up the road and a ditch dug out at my feet.

I must have hit the spikes, not realizing it until my wheel went into the ditch. With nothing to buffer the hit, I spun out.

I lift my head.

I've been gone less than forty minutes. There's no way anybody knew I was gone.

Then, it hits me—the man standing by the stalled truck was Elijah McClaine.

*This is a trap.*

Fear clamps down on my chest like a vise. This means, somehow, they tracked me. They knew I left the ranch. Heart pounding, I spin on my heel and go to the side of my truck where Aiden hit it just over an hour ago. I dip my hand into the bed, and there it is—a little metal tracker stuck to the side.

I look down at it, gray in my palm.

They know Freya is alone.

My feet start going before I know what's happening. I'm running up the road, going as hard as I can toward where the trees open. My heart is in my throat.

The world spins out.

I haven't been this scared before in my life, not even when Henderson stuck me to a tree and left me to bleed out.

I don't remember running down the road and up the driveway. All I know is suddenly, I'm tearing up to the porch with my rifle in my hand and my lungs on fire. The door to the house is ajar, swinging in the breeze. The gravel of the drive has two deep marks where someone spun out.

Inside, Stu yaps and whines pitifully.

I lift my rifle, moving up the porch, and kick the door wide open. It swings in, revealing an empty hall. Swiftly, I move along, checking behind every door, even though I know the truth.

There's nobody here, but I already know who's responsible for breaking in. I know who did this, and he's got a vested interest in taking what's most precious to me and disappearing fast.

My boots echo as I go upstairs and burst through the open door of our bedroom. The covers are pulled back. The bed is empty.

The pillow on her side is bloody. Not a lot, like she scraped herself. Maybe bumped her face and split her lip.

If Aiden hit her... Fuck.

My vision flashes. If they hurt her, God help them. I'm going to gun down every man who had a hand in this and burn their bodies at the top of Deacon's Hill so everyone sees the smoke.

I'm not an angry man, not the way she was afraid I'd be. But I lose it and lash out, kicking the center of the bed frame so hard, the solid wood splinters.

It bows in the middle, the bed where I fell in love with her, where I coaxed her to trust me.

Maybe the place we made our baby.

Deep down, I want to believe she's pregnant.

The test burns a hole in my pocket. I take it out with unsteady fingers, chest heaving as I stare down at it. In the distance, I feel something snap deep inside. It's the same thing that happened the night Henderson stabbed me. The man drained out of me, and all that was left was the animal.

I want my family back, and I'm going to make it everyone's problem until she's safe in my arms.

Dust settles slowly around the broken bed. I take out my phone.

It's time to call in that favor.

# CHAPTER THIRTY-NINE
# FREYA

I can tell I'm in the back seat of Aiden's truck by the familiar oil and leather scent.

I was asleep. Then, I was ripped from our bed, my eyes covered with a rag. All I remember clearly was Stu yapping his head off. Hands were on me, gripping hard enough to hurt. I heard my own voice, begging those hands not to hurt me. The only thought in my head was the baby who might be waiting in my belly.

I was dragged across the bed. Then, they slung me over their shoulder, and right away, I knew it was one of two people by the way they walked.

Deacon or Aiden.

And only one of those men wants to hurt me.

My arms prickle with goosebumps. After Deacon left, I changed into my black slip so I could take a nap, and it's freezing outside. I'm still wearing the chastity harness without that strap underneath. Deacon doesn't take it off unless I have a reason for it.

My nose drips. I'm cold, exposed, and scared. Every time the truck goes over a bump, I jostle and my stomach flops. My hands are bound behind my back with what feels like cloth. It doesn't hurt, but it's jarringly different from when Deacon binds my wrists.

The truck goes until I feel it shift from the road to gravel. I brace my feet on the floor, my body flopping from side to side. My center of gravity stabilizes, and we're going up a hill. I lean my head against the rest.

"Aiden," I whisper.

"Shut up."

His voice is gruff.

"Please don't do this," I say, keeping my voice sweet and low.

He doesn't answer. The truck comes to a halt and the door slams. His hand wraps around my elbow, and he drags me out, slinging me back over his shoulder. All the blood rushes to my head. It's disorienting to move without knowing where we're heading.

A door slams. Boots ring out. Another door opens. I'm laid on a bed, and the door shuts again.

I keep perfectly still. The room smells faintly of whiskey and dampness.

My heart beats like it's trying to jump from my chest. In the darkness, I try to figure out what this horrible feeling is knotted in my belly, creeping through my veins like cold.

I thought it was terror, but it's something worse—acceptance of my fate.

I always knew this would come.

Aiden taught me that violence is inevitable. The same cycle that forced him into the factory, that forced Bittern down into that mine, has brought me here.

Desperation.

We're all just clawing over each other, trying to get a leg up, hoping for relief that never comes. The deck was stacked against all of us, some of us more than others. Now, we're all trying to figure out how to play a game we're bound to lose.

The door creaks. Boots sound on the floor, and the bed sinks. Unsteady fingers pull the blindfold up, and the light blinds me for a second. Bittern's haggard face swims into view. He looks so much older than thirty, and the heavy, dull expression in his eyes is worse than usual.

"Hey, Frey," he says.

"Bittern." The word bursts out.

He runs a hand over his face, rubbing his temples. "I didn't want this to happen. I told Aiden to just let you stay put, but he's angry."

"I know," I whisper.

He shakes his head. "No, Frey, he's really fucking angry. I've never seen him like this. He doesn't sleep. It's not like before."

My stomach sinks. I've seen Aiden so angry, it made me hole up in my room for two days, but I can tell by Bittern's face that this is different.

I reach out and grip his forearm. Beneath my palm, there's a scar—white, twisted in a circle, like he got it caught in something and tore it out.

I never asked where he got that. I always assumed it was from the mine.

"Bittern," I whisper, "I need you to get me out of here."

His throat bobs. He's pale, like he's cold, but sweat drips down his temple. "I don't know what I can do," he says. "I've never been a match for Aiden."

"Bittern—"

"Frey, listen, I—"

Desperate, I yank his arm so he has to look me in the eyes.

"Bittern, I think I'm pregnant," I whisper, fear cracking my voice. "I need to get back to Deacon."

He goes still, only his eyes darting down to my waistline. Suddenly, we're not in this tiny room with the world falling apart around us. We're right back home, tucked in the Appalachian Mountains. The porch steps, worn by generations of Aiden's family before us, are warm from the sun on our bare feet.

Back then, we were delusional enough to think we had a say over our futures. I was young, but I remember Bittern saying he'd like to meet somebody and have a family one day. This was all before the mines, before his light went out.

He clears his throat.

"You sure?"

I shrug. "I don't know. There's a good chance."

His brows rise. "And it's Deacon's?"

I laugh, although I'm not sure why. "Yeah, of course it is."

He shrugs, a little smile creeping over his mouth. "Didn't think it'd be you having babies before me," he says finally. "I'm happy for you, Frey, but I don't know what I can do to get you out."

My mouth is so dry, my lip keeps splitting. I wet it, tasting metal. My fingers trail up and come away bloody. Did I hit my face on the table when Aiden tore me from the bed? Bittern digs in his pocket, brings up a handkerchief, and hands it over.

"Can you get to Deacon?" I whisper. "Maybe tell him where I'm at?"

His jaw works. He wipes his face again.

"I can try," he says. "Aiden's watching me. I think he's been watching me since I hit him the night he smashed your bugs up. But it isn't about that. There's other stuff stopping me."

His voice cracks, as if he might cry. I tighten my grip on his arm, and he looks away.

"Bittern," I ask. "What's he doing?"

To my shock, he sniffs. "I'm all fucked up, Frey. I never talked to you about it, but when the collapse happened, it just fucked me up."

My heart pumps, making my breath come shallow. "I know, I'm sorry."

He shakes his head. "No. It wasn't just... Look, I was down there for six and a half days. Wayland, he was with me but separated by the rocks. I heard him calling out, heard him dying. I never told Aiden this. He doesn't need to hear it. But I sat there, in this little area, about five by five, where the rocks missed me. It was hell. We dug down to hell, and it's not very far, just below the surface."

My stomach turns, and sickness passes over me in a wave.

"Solitary confinement. That's torture for a reason," Bittern says slowly. "I tried killing myself, but I couldn't do it. My ribs were fucked up, but it wasn't what hurt the most. It was sitting in the dark, listening to Wayland die. It was knowing I was dying, that it wouldn't be quick. I was gonna have to live every second of my death."

Tears slip out, hot trails down my neck.

"Bittern, I'm so sorry."

He shakes his head once. "I close my eyes, and I'm still down there. I can't get out. I'm still down there in the dark. The pills they gave me for my ribs...they help. They turn my brain off. Make it shut up."

Something clicks into place. The deadness in Bittern's eyes didn't come from the memory of being underground. It came from the monster that always lurks in the shadows of desperation. Offering hope where there is none.

"Oh no," I whisper.

He drags his tortured gaze up. "Aiden gets me the pills. I can sleep at night. I don't have to replay my own death in my head every second."

I crush the handkerchief in my hand.

I'm so tired. Maybe my mother and grandmother were tired of carrying all the darkness and despair too. It's not Aiden's fault he had a father with an iron fist and a penchant for violence. It's not his fault there was nowhere for men to work but the factory and the mines.

But it's his fault he dragged all that pain in like the cold and let it infect us all.

And now, sweet Bittern can't sleep because Aiden's a copy of a copy of a copy of the men who came before him.

I squeeze my eyes shut, but a tear slips out. Bittern takes the handkerchief and uses it to clumsily wipe my face.

"I'm sorry," I whisper.

"Aw, Frey, it's not your fault," he says.

I shake my head, opening my eyes. "I'm sorry Aiden was your father. I'm sorry the factory closed, sorry you went to the mines. I'm so sorry all he's done is give you pills. You deserve to get better."

His face goes still. "It's okay," he says.

I shake my head hard. "No, it's not okay. It's awful, and it shouldn't be this way."

His gaze flicks up and fixes to mine. There's a spark of life in it.

"But it is," he says. "Fair or not, it just is."

My throat catches. I reach out and take his hand.

"I want more, Bittern, and I'm getting it," I whisper. "Aiden won't change. Neither will Ryland. But you deserve to get better, and I'm in love with Deacon Ryder. I want to be his wife."

He's so sad, eyes soft.

"You want to get married?" he asks.

My eyes are streaming. My throat is so tight. "He showed me it's possible to get out."

He smiles, and that light flickers, a hint of gold through the woods.

"I like that," he says, voice like gravel. "I always wanted something like that for you."

"You come with me," I whisper. "Deacon can help me help you."

He laughs, but there's no humor in it.

"I helped kidnap you," he says. "I've been surveying the land for the easement. Deacon won't forgive me for that. I'm a fucking coward, Frey."

My stomach goes cold. I pull my hands free, covering my mouth.

"You have?"

He runs a hand over his face. "I want to choose you, but I don't see any way out of this."

"Deacon won't hurt you if I ask him not to. I get it, I do. I forgive you for anything, everything."

He shakes his head hard. "Maybe I deserve for Deacon to hurt me. Maybe it'd be better if he just...you know, put a bullet in my head."

I'm so sick inside, it's making the room spin. I take his hand and squeeze it.

"Deacon will come for me," I say. "I'll make sure you get out of this alive, that you get clean, that you get a chance to be happy. I promise."

I don't know how I can promise this much, but I know it's true. Deacon is a good man. A complicated one who sometimes does the wrong thing, but his heart is good. I trust that he won't let me down.

He isn't like Aiden at all.

"I promise," I repeat.

Bittern stands slowly, like his body hurts. He coughs, a damning rattle in his chest.

"I don't know, Frey," he says. "I think all the bravery I had got used up."

He leaves, just walks out and shuts the door. I sit there, stunned.

Out of everything that's happened in the last few years, the harsh click of Bittern closing the door on me hurts the most.

I lay back on the bed. Deacon will come for me, I know he will. Through my slip, I dig my fingers into the delicate straps of the chastity harness. The lengths he went to get me were reprehensible, but his hands, once they were on me, were so gentle.

I can never go back. I have something to live for now, and I want to live so badly, to be Deacon's wife, to have his babies. To let him love me with all his obsession, his dark desire, his steadfast certainty.

I need him the way I need the stars, and I believe with every fiber of my body that, like those stars, at the darkest hour, he'll appear.

# CHAPTER FORTY
# DEACON

My heart fights like a live animal against the cage of my ribs.
*Thump.*
*Thump.*
*Thump.*
The rest of me is perfectly still.

I'm standing by the kitchen window, staring out at the gray hills. The window is cracked, the cigarette in my lip trails smoke. November air bites my skin.

Nothing wakes me up out of this nightmare.

Jack Russell is on his way to Ryder Ranch. Jensen Childress is going for back-up, says he can get Sovereign Mountain behind me.

Slowly, I bring the cigarette down and stab it into the sink. The buzz of my phone vibrating against the sink jerks me out of my reverie. It takes a second, and then the screen flashes the letter B. Without thinking, I swipe it and bring it to my ear.

"Deacon Ryder." The tone is soft, drawling.

"Brothers Boyd."

My voice cracks and I clear my throat.

"I called to say Whitaker is dead," he says.

Right now, it feels like years ago when I spoke to him last. It takes me a second to remember what he's talking about. Then, it clicks.

"How much do I owe you?" I say.

"Not a thing," Boyd says. "It wasn't my boys who killed him. He's been dead for a good four or five years."

Faint disappointment rises in my chest. Maybe I was hoping for this small win in light of the woman I love being torn from me.

"Who killed him?"

"Well now," Boyd drawls, papers shuffling in the background. "Looks to be an Aiden Hatfield. I can't for the life of me see what the issue was between them. Hatfield has multiple prior arrests, drunk and disorderly kind of thing, but he was friends with the sheriff, so he never got more than a slap on the wrist. If I had to guess, it was a drug dispute gone wrong."

"Aiden Hatfield," I repeat.

"Does that mean something to you?"

My stomach turns. A lot of things would make sense if I could just get myself to accept the thought lurking in the back of my brain—that Aiden has a twisted obsession with Freya.

Maybe I'm assuming too much. I know Aiden is a prideful man. He'd probably consider it a slight that some man got his stepdaughter down in the dirt and left. Maybe he went to talk about making her an honest woman, getting her off his hands, and Whitaker refused.

Or, deep down, it's about desire. What doesn't make sense is why he hasn't acted on it yet.

"No, nothing," I say. "Let me pay you for your time."

"Oh, just stop by and see me next time you're in the commonwealth," he says. "You have a good day, Ryder. I'll chat anytime. Maybe let me see some more of those horses. Alright?"

"Yes, sir," I say.

He hangs up. I go upstairs and take my semi-automatic out of the gun cabinet. I have hundreds of rounds in there, and every one of them has that motherfucker's name on it.

A truck pulls up the drive. I use the barrel of my rifle to push the curtain aside. Down below, Jack swings out of his truck, black cowboy hat on his head. He has a pistol in his hand, and he checks the magazine as he heads up the front steps. I leave the bedroom and move downstairs to let him in.

The door must be unlocked still, because he walks in as I enter the hall.

"Anybody else here?" he asks.

I shake my head. "Andy went with some of the cowboys to check the back gates and lock everything up. I wanted men and dogs at every entrance to the ranch."

"Good," he says. "Let me see the bedroom where they took her."

We go back upstairs. Jack's eyes move over the floor and walls as we go, taking everything in. I push open the bedroom door, and he holds out a hand to keep me back.

"How likely are they to hurt her?" he asks.

I shake my head. "I don't know. I—"

My voice cracks. Jack's eyes snap up, narrowing.

"What do you know that you're not saying?" he says.

I shake my head.

"You want my help? Be honest with me, Ryder," he says, voice hard. "What do you know?"

I clear my throat. "I talked to Brothers Boyd. I asked him to kill the man who took Freya's virginity."

"Because?"

"Because he was a cunt," I say. "Because she cried when she told me about it, and, more likely than not, that's the mother of my baby."

"Congratulations," says Jack, not missing a beat.

"He was already dead," I say harshly. "Aiden killed him years ago, after that man fucked her. And then, she collects all these fucking bugs and pins them in cases. It's something that means a lot to her—she had years of these things in a box. When Aiden found out she was fucking me, he smashed that shit to dust."

Jack's forest green eyes are black. He leans down and pulls the sheet back, revealing the pillow with a few smears of crimson.

"Are you saying he fucks her?" he clips, no emotion.

I shake my head. "I'm saying he's got some kind of weird attachment, and he can't stand the thought of anybody else being with her. She's talked about how she looks just like her mother. She talks about how he shames her, calls her a whore."

"I don't think he wants her like that," Jack says.

I stare at him, jaw working. "We've been friends a while, Jack. Don't bullshit me."

"What do you want from me?" He lifts his hand. "How am I supposed to know if Aiden wants to fuck his stepdaughter?"

"Because you know shit."

"Not shit like this. Do you know?"

I push the semi-automatic back over my shoulder and run my hand over my face. Sweat drips from my temples, stinging down my neck. Every conversation I've ever had with Freya, in our most intimate moments, spins through my mind.

"I don't," I say.

"Deacon—"

"I don't know." My voice raises. "I don't know what he's thinking, but I know she doesn't know. I don't want her to know."

"Why can't she know?" Jack circles the bed.

"Because she doesn't deserve to have to carry that around."

Jack takes off his hat and stands with it hanging by his thigh, like he's thinking hard. "I get it," he says. "But I don't think she's in danger like that from him right now."

He sounds confident. Or maybe he's just trying to keep me calm. That's more likely.

"Why do you think that?" I press.

"Why now?" Jack says. "If he was going to, he'd have done it already. He wants what he said he wants. Land, money, power. If he and the McClaines get the highway and development through, he's set up to be one of the wealthiest landowners in the state."

I turn, heading back down the hall. Jack comes after me.

"Deacon," he snaps.

"Don't patronize me," I retort, heading downstairs. I grab my jacket and pull it on before stepping onto the icy porch. Jack follows me just as my phone starts ringing.

I pick up. It's Jensen, walking fast. I can hear it in his breath.

"What's the situation?" he says.

"The same," I say. "Jack is here."

"Sovereign and Westin are coming. They can be there by nightfall, but we need a plan. We need to figure out where they're keeping her first."

"Good," I say. "Get them here. I'll do everything else."

He hangs up. I stand, heart refusing to slow down. I've been in situations where I was sure I was going to die, but I've never felt anything like this anger.

They have her, and maybe our baby too. There's no fucking way I'll let Aiden get away with this.

I alight the porch and head for the blacksmith shop.

"Where are you going?"

I stop, looking down at my boots. Jack knows who I am. He's been my friend for over a decade and a half. None of the violence I'm about to commit will shock him. I turn, looking back. He's gazing at me from beneath the brim of his black hat.

"Aiden Hatfield needs to be put down," I say. "But I'm not doing that with a gun. That's too good for him."

Jack's face doesn't change. "What do you need?"

"I need the rest of you to handle the other men," I say. "Aiden's mine."

# CHAPTER FORTY-ONE
# FREYA

It's getting on towards night.

After Bittern left, nobody came again, but I can hear men moving about the house. I'm in a bedroom with the window boarded shut. Luckily, there's a small adjoining bathroom with a toilet and a sink. Otherwise, all I can do is pace the room or sit on the bed with my arms wrapped around my legs, staring into space.

Once or twice, I touch my stomach and wonder what will happen.

I'm exhausted, my head blurry, but I can't sleep.

Deacon will come for me, I know that. What scares me is wondering what kind of carnage he'll cause and who will make it out alive. My heart aches, and all I can do is fantasize about getting free.

Getting home to Deacon.

The doorknob turns. My pulse spikes, and I push myself up, crawling back against the headboard. The door creaks open, and the bottom falls out of my stomach as Aiden walks in and shuts it behind him.

Our eyes lock. I wet my lips.

"Please let me go," I whisper.

Aiden shakes his head once. He looks tired, but his eyes are alert. I can tell he's been up for hours. He's wearing one of his old shirts, dusty, eaten away at the collar, and he's got a backward ball cap on his head. He only wears that inside when he hasn't gotten a chance to shower in a while.

He kicks out a chair in the corner and sits, splayed out like Deacon.

"Please," I whisper.

He shakes his head again. "I need Ryder to back down and give me that easement. He won't do that for anybody but you. For once, you being a whore has paid off for me."

He's called me that so many times, but this time it hurts the most. Silence falls. He sits there, one leg jiggling, not taking his eyes from me.

"You look so much like her," he says, voice low.

All at once, years of pain fill the room like a palpable ache. His throat bobs as he swallows.

"You loved her," I whisper.

It tumbles out before I can stop it. All my life, I assumed he just wanted to own her, to take something beautiful and snuff it out. But the moment I say those words, a flicker of pain moves through his eyes.

"When she left, I ignored you for years," he says distantly. "I don't remember much of you from then, but after you said the Whitaker boy fucked you, I woke up and noticed you looked just like her."

My mouth is dust-dry.

"You can say her name," I whisper.

The corner of his mouth jerks up. "I called her Laurie. She used to get so mad because she wanted to be Laurel Rose."

I can't speak. Not even dead drunk has Aiden been this vulnerable before. Now, he's sober, and his eyes are like open sores.

He runs a hand over his face. Silence falls again.

"Why did she really leave?" I whisper.

He lets out a slow sigh and reaches into his pocket to take out a pack of cigarettes. He turns it over in his hands. The corner is crushed, and he keeps worrying it with his thumb.

"We had a fight, things got heated," he says. "I might have done some things...I didn't mean."

Sickness passes over me in a wave, making my breathing come short and fast. Aiden snorts, looking toward the boarded up window.

"She overreacted," he says. "And she did the same thing Lady did, threatened to take my kids. I told her she couldn't leave with the boys. So, she decided to stay, but she wasn't right after that. Started getting high, just bottomed out. She left for good six months later."

He leans forward, resting his elbows on his knees.

"Nobody takes my kids," he says softly. "You call me what you want, but I was never a fucking deadbeat. I raised you all."

Anger rises like a storm in me.

"I'm not your daughter," I snap. "You didn't raise me. I raised myself."

He stands, shoving the cigarettes in his pocket. "Yeah, you're not. You were never anything but another mouth to feed. Which is why I don't mind to use you as bait."

Hatred like I've never felt pours through me. "Is this about Deacon? Or about me?"

He gives me a long stare. "Not everything is about you."

"But this is," I say. "This is personal. There was no reason you had to smash my collection."

"Jesus," he says under his breath. "You still fixated on that shit?"

I stand up, aware there's nothing intimidating about me. He's over a foot taller and has a hundred pounds of muscle on me. I'm shivering in nothing but my slip, blood still caked on the split on my mouth.

"It meant *everything* to me," I whisper, fists clenched.

His eyes flare. "Nobody ever fucking laid their hands on you, and all you do is bitch like they did."

The anger I've pushed down for years boils over. Without thinking, I surge forward and swipe at him. Quick like a snake, he grabs my wrist, spins me, and slams my front into the wall. Pain splits through my head, a hot throbbing below my right eye.

He's breathing hard, forearm against my lower back.

"I will break you," he says, voice harsh.

A sob works its way up my throat. He already broke me so badly, I don't know if I'll ever be fully healed. And for years, he sat at his place at the head of the table and watched me try to put myself back together again and again, like a bug squirming on its back.

Aiden has left scars on me I'll always live with. It's how my brain formed, like a tree growing around a thick chain. I can extract him, but I'll always have the empty places he left behind.

He lets me go. Slowly, I turn around to face him.

His eyes are so close, burning black and blue. Sweat etches down his chest, down his neck, down to the collar of the shirt I scrubbed with my bare hands. The shirt he wore out putting food on my plate.

My heart thumps in my mouth. His hand comes up, and I tense, waiting for the blow. Then, his hand stops, palm open, but relaxed, like he's reaching.

Then, he touches me, middle finger on my jaw.

The world spins.

His chest heaves. The room is gone. We're standing in the kitchen, and I'm telling him what Braxton Whitaker did, that he fucked, but didn't force, me, but Aiden is livid all the same. The bottom drops out of my stomach as pieces click into place.

"You did it," I whisper. "You're the reason Braxton never came back. What did you do to him?"

His pale eyes flick up then go back to his finger. He's watching it drag down my jawline, to my chin. Now I understand, like never before, the thin, thin line between hatred and desire.

"Aiden." The word is so quiet.

His finger and thumb are on my chin. My chest heaves, straining through the thin fabric. The corner of his lips curls.

"I snorted, took pills," he says hoarsely. "But there's some shit I never touched. There's shit you can't come back from."

"Did you abuse it too?" I whisper. "Just because you couldn't have it?"

His fingers leave my chin and wrap around my neck. They don't feel too different from Deacon's hands—until they start tightening.

"Don't," I gasp. "Please, just leave me with this one thing you didn't do."

His jaw flexes. Dots appear in my vision.

"Please, Aiden," I manage. "I'm begging you. I'm pregnant."

All the fleeting emotion in his eyes vanishes. There's nothing left but rage. Decades of it, boiling over. He lets me go, shoving my head back.

"You'd better pray Deacon Ryder can really fucking fight," he spits.

He turns, boots ringing on the floor, and leaves. The door slams so hard, the room shakes. My hands are numb as I slide to the floor and drop my head to my knees. How could I have misunderstood Aiden so deeply for so long? The world has turned upside down.

The only thing I know for certain is that Deacon Ryder can fight like hell.

And not even Aiden is a match for him.

# CHAPTER FORTY-TWO
## DEACON

I go to the blacksmith shop. It's icy cold, and all the metalworking materials I left after making her chastity belt are still laid out. The smooth-topped fence stake still sits on the anvil from the night I fucked her with it.

My mind goes back to when she told me Aiden smashed her collection. I've heard a lot of sad stories in my life, but nothing that tugged at my heart like that, especially in the context of everything else she's told me, how scared she's been her entire life.

I pick up the stake. It brings back the memory of that night—of Freya draped over the anvil, firelight glimmering over her beautiful body.

My fingers tighten.

Beneath all the good she brings out in me, I'm still the same animal who drove metal into Henderson's skull, again and again, long after he was dead. All those years of torment poured out of me. I should have hit him the minute Phil died, but I let it build until there was so much bad blood, nothing but death could fix it.

That was when I realized there was something different about me.

Something dark.

It lifts its head, sniffing the air. I bring the stake to my face and inhale. Just metal, nothing else. Head blank, I run my tongue along it, and that's when I taste a faint sweetness.

My eyes snap open.

It's time to pin that motherfucker to a wall like one of the bugs he crushed to dust from her collection.

It's almost dark when I step out of the blacksmith shop. Jack went out and rode the property. He came back, certain that with the number of trucks on the McClaine land, they took Freya to the farmhouse at the top of the hill. He went by the Hatfield property to find their house locked up and the lights off. The McClaine house is a fortress with the best vantage point.

Now, he sits on the porch, hat low and cigarette tip glinting. Stu rolls lazily at his feet. Ryder Ranch is quiet even though everyone is on high alert. The wranglers are stationed along the border. Andy has his best at the gates.

I hear the vehicles approach and move to the edge of the driveway. A black truck pulling a horse trailer comes up first. Riding on either side of it, at an easy posting trot, are Gerard Sovereign and Westin Quinn. The silver Sovereign Mountain logos on their hats and side of the trailer glint in the barn lights.

Jensen swings out of the truck, eyes tired and shirt damp with sweat. Westin pulls his horse to a halt. He's a tall man, a year or two younger than me, with a grim face and bright, piercing eyes. When he needed me most, I was there. Now, he's back to return the favor.

Gerard circles him and pulls to a halt. He's the only man I know who's bigger than I am. Not by much though. His body is broad, his shoulders like cinder blocks. Even the horse he rides, Shadow, is a giant of an animal.

Slowly, he takes off his hat and gives me a long stare.

"Get me back alive," he says. "I got a pregnant wife at home."

I nod, jerking my head at the house. They both dismount, and one of Sovereign's cowboys gets out to bring the horses into the barn. We head up to the front porch and go inside. Jack Russell is in the kitchen, taking down a bottle of whiskey and setting glasses out on the counter.

"Westin," I say.

He glances up. Over the summer, he found himself up against some powerful men, ones who hurt his wife. I was there, helping, the night he killed them all. Since then, there's been an unspoken bond of brotherhood. Out of anyone, he'll understand what I'm feeling.

"Cigarette?"

He nods, following me through the side door to the porch. I shut it behind me and light two cigarettes, passing him one.

"Jack thinks Freya is in the McClaine farmhouse," I say.

Westin inhales, eyes glinting below his hat. "We can't attack if she's inside."

I shake my head. My throat feels tight.

"There's something else," he says. "What?"

"She thinks she's pregnant."

Westin glances at me sharply. "By you?"

"What the fuck? Yeah, by me."

Desperation cracks my voice. Westin puts his hand on my shoulder.

"I get it," he says. "We'll get her back. They don't say all roads lead to Sovereign Mountain for nothing—you've got us. Between the five of us, we can figure this shit out. Okay?"

I nod, wordless.

"You eat today?" he asks.

"Not since early morning."

Westin stubs out his cigarette and pulls the door open. "Go shower, get some clean clothes on. We'll make some food and get a plan together."

He's right—I need to be sharp and have a clear head. I move through the bodies in my kitchen without speaking and go upstairs. With the bedroom door shut, everything is quiet.

I go to the bed and sink down. The pillow, smeared with a bit of blood, stares back at me.

I pick it up and bring it to my face.

Sweet, warm vanilla. Like home, the home I never had.

The home she'll give me.

Without her, I'm not a man. I'm a shell, a machine made of nothing but hurt and scars. I can fight, can hit back better than I know how to breathe, but to be whole, I need her. She's the heart in my chest. She breathed life into my empty body.

I set the pillow aside. One of her fern-green ribbons sits on the bedside table. I shove it in my pocket before I go into the bathroom and strip my shirt off. The fear is ebbing away—maybe because I have the best men I can get downstairs, maybe because I know there's no world where I don't get her back.

My eyes lock with my reflection.

I'm not the man I was a week ago, a month. Freya has changed me, deep inside. There's no confusion about who I am.

John, the boy who got kicked around, is gone. Now, there's only Deacon Ryder, a man who doesn't question himself.

I want blood the way I needed it the night I put a stake into Henderson's temple. I can be a gentle beast for her, but not for the rest of the world. Whatever son of a bitch fathered me put something in my veins that's stronger than conditioning.

I've always wondered who he was, what he was like. Now, I think I'm looking at him. I've tried to change, to not be this brutal kind of man, but I always come back to myself in the end.

Numbly, I open the drawer and take out a silver chain, threading Freya's ring on it and hanging it around my neck. Then, I turn on the shower and let it run while I take out the buzzer and run it over my head until there's nothing left but a dark shadow.

There it is: the haunted dark eyes of the man who burnt the dead body of his brother, standing drenched in hot blood, watching the funeral pyre disappear into the sky.

Cain, left to wander the Earth.

I get in the shower and wash quickly. I'm fastening my belt and pulling a Henley over my head when I hear a faint shout from outside. My pulse spikes, and I pull on my boots and move down the stairs. Jack stands in the front door, body relaxed, rifle laying over his thigh. He glances at me and jerks his head, disappearing onto the porch.

I follow him.

"Westin and Jensen went out," he says. "There's a man crossing the fence line."

I scan the darkness, gaze fixing on bobbing lights near Deacon's Hill. "Don't shoot," I say.

"They won't," he says. "They're bringing him in."

I alight the steps and watch the lights bob closer. Voices rise and fall. Three figures come into view: Westin and Jensen, a limp-shouldered man walking between them. They get closer, and I can see his hands are tied in front of him and he's walking with difficulty.

Jensen steadies him as they reach the bottom step.

Bittern Hatfield.

He drags his head up. His skin is moonlight white and dewy with sweat.

"Jesus, you look like shit," I say.

His chest heaves. "Can't breathe good."

I jerk my head. "Get him inside. He's no good to us dead."

They drag him into the kitchen, and I watch from the hallway while Jensen sets him down and gives him a glass of water and a shot of moonshine. Sovereign stands in the doorway between the kitchen and the porch, arms crossed. When he sees Bittern, he narrows his eyes and studies him without speaking.

"Where's Freya?" I ask.

The kitchen goes quiet. Bittern drags his eyes to mine.

"She's at the McClaine's," he manages. "She asked me to help her. I don't know how."

There's a short silence. I sink down in the chair opposite him.

"Aiden put a tracker in my truck," I say. "He trapped me."

Bittern wipes his drenched face with his palm. "Yeah, he did. He didn't expect you to leave so soon, but he had everything he needed with him. Ryland had his truck parked at the pull-off from the night before."

I take a moment to digest that. Aiden disgusts me, but he's smart. I underestimated how smart.

"So how do I know this isn't a trap too?" I ask.

He shrugs.

I take my pistol out and set it on the table. "Maybe I should just shoot you right now."

His eyes drag up, and a chill goes down my spine. There's weariness in them I've never seen before. It's as if, deep down, in the fibers of his body, he's ready to go out at any moment.

"You can do that," he sighs. "Just get Freya out. She doesn't deserve the things Aiden does to her."

The mood in the room shifts. I glance at Westin, and he's giving me a faintly disgusted look, like I'm playing with a wounded animal.

"What does Aiden do to her?" I ask.

Bittern shakes his head once. "Makes her cry. I always say, don't fucking make Frey cry, but all I get for it is the shit beat out of me."

I get up and take a cigarette from the everything drawer. He leans back in the chair, putting it to his lips with shaking fingers. I snap the lighter, he inhales.

"Does he do anything else?"

Bittern glances up. "If you're asking if he touches her, he doesn't," he says. "He thinks about it, but he doesn't."

"Jesus fucking Christ," says Sovereign from the corner.

The corner of Bittern's mouth turns up, but there's no humor in his face.

"Nobody hates Aiden more than Aiden," he says.

I don't know what that means, but I have bigger concerns. I sink down in the chair beside him. "You say you want to help. What do you want in return?"

He shakes his head. "Nothing. Keep me here, send me back. Either way, I'm dying."

"The fuck's wrong with you, other than being a pill addict?" Westin says.

Bittern goes quiet for a second. Then, he takes a drag. "Got fucked up in the mines," he says. "Nowhere for men to work but the factory and the mines. Nothing for men to do after but die. Get pills to help you there, if you're lucky. I'm ready to go."

The kitchen is dead quiet. I get the feeling Bittern hasn't spoken this many words in a long time.

"Does Freya know you're here?" I ask.

"No, I told her I couldn't help her. But I came anyway."

"Why?" I press.

"Because if anybody deserves to make it out, it's Freya," Bittern says. "If you're going to save her, I gotta go back and pretend like I wasn't here. You can't shoot into that house with her in it. She says she's pregnant."

Everyone looks right at me.

"Yeah, not sure, but likely," I say.

"You know, they got a test for that now," says Jensen.

I give him a look. "Thanks."

Bittern clears his throat. "I'm going back," he says. "I think I can get Freya out, but I can't get her further than the land where the easement was supposed to go. Don't have the lungs for it."

"We can have someone get her there," Jack says from where he leans against the wall. "I'll go and Westin can spot me. Unless you wanted to go, Deacon?"

I shake my head. "I want someone to take her as far from that house as possible. There won't be anybody alive by morning. She doesn't need to see that."

Sovereign clears his throat, pushing off the doorway. "Let's get moving," he says. "It's already nine."

I look at Bittern, studying him. His eyes focus for the first time, and a chill goes down my spine. He might not be her blood, but he is a piece of Freya. He looks at me with her haunted eyes. There's a deep trauma bond between them.

I lean in. He doesn't break eye contact.

"When this is done, you're going to rehab," I say. "You're getting help, getting whatever is fucked up in your lungs taken care of. And if you try to leave wherever the fuck I lock you up before you're stone cold sober, I'll put a bullet between your eyes. We clear?"

His lack of reaction tells me everything I need to know.

He fears death, but he loves Freya enough to face it. I admire him for that, and I'll keep my promise and do my best to save him.

"I got it," he whispers.

I stand up and pour a shot. "Alright, let's make a plan."

He clears his throat, hitting his chest with his fist. "There's one more thing you should probably know about Aiden, Freya, and me," he says. "Everything makes a little more sense in light of it."

I sit back down. "Go on."

# CHAPTER FORTY-THREE
# FREYA

I'm on my side, palm on my lower stomach. If I press my eye to the boarded windows, I can see a sliver of the sky. By the position of the moon, I think it's around midnight. The men in the house haven't slept. I can tell there are a lot of them, maybe a dozen. They pass the hallway outside my door frequently.

Deacon once said he didn't want to have to choose between his land and me, but I'm afraid he's going to have to. And I know what he'll choose, even if it breaks him.

My finger traces over my belly.

He'll pick us.

I squeeze my eyes shut and open them. There's a little glow from the nightlight in the corner, and it brings me back to my childhood.

I don't have many memories of my mother, but I do remember her putting me to bed. She'd sit on the other side of the crib bars while I fell asleep. I remember the nightlight on the wall. It was a single bulb, the cover made out of a mason jar.

I wonder if she was as scared as I am now.

The floor creaks outside the door. Slowly, I sit up. It sounds different than the heavy tread of the men. It's cautious, quiet.

The knob turns. My stomach tightens, my mind going right back to when Aiden grabbed my arm and touched my face.

I push back against the wall. The door swings, and I let out a harsh gasp as Bittern steps in.

"Bittern," I whisper.

He shuts the door. "We have to go," he says.

A tingle shocks through me. "What?"

"There's a man waiting for you at the strip of Deacon's land between ours and the McClaine's," he says.

"Deacon's Hill," I whisper. "Who's waiting?"

"His name's Jack," he says. "He'll take you to safety."

"And Deacon?"

"Deacon is going to…stay behind to clean up."

The ceiling creaks, boots move. We both freeze, but nobody comes downstairs. Bittern runs a hand over his face, wiping the layer of sweat off his forehead. I wonder if Aiden gave him his pills today.

"I need you to help me get the boards off the window," he says, reaching into his pocket and taking out a small hammer. He crosses the room and kneels by the windowsill.

I scramble up and tiptoe on bare feet to him. He fits the hammer beneath the bottom board and pulls slowly, trying hard not to make a sound. It pulls off, but it feels like it takes an age to come free. I catch it before it hits the ground, and he starts on another.

"We need to pull five boards off for us to fit through," I whisper.

He glances up. "I'm not going."

I shake my head. "No, you're going. I can't go without you."

He eases the second board off and hands it to me. "No, you're small and quick. I'm slow."

"I won't go," I whisper.

He glances at me briefly. "Yeah, you will. Got a baby, that comes first."

He's right. I blink, a hot tear etching down my cheek. Bittern eases the third board off, and I stack it with the others. The fourth board is giving him trouble, the nail running through a knot. It won't pull free the way the others did.

His hands shake. He wipes his eyes.

"Can I tell you something, Frey?" he says, voice hoarse. "Something I just told Deacon."

I sink to a crouch. "What?"

He's in profile, a bead of sweat hanging off his nose.

"I'm not Aiden's boy," he says.

My heart hurts so badly, I don't know how to absorb another hit out of nowhere. Bittern sets the hammer down for a second and takes a deep breath. I scramble up and get the half-empty bottle of water sitting on the floor by the bed. He takes it and has some before he shakes and spills it down his shirt.

"How do you know that?" I whisper.

He glances at me. "Lady came from a real rough place. Her family moved down from up north when her mother married a man who worked in the mountains. Aiden got Lady pregnant with Wayland and Ryland when they were teenagers, and he took her to live with him. But she went back to her family real quick, begging for refuge, and her stepdad... He got her knocked up."

Sickness rises in my throat.

"Oh my God," I whisper. "Did he go to jail?"

"Lady was just eighteen when she ran home. She got groomed is my understanding." Bittern sets the bottle aside and takes up the hammer again. "Aiden was humiliated. Never wanted anybody to know, so he made Lady go back with him and raised me."

It makes sense now why Aiden never liked Bittern the way he liked Wayland and Ryland. I'm speechless. Bittern spits on the ground, struggling to get the tines of the hammer under the last board.

"Nobody in this goddamn family stood a chance," he says under his breath.

I'm silent, remembering the disgust on Aiden's face when I begged him not to touch me. This is why he never acted on his feelings. He's a broken man, haunted by ghosts.

"Did you ever meet your father?" I whisper.

Bittern shakes his head. "Aiden went to his house with a shotgun and told him if he ever came near his family, he'd blow his head open. Might be one of the few good things Aiden ever did."

The board starts easing off. Bittern gets excited, his eyes flashing, and the board lets out a squeak.

"Slow," I say.

He nods and takes a breath.

"Bittern, can I ask you something?"

He nods again. I realize now where I got into the habit of doing that. It's because Bittern never asks or tells without checking with a person first. I think I just picked it up from him without knowing.

"Aiden hates me because of my mother. But that's not the whole story, is it?"

He goes still, lids lowered.

"I think because...he was always one wrong move from becoming just like Lady's stepfather," he says finally. "He was really fucked up from what happened. I'm sorry he took it out on you."

He's right, but my brain is so tired, I can't absorb his words. The board eases off, and I dart forward to catch it before it clatters to the ground. The window is halfway exposed.

"Take the next board off," I say, gripping his arm. "Please. For me."

His jaw works. A second etches by. Then, he pushes the hammer underneath and starts tugging. This one is the easiest. It comes off cleanly, and he sets it aside. Behind it, the window is grimy, like it's been closed up for a while.

"Alright, let's go," Bittern says, digging his fingers in and pushing the glass up. The wood squeaks, but he keeps going until it's big enough for him to get his broad body through.

Working quickly, he unlatches the screen and puts his head out. A gust of cold air tears through, raising goosebumps on my arms.

"All clear," he says.

He wriggles himself halfway out, swinging both legs over the edge. Our eyes meet, and then he falls. Heart in my throat, I lean out.

Thank God, it's barely five feet off the ground. He's standing there, unscathed, holding his hands up.

"Come on, Frey," he says. "We gotta go before someone comes out on the porch."

I swing the lower half of my body out, the cold air biting my bare skin. All I have to cover me is my slip and the chastity belt underneath.

"What if they chase us?" I whisper.

He looks up at me, and for a second, I see him the way he was before the mines—quiet, sweetness in those blue eyes.

"I got a gun in my belt," he says. "I'm ready to go out in a blaze of glory."

He says it with a smile, but my heart aches. I drop into his arms, and he sets me on my feet, taking my hand. The ground is cold on my feet, but I don't have a choice. We get across the yard to the edge of the woods when Bittern stops. He pulls his flannel shirt off, leaving him in just his undershirt, and wraps it around me.

"I got no shoes," he says.

"It's fine," I say. "We just have to get to Jack."

The front door slams open. Bittern doesn't wait. He takes my arm and drags me into the shadows. The moon casts enough glow to highlight the worn path ahead, but I cling to him as we move quickly through the dark.

My feet are ice cold when we break from the woods. In the distance, I think I see a figure on horseback. My heart flutters at the thought of it being Deacon, even though I know it's not.

*Click.*

My heart leaps. Bittern spins and shoves me behind him.

Aiden stands behind us, pistol up. He's carrying his father's revolver, the one he kept his entire life. It's old, but it works. I know because I've seen him use it. His chest heaves, the buttons of his shirt mismatched, like he got dressed quickly.

"Don't fucking move," he snarls.

Bittern raises his hand. "Don't point that at her."

Aiden's eyes flash. "What is she to you? Why're you always sticking your neck out for her?"

Bittern doesn't speak for a long time. I see Aiden's patience wearing thin. Bittern's hand lowers. He's sweating so hard, there's no doubt he hasn't gotten his pills in hours.

"It wasn't right, what you done," he says finally.

"What I did?" Aiden repeats. "What did I do but raise you all?"

"You smashed it," Bittern says, voice shaking. "You smashed all her shit."

Voices sound from the woods. I hear horses coming closer with a steady beat. My stomach sinks. We got close, but we're not getting out of this one. There's nowhere to run except out into the open field. The men and dogs will take us down before we get halfway there.

Another set of hooves joins the chorus.

Pounding from behind.

Cowed, I turn and tip over onto my ass in the dirt. A pale white horse skids to a halt, grass spraying, and a man swings down, coat whipping around his body. He pulls a shotgun from the saddle as his boots hit the ground.

His body turns in a graceful arc. The shotgun spins in his hand. The butt hits Aiden across the head with a sickening thud.

Someone is screaming. I think it might be me. Quicker than I can see what's happening, Jack is in the saddle again, his huge ghost of a horse spinning on a dime. A hand comes down and grabs me by the scruff of Bittern's flannel shirt, yanking me painfully off my feet.

Then, I'm in the saddle, an arm clamped around my body, and we're riding hard into the dark.

My eyes stream. The air feels like icy cold fingers raking over my half-naked body. Exile runs like it's the last time he'll ever run. His huge body takes us through the dark so fast, I can barely focus on the trees flying by.

I squirm, trying to turn. Jack makes a sound in his throat, a harsh warning.

"Stay," he shouts.

In the distance, the lights of the McClaine house fade. Bittern is back there with the men. He's a defenseless bird, just like his namesake, and they'll crush what life he has left in him.

"Bittern," I scream, sick with desperation.

"He's got a gun," Jack says. "He can fight."

He doesn't know Bittern. Aiden will beat him and leave him bleeding out on the hill. When the frost comes tonight, he'll die frozen, far away from his home.

"Where are we going?" I beg through the tears falling fast and hard.

He puts an arm around my body, locking me against his side.

"Hold on tight. We're going to Sovereign Mountain."

I think I misheard him—I've seen the road signs and heard people talk about that place. There's no way he can make the run to Sovereign Mountain tonight, not when it's down the highway past South Platte. By the map, it's a two and a half hour drive via the most direct route.

I turn my head. In the distance, the mountains loom closer.

My stomach churns.

We're not going by the map. He's taking us into the mountains, the ones I don't trust because they're nothing like the cradle of the Appalachians. I squeeze my eyes shut and burrow my face into the shoulder of his coat. There's nothing I can do but let him urge Exile on, the shadows deep from the overhead moon.

Deacon trusts Jack Russell to keep me safe.

That's all I need to know.

# CHAPTER FORTY-FOUR
## DEACON

I'm stretched out beside Westin, on the rise of the hill that overlooks McClaine Ranch. He's the best sharpshooter I know. It's why they call him Gunslinger, and it's pissing him off that I won't let him just pick Aiden off through the window.

Behind him, Sovereign waits with a rifle over his shoulder. He's going to spot us going down the hill and take out Aiden if, God forbid, I lose against him and he runs.

"I can fucking see him," Westin whispers, breath frosty. "An inch to the left, and all your problems are gone."

"Down boy," I say.

"Yeah, fuck you."

I glance over at the hillside, where Jensen is waiting to signal the second Jack has Freya safe on his horse. It's dark, just the outline of the trees visible. In the distance, I can hear horses pounding through the woods.

My heart is in my throat.

Jack swore he'd keep her safe. If anyone can, it's Jack Russell.

But that doesn't mean it's not killing me that I'm the executioner in all this, not the savior.

There's a faint thud to the north. We both turn our heads at the echo. Hooves pound. Then, I see it—a light flickers three times through the trees.

"Jesus fuck," I breathe, relief flooding through me.

"Let me do it," Westin says, flitting his eye to the sight again. "She's safe. Let me take out this motherfucker."

I shift off my stomach and into a crouch. "No, I need to do it. With my hands."

I stand and head to where Bones waits just below the rise of the hill. Sovereign stays where he's at, arm crossed, rifle against his thigh. He's like a rock. He won't move until it's time. Westin sighs, getting up and following me to where his horse stands and mounts up. I do the same, and we head east, taking the long way around Deacon's Hill to come at the house from the other side.

We just have to wait until the men come back to the house. They're not dumb enough to follow Jack into the mountains. They couldn't catch up with Exile if they tried anyway.

We move through the shadows until I can hear the faint sound of talking in the house.

Horses thunder down the hill. I see Aiden leading the way. They all pull to a halt in a spray of dirt and frozen grass. He's livid—I see it in the way he moves to the house. He walks like me when I'm angry, jaw set and fists clenched. It's no wonder Freya was scared of me at first.

"They go inside, we move," I say. "You got my back?"

Westin jerks his chin in a nod. "Don't tell my wife, but it feels good to be back in the saddle, even just for a night."

I laugh. "Won't say a word."

There's a short silence. Westin clears his throat and checks his rifle.

"What's it feel like, knowing she's pregnant?" he says. "I think Diane and I... We'll start trying soon."

"I don't know, but more likely than not, she is," I say.

"What's it feel like?" he repeats.

I clear my throat, tapping my chest. "Feels like all this is on the outside now."

There's a long silence.

"Makes sense," he says gruffly. "Alright. They're in. Let's move."

"Remember, your job is to cover me and get me to Aiden," I say. "Pick anybody else off who shoots at you. It'd be best if you let the randoms just run. Less paperwork that way."

He jerks his head, adjusting in his stirrups as his horse prances. I click at Bones, and he starts trotting up the hill, breaking into a canter. Westin keeps pace beside me. The sound of our approaching horses doesn't reach the men circled by the door and on the porch until we're breaking out of the field and into the yard.

Then, they hear us, and everything is chaos. Someone starts shouting, trying to raise the alarm. Westin lifts his rifle and fires a row of warning shots over the house. I let Bones take me right into the middle of it and swing off, slapping his hindquarters hard enough so he knows to keep moving. I don't want anybody killing my horse.

A man with a rifle bursts from the front door. Westin spins and shoots, and the man crumples before he can lift his gun. Through the haze, I hear another set of hoofbeats behind me, and I know Jensen is here. It takes a half second before I see him barreling around the corner and running right over someone with a sickening crunch.

Jensen dismounts, taking a pistol out, and starts shooting like he's got no fear in his body. That's the thing about these people from the eastern hills: they're fucking scrappy, Freya and Jensen both.

A bullet flicks past my ear. Blood trickles down my neck. Through the screaming and the doors slamming, I hear someone's voice shouting orders.

Aiden.

Gripping my gun, I move through the men, knowing Westin is picking off anybody who tries to shoot at me. My boots clatter up the steps. Through the screen door, I catch a glimpse of Aiden disappearing down the hall.

Rage floods my veins. He took my wife and my baby.

Time to pay up.

One-handed, I grip the door and rip it to the side, shattering the hinges. The interior door hits the wall so hard, the knob sinks into the drywall. I step inside, just in time to see Ryland come around the corner with his gun raised.

I freeze for a beat.

There's a coat rack to my left. I pick it up and launch it down the hall so quickly, Ryland can't move. It hits him across the chest and sends him flying into the kitchen beyond.

Another man takes his place. I flip up my rifle and pull the trigger, and he falls on top of Ryland's squirming body. There's a stomach turning crunch. Then, they both go still.

Unphased, I step over them and look to the left. It's a big house, but if I had to guess, Aiden went upstairs because the back door is still locked by a hook and eye catch on the inside. I veer to the right, moving through the living room.

Pain explodes in my shoulder, and I spin, falling to my back so hard, the house shudders.

Aiden stands over me, a rifle in his hand. There's a second where we look at each other, and we both know where this ends without saying a word.

Someone walks away.

Someone doesn't.

I lift my boot and shove my body down the floor hard until I'm close enough to kick as hard as I can into his shin. It's so quick, he can't sidestep before he swears, falling back against the wall. The glass cabinet behind him shatters, spraying the floor around us.

I roll to my stomach, blood trickling from my palms, and get up. Aiden picks up a chair. I see it like a flash, and then it's flying toward me before I can duck. Hands up, I catch it and slam it down on the floor, ripping the leg off.

This time, I sling it hard. It hits his arm, knocking the gun from his hand. I kick it back, leaving my gun with it. Now, we're both unarmed.

"You're fucking insane," he breathes.

I tilt my head and take a step closer. We're locked in, wolves circling.

"She's gone," he breathes. "Get out."

I shake my head. "No, I'm going to make you pay for every fucking thing you've ever done to her, you sick fuck."

He takes a step back. Before I can react, he spins and bolts toward the back of the house. I take off after him, our boots thundering. He disappears around the corner. I follow, catching a glimpse of him at the top of the stairs as he turns.

I go after him.

I'm not scared of Aiden Hatfield.

There's nobody there. I kick in the first door, tearing it from the hinges. Empty.

And then the second. And the third.

I move down the hall, putting my boot through every door and leaving them a mangled mess. They crash, one after the other, shooting up dust. At the last one, I turn the corner and *bam*—Aiden comes out of nowhere, colliding with me.

The wind knocks out of my lungs. Pain explodes.

We hit the ground, and he draws back, punching me in the side of the face.

Motherfucker, he's got a right arm like a mule's kick. Pain bursts right after the impact, like white heat. My eyes are unfocused, and I blink, his contorted face swimming over mine. His eyes are burning, raging.

That's the advantage I have over him. I can hold my shit together and he can't.

I think that's what makes us different.

I stop moving and spit, hard enough that it hits him. He freezes. Blood and saliva drip from his face. My mouth must be bleeding, I can't tell. Everything tastes the way it does in a fight, like the raw end of a gun.

"You got any last words?" he seethes, lifting what looks like a chair leg.

Clearly, he underestimated the amount of times I've had the shit beat out of me if he thinks this is the end. I tighten my hips and thighs, wrapping them around his free leg, and flip him to the side. Before he can react, I grip him by the collar and slam him into the floor.

"Yeah, how's it feel to be a little bitch?" I pant.

He gnashes his teeth, slams them together, foam gathering at the corner of his mouth.

"You want that whore, you have her," he spits. "She's fucking ran through."

I hit him hard enough to stun him for a second. My fingers dig into his hair, pushing his head back against the floor. I lean in, our breath mingling. Blood drips from my mouth and hits his chin.

"Is that why you never touched her?" I say, teeth gritted.

His eyes widen.

"What? You think I don't know?" I spit. "You thought you'd be the first, huh? Couldn't stand it when you weren't."

I'm just shit-talking based on my assumptions, but I'm clearly right, because the deepest rage mixed with self-loathing floods his eyes.

"Oh, yeah, Bittern spilled everything," I say. "How he's not your boy. Does it eat you up that you're the same as his father?"

His throat moves as he swallows. My blood slips down his jaw.

"Do you look in the mirror and see him?" I whisper, getting closer. "And then think about touching her anyway? Filthy fucking pervert."

He snaps into action, whipping his head back and butting me in the face. My nose crunches for the third or fourth time in my life, and I feel it snap. Blood surges down my chin and over his face.

The tension, the blood spattering over us, throws my balance. Aiden flips, scrambling to his feet, and runs. This time, he's not trying to do anything but get away. I scramble upright, the room swaying.

My hand finds my nose through slippery, metallic red and pinches it hard, pulling it down and back into place. Pain hits me so hard, my eyes cross for a second. I lean over and spit, trying to get the blood out of my sinuses so I can run like hell after him.

He's disappearing through the back door. There's nowhere to go. It takes my eyes a second to adjust, before I clock his shadow moving toward the barn. Then, it appears in full color as the motion activated lights come on, flooding the yard.

I sprint after him, stopping only to grab the table leg off the living room floor. Neither of us were made for this kind of running. We're both big and carry a lot of muscle. I can fight, but not for longer than a reasonable amount of time.

That's why I prefer to finish my fights within fifteen to twenty minutes. After that, I need a beer or something.

We enter the barn, and he spins, hands up. The whites of his eyes flash.

"Walk away," he pants. "This doesn't have to end like this."

"Yeah, it does," I say.

He shakes his head. My blood is all over his face, making his teeth stand out starkly as he struggles to get his breath.

"Just fucking take her," he says.

I cock my head. "And my land?"

"We'll talk."

Every time Freya has brokenly admitted bits and pieces of her past runs through my mind. She came to me shattered, too scared to look me in the eye sometimes. Aiden did that. He made her afraid. Abuse is complicated, I know that. He might not have hit her, but he abused her for years over things that were never her fault.

That pisses me the fuck off.

Abuse against those who can't fight back is unforgivable. The people who perpetuate that are evil, sick fucks just like Aiden. He's weak inside, tied up in knots over his hatred and lust for what he wants but doesn't understand.

I take a step closer. He backs up.

We're a dozen feet from the back wall of the barn. On either side are shadows. The outside light cuts through and hits Aiden like a spotlight. Blue light, black shadows, and red blood drench his body.

"She's all fucked up," I say, voice dropping.

His eyes dart over me. "Who?"

"Freya," I say. "She's all fucked up from the shit you did."

"No one laid their hands on that girl." His jaw flexes, pushing out defiantly.

I take a step closer. "So if it didn't leave a bruise, she's alright, huh? You think she's okay after what you did, smashing all her shit?"

I take another step. He doesn't move back this time. He drops his hands, letting them hang by his sides. His shoulders go back, squaring. I get closer, until we're a few feet apart. Eye to eye.

"You want to bully somebody, bully me, motherfucker," I say, voice dropping. "I'll bet you won't because I'm not half your size."

He lurches like he's going to skirt around me and make a run for it. In that millisecond, I think of Freya in tears, in my arms, trying to cover all her wounds because, deep down, she's still afraid she'll be punished for reacting to her pain. I know that doesn't go away. I can give her safety for the rest of her life, but she'll still always cringe inside every time she messes up, expecting to be abused.

She can sort it all out. She can go through therapy.

She can put it in boxes with the right labels.

But she can't change that it happened.

Not any more than I can erase my past and make myself anyone but Deacon Ryder. Our pasts are set in stone. I'll be picking up the pieces of what Aiden did for the rest of my life. I'll sleep beside it, hold it in my arms, talk around in circles about it past midnight.

I love her enough to hold her pain forever, but that doesn't mean I can't get some good, old-fashioned revenge for it.

My arm shoots out, blocking Aiden. Before he can move, I pull the metal stake from my pocket and body him so hard, we both smash into the barn wall. It shudders with a colossal bang.

Our eyes meet, his wild. Our faces are inches apart.

"You're getting off easy with this," I whisper. "This is just for fucking with her bugs."

All the rage in my body explodes into inhuman strength. My hand comes up, and I drive the stake into his chest, stabbing halfway through and ripping it out.

His eyes widen, his body convulsing.

I'm right back where I was twenty years ago. Blood on my knuckles. Life draining away in front of me. This time, I don't have regrets. Aiden needed fucking put down. After what he did to my woman, I'm happy to be the one to rid the world of one more asshole.

I bring the stake down as hard as I can. It rips through his chest, going between his ribs, and sinks into the soft wood, pinning him like one of the bugs in her collection. Satisfaction floods me.

Justice tastes good.

Chest heaving, I step back. He hangs from the wall, eyes glazed. He's gone. Maybe I went too easy on him, maybe it was too painless, but it's done.

I stand, bloody chest heaving. Aiden and I were similar, Freya was right about that. But somewhere along the way, our paths broke apart. I don't know what makes that happen. It's not fair. It's an unbalanced world.

A part of me is sorry for him.

But not sorry enough for mercy.

Exhaustion hits me like a freight train. Limping, I leave the barn and start across the yard. My body aches. I'm wet from head to foot with blood. There's a soft, hot heartbeat in my nose. Now that I'm calming, I can feel the icy air biting at my bloody skin.

It smells like something new, like the eve before a new year.

Morning after a long night.

I've walked a hard road, and it made me a rougher man than I set out to be. But if she's at the end of it, I don't mind what brought me here.

All water under the bridge, as they say.

My left leg hurts like hell. I think there's something jammed in it, but I keep walking because my heart feels her distant presence and my feet will get me there eventually. Up ahead, the yard is empty. There are two bodies on the porch. Jensen sits on the steps, elbows on his knees, a cigarette hanging from his lips.

"Westin's gone to get Bittern," he says.

I stop, one foot on the bottom step. "You think we're getting too old for this shit?"

He sighs, taking in my bloodstained face. "I don't think Deacon Ryder's ever too old for this shit. Me? You got me thinking about settling down."

The yard is silent. He hands me his cigarette, and I take a drag, leaving a bloody stain on the white paper.

"Really?"

He nods. "Yeah...this whole home thing is starting to sound good."

I pass the cigarette back. "Nobody to keep you warm, huh?"

His eyes rest on the mountains. In the distance, we can see the shape of Westin riding back. He smiles in the dark. The cigarette glows as he inhales.

"Nobody waiting for me at home," he says.

Westin draws near and Jensen stands. His hand claps my shoulder as he heads toward him. I follow, drawing close enough to see the limp body thrown over the back of Westin's horse. My stomach drops, and I lift Bittern's head by the hair, pushing my finger beneath his nose to feel his breath.

He's alive.

"Let's get him back to Ryder Ranch," I say. "He needs the hospital."

"Where we headed?" Jensen asks.

"Sovereign Mountain," I say.

"You know what they say," Jensen says, putting on his hat and looking around for Godspeed. "All roads lead to Sovereign Mountain."

"Speak of the devil," Jensen says.

Sovereign appears, spurs jingling. He draws up beside us, Shadow's giant hooves shaking the ground.

"We ready to haul ass out of here?" he asks. "I think we're done."

"Yeah, I need to get to Freya," I say.

"Just...don't tell our wives about this," Westin says firmly, glancing around. "They know we're helping out, but not the particulars. It's just not necessary that they know."

"Nobody tell Freya I stuck Aiden to the barn wall," I say. "Let's just pour some gas, light a match, and get the fuck out of here."

Everyone nods in agreement. I go inside and pause just outside the kitchen. Ryland is on his back, the coat rack still lying across his body. I kneel, placing two fingers against his neck. He's gone—still warm, but without a pulse.

Maybe I killed him when I hit him with the coat rack. Maybe it was a stray bullet.

It doesn't matter anymore.

The house is ravaged. I walk through it as Jensen pours gas and steps out the back door. Westin is by the barn, standing in the doorway. I limp to him, pausing. At the back hangs Aiden, chest mutilated, head down. Blood drips black on his boots.

"Remind me not to cross you," he says.

I look away. "Let's light this motherfucker up. I got somewhere to be tonight."

We stand on the hill for a moment, watching fire blaze through the windows of the house and eat up the open barn. The ground is too cold and wet for it to travel beyond the buildings. When the police get here tomorrow, there will be nothing left but a shell.

# CHAPTER FORTY-FIVE
# FREYA

I'm so cold, I can't move.

The mountains pass by on either side of us, blocking out the sky. Exile scares here and there, but Jack has a steady hand, and he guides him through it. I have a vague impression of passing through two cliffs, the ground winnowing down to a path between them.

A deep sense of foreboding lingers until we're through the pass and heading down a hill.

"Look up," Jack says.

He's slowing, letting Exile catch his breath. I turn my head, the wind whipping my hair. Down below glitter the lights of a ranch. So close, but so far. I've never been, but I can guess that's Sovereign Mountain. To the left of us sits a placid lake, and to the right is a little village of chimneys puffing smoke that must be employee housing.

It looks like warm heaven.

"One last ride," Jack says. "Hold tight."

I grip his arm. He lets Exile's reins loose, and we're running again. This time, it's downhill and harder to hold on. I bounce like a sack of rocks, teeth chattering. Then, after what feels like forever, we move to a slow walk and, finally, a halt.

Jack dismounts, taking me with him. My legs are water, so cold, I can't stand. He half carries me up a set of stairs. Then, he beats so hard on the door, it echoes off the hills.

It opens. I hear a soft gasp.

I'm clinging to consciousness. Sleep is coming, pulling me under. I can't tell what's happening. All I know is Jack is carrying me into a warm house and I'm being laid down. Blankets are packed around me, a fireplace glittering before my eyes. Deacon isn't there, but I feel him drawing closer, like a silvery string tied to my heart and his.

I shut my eyes and sleep.

At some point, it feels like hours later, I become aware of someone gently shaking my shoulder. A groan works its way out as I roll my head to the side. My eyes are stuck shut. It takes a minute to peel them open.

Did I die?

There's an angel leaning over me. Soft red waves fall down her back, framing bright blue eyes, little freckles like stars over her pale beige skin. She grips my shoulder with a hand laden with a fern-green ring. I shift my gaze, confused. A fireplace roars in the hearth across from my bed. Early morning light spills through the window.

"Freya," she whispers.

I turn my head. "Where am I? Who are you?"

Her shoulders sink. "I'm Keira, Sovereign's wife. You're at our ranch."

I just stare, waiting for it to click into place. "Sovereign Mountain."

"My husband went to help Deacon get you back," she says. "Jack brought you here, but he had to take the shortcut through the mountains. You're half frozen, but the doctor is coming at noon to check you over. Can you feel your hands and feet?"

I flex both. "Yes, they feel alright. Just stiff. Where's Deacon?"

She gives me a warm smile. "He's coming."

I sit upright. "He's alive? What about Bittern?"

She shakes her head, forehead creased. "I spoke to Sovereign, and he just said Deacon got what he came for and he was on his way to Sovereign Mountain to bring you home."

My throat is knotted. Half of my heart is overjoyed that Deacon is alright. Half is in deep mourning for the inevitable news that Aiden killed Bittern. I crook my legs, wrapping my arms around them. Keira makes a soothing sound and brushes back my hair.

"Can I get you into the bath?" she asks. "You're very unsteady, but I think some warm water would help."

I nod. Deep inside, I'm still chilled. She stands and my eyes fall to the tie of her dressing gown—knotted over the swell of her pregnant stomach.

Oh God, how could I forget?

My mouth is parched. I need some water. There's a glass on the bedside table. I lift it with unsteady hands and take a sip while Keira disappears into the bathroom to my right. Water runs, and the soft scent of lavender follows.

She returns, leaning in the doorway.

"Do you need help getting in?" she asks.

I look up, unable to speak. She goes to me and sinks down on the bed. "What's wrong?"

Hand shaking, I set the glass down. "I need a test."

Her eyes widen and drop to my waist. I'm out of the slip and in a man's shirt, my body swamped. I touch my palm to my stomach.

"I have one," she says.

She holds out her arm, and I get to my feet slowly. My legs look small and shaky as I move across the floorboards into the bathroom. It smells good, a little steam rising from the foamy bath. Keira lifts the toilet lid and helps me to sit down. I don't protest. Now isn't the time to worry about my dignity.

Keira kneels and takes a little box from beneath the sink. Inside is a blue and white plastic test. She uncaps it and hands it over.

"You just pee on the exposed end," she says. "For about five seconds. Can you do that?"

I nod, cheeks pink. She gets up and pretends she's busy checking the water while I put the test between my legs. When I'm done, I set it on the counter and finish emptying my bladder. Keira, clearly not bothered by germs, pops the cap back on and sets it aside.

"Alright, let's get you in the bath," she says, helping me up. "It's lukewarm. We don't want to shock your body."

She helps me in. Tears gather at the corners of my eyes.

"You're very kind," I whisper. "Thank you."

She gives me a kind smile. I offer a shaky one back. I think she understands. After so many years of cruelty, it's hard to comprehend kindness. She just pats my arm and goes back to the test, picking it up.

"Almost there," she says.

My stomach churns. "Do you like this? Living on a ranch out here, married to one of these Montana men?"

She thinks hard, her lids lowered. Then, she looks up. "Yes, this is my home," she says. "I was afraid, but I'm not afraid anymore."

She doesn't have to say anything else. I hear it all in the timbre of her words. She knows the kind of fear I lived with. I can tell without asking. She moves confidently, but there's still a lingering hesitancy, like she wasn't always as safe as she is now.

"Do you want me to tell you what it says?" she asks.

Heart racing, I nod.

"You're pregnant, honey."

To my surprise, all I feel is the deepest sense of relief. If the last few weeks have taught me anything, it's that Deacon is in this for the long haul. When I tell him, he's going to be so happy, and it's going to make me sob.

For the first time in my life, someone chose me, wanted me, and followed through all the way to the end.

Now, he's on his way here, and suddenly, I'm terrified to tell him.

"Keira," I whisper, my voice shaking. "Will Deacon go to jail for what he did last night? I know he killed everyone."

She laughs, which catches me off guard. "No, Sovereign will probably pull some strings. Jay Reed will get a little grayer. They'll kick the case around for a few months. Then, it'll be ruled a gas leak or an accidental fire."

My jaw is on the floor. "How?"

"Don't ask," she says. "That's my advice if you want to be with one of these men. Just don't ask."

I nod, wordless. There's so much happening. I can't absorb it all. Keira comes to the edge of the tub and sinks down on the chair. Without speaking, she takes a comb and starts working the tangles from my curls. I wrap my arms around my knees and let her work on it. It feels so good to speak with another woman, but it feels better to have one fuss over me, almost how I imagine a mother might.

It takes her a half hour and a lot of conditioner, but she gets my hair fixed and braided tightly down my back. Then, she helps me back into the shirt and walks with me to the bed.

"Thank you," I whisper. "I'm sorry. You must be tired too."

She shakes her head. "When I needed help, others helped me. Now, go to sleep."

"Will you tell Deacon for me?" I blurt out. "As soon as he gets here? I know he's frantic."

Her eyes go soft. "Of course. Now, you try to get some sleep until Deacon arrives. Then, I'd like you to try to eat something."

I nod, sliding onto my side, my eyes heavy. She goes out, leaving the door open. Less than five minutes after she's gone, I hear a faint snuffle under the door. A gray nose peaks around the corner, and a little dog that looks like a black fox peers in. I lift my head.

"Come here," I whisper.

He toddles in and, amazingly, makes the jump onto the bed. His salt and pepper fur is like satin. I brush my fingertips through it as he curls up against my stomach and passes out.

There are so many things I can't control, but that doesn't scare me anymore. He'll handle it, like he handles everything else. He'll take care of me and the babies we have together. He's so good at caring for people.

I found somebody to love me the way my heart wants to be loved. For the first time, I'm a girl with a future worth living for.

# CHAPTER FORTY-SIX
## DEACON

Westin drives my truck. I sit in the passenger side with a handkerchief shoved in the hole in my leg. It's right below the last place I got stabbed, but this time, it's wider and not as deep. I'll be fine once I get a chance to make sure there aren't any wood splinters in it. I can just wrap it up and take an aspirin.

Jensen stayed behind to take Bittern in. His body was cold, breathing shallow but his vitals stable. We loaded him into his truck, and Jensen took off toward the hospital in South Platte, driving like hell.

I told him to make sure the doctors knew I wanted him put directly into rehab the minute he recovers. Freya loves him, so he's getting better whether he likes it or not.

I can't think of anything else but Freya. Keira called Sovereign as we were standing on the hill, watching the flames roar, to let us know Jack got her to Sovereign Mountain safely, but I can't keep rolling through the same two questions in my mind.

If she's pregnant.

If she'll say yes to being my wife.

Morning is breaking as we pull the trucks up the driveway of Sovereign Mountain. Westin gets out and goes to unload the horses, leaving Sovereign and I standing in the driveway.

I hold out my hand, and he shakes it, always a man of few words and fewer emotions. "Better get inside," he says. "You got somebody waiting on you. Maybe two somebodies."

My stomach flips. He heads up the path, and we enter the front hall of the ranch house. It smells like breakfast, and that calms me. Surely, if something were wrong, Keira wouldn't be cooking.

Sovereign leads the way to the kitchen. Keira is putting a pan of biscuits into the oven. She straightens, and relief passes over her face as her eyes fall on her husband. He wraps an arm around her, pressing his lips to her forehead.

"Everybody's safe," he says.

She nods, eyes moving to me. "Oh God, you're bleeding."

"It's fine. Where's Freya?" My voice cracks.

She untangles herself from Sovereign and skirts around the table, putting her hand on my elbow to push me toward the door. I go eagerly, but she stops me in the living room.

"Freya is alright. She's sleeping," she says, her voice lowering, "but she's been through a lot. The doctor is coming at noon just to check her over."

I nod, wordless.

"And Deacon, she wanted me to tell you she's pregnant. She didn't want you to have to wait until she woke up to let you know."

My shoulders drop and my head falls back. Everything tingles, but maybe that's from the blood seeping down my leg or the ringing in my ears.

I don't remember leaving Keira, but she must have told me where to go, because my feet are moving. I'm floating up the stairs and down the hall. Every step seems to take forever. Then, I find the bedroom with an ajar door, and I push it all the way open.

Sleeping curled up with one of Sovereign's dogs is Freya.

I swear, I almost fall to my knees. Part of me was so scared, despite my rage at Aiden and my mission to wipe them all out, that Jack wouldn't pull through and get her out safe. But here she is, without a scratch on her.

That favor was worth every penny I spent on Exile.

Freya is sound asleep. The small dog lifts its head but lays back down. I limp across the room and push the curtain open. The sky is pale blue, the stars winking out between gathering clouds. It's starting to snow, little flakes that swirl and fall lightly before hitting the frozen ground.

My eyes move up to the crest of the hill. I see it, a trail through the frost, leading in the direction of the mountains.

Jack Russell has come and gone. I'll see him again when he decides to call on me, but for now, his work here is done.

I sink down into the armchair. My leg is halfway numb, the pain a dull throb that won't quit. But in my chest, I'm whole. There's no hoping, no longing anymore. Now, I realize as I sit, miles from the house I built, that home was never a place. It was always this woman.

It was the baby she'll have when summer comes.

It's all the years I get to love her and have her love me back.

A dog barks outside. Freya stirs, rolling onto her back. Her lids open, and her eyes move over the room and fall on me.

She sits bolt upright, and I'm by her side in a second.

"Hey, you're okay. Sit back." I take her shoulders.

Her face crumples, and she throws her arms around my neck, clinging to me as sobs wrack her body. I pull her into my lap, brushing my hand over her head, holding it against my shoulder. My hands move absently over her body, checking for injuries, but she's whole.

"I'm having a baby," she sobs.

I kiss her temple. "I know, sweetheart. It's alright. I'll take care of you both."

She cries herself out. I just hold her, knowing how stressed she is after everything she's been through. Finally, she lifts her swollen face.

"Please," she whispers. "Promise me something."

"Anything." I cradle her chin in my fingers.

"Don't leave me," she begs.

"There's no leaving," I say. "Love me. Marry me."

Her mouth shakes. She bites her lip and lets it go.

"I do love you," she whispers. "And I'll marry you, but only if you promise to never hate me or hurt me."

She knows I wouldn't, but I understand why she says it.

"I know he hurt you," I say, my voice hushed, "but I'm not him. Been waiting all my life for you, sweetheart. I promise."

Something about those words get right to her heart. The tension in her body eases, and she sags against me.

"I trust you," she breathes.

I stroke her hair. "I've been lonely for a long time. But not anymore, not since the night you slept with me. I've been tired for years, but you make me feel like I'm ready to start at the beginning. I want to do this with you. I want you as my wife. Let's go home, have some babies, just live for a while."

She hiccups.

"You think you want that?"

"Yes," she whispers. "I want that."

Gently, I shift her around to lay in my lap and lean back against the pillows. My leg is bleeding through the handkerchief, but I don't feel it. Maybe there's nerve damage, but it's more likely the warmth burning in my chest.

She lit a fire in me. My heart was nothing but an empty hearth, and no matter how hard I struck the tinder and fanned the flames, it was always so cold until I laid eyes on her.

I let my lips fall to her hair.

My family, right here in my arms.

"What do you think it is?" she whispers.

"I think it's a boy," I say.

She smiles, and I feel it against my chest. "I think it's a girl."

"I guess we'll find out."

A shuddering breath slips out of her. She wipes her cheek. "Bittern?" Her voice cracks.

"He's safe, in the hospital," I say. "He's just fine, but I'm sending him to rehab outside the city as soon as it's safe."

"Deacon—"

"Freya, let me handle this."

"Are they gone?" There's a clear note of panic. "Ryland? Aiden?"

I bend in, holding her, and kiss her forehead. I keep my lips to her skin until her breathing slows.

"Yes," I say. "But that's not your worry. You need to rest and do what's right for you and the baby."

I see it in her eyes, the complexity of grief. I know it well. Grieving an abuser is grief all the same, even when it goes hand in hand with anger and relief.

"Okay," she whispers.

There's so much exhaustion in that word. She nestles her head against my shoulder, one arm slung over my neck. I close my eyes and lean back, my body exhausted from my fight with Aiden. I'm glad she's in my arms, just letting me hold her, because I couldn't move off this bed if I tried.

# CHAPTER FORTY-SEVEN
# FREYA

The doctor comes at noon. He checks me over carefully and lets us listen to the baby's heartbeat. Deacon sits in the chair by the bed, eyes exhausted. When the little *thump-thump* fills the room, he drops his head. His hand comes up over his face, covering his eyes. I weave my fingers into his, holding tight.

I think Deacon Ryder might be in tears.

My heart breaks, and warmth like starlight spills out. This man is going to be the best father when this baby comes.

He doesn't want to leave me for a second, but the doctor forces him into the bathroom so he can clean his wound. I hear them arguing through the door. I can't help but roll my eyes. Even at forty, Deacon still thinks he's invincible. He'd just as soon spit on his hand, rub the blood off, and say it's fine.

When they return, Deacon's wearing a pair of Gerard's old sweatpants, a bandage just showing over his waistband. The doctor leaves, and Keira comes back upstairs, this time with more food.

"What are your plans?" she asks Deacon.

He sits on the edge of the bed. "I thought we'd head out. I'd like to get back to Ryder Ranch as soon as we can."

"You can stay as long as you need to," she says.

"I know. Thank you," he says, "but I'd like to get Freya home."

The way he says that word—home—makes me feel like I finally understand what it means. Keira excuses herself, and silence falls as Deacon sinks down onto the chair. I shift to my side, laying my cheek on my arm. Now that the dust has settled, I have questions about what we went through in the past twenty-four hours—and before that.

"What is it, sweetheart?"

"There are some things you did, and I don't know how to feel about them," I whisper.

He sinks from the chair to his knees by the bed. His touch skims my cheek, brushing my hair back.

"Are you talking about tapping your phone?"

My brows rise. "No, I didn't know about that part."

There's a short silence.

His jaw works, a crease appearing on his forehead. His dark gaze is soft as ever. Tonight, that softness drives the fear that's been in my chest for years away. I know he's psychotic, but with me, he's so gentle. It heals the damaged parts of my heart.

None of this matters. I've made my choice.

"I know there was no accident on the highway," I whisper. "And I know you've been trying to get me pregnant this whole time."

He doesn't speak for a second. Then, he clears his throat.

"How does that make you feel?" he asks.

I touch his hand, gripping it. Tonight, he risked everything. He was faced with an impossible situation, a losing battle. Yet, he found a way through and got me safely to Sovereign Mountain, away from the bloodshed. He might be a hurricane, but I was always safe in the eye of it.

"It makes me feel safe," I manage. "And scared for anybody who makes you their enemy."

The corner of his mouth turns up. He bends in, kissing my temple. His hands slides down my waist, lingering on my lower belly. I remember all the times he came in me when he should have pulled out.

I can't totally blame him for this pregnancy. I'm guilty of being just as careless about birth control. I was just too scared of the past to consider the possibility of a family with him.

"Tell me what it looks like," I whisper.

He shifts onto the bed, stretching out to face me. "Our future?"

I nod. He draws me closer, letting me curl up against his chest. When I turn my head, I can hear his heart thump under my ear.

"It looks like you being happy," he says. "We have a family. I'll get you the help you need so that you still have time to do whatever you want. You can collect bugs. Hell, you can go to college and study bugs if you want."

I laugh. "I'm happy to just collect," I whisper. "I don't want my life to be complicated. All I want is peace."

"I'll spend the rest of my life making sure you get that," he promises.

My throat is tight with unshed tears. The generations of people who came before me were mired in pain. I thought that avoiding men like Deacon would save me, but I was completely wrong about him. He might look rough, but inside, he's the purist person I've met.

He's the cycle breaker, the person who steps in and changes everything.

"Let's sleep for a bit then go home," I whisper, offering a weak smile.

He clears his throat. "You don't know what it means to hear you call Ryder Ranch home."

I don't answer. Instead, I just close my eyes and reach for his hand.

It feels like a long ride back to Ryder Ranch. Deacon puts me in the passenger seat wrapped in a blanket. He put his old clothes on after Keira took them out of the dryer, and I try not to notice the bloodstains on his shirt. Instead, I focus on his hand wrapped around mine all the way home.

The days that follow are the quietest of my life. Deacon sets up another appointment with a doctor in South Platte, but it's a few weeks away, so there's nothing for me to do but try to adjust to everything. Ginny stays at the house with me while Deacon cleans up at the McClaine Ranch. Tracy comes to visit, bringing pastries.

Jay Reed, his lawyer, is at the house a lot. They both seem concerned. Then, there's silence. Jay probably did something illegal. Now, the weight that's been hanging over Deacon's head is gone. He shifts into talking about safeguarding the ranch against future encroachments. Late one night, he floats the idea of offering the remaining McClaine brother a deal for the land. I tell him he should do what he wants. He doesn't need my permission.

He says he wants my input. I tell him it can't hurt to have more land to buffer the property. I don't want what happened to ever happen again.

The snow starts coming a few days later. It blankets Ryder Ranch and turns the gray hills and mountains sparkling white. I try to distract myself with anything. There's a lot of fabric in the chest upstairs. I find a bolt of pink, dotted cotton and start making a baby blanket with it, fuzzy gray on one side, soft pink on the other.

It keeps my mind off Bittern.

"When can I see him?" I ask.

We're in the kitchen, having coffee. Ginny says I'm having an easy pregnancy. There're only fleeting moments of sickness. Mostly, I'm just exhausted. I could wrap myself up in a quilt and sleep until spring.

Deacon just got in from chores. He still has snow melting on his buzzed hair. He did that when I was kidnapped. I asked him why, and he said so he didn't have to wash the blood from his hair.

Typical Deacon answer.

"Bittern?"

I nod, taking a sip of my mostly-creamer coffee. He reaches for his mug, sinking into his chair.

"He's already in rehab, sweetheart."

My heart sinks. "Really? I wanted to say goodbye to him."

He gives me the softest look and holds out his arm. I sink onto his knee.

"I think Bittern would rather you see him next when he's clean," he says. "I spoke with him on the phone."

That hurts, but I understand. Into my mind comes everything Bittern and I talked about the night I was kidnapped—and the conversation I had with Aiden.

Deacon and I haven't spoken about either of those things.

Late that night, we're laying in each other's arms. I sleep on the side of the bed closest to the window. That way, I can watch the stars come out. Deacon rests against my back, reminding me to stay down here on Earth with an arm around my body.

I don't long for the stars anymore.

My home is safe. My love is right here, holding me. Slowly, I'm finding that was all I ever wanted.

"Deacon," I whisper.

He stirs but doesn't move. His chest is firm, and I lean into his warmth.

"Bittern told me Aiden wasn't his father," I manage.

"Told me that too."

Curious, I roll over. He's watching me intently, with no expression.

"Aiden said... He said some things to me that made a lot of other things make more sense," I manage.

"I know," he says. "I noticed there was something...off with him a while ago. It was why I pulled you from that truck and brought you to Ryder Ranch. Couldn't put my finger on it, but everything clicked the night he took you."

I feel my lip tremble.

"You suspected?"

He nods. "You were a frog in a pot of heating water: too hot for too long to realize there was a boiling point. Someone needed to reach in and get you out."

I swallow the lump in my throat. "I should have known when Braxton Whitaker disappeared."

"No," he says, tucking my hair behind my ear. "You shouldn't have. Nobody should worry about shit like that."

"But it happens," I whisper.

He's quiet for a moment. "The world is a hard place. Darkness comes in through the cracks."

For Deacon, he's being surprisingly eloquent. I push myself up on my elbow, pressing close so I can drape my leg over his waist. He's so handsome, with big, dark eyes, a crooked nose, a clean-cut mouth.

"I don't hate him," I say. "It's just sad."

"Yeah, some things are just sad," he says.

I know he doesn't feel the same way, but it's different for him. I know how hard life was for Aiden and my brothers. We shared that hardship for years. Deacon saw him as a threat to me and nothing more.

Maybe I'm wrong, but I forgive Aiden now that I understand his past. But I'm not sorry he's dead.

# CHAPTER FORTY-EIGHT
## FREYA

**EIGHT MONTHS LATER**

It's the middle of the afternoon in early summer. The windows are open, the breeze fluttering them. I'm on my side of the couch, a pillow under my stomach and between my knees. It helps, but I'm still panting, laying perfectly still.

"You want some water?"

I lift my head. Ginny comes out of the kitchen, a glass in her hand. Slowly, I ease myself up and shift back against the couch. I'm supposed to keep my legs elevated, but it compresses my lower stomach. I'm carrying low, and my stomach hasn't stretched a lot, which means my lungs are getting crushed.

"Thank you," I manage.

She sets it down and goes to look out over the driveway. "You want to take a nap?"

I shake my head. "I want to see them."

Today is a day I've waited for for months. Bittern is getting out of rehab today. Clean. Heavily pregnant or not, I'm going to be out on the porch waiting for him.

I get up with difficulty and join Ginny by the window. As if on cue, Deacon's truck appears over the hill. He parks, and I'm out the door as fast as I can go. Bittern steps out onto the gravel at the same time as the back door swings open. A sob erupts from my throat, and I clap a hand over my mouth.

He's standing tall, his head down but his eyes up. He's put on a little weight, and it looks good on him, filling out the shoulders of his shirt. Somebody gave him a good haircut and trimmed his beard short. He stops and looks at me. Then, he shakes his head.

"Hey, Frey," he says.

Tears pour out. I can't stop them.

"Hey, Bittern," I whisper.

He comes up the drive, walking in that easy way I haven't seen since before the mines. I'm speechless as he takes me in his arms, pulling me close. He smells good, like soap and nice clothes. I close my eyes and press my wet face into his shoulder.

This is all I wanted. Clean, happy Bittern.

He pulls back and looks down. "Well, looks like you were pregnant, huh?"

I laugh, wiping my face. "Yeah, I'm due in a few weeks."

"What is it?"

I shrug. "We decided not to find out. Deacon is dead set on thinking it's a boy, but I'm pretty sure it's a girl."

"Well, I think whatever it is, it's lucky to have you, Frey," he says, giving me a soft stare.

God, there he is. The dullness is gone, and the Bittern I love shines right through.

I wipe my puffy face. "You hungry?"

"Yeah, I'm starving."

My throat is so tight, I can't do anything but nod. Ginny appears behind me and waves Bittern up the stairs. This is their first meeting, but I hear her scolding him about being too thin as they head down the hall—didn't they feed him anything in that rehab? For all the money it costs, they should have. Smiling, I linger by the door for Deacon. He comes up the walkway, sauntering like he owns the world.

He wraps an arm around my waist, one hand on my belly.

"You're beautiful," he says, kissing me.

"I'm crying and pregnant, but thank you," I say, kissing him back.

He guides me into the house, shutting the door. Stu comes tearing around the corner, almost doubled in size since the day I found him. I found out from Jensen, after cornering him in the café one day, that Stu wasn't a stray. Deacon bought him from a neighboring farm and put him in the alley. Then, Jensen stuck around to make sure I found him and pointed me in the direction of Ryder Ranch.

I was speechless. The nerve of Deacon Ryder to set a trap with a puppy as bait. And I fell for it.

He's a wild man, but I love it. I'm never bored.

I scratch Stu behind the ears, adjusting his plaid bandana. Deacon says he'd make a good hunting dog when fall comes around. Stu thinks that's too much work, I can tell. He'd much rather hang out at the house than go out into the cold. He's been glued to my side every moment of this pregnancy, so it's easy to see who he likes best anyway.

In the kitchen, Andy leans on the stove, talking to Bittern. The other day, he cleaned out one of the unused employee houses. Bittern will live there for as long as he wants, and he'll work for the ranch. That was Deacon's idea, to help give Bittern a soft landing so all that rehab sticks.

That's what he says, but I know he wants Bittern close for my sake.

Ginny piles the table with thick, cheesy potato soup and garlic bread. We sit down, and Deacon puts his hand on my thigh under the table. I nibble—I'm so pregnant, it's hard to find room for a full meal—and look around the table with my heart full.

Bittern is alert, talking with Ginny and Andy like the accident never happened. Deacon is listening, absently stroking my leg. My heart is so full. I lay my hand on my stomach, grateful I didn't run when I had the chance.

Sometimes, it feels like a dream. But then, I look at him, and he's so real, I know it's not.

This is my life. I love and I'm loved back.

After dinner, when the house is quiet and we're alone, I go upstairs and undress for bed. I hear Deacon turn out the lights and say goodnight to Stu before heading up. He walks down the hallway and into our room, shutting the door behind him.

I'm on my side, feeling incredibly pregnant, but not too pregnant to notice he's looking good. My hormones have been raging. We've had more sex than ever in the last eight months.

He strips off and gets in the shower. I flip on my other side so I can watch the stars come out over the mountains. I'm drowsy by the time he comes out and gets into bed, his warm, naked skin sending shivers of pleasure through me.

"Mind if I borrow that pussy for a minute?" he says, kissing up my neck.

"It's all yours, daddy," I murmur.

I let him shift my thigh to rest over his knee. I've had some swelling, so I'm not wearing the chastity belt, but he gave me a silver bracelet to wear instead. It's a beautiful circlet, with our initials entwined on the clasp.

He spits in his hand and guides his cock into me, groaning. The sensation of hard smoothness and the four points of his piercings make my eyes roll back.

"It feels good," I whisper, letting my head sink into the pillow.

"Better than good," he breathes.

He fucks me, slow and deep. I bite my lip when he strokes my clit, pumping lazily, until I orgasm with a breathy gasp. Dimly, I hear him call me his good girl, his hand on my throat. He's so hard, I'm filled with the sweetest pressure as he comes, emptying into my pussy.

I love our casual intimacy—the kinky things he does, the intense scenes, they burn me up. They're a place where we can work everything out, and I feel so safe with him. But the little things about being his wife are the things that make me feel the most loved.

The kisses pressed to my cheek before he leaves in the morning. When he grabs my ass as he goes by. The quickies we have when he's in a hurry or comes in late. The sleepy morning sex before he goes out to do chores.

I always feel loved now. That has changed me, fundamentally rewiring my brain, healing my heart.

After he cleans me up, he arranges my pillows to support my stomach. I sigh in satisfaction as he starts absently rubbing my lower back. Satisfied silence falls.

"Thank you," I whisper. "For everything."

"You don't have to thank me, sweetheart," he says. "Just love me."

That makes me smile in the dark. My eyelids are heavy. I'm always sleepy now, so it doesn't take long to fall asleep. It's staying asleep that gets me some nights. Most of the time, the baby starts kicking around three, and I have to get up to use the bathroom. Tonight, I'm grateful we both sleep soundly.

I'm more rested than usual when I get up the next morning. Deacon is already gone. My clothes are laid out. He chose a matching pair of panties and a new bra to accommodate me being pregnant. Slowly, I put it on and pull the dress he laid on the chair over it.

Downstairs, Ginny stands by the stove, frying up bacon. When I sit, she turns and offers me a smile. "You want some tea, honey?"

I nod. I'm incredibly grateful to have her right now, especially as I get closer to my due date. I'd always assumed that when I had a family, I wouldn't have any women to help me. But now, I find myself with one of the kindest women I've ever met helping me out every day, even when she's off the clock. Tracy comes too, at least once a week, just to chat. That means a lot.

"How do you feel?" Ginny asks.

I clear my throat. "Alright. Just very pregnant. I've been having a lot of Braxton Hicks. Everything goes tight and then relaxes."

"I had a lot of those with my son," she says. "My daughter, not so much."

Somebody saunters down the steps. Bittern appears in the doorway. I take a second just to look at him. He's freshly showered, more alert than I've ever seen him.

"Hey, Frey," he says, circling the table and sinking down into a chair.

"How'd you sleep?" I ask.

He nods. "Real good. It's quiet out here on the ranch. Where's Deacon at? He need me to help with chores?"

"He's got Andy and the other cowboys," Ginny says, handing him a plate of bacon and eggs. "You eat."

I pick up my tea and get to my feet, only to set the mug back down. Ginny is filling my plate, her back to me. Bittern stops mid-bite and looks up.

"You alright?" he asks.

I stare at the ground. There's nothing on the floor, no gush of water, but it feels like...I'm peeing myself. Mortified, I tug my skirt to my knee and look for a wet spot.

"Honey, you okay?" Ginny sets the plate down.

"I don't know. My water might have broken," I say, blushing furiously. "It's sort of...wet."

Bittern shoots to his feet. "I'm getting Deacon."

He disappears out the side door. Grateful he's gone, I hitch my skirt up a little higher. That's when something warm trickles down the inside of my thigh, followed by a few more drops that reach my ankle. I look up at Ginny, frightened.

"I think it's time," she says.

"Is that my water?" I whisper.

She nods. "Let's get you laid down on the couch while Bittern gets Deacon."

She gets me to the living room and tucks a towel between my thighs. I can tell she's being calm on purpose so I won't be frightened. I appreciate it, but I'm terrified. She pats my hand and goes down the hall. I hear boots on the porch, and Deacon's coming around the corner and at my side in a second. He kneels, looking up at me.

"You alright?" he asks.

I nod wordlessly.

"Any contractions?" His voice is steady. I cling to how calm he is.

I shake my head then nod. "I don't know. I thought they were Braxton Hicks."

"Ginny's calling into the hospital now," he says. "They'll let us know if you should go in yet or wait."

I nod, swallowing. He takes my hands, looking into my eyes.

"Hey, I'm right here, sweetheart," he says. "I won't leave you for a minute."

I look into his eyes, and I'm not scared anymore. He's here. He always is, no matter what I need. I swallow and offer him a weak smile.

"I'm ready," I whisper.

Ginny walks in, holding the phone to her ear. "They're saying because of the distance, you should start gathering things up and head in now. It's not a hurry, but we need to head in that direction."

Shakily, I turn to Deacon. His fingers grip mine hard.

"You ready, sweetheart?"

I look into his eyes, dark and soft. I squeeze his hand back.

"Ready as I'll ever be," I whisper.

It's ten hours later when I'm on my back with the ceiling spinning, floating in and out of euphoria that it's over. I can hear my baby mewling angrily in the nurse's arms. Deacon's saying something, and I can tell he's somewhere beyond happy.

The nurse gets me cleaned up and helps me sit up against the pillows. Another nurse holds our baby, wrapped in a blue blanket. My heart is going so fast, I might pass out. Deacon says something to the nurse in a low voice. Smiling, she puts our little bundle in his arms. Our baby is so small, Deacon can hold it in just his hands. But then, he's always had huge hands.

"Deacon," I say.

He looks up. I've never seen him like this before. His dark eyes are wide, his lashes wet.

"You seeing this, sweetheart?" he says, looking down. "That's our baby."

"I could see better if you bring her over," I say.

He walks over, like he's afraid he'll break something, and sinks onto the edge of the bed.

"It's a boy," he says.

My brows shoot up. All through the pregnancy, I was so convinced I was carrying a girl. It takes me a second to calibrate myself.

"You alright?" Deacon asks.

I nod, sniffing. "He's perfect."

Smiling through my tears, I realize I never cared. I just want my family to be happy and whole. I'm worn out but not too tired to let him put our baby in my arms. He's the cutest thing I've ever seen, red and scrunched up with dark hair. Right away, I can tell he's going to favor his father. When he cracks a blurry eye, I see a hint of the same bullheadedness I know so well.

I just hope he's less of a daredevil.

"What do you want to name him?" Deacon asks, leaning in.

I reach out my free hand and slip it into his. All through the labor, which the doctor said was easy and short, Deacon held my hand. He brushed my hair back and fed me chips of ice with a spoon. When the pain made me want to give up, he kissed my sweaty forehead and let me cuss him out for doing this to me.

Now, all that's faded, and we're in the thick of the new baby haze. We stare down at him, holding onto each other hard.

"I just had girl names on my list," I say.

"I didn't have any names," Deacon admits. "You seemed pretty set on the ones you had."

I glance at Deacon. He's in his work pants, steel-toed boots, and charcoal gray shirt. Behind him, through the hospital window, runs the highway, and beyond it are the mountains. I never noticed until now, but in this light, they're the same color as the shirt he always wears, a shade brighter than his eyes.

"Slate," I say. "You like Slate Ryder?"

He nods. "Yeah, it's practical, sturdy. I reckon he could be somebody with a name like that."

"Alright, Slate is fine by me," I whisper.

He bends in, pressing a kiss to the back of my hand. I look back through the window, realizing I've finally made peace with these mountains. I'll always miss the Appalachian hills—they raised me, but I've found something just as beautiful here.

Montana is my home now. We'll raise our children in these fields. When Deacon and I are gone, the hard-packed earth will cradle us while we sleep.

I'm at peace.

It doesn't take long for us to fall into a new routine when we finally get home to Ryder Ranch. Deacon already had the nursery set up. During the pregnancy, I sat in a rocking chair and watched him prepare the room and build a crib with his bare hands.

That's when I realized, deep down, I made the right choice. For all his faults and questionable choices in the past, Deacon was made to care for a family. He's the most selfless man I've ever met.

The weeks blur together. Bittern lives in employee housing and works on the ranch. He's thriving as Deacon trains him to work with the horses, and he's making strides in his personal life as well. One day, he walks into the kitchen while Ginny's youngest daughter, Janie, is visiting. After that, he's a goner, hanging around the porch like a stray dog every day.

Finally, Deacon gets so fed up that he goes right up to Janie and tells her that Bittern's taking her out Saturday night. The next morning, I'm going for my daily walk with Slate, and I see them both sitting on his porch, having coffee with messy hair.

I smile and keep on walking.

Some of us made it, some didn't. You reap what you sow. I'm so glad it was Bittern who made it out.

Being a mother is difficult, but I love it more than anything. Slate is a pleasant baby. Ginny says he's easier than any of her children. He doesn't cause much fuss until his teeth start coming in, and then I switch him to bottles because he won't quit biting. Soon, he's crawling. Pretty quickly, he's Mr. Independent, walking around the house.

I cry to Deacon about it—my baby is growing up so fast.

"He's just got a lot of get up and go, sweetheart," he says. "He'll need it on the ranch."

I wipe my eyes, sniffing. We're standing in the bathroom, getting ready for bed.

"I think I'm ready to have another one," I say.

His brows shoot to his hairline. "What's that?"

I turn, leaning on the sink, hands behind my back.

"I want another baby," I say. "It's not like you can't afford all the babies we want."

He's in just his sweats and, God, he looks good, all tattoos and muscles. He leans on the counter and looks me in the eyes.

"I want lots of babies," he says. "But I aim to marry you first. I've waited long enough."

I scowl, but inside, I'm secretly pleased. "Okay."

He turns me around, bends me over the counter, and spanks my ass. "We can start trying on our wedding night."

I laugh and he picks me up, carrying me to our bed. We fall onto the flannel, the way we did the first night we spent together. Our mouths meet, and sparks burst like fireworks, warming me to my toes.

When we break apart, I wrap my arms around his neck. "I don't want a big wedding," I whisper. "I'd like to get up, put on my nice dress, pick some flowers from the field, and go to the courthouse. Bittern can be the witness. Then, we can have dinner at the ranch. Is that...alright?"

He cocks his head. "Is that really what you want?"

I nod, confident. "I never dreamed of a big wedding, just somebody who loves me for all the days afterward."

The corner of his mouth curls in a smile. His mouth brushes my forehead.

"Let's do it," he says.

He bends in, and we kiss deeply. My heart that longed for home finally found it. I know he feels the same way. Our house is happy and we're all together.

I'm always safe. He's always loved.

We both got everything we wanted. I can't wait to see what the future holds.

# CHAPTER FORTY-NINE
# DEACON

**FIVE YEARS LATER**

---

It's autumn. The fields smell like sweet grass. The woods smell like earth and ferns.

Bittern and I have been out haying the fields all day. The sun is just starting to drop. He went back to employee housing, to his wife, Janie, who's a few months pregnant with their first baby. I'm closing the gates to the back pasture and locking it for the night.

In the distance, I hear a door fly open. That'll be the boys, probably on the run from Ginny. I turn and see them, streaking up the hill at top speed. Slate wears a pair of muddy shorts, and his younger brother, Gage, runs after him in just a diaper. He's so young, but he's already climbing through the fields and woods of Ryder Ranch, every bit as wild as his brother.

I married a woman in love with the outdoors. She's happy to let the fields and streams raise her babies to be wild and free, and I have no complaints. I'm proud of how strong my sons are. Slate is bold and chatters about anything and everything. Gage is the strong, silent type, an ever-present scowl on his tiny forehead.

"Dad," Slate yells.

I break into a slow run, catching him with one arm. I grab Gage with the other and carry them giggling down the hill, tucked under each arm. We burst into the house, waking Stu from his spot on the living room rug. He shakes his heavy coat and barks, chasing after the boys as they spill onto the couch.

A door shuts upstairs. I look up to see my wife's legs appear, the hem of her skirt and her beautiful face following. She's changed since we met, for the better. When she moves through the house, it's clear she's comfortable. This is her home and she knows it.

I lean on the railing, and she stops, bending to kiss me. I linger, tasting her on my tongue. When I draw back, she's smiling.

"You're a little horny," she whispers.

"I'm always horny when I see you," I say quietly, even though the boys are yelling so loudly, they couldn't hear us anyway. "Let's get these kids in bed."

She touches my temple, tracing the tattoos under my buzzed hair. "I'm wearing what you set out," she murmurs.

I glance down, warmth tingling in my veins. This morning, I laid out a set of deep red lingerie and the dress she's wearing. She lifts her neckline an inch, and I see the crimson strap of her bra.

Alright, time to get these kids in bed.

I turn. "Boys, go brush your teeth," I holler.

She laughs, shaking her curls back and floating down the stairs. My sons start arguing like a pair of lawyers, running through every reason under the sun why they shouldn't be in bed. I duck around the couch and grab them both, turning them in the direction of the stairs.

"Go on, let's go," I order.

They obey, already arguing about who gets to brush their teeth first. I follow them, herding them to the bedroom at the far end of the hall. They have a set of bunk beds I made and Freya painted with forest animals. I built a fort in the corner, complete with a fake tree that reaches the ceiling. It's the room every child dreams of, the kind neither Freya nor I would have dared to dream of as children.

"Dad," Slate yells from the bathroom. "Gage is pouring the toothpaste in the toilet."

I sigh, stepping in just in time to snatch the toothpaste from Gage as he squeezes it into the toilet. Slate is brushing his teeth, but only the front two. I correct him, even though I've done it a hundred times before. Gage clings onto my leg, begging for the toothpaste back.

I set him on the sink. "Alright, show your teeth," I order.

A glint appears in his eyes. Grinning, he clamps his jaws shut.

Damn kids. I do the best I can to brush his teeth, even though he's giggling. Apparently, this is the funniest thing he's ever done, because he's gasping for breath by the time I give up and put the toothbrush away. I turn on the shower and toss them both in, scrubbing all the dirt from the garden off, and get them into their pajamas.

They give me hell, but my life is perfect.

A son under each arm, I carry them out to the bunk beds and sling them into bed. Freya appears with two cups of water and a storybook. Immediately, they straighten up and pretend they weren't acting like little animals.

I tuck them both in. Freya reads them a story. We kiss them on the head and turn out the lights. On the other side of the door, I cock my head. They're both silent, tired out from the day.

"I'm going to the attic for a minute," Freya whispers.

I nod. "Don't be too long. I'm going to have a shower. After that, you're all mine."

She blushes, glancing over her shoulder as she opens the attic door. "Yes, daddy."

I think about her the entire time I'm in the shower, but I'm always thinking about her. I never stop marveling at how much she's changed my life. I went from being lonely every night to having a full house.

Never in my wildest dreams did I dare to hope my life would end up this good.

I towel off and pull on my sweats. Then, walking quietly, I head up the stairs to the attic. She's sitting at her desk, chin in her palm, flipping through a book. The fern-green walls are covered in her sketches. Beetles, butterflies, and other insects are preserved behind glass and mounted on the walls. Dried flowers hang in bunches by the windows. Books are stacked by the couch and fill the shelves. Everything smells faintly of vanilla.

She still works a few days a month at the café, helping Tracy, and the scent of baked goods still clings to her curls and soft skin.

I cross the room and bend, pressing a kiss to the nape of her neck. "You ready for bed, sweetheart?"

She turns, looking up at me with those big blue eyes.

"Does bed mean sleep? Or fun?"

I pick her up, and she wraps her legs around my waist. "Bed means fun, then sleep."

She smiles as I kiss her mouth, velvety and tasting of my wife. "Good, because I'm horny. Let's make another baby."

My brows rise. She wriggles out of my arm, gives me a look over her shoulder, and dashes down the stairs. I'm hot on her heels, catching her as she ducks into our room. She yelps as I toss her onto the bed and climb over her, pinning her by the wrists.

"Do you mean that?"

She bites her lip, releasing it. "Maybe we just fuck and see what happens?"

"No birth control?"

She shakes her head. In my sweats, my cock is rock hard. Slowly, I lift her skirt and ease her dress up over her head. Her lovely, curvy body is decorated with deep red lingerie and the silver chastity belt. I hate that she can't wear it while she's pregnant. It's so pretty on her hips.

I bend my head, running the tip of my tongue along the straps that cradle her hips. She moans, lashes fluttering. I bite, feeling her flesh sink under my teeth. Her spine arches. I slide my fingers between it and the bed, tracing the delicate bones.

*My wife. My now, my forever.*

"I'll give you anything you want, sweetheart," I murmur.

She breathes, lifting her hips, begging for my mouth between her thighs. I glance up, and she touches my face, tracing up to the tattoos showing through my hair. I never got any more cover ups. There's no need. She thinks I'm perfect, and that's all that matters.

"Eat my pussy, daddy," she breathes.

I cock my head. "What do you say?"

"Please?"

I unfasten the chastity belt and lay it aside. Then, I bend my head, peeling her panties aside. The soft scent of her pussy reaches my nose. I press my mouth to her sex, sliding my tongue over her. She tastes like heaven, like Freya. Moaning, I eat her until she's got her thighs clamped over my ears. It doesn't take her long to gasp and shudder. Wetness drips down my chin, her nails digging into my shoulder.

I lick her clean and take her panties down. Then, I lift her into my lap and unhook her bra, letting her breasts fall free. Every time, they take my breath away. Now, the first time, even when we're old.

She's naked except for the soft chains that make her mine. Our eyes connect. We both shudder as I push down the front of my pants and slide her onto my cock.

Her spine arches, her hair tumbling down her naked back. I grit my teeth, controlling the first thrust. I want to feel every inch.

"God," she gasps. "You feel so good."

I shift up against the headboard, pulling her close. She moans, one hand on my chest to steady herself, and starts moving. If my only purpose in life is to fuck my wife, that would be enough. Just to watch her pleasure is enough.

She rises and falls, riding hard. She takes pleasure the way she gives it—without any shame. She's come such a long way from the scared girl I saw in that alleyway. Now, she's as confident as she is beautiful.

We fuck the way we have nearly every night since our marriage. Then, we fall exhausted into bed. She snuggles close, her back warm against my stomach. I turn out the light, and my eyes adjust.

"Look," I whisper.

She lifts her head, following my finger to where I'm pointing out the window. Over the inky mountains shimmers pink and a shadow of green. Neither of us speak. We don't have to. We hold each other and watch the colors ripple over the sky until they fade to darkness.

Then, the stars come out.

THE END

# Acknowledgments

Thank you to everyone who worked on this book with me. Thank you to Corinne, who read this book multiple times during the alpha reading process and was so supportive as I worked through the writing process.

Thank you to my developmental editor, Lexie, and my copy and proof editor, Alexa, for all your hard work on Deacon.

Thank you to my beta and early readers, especially Emilie and Lex. Thank you to my street team, my ARC readers, my PR team, and all my readers for being so supportive of this series.

Thank you to my designer Sandra and photographer Michelle for the wonderful covers!

And last, but not least, thank you to the love of my life, my husband, who worked at a cabinet factory in rural Kentucky and allowed me to share some of his story here.

Made in the USA
Columbia, SC
27 June 2025